Red Phone Box

A Darkly Magical Story Cycle

GHOSTWOODS

THIS IS A GHOSTWOODS BOOK

11 12 1 2 3 4 5 6 7 8 9 10

Copyright ©2013 Ghostwoods Books. Copyright of each story belongs to its listed author. All stories, artworks, fonts, and textures appear under license.

Executive Editor: Salomé Jones
Cover: Gábor Csigás
Copy Editor: Tim Dedopulos
Image Credits: Interior art by Kara Y. Frame. Main cover image "Lonely in London" by Trey Ratcliff (stuckincustoms.com). Cover textures by Dustin Schmiedling (valleysinthevinyl.com); Lost and Taken (lostandtaken.com); and Sirius-sdz (sirius-sdz. deviantart.com). Fonts "Faustant" by Manfred Klein (manfred-klein.ina-mar.com); "VAL" by Fontfabric (fontfabric.com); "Drop Cap One" by Rae Kaiser (outside-the-line.com) via Font Bros (fontbros.com); and Garamond by Claude Garamond via Christophe Plantin and Adobe. Editor's portrait photo "Salomé" by Brown Cathell.

ISBN: 978-0-957627-10-9

This edition published November 2013 by:
    Ghostwoods Books
    Maida Vale
    London W9
    United Kingdom

http://www.gwdbooks.com

If you are interested in writing for Ghostwoods Books, please head over to:
http://www.gwdbooks.com/submission-guidelines.html
for details of our submissions policies.

For my insane genius, Tim.

A Note from the Editor

Warning. You are about to step inside the collective mind of some dangerously creative people.

Though it's not a standard novel, this book should be read like one. The 58 story-chapters it's composed of have been arranged so that they depend on those that precede and follow them to make sense. They won't work if you read them out of order. Such is the way of story cycles.

Red Phone Box has mostly been punctuated and spelled according to British standards. However, the American characters' stories – that is, those whose viewpoint character is American – have American spelling and punctuation where applicable.

The book began its life as a series of loosely-connected short stories written by people who mostly never met or spoke to each other. Through the magic of editing and additional writing, author/puzzle designer Tim Dedopulos and I have taken the pieces and transformed them into a collective novel.

Strange things will happen when you enter here. The pages of this book are infused with the energy of London and tinged with distant cultures and rhythms. But the clearest view inside this book is of the dark places within the heads of the people who wrote it.

We are a frightening crowd of rebels, revolutionaries, artists, geeks, apocalypse prophets, and *writers*. Perhaps you are one of us.

You are advised to stay on the path. Even so, you may find yourself pulled into the box, wanting to know where it would take you if you should enter the imaginary world yourself.

Salomé Jones,
July 2013

PS: There's a list of characters on p357, if you're interested.

1. Oh Aye, Crofton
by Gethin A. Lynes

Iain sat atop the gothic bulk of the Crags with a bottle of Black Isle Stout and a fag, and looked down between his knees at the path below. Angus was laughing, wild black hair and beard blowing in the wind as he came up the steep track from Holyrood Palace. He had one arm around some bird's shoulders, and they passed a bottle of Buckie back and forth.

Gazing up and over the city, Iain tried not to be disappointed that his cousin had brought a girl with him again. *Not even like she's his bird*, Iain thought. *Just some bit of minge he picked up on the train.* The street lights were beginning to come on, their orange shroud settling over the city beneath the lively blue of the evening sky.

There was a great pulse in the city at this time of year: the endless daylight, the warm, damp air, the steady rhythm of the Festival. Most locals hated the Edinburgh Festival, the dour bastards, but Iain thought it was brilliant. Aye, he was jeeked come September, but Jesus, they had all bloody winter to do fuck-all but sleep and hide from the cold. The tourists were all right, just tourists.

The wind, all bluster and full of yeast from the brewery, pulled at his jacket and whipped his hair about his eyes. Every once in a while, in a lull, he would catch the faint air of some lone piper playing somewhere up the Mile, or snatches of conversation from the path beneath him.

A peal of laughter blew up to him, and he looked between his knees again. Angus had the girl pressed up against the face of the Crags, his hand up her skirt. Iain grimaced. *For fuck's sake*, he thought, sitting back and taking a long swig from his bottle. *They'll be at it all bloody night. Angus'll not even ken I'm here.*

The wind died away a moment, and Iain heard Angus as clear as day itself.

"Right, on you go, lass. It's aw men's business the night."

He looked down, but the wind rose again and carried the rest of their words away. Whatever was said, the lassie was clearly raging. She hurled the empty Buckie bottle at Angus. He ducked away from it, and when the lass stormed off back down the path, he turned and continued on his way.

Iain sat back again, smiled to himself, and took another long swig.

* * *

What was taking Angus so long? Iain was about to stand up and go look for him when, from behind, a cold, smelly hand clamped over his mouth and nose.

Angus leant in close to his ear. "Nothing like a wee whiff of quim to a virgin boy, eh?"

Iain twisted around. "Get tae fuck, you weegie bastard," he growled, shoving Angus away, and getting to his feet. They stood staring at each other threateningly. Then a grin split Angus's beard, and he caught Iain in a fierce hug, lifting him off his feet.

When Angus had put him down, Iain reached into his jacket and produced a long, fat spliff.

"Areet! Good man." Angus took it from him. "Now, get your kit. We'll smoke it on the way."

"On the way where?" Iain asked.

"Penicuik."

Iain stopped, halfway through lifting his weighty backpack. "Why the fuck would we want to go to Penicuik?"

"Tell me, my young padewan," Angus said, pausing to light the spliff. "What do you know about Aleister Crowley?"

"Bugger all. Intae black magic or the like, aye?"

"Come on, I'll explain on the way," Angus said, starting off back down towards the city. "If we dinnae dawdle, we'll get on the bus before all the radge bastards are headed home tae the countryside."

Iain shouldered his pack, and followed.

* * *

Iain reluctantly trailed Angus off the bus. He was feeling far from happy about things, but Angus was a force of nature, and there was no denying him once he'd got an idea in his head.

About a mile along the twilit road south of Penicuik, they came to the firmly locked gates of an estate, where according to rumour (and Angus) old Aleister Crowley had once practised dark rituals in the now-ruined Penicuik House. In fact, Angus reckoned, it was one of Crowley's rituals that had caused the fire that had gutted the original House.

Iain stopped him on the verge of clambering over the stone wall to one side of the gate. "Angus, what are you doing?"

"What does it look like?"

"I don't know, man. It doesnae seem right tae sneak into a locked estate?"

"Iain," Angus said, shaking his head. "That's the propaganda of oppression talking wi' your mouth, man. We have right of access in this country. That means we can go wherever we please, and bugger they rich bastards that think they own the whole place. This'll be here for everyone long after these gates have gone to dust."

"You want tae claim right of access tae fucking camp on grounds that Aleister Crowley practised black magic on?"

"Aye, fucking brilliant, eh?" And with that, Angus leapt up, pulled himself over the wall and was gone.

Iain shrugged to himself and threw his pack over the wall and climbed after Angus. On the other side, in the gloom beneath the trees, Angus had just lit the spliff he'd rolled on the bus. He handed it to Iain, and picked up Iain's pack for him.

"Areet, son?"

Iain hesitated a moment before saying "Aye."

"Come on then." Angus turned and led the way along a narrow path through the woods. Before long, Iain had lost sight of Angus, and continued slowly along the path, stoned and getting steadily more nervous in the growing dark.

Eventually, the path emerged from the trees by a small stream. There was no sign of Angus, and Iain stood silent and uneasy, unsure of which way to go. It seemed that the more he strained to hear any

7

sound of Angus, the quieter everything became. He began to hear strange noises, like the call of some eerie bird, and scurryings in the undergrowth, and he became afraid. He felt that something was coming near, some dark presence, and he wanted to run.

Then away to the right, Angus wandered back around a bend in the path. "What're you doing?"

The pall of fear shattered, and Iain grinned foolishly and shrugged. As Angus approached, he held out the half-smoked spliff in explanation.

Angus shook his head and took the joint. "Come on, ya eejit," he said, and turned away again.

They came around a bend, past a thick stand of copper beech, to a place where the path split, one fork crossing an old stone bridge over the stream and disappearing into the thick trees that covered the hillside beyond. At the foot of the bridge, Angus pointed down to the opposite bank. There, next to the bridge, two ancient yew trees stood, their twined branches reaching down so that they nearly trailed in the babbling water.

"Who needs a fucking tent, eh?" he said.

Angus reached into the pack and pulled out another bottle of Black Isle. They shared it, leaning on the edge of the bridge for a while in silence, listening to the splash and murmur of the water, the soft susurrus of wind in the trees. The beer was nearly empty when Iain broke the quiet, slapping at a midge on his neck.

Angus stood up. "Areet," he said. "Let's get some firewood." He picked up the backpack, and Iain followed him down beneath the patient yew trees.

A small fire pit, circled by stones and filled with the remains of recent use, sat between the two trees. Angus dropped the pack, and immediately began gathering kindling. After a moment, Iain wandered off to look for larger branches.

It was almost completely dark now, and with returning unease, Iain went back to the path, out from beneath the cover of the forbidding trees. He followed it up the hill from the bridge, scooping up fallen branches along the tree line. As the path wound up the slope, the noise of the water faded and the wind died.

He found himself once more in silent woods, surrounded by darkness, and once again he had the growing sense of some ominous presence nearby. He looked wildly about him, trying to spot anything amongst the trees. He could barely make out the pale line of the path going back down to the bridge. Off in the trees he heard the snap of twigs. He froze, hardly daring to breathe. Again, the crack of a twig underfoot, closer this time.

He panicked, flung aside his bundle of firewood, and fled down the path.

Beneath the yew trees a small fire burned. Angus was nowhere to be seen. Iain rummaged around in the backpack until he found his pocket-knife. He opened the blade and crouched down with his back to the fire. After a few minutes Angus emerged from the darkness of the path. He had Iain's bundle of wood in his arms.

"Fuck you, Angus," Iain said, as Angus broke into laughter.

"Ya big bloody Jessie." Angus dropped the wood beside the fire. "Go on, you jumpy bugger. Open another one of they beers."

* * *

Iain awoke from black dreams, from fire and chanting and a blood-red telephone box. He sat up. The fire was still burning, casting spectral shadows among the branches of the trees above him. Angus was gone, and his blanket, the empty bottles and Iain's backpack with him. Iain reached into his pocket and pulled out his knife. He did not feel reassured.

He didn't like the idea of wandering through the woods on his own, but he wasn't going to sit where he was. He got to his feet and walked out to the bridge. On the other side of the stream, and off down the path, away from where they'd come, he saw the twinkling of fire moving amongst the trees. He stopped dead still and waited. A moment later it appeared on a patch of open path, moving away from him. It was the unmistakeable silhouette of Angus, carrying a burning torch. Curious despite himself, Iain crossed the bridge and followed.

* * *

The path eventually emerged from the trees, and skirted the edge of a wide paddock. The occasional bleat of unseen sheep accompanied Iain as he followed Angus at a distance. Beyond it, the path plunged once more into woods and climbed a steep slope.

Iain stopped within the tree line, and watched as Angus approached the ruin of what must have been Penicuik House. Through the windows and broken stone, he could see the flicker of firelight from within.

Some time later, Iain crept up the wide, uneven steps of the once-grand entrance to the house. The front was covered in the scaffolding of some barely-begun restoration project. He stood beneath it for a moment, considering. *Jesus, do I really want to know what's going on in there? What the fuck has Angus got himself mixed up in?* But despite the pit in his stomach, he knew he was going to find out.

Careful not to make a noise on the uneven stone, he crossed the entrance hall, and followed the dancing glow of light through a doorway to the right. At the far end of the building, he stood in the shadow outside a room ablaze in torchlight. Taking a deep breath to steady himself, he stepped into the doorway.

Every inch of stone was covered in chalk. A pattern of strange sigils, shapes, and runes danced in the torchlight. On the floor were five wide circles, marking the points of a huge pentagram, in the centre of which four manacles were chained to the floor.

Iain walked slowly into the middle of the room, looking about in amazement. The circles held a strange array of things: a small silver knife, a carving of a deer, a book bound in red leather, a severed arm. At the far end of the room, in the circle that marked the upper point of the pentagram, stood a red telephone box.

As he gaped, the door of the telephone box opened, and out stepped a man in a long black coat. Tall and dark-haired, with an aquiline nose and an imperious forehead, his black eyes glittered in the light. He smiled a thin, dark smile at Iain. "Whenever you are ready, Angus," he said, his voice dry and cold as steel.

Iain turned to see Angus standing behind him, his bare chest and arms covered in symbols, a mirror of the walls. In one hand he held a long, curved dagger.

"Y-You know this man, Angus?" Iain stammered, taking a step back from the knife.

"Oh aye, Crofton." Angus stared at Iain, his eyes glazed. "Now," he said, raising the knife. "Get your clothes off."

2. What a Little Moonlight Can Do
by Salomé Jones

It was not a normal London night. Amber gazed up at the full moon through the glass balcony doors. It was strange how the light it cast left the sky dark, but coated the tops of buildings and trees, cars and streets with a ghostly glow. It stencilled black outlines around places it couldn't reach, more like ethereal rain than actual light.

She slid the glass door open and stepped out onto the balcony. The air was absolutely still, not like normal, windy London at all. She leaned against the railing and looked out over the city. As she did, she noticed that her arms and the front of her blouse were glowing. If only that liquid light could get inside her, sink into her veins, maybe she would brighten, stop missing Jon.

The sounds of the city floated up to her, perfectly clear, even though the street was over a hundred feet down. The hum of car engines, an occasional siren, the isolated sound of people laughing like they were the only ones in a big, dark room.

She looked through the window at the clock. 2:22 in the morning and still she couldn't sleep. Two two two. Even the clock was mocking her now. There was no 'two' any more. Jon wasn't coming back.

She had to do something, or she was going to cry. Again. She was so tired of crying. *A walk.* It was the perfect night for it. She went back into the flat, leaving the glass doors open to the night air. She crossed the room and stared at herself in the mirror on the wall above the sofa. Her hair needed combing, but she only ran her fingers through it. It would do. It was dark, after all. Who would see her?

She flipped the lights off. As she slid her jacket on, she noticed her arms and her shirt still looked like they were glowing. Funny. Did moonlight always do that?

She took the lift down to the ground floor and walked past the porter. He was watching TV behind the counter.

"Amber." He inclined his head. "Going out late?"

"Just need a walk, James." She forced a smile.

He nodded, like he knew the feeling. He said something else then. His Filipino accent sometimes confused her.

"Indigo starfish?" She repeated what she thought she'd heard.

"Riiiight." He grinned and waved.

She waited until she was out the front door before she shook her head. Who knew what James meant? She turned left at the gate and kept going. She walked fast, the clicking of her heels echoing between the buildings on either side of the nearly empty street. The trouble was, she couldn't escape her own thoughts.

Jon had left her for someone else. He'd never said so, but she knew it.

She crossed over the road when she reached the roundabout, and slowed for a moment at the corner, deciding which way to go. *Probably that Alice. The one with the perfect teeth. It was always a risk, letting him play away from home.* She peered down the first right, a dark, narrow street, a row of terraces and the entrance to a park. *Maybe it was the redhead, the Spanish girl. What was her name? Gloria?* She took a few steps toward the second right, bigger and brighter, more traffic, a pub. No, she was sure it was Alice. She retraced her steps and took the first right, picking up her pace again, moving in and out from under street lights, light dark light dark light, like the windows of a passing train.

He was undoubtedly with her right now. Maybe they were still awake. So new in the relationship, two in the morning, they were probably...

A shadow stepped out in front of her, right out of a terrace gate. Just a shadow, nothing in sight to have cast it. It meowed.

"Hi, kitty." She'd never seen a cat out on the street in London before. Was it feral? As if answering her question it brushed up against her shins. She crouched down.

"Hello, little one." She extended her index finger in greeting. The cat touched its nose to her fingertip. Its black fur made it all but invisible in the dark. When it looked up at her, its eyes glowed yellow gold. "What are you doing out here? You're not lost, are you?"

The cat rubbed the side of its face against her hand.

"Ah. You, too, eh?" She smiled. "Night-time's the worst, isn't it?"

She ran her hand down the cat's sleek back.

A light came on inside the terrace whose gate the cat had appeared from. The door opened a crack and a woman's voice hissed, "Max!" The cat turned and ran back through the gate and into the house. The door closed.

Amber straightened up and dusted her hands on the seat of her trousers. "Bye, Max. It was nice to meet you." A wave of sadness welled up in her and something warm tickled down her cheek. *Oh god, not again. So much fucking crying.*

She started walking again, past more terraces, a bicycle stand, parked cars. She wished she could hear Jon's voice. That would calm her down. If she could just talk to him... But she couldn't. She'd tried. His mobile was disconnected, and she had no idea where he lived now. She reached the gate to the park. It was closed and locked. She guessed they didn't want people in there after dark.

When she really needed to hear his voice, she called home and listened to his low rumble on the answer-phone. *Hi, this is Jon. Leave a message for me or Amber and we'll call you when we get in.* She still couldn't make herself change the recording, even though he'd been gone three weeks. Hearing it was like time-travelling back to when they were happy together.

She should call it now. Maybe it would help her stop crying. She paused along the low brick wall in front of the park, unzipped her jacket pocket, and fished inside for her cell phone. It wasn't there. She had a sudden flash of it sitting on the nightstand, plugged into the charger. *Damn.* Her nose stung with tears. *Pathetic.* She wiped her face with the back of her hand and blinked to clear her vision.

She focussed her eyes on a spot of light across the street. A red phone box! That couldn't be a coincidence. It was a sign. She was meant to call. She'd never actually used a phone box. She patted her pockets. She had some change, but she wasn't sure how much it would be. There was only one way to find out.

She darted across the street and peered through the one of the glass window panes. It was lit from the inside. '60p Minimum,' said a notice on the phone. She opened the door and stepped inside. She dug some coins out of her jacket pocket. She lifted the receiver and put the coins in the slot. The black plastic was cold against her ear. It felt strange, old and unwieldy. She dialled her own number and listened to it ringing.

There was a click right after the first ring. Weird. She thought it went over to the answer-phone on the third –

"Hello?" A man's voice.

Oh good Christ. She'd dialled the wrong number. "I'm sorry. I must've –"

"Amber?"

"Who is this?" Her heart jumped.

"Who do you think it is, loon? Where are you?"

"What?" How could this be? "You're home?"

"That's the sensible place to be at three in the morning." It was Jon. It was really Jon.

"Don't go anywhere. I'll be right there. Just don't move." She replaced the receiver in a rush. It fell from the cradle and dangled from its silver cord, but she didn't care. She pushed open the door and hurtled out into the street, breaking into a run. He was home. She ran back past the terraces, the bike rack. He was home. She rounded the corner and crossed at the roundabout.

Oh god, she wasn't even wearing any makeup. She must look like hell. At the front door, James buzzed her in.

"Hey," he said.

"Indigo starfish?" She flashed him a smile.

"Yeah." He laughed.

She got into the lift and pushed the button for her floor. Her heart raced almost painfully. The lift doors opened and she got off, holding herself to a fast walk. At the door to her flat, she ran her hands over her hair, licked her finger and wiped it under each eye, hoping she didn't look like a raccoon. She put her key in the lock and turned the latch, pushing the door open. It was dark inside. She went in, not bothering to flip the light on.

"Hello?" She took off her jacket and hung it up. It gave off a faint glow. She looked at it more closely. Definitely glowing. So weird. She took off her shoes and put them on the shoe rack. Parts of them were glowing, too. She shook her head.

The flat was quiet.

Amber tiptoed across the lounge. Maybe he'd gone to bed already. It was late after all. God, it *was* late. Fatigue hit her all at once. She went into the bedroom. "Honey?"

There was a groan from the bed.

"Oh, thank God." Amber stood staring at Jon's dark form under the blankets.

"Where've you been?"

I could ask the same about you. But she didn't. "Out for a walk. Couldn't sleep." She unbuttoned her blouse.

"You're glowing."

"I know. It's just the moonlight." She unzipped her trousers and pulled them off.

"Moonlight?"

"Yeah, it's some crazy full moon." She unfastened her bra and slipped her panties down, adding them to the pile of her clothes on the floor.

"I don't think moonlight makes people glow."

She sat down on the edge of the bed and slid under the covers. "Neither did I." He must have been there a while. It was warm already. God, she was *so* tired, like she'd been running marathons. "But it does." She snuggled up against him.

"Amber?"

"Let's not talk about it now," she whispered. "I missed you."

* * *

She woke up to a darkened room. The curtains were drawn, but she could tell it was daylight by the glow seeping in at the bottom of the window. She sat up and looked at the clock. 7:30. Jon was still asleep next to her, his broad back facing her, his hair spread out on his pillow.

Wow, she'd had such a crazy dream. Moonlight makes you glow? And Jon running off with some girl named Alice? What was that about? Such a sense of relief to wake up and find him right next to her where he belonged.

She left him sleeping and went out to phone work. She was ill, she said. She'd be in tomorrow.

She went into the kitchen, still naked, and put some coffee on. While it was brewing, she went into the bathroom and brushed her hair and put on a little mascara. She heard Jon moving around in the bedroom. She went back to the kitchen and made his coffee, just the way he liked it. Cream and two sugars, right to the brim. She poured herself a cup and carried them both out to the coffee table. Jon was sitting at his desk. She could hear him typing. She walked past him, concentrating on the cups of coffee to make sure she didn't spill any. She bent over to put them on the table.

"Nice arse."

She grinned and turned around. "Come and get—"

The man in Jon's chair smiled at her. She screamed and took three steps back. In Jon's chair, in Jon's body. But his face wasn't Jon's.

"Amber? What's the matter?"

"Who are you?" She was breathing hard. She reached over and grabbed the shawl she kept on the couch and held it up in front of herself.

"What the hell?" The man squinted at her. "What's wrong with you? It's me."

"Me who?" She took another step back. "Who are you? How did you get in?" Her voice was getting shrill. God, what was happening?

"For Christsake, Amber." The man was staring at her now, looking quite alarmed. "It's me. Stuart!"

'The sounds of the city floated up to her, perfectly clear,
even though the street was over a hundred feet down.'

3. For Whom the Phone Rings
by Matthew Scoppetta

It was 2:22. Strange to even be up, let alone walking along the street
at this hour. Stranger still was that he actually regarded this new city
as home. *London, so many new sights to see and new avenues to explore.* That's
what he'd thought. He shook his head. Not since he'd first arrived
after leaving the States six months before had he felt more alone.
True, he'd never been one for attachment. Still, the pettiness of 'being
in a couple,' the notion of 'friends,' hell even the fucking joke that
sometimes qualified for a family never seemed more alien to him than
it did now.

"Well, Jarreth, my friend, you certainly are fucked in the head,"
he said aloud. There was no-one else to talk to, even on this temperate
London night.

Tonight's stroll was supposed to offer breathing room rather than
an excursion into melodrama. But he knew perfectly well that he was
broken. Hell, he still carried his heart in its burgundy box.

Useless polished lump of coal. What good are you to me now? "Did I
really just fucking think that?" He was aware of the irony in talking to
himself out loud about his thoughts. "You're really losing it this time,
Jarreth."

He came to a crossroads, and a simple choice – continue 'home'
or, as the young lady at the café had said, "Get lost." He decided
to continue straight on, with his shadow stretched out before him
under the big moon. He *wanted* to get lost in this new city, but without
trying, he took in the local landmarks, mapping and geo-locating
their positions as if his brain was a living, breathing GPS unit. The
legacy of years of work in architecture. The simple pattern in the
cobblestones told his mind that if he turned left, there was less than a
mile before he'd be at his door.

A right turn here, a left turn there, going straight, doubling
back, closing his eyes and spinning around, still he'd *know* his path

home. Besides, this particular walk was becoming almost routine. He continued as he had a few nights before – the double lamp, and then the silver Porsche, followed by that low wall beneath the elder tree. Jarreth eased himself down onto the sidewalk, his back against the wall, and absorbed his surroundings. Terraced Victorian buildings set against an alien backdrop. Sure he had seen sights like this before – New York came to mind – but he was never comfortable in cities. Too much hustle and bustle. But he did enjoy looking at the throwback phone box, its regal red standing out defiantly against the yellow-hued street corner.

Funny how you pick up on the oddest things. Maybe it wasn't the box, but its occupant. Narrowing his eyes against the glare of the street light, Jarreth could just make her out. The light seemed to be playing tricks. There was an odd glow coming from her jacket. "Some new high priced LED-lined jacket," he whispered, trying to convince himself.

Must be one of those rich London girls... Still, he did what he always did, scanned her fingers for a ring. He'd discovered, as he entered his thirties, that he actually cared about that. Just a few years ago, he'd have kept his gaze a lot higher. No ring as far as he could see. She was animated on the phone. *Hope it's good news*, he thought. It would make for a fantastic cheesy movie, if she was being courted or dumped in a London red phone box. He sat still so she wouldn't see him. He didn't want to disrupt her conversation. Maybe he would come back here and sketch the surroundings, and this new Muse he'd found in the box...

The fantasy was broken by the woman vacating it with quite a speed. The glow Jarreth had noticed shot off into the night.

He watched her run, and when she had rounded the street corner and disappeared from sight, he turned back to the box. Taking his hands and forming a small frame – how many times had he done that – he noticed something wrong. The purity of the box had been compromised.

"Crazy bitch left the phone off the hook," he muttered. Slowly getting up from the sidewalk, he headed over to fix the disorder.

The question came to him as he stood in front of the phone:

if he put the receiver back, would it ring? Gingerly picking up the phone, making sure to let the silver cord untangle, Jarreth placed it back within its cradle.

Nothing. No sudden life-changing call. Self-consciously aware of his disappointment, he left the box and closed its door.

"Now you're really losing it." He turned to walk back to the spot he'd found so comfortable before. One step, two steps, three, five, ten... He was just about to sit –

Riiiiing! Riiiiing!

"Fucking knew it!" He took his place against the wall.

Riiiiiing! Riiiiiing!

"I am *not* getting that," he yelled at the box from across the street, "so you can keep on ringing." It did. "Fuck you, I'm not answering that," he muttered. It would stop in a minute. It would stop and he'd never know.

Curiosity had always been his greatest flaw. Leaving his wall and running to the box, Jarreth picked up the receiver. "Hello?"

"You have to help me," a soft female voice answered. The static on the line cut out what she said next. And then, "Find me. I'm at corner of –" Silence, followed by static.

"Listen, I couldn't make out a thing you said. You keep cutting out. Say it slower." Nothing but the din of white noise answered him back. "Hello? Can you hear me? Am I coming through? There's nothing but static on the line."

Once again the voice said, "You have to help me... Find me. I'm at corner of *static* and –" Eerie and utter silence.

"I still can't hear..."

Two loud, metallic sounds tore the silence. Jarreth stumbled, oddly off-balance, and dropped the receiver. The phone box seemed to be closing in on him. Looking around, scared and confused, he noticed two dime-sized holes in the glass and a silver cylindrical object sticking out of his abdomen.

"Would fucking figure... I'm in a damned cliché." Jarreth fell backward against the door, and spilled out of the box. He grasped for the cylinder in his stomach, and felt a sharp pain in his neck as he turned his head. Wincing at the sudden sting, he brought his hand up.

Another object was stuck in his neck. The cold, smooth metal hurt like fuck as he tried to pull it out, and he found his fingers refusing to obey. The light began to fade.

A sudden rush of footfalls was followed by disembodied voices. "Stabilize him first, you idiot. We don't want a repeat of last night. Dixon will kill us if we lose another one."

The voice growled through the deepening dark.

"Why this one, Steve? He don't seem like nothing..."

"You getting a curiosity, now? Don't be bloody thick. Just do your job, get those darts out of him, stabilize him and get him in the truck. Now!"

Jarreth could feel damp concrete scraping across his back and legs, could feel the sudden bump of his head hitting a metallic surface, but it was all so very far away, happening to someone else.

It was strange, this sensation of nothingness. A seemingly endless void of blackness, punctuated by random sounds and unfamiliar smells, and none of it meant a damn thing.

Until a soft, feminine voice echoed inside his head. "You're stronger than you think. Just be still and don't try to fight them. You'll be fine." The voice created a warm spot in the endless dark. "I'm always with you, my love."

Glimpses of family, of friends long past, places he had been, buildings that had once meant something to him, they all seemed to rush to this warm spot, adding to the blanket that covered him inside his numbed mind. The image of a ring formed, wrapping itself around the whole motley collection of faces, places, and times. Punctuating the ring was a large stone, upon whose multifaceted shape Jarreth imprinted himself. A ring in a burgundy box... The walls came down, and he went away.

* * *

"Well? The Phrygian charged more for this idiot's name than I paid that leech for the last twenty specimens. He'd better *not* be another near miss." The disembodied voice echoed out from an intercom.

A group of professionally expressionless techs in black vinyl coats were gathered around the American. Pale and naked, he was strapped down to a white marble table, tubes and electrodes jutting from his body. A small machine balanced upon his abdomen was busily knitting damaged flesh back together, leaving barely a mark behind.

"He's already surpassing all expectations," one of the techs replied, speaking in the direction of the intercom. "We haven't seen promise like this since experiment ten. We believe we've found the correct genetic sequence. His is the key this time, definitely."

"That would make a pleasant change. Keep me informed. Make sure this one stays sedated, but do try not to lobotomise him in the process, eh? We might want to use him for something afterwards."

"I'll have the report on 101 in your office by the morning, Mr. Dixon. I am confident of a hundred percent success. His initial uptake has been exceptional, with no sign of the instability we saw with 89 or 93. All the markers are solid." The intercom clicked off, and the tech returned to the machines that flanked the table where 101's body lay.

In the control room, the man who'd been speaking through the intercom nodded to his compatriot. He watched the lab below, the view tainted a little by the one-way mirror. He allowed a certain perverse satisfaction to creep through him and onto his face. His ears pulled as the smile tightened the scar that ran between them.

Grabbing a large black trench-coat from a spinning chair, the heavy-set man walked toward the single entrance to the room. "Remind me to visit Nadia in the coffee shop," he said, forcing open the rusty door with his elbow. "She's served her purpose and must be rewarded." He slammed his gloved hand on the switch next to the steel frame, and behind him the room went black.

4. Tourist Trap
by Steven Sautter

For the third day in a row, Henry Bannister sat in the Café McLaughlin and sipped his nasty tea. He found it difficult to stomach, even loaded with sugar to disguise the taste. But it was cheap and warm, and for that he was grateful. The café, with its round tables and elegant, hard chairs, was a far cry from the campus coffee house and its comfy sofas. If he'd had any choice, he would have been elsewhere.

Taking another sip, he looked out the window at the street. There were surprisingly few people he recognised. He'd thought he would see the same people walk by at about the same time every day, but apart from the dog walker, and a gaggle of mums – or nannies, or both – taking their charges to a nearby park, the faces changed from day to day. Or maybe they didn't, and he was losing his memory for people.

He looked down at the table where the pages of a photocopied article from *Annals of Middle Eastern Literature* were spread out. It was quite intriguing, but he supposed it was too late to follow up on any of its leads on this trip.

Henry glanced at his watch. 9:17. He didn't have much time left, and his contact was late. He was supposed to have been in touch three days ago, but there had been no word. So Henry waited mournfully at the café, drinking tea as per his instructions, day upon day. The barista girl probably thought he was mad. Not for much longer, though. His flight back to Fairfield left at two, and customs were always a pain. As lucrative as this trip had promised to be, he wanted to get back to McMurtry. No, strike that. He wanted to get back to McMurtry's archaeology professor. To Kelly.

An unpleasantly tinny version of a song that'd reached number five on the charts in 1978 blared out from Henry's pocket. He sheepishly pulled out his cell, and the few people around him who hadn't been annoyed by the ringing were soon nettled by his answering it without stepping outside.

"You got the envelope?" The voice was strongly London-accented, and thick with menace.

"Y-yes?"

"You seem a bit uncertain, mate. That'd be a mistake, that would."

"I have it in my pocket."

"Better. See that phone box across the street? You'll get your instructions there." There was a click and the line went dead.

Heart pounding, he tossed a couple of bills down to cover his tab and got up, abandoning the article to its fate. A small black cat nearly tripped him as he went outside. He hoped it wasn't an omen. Making his way across the street, Henry stopped at the big red tourist trap, stepped inside and settled in to wait some more. The interior was plastered with fliers for English classes, housing opportunities and offers to do things to nether regions that ought not be mentioned in polite society.

The box's telephone rang. Henry's hand hovered over the receiver. Last chance to back out, but Kelly would never forgive his spinelessness if she found out. Summoning his courage, Henry answered the phone.

"Yes?"

"Now listen up, Mr. B. Real careful, please. Right this instant, a bloke of mine is up on a lofty little perch with a very big rifle aimed right at your forehead."

A thin trickle of sweat began to form on Henry's brow.

"Open the envelope and take out the cash so my spotter can see it."

"The bank wouldn't let me withdraw that much cash. I have a banker's draft. Is that okay?"

There was a resigned sigh from the other end of the line, followed by a very long moment of silence. "Jesus. Amateurs. All right then, Hank my buddy. Best make it out to 'Horace Vandenbussche'."

"A pseudonym."

25

"No, it was given to me by my dear old mum herself." The voice was heavy with sarcasm. "Fill the fucking thing out, hold it up in front of your face, then seal the envelope and fix it to the base of the phone."

Henry did as instructed, the pen wavering in his hand as he scrawled the name. There was a piece of duct tape waiting underneath the phone for the envelope. *Quite helpful*, he thought.

"All right, I've held up my end of the bargain. Where is my merchandise?" Henry could only hope that he'd managed to fill his voice with conviction.

The man on the other end rattled off a series of long and somewhat contradictory instructions. "My bloke will be keeping tabs on you. Anything happens to the draft before we pick it up, you're dead. Ignore my instructions, you're dead – and it won't be my fault this time. Take more than an hour to get the piece, and the deal's off, no refunds, plus I might have you shot just for being a fuck. Well? Go on then!" The man snorted, and hung up.

Henry dropped the receiver back on the hook and turned round to race outside. He ran smack into the door, then stepped back and rubbed the bridge of his nose where it had hit the frame.

As he reached for the door again, he noticed two round holes in the glass, about the size of dimes. "I wonder what those are for," he murmured. He carefully opened the door and strode back out on the street.

The directions were peculiar, of course. Through the nearby park, out the other side, then back into it, to walk three times widdershins around its central green. After that, they got plain strange. A diner that transcended time and space? Henry swallowed his pride and obeyed his orders as hastily as possible, shoulders crawling at the thought of the hidden gunman.

Finally, he found himself standing in front of a battered green Ford at the end of a very run-down cul-de-sac. Dust outside and in made it clear that the vehicle hadn't been touched in months, years even. He tried the door, found it unlocked, and slid into the passenger seat. In the glove compartment, as promised, was a small parcel wrapped in cardboard and string.

Taking great care, he opened it. Inside was a small wooden carving of a deer. It was pretty, in a seemingly insignificant way. He knew exactly what it was, though. Carved by an unknown Celt out of the remains of one of the sacred trees at Anglesey after the massacre, the totem was hugely important. Legend claimed it was one of the last links to ancient Druidic forces. Kelly would be blown away, her tenure assured for years to come.

As Henry was musing about how he'd get the carving past customs, a man came up to the car. He was dressed in a nearly-blinding green suit, and had a floppy grey-green hat pulled down almost over his eyes. He raised his head and fixed Henry with a steely gaze.

"V-vandenbussche?" Henry asked hesitantly.

"I know not of what you speak," the garish old man said. "You must come with me." His voice was oddly lacking in inflection.

Henry looked at his watch. "Look, I'd love to, but I have an urgent plane to catch and..."

"You must come with me," the man repeated.

He passed a hand over Henry's face. Henry's eyes crossed, and before he knew what had happened, he found himself sprawled on the pavement. The last words he heard as he passed out were the old man's flat voice again.

"You must come with me."

'Taking great care, he opened it.
Inside was a small wooden carving of a deer.'

5. The Crimson Tower
by J.F. Lawrence

From <u>Annals of Middle Eastern Literature</u>, July 2011, Vol. 47: 3; pp. 161 – 174.

Editorial note: I found this fragmentary document in Southampton's city archives. I was researching local poet Harmsworth Fountainhead for my PhD, going through a proof copy of his collected works 1962-1980. This piece was nestled between the pages, untitled, anonymous and undated. The penmanship is elegant but highly stylised, and yields no clues. It may be from a first draft of Fountainhead's rumoured epic prose work, 'God's Own City', if that was ever committed to paper. If he is not the author, then I am tempted to suggest Gilbert Frotte. The man was a notorious literary prankster, and his role as Fountainhead's secret lover during the years of the poet's political marriage would have given ample opportunity. The style certainly does not reflect Frotte's typical work – it is neither blasphemous nor pornographic – but it could fit his sense of humour. It doesn't echo Fountainhead's usual writing either, though: the ludic spirit of the fragment is out of keeping with his famously dour demeanour. Some scholars have suggested that God's Own City took the form of an experimental serio-comic work, however. The epic is typically thought to be a fictionalised history of Southampton, so the possibility that the fragment belongs there is not entirely far-fetched. Still, given that archives can prove somewhat random when it comes to the placement of documents, the fragment may be the work of someone else entirely. JFL

"I have discovered a rather strange scrap of translated text. It lay within an antiquarian bookshop which I encountered on one of my regular walks in the more far-flung streets of Southampton. It was a dark-windowed little building, deep inside an alleyway that does not appear on any street-plan of the city. Neither the ever-reliable Ordnance Survey A-Zs nor Kelly's Directories have betrayed any hint of its presence in my library searches. I know the city intimately, being a lifelong wanderer of its thoroughfares and purlieus, but this alleyway was far off the beaten track. I have never come across it before, nor have I found it again since, as I was somewhat distracted when I first encountered it, and absorbed in my treasure by the time I left.

"Orbis Books. The name caught my attention, pulled me out of my reverie. It was written in gothic lettering above a leaded glass door. A bell tinkled as I entered. A musty suffusion of pipe smoke, mould and dust wafted over me. Gloomy light filtered in from the mullioned windows, and cast devious shadows over muddled shelves. Serious dealers in aged tomes are invariably cleaner, tidier and better organised. However, as an ardent collector, it was impossible that I would have not been familiar with one of those serious dealers. This was the kind of ramshackle place where the most surprising oddities might be discovered – the rarest of rare literary works, the most obscure and the most clandestine. There was a particular quarry I had been chasing for years, relying on the say-so of the whispering network of scheming paranoiacs, fantasists, quasi-criminals and lovelorn romantics who comprise the *demimonde* of the antiquarian books world. Naturally, I was captivated.

"A spindly Dickensian fellow with a long, narrow face peered up at me through Roger McGuinn spectacles. He stood up behind his counter, obscured in half-shadow, and gently set down a shiny little metallic cone. He had been caressing the object, his fingers unusually long and sleek. He offered me a cartilaginous handshake. He had an ancient face, a tapestry of lines and seams, but his eyes were dark and penetrating.

"He smiled slowly at me. 'Good afternoon. I am Orbis, the proprietor of this establishment. I can see that you are in search of something in particular, a special item. I can usually sense the spirit of the true enthusiast, sir. Am I right?' His voice was stronger than I had expected from such a decrepit specimen, and carried a mischievous edge.

"'Yes, indeed,' I replied. 'I doubt that you have it though, or even know of its possible whereabouts. It is a children's book, *The Red Telephone Box* by Crofton Wingwalker. Only a thousand copies were ever printed.'

"'Ah, of course. I think I'm right in saying that a mere handful of copies are known to have survived the gas explosion that destroyed the publishing house. Let me see...' Orbis lurched off into the recesses of his shop.

"Wingwalker is something of a fascination of mine. A noted eccentric, he wrote dense, unreadable tomes on Sufism, Swedenborg and Turkish love poetry. He'd produced a ten-volume history of the lives of the Scholastics. More compellingly, he was linked to some of the most famous and notorious figures in 20th century history – an *eminence grise,* who trailed vortices of hinted influence and occulted knowledge. Pick any important figure in politics, art, science or philosophy, and Crofton Wingwalker was associated in some not-too-far-removed capacity or another. *The Red Telephone Box* was his one attempt at commercial writing, an ostensibly innocent cover for his philosophical and magical theories, and his subversive moral programme. The book tells the story of a little girl who gets lost in a big city, and discovers a magic telephone box which is a portal to a version of this world where things are very different. Naturally, she emerges from her journey profoundly and disturbingly changed.

"Wingwalker was a mystic alchemist, and an Anarchist in the Bakunin mould. A visionary who formed secret cadres and conceived complex plots, he loved playing individuals and groups off against each other in dense strategies. These ultimately may have been so unfathomably involved as to confuse even Wingwalker himself, let alone his hapless puppets. A labour, truly, of love. The man died in the explosion that destroyed his last work, and conspiracy theories abound regarding his demise. Some even claim he faked his death and is still behind the scenes, though if he were alive today, he would be a very old man indeed. I have followed biographical clues around Europe, North Africa, Turkey, Israel, India and Mongolia, seeking out his writings and uncovering scraps of information. Often, my efforts have brought me to dead ends, or meetings with characters whose relationships with consensus reality have been problematic, to say the least. I suppose Wingwalker is an obsession. That state of mind is a psychic risk to which collectors of esoteric literature – and historians of the marginal – are all too susceptible.

"Orbis returned bearing a small red-leather-bound volume interleaved with loose papers."[1]

"... I have not been able to identify the 'famed' Ghirgiz al-Uqbar who features in the story. Nothing appears to remain of his works, and it seems that history has not recorded him. Thus the celebrity of discovering a lost piece by an overlooked great amongst Arab mystics and scholars is, alas, denied to me. More seriously, connections between *The Crimson Tower* and *The Red Telephone Box* remain purely speculative, despite the tantalising indicators to which I have already referred.[2]

"The translation is missing significant parts, including the name of the author of the piece, and the editorial notes are unhelpful. The named translator, LJ Osberg, may have been one Linus Osberg, an obscure Swedish academic who is mainly remembered for his spectacularly fatal heart-attack on an Oslo dock. However, this LJ Osberg may just as plausibly be a complete fiction. The surviving text is as follows.

THE CRIMSON TOWER

"Ghirgiz al-Uqbar, feted Sufi poet and translator, a scholar famed in all Arabia, was visited nightly by a dream from God. He would travel alone across the desert for many days, time compressing in the manner of dreams, until he saw before him, distant and seductive as a mirage, a great crimson tower. He would ride up to its gates, where a veiled woman always stopped him. "You may not enter here unless you can answer me this," she would say, then whisper something he could not understand into his ear. A powerful voice would echo in his mind: "Go to her,

---

1   *(JFL: The fragment breaks off here. There appear to be a number of missing pages, though it is impossible to say how many, since the document is not numbered. In the following section, the author is describing the translated item he mentions at the beginning. I presume it is within the red leather book, although it may not be. I have failed to unearth any information whatsoever on Wingwalker, who seems reminiscent of the likes of Crowley and Gurdjieff.)*

2   *(JFL: I, too, have failed to uncover any references to this putative poet, or to his writings, the piece itself, or even the translator. Did al-Uqbar even exist?)*

Ghirgiz, she is your destiny." Then he would awake with a feeling of unease.

"He was highly troubled by this recurrent vision, wondering if it was truly a message from God. If not, then it would be madness to follow its injunction; if so, then to ignore it would be disobedience to his maker. He consulted the Holy Qur'an for guidance, and discussed the dream with fellow poets and philosophers. When in the throes of the dervish dance he saw visions of the crimson tower flickering in the shadows thrown against the cave walls by the holy fire.

"One morning as he sat in his courtyard, contemplating the beauty of the sunrise above the city and enjoying the incipient warming of the day, he saw a sign that gave him the answer he sought. He ...

"[Ed. A lost page interrupts the story here, which resumes with Ghirgiz at the gates of the tower. A pity, for Ghirgiz was famed for his beautiful evocations of religious symbolism. Alas, fate has denied to us the pleasure of reading his description of the fateful sign. LJO]

"He ran, stumbling, from the room of infinitely reflecting crystal mirrors, maddened by the visions that teemed in his terrorised, disoriented mind: demons riding on eagles' wings, chanting obscene verses from a red book, verses of a wicked poem that told of a devilish chariot made of glass and red metals that carried the ungodly to Hell, where they disported themselves in frenzies of lewdness, gluttony and violence. He was struck blind by the burning light of the mirrors and the apocalyptic scenes they displayed.

"Falling to his knees at the gates of the tower, he faced upwards sightlessly, pleading, as the veiled woman said: 'You have been deprived of sight for the sin of devoting yourself to the word of man more than to the word of God. Your judgment is this: you will wander the city for the rest of your days as a blind beggar, exhorting all to reject the unholy writings of men and live only by the word of the Creator. Only by this may you repent of your blasphemous foolishness.'

"And so it was. Ghirgiz lived out his life as a mendicant railing against the vanity of humans who do not look with sufficient diligence upon God. He would stop passers-by in the marketplace each day and fix them with his unseeing eyes. Fascinated, they would hear his terrible tale, then hurry away with this exhortation echoing behind them: 'Remember the name of poor Ghirgiz al-Uqbar! Tell his story wherever you go!'"

33

"[Ed. This is the story's end. The legend of al-Uqbar's blindness has been handed down in numerous versions through the last five centuries, via the Arab nations, Persia, Turkey and the Maghreb. It is a shame that The Crimson Tower itself is so hard to find, and that this version is incomplete. My translation is the first into English, the language I love most after my native tongue. I console myself that its incomplete nature is justified by the hope that it will be a harbinger, to the Anglophone nations, of the beauty and profundity of the writings of the great and mysterious Ghirgiz al-Uqbar. –L.J. Osberg, Buenos Aires.]"[3]

"Having retrieved the required document, I returned to my desk. As I sat, I saw a lanky old man leave the archive through the glass double doors. I could not be certain, but I thought it was Orbis. I was wondering what he was doing there when my eye was drawn to the folder of documents I had been studying before I got up. A copperplate handwritten note was sitting on top of the folder's cover. I can state with certainty that it had not been in the folder previously; I had already been through its contents thoroughly. It said simply this:
"'If you go to the Infinite Library, there you will find me.'"

JFL: There is nothing more. It might be the end of the tale, although there might as easily be far more. It is possible that the archive referred to is the very same Southampton city archive where I conduct my research; the mention of glass double doors certainly fits, as does the presence of the fragment. I maintain the hope that one day more of this document will come to light – or that I will find some evidence for the existence of Crofton Wingwalker or Ghirgiz al-Uqbar.
J.F. Lawrence, Cap d'Antibes, 2011

---

3   *(JFL: The fragmentary document is missing another section here. Once again, it is impossible to know how many pages were omitted. There is one last page, which starts at a point where the scene has changed to an unnamed public archive.)*

6. Echo
by James 'Grim' Desborough

The bus was late. Talbot was late.

Work dragged on too often nowadays. You were expected to work overtime – no question of any extra money for your efforts of course, you just got to keep your job. The apologetic weeknight calls to his wife had come to take on the hollow emptiness of ritualised Catholic guilt.

It was that half-lit time of the evening where the grey of the sky bled into the dull concrete and the exhaust-stained fascia of the older, pigeon-speckled, brick buildings. The light was oddly flat, and one colour bled into another, neither day nor night. The street lights were just waking up from their daytime slumber, their cider-yellow glow just bright enough to make them irritating, but not enough to help you actually see anything with.

A chill was setting in as the sun clocked off for the day, and the wind gusted around the quiet street sending old crisp packets and cigarette butts scuttling for cover. He waited, bored, feet thrumming on the pavement like some spastic tap-dancer. God, he wished he smoked. Something. Anything to pass the time, to give him something to do with his hands while time stretched out in front of him like an abyss. There was nothing like lighting a cigarette to make a bus turn up. That was the only time, these days, where he missed sparking up – when he was bored.

London was strange that way, leaving you alone amongst so many people. The blocks of flats around the bus stop were a mix of light and dark. A living map of impatience – or fear of the dark. Silhouettes moved against the windows where they were lit, a shadow play of other people's domesticity and warmth, the indecipherable chatter of a dozen distant televisions.

The utter bastards, all warm and snug and distracted in their homes. He was jealous.

The wind picked up again, and with the abrupt shock of a hammer blow, the rain tumbled down in ropes. He gasped at the sudden chill, soaked to the skin within instants. He held his hand pointlessly over his head against the drumbeat rain, and looked for cover. The bus stop had none, just a bench with broken seats. A car crash – or vandals – had taken the shelter. He didn't much care which, at this point. He couldn't very well barge into someone's flat and beg for shelter, and he didn't want to miss the bus.

There was one place.

Glowing dimly in the sudden darkness was an old, peeling telephone box. An endangered species, these days. Preserved, here and there, when a nostalgic council or determined locals felt it brought something to the area. That conservative love of the old that so many British shared. He lunged for it, hauling open the protesting door with a shriek of metal. As he wedged himself through the gap, a black cat – also seeking shelter – slipped between his legs and darted into the box. It nearly tripped him as he struggled to yank his coat in after him.

"Bloody mog," he growled. Its tawny yellow eyes looked up at him with practised indifference and it began to enthusiastically lick its genitals. He supposed he didn't really begrudge it. They both needed shelter, and it was nice to have some company.

Faded cards, blu-tacked to the back of the booth, advertised perverted wares with sweet-sounding lies. Most of it seemed to be in some secret prostitute's code he couldn't decipher. There was nothing in this tiny room to ease his boredom.

Cold, with nothing else to do, he stamped his feet to shake off the raindrops and get a little warmth back into him. There was a "murph" of protest from the cat as his foot clipped the tip of its tail, and he caught himself, just, before he apologised. It was only a cat.

His eyes ran over everything inside: the peeling paint, the tags scratched into the panes, the pitted, scarred surface of the phone itself, a glimmer of broken glass on the floor. Something had punched out two small circles from one of the window panes. There was a faint stink of stale piss, the fossil evidence of some feral Friday night, but that was just unpleasant, not interesting.

Toilet. Shelter. Prostitute's yellow pages. Billboard for the tags of the local gangs. God, how he missed 'proper' graffiti. It seemed this venerable old red box was used for anything and everything except making calls. No dirty old men making furtive assignations. No teenagers kiss-calling the loves of their lives, away from their parents. Nobody dialling home to say they'd be late for dinner. The mobile phone had put an end to all of that.

Still no bus. He peered through the tag-scratched glass looking for any sign of it, the gleam of headlights rounding the corner.

Nothing.

Then the phone rang. He jumped at the sudden noise, the familiar yet unfamiliar sound of a ringing phone in a world of ring*tones*. For a moment it threw him entirely, his brain struggling to string the noise and the expected action together. He stared at the handset for a seemingly endless moment and then, tentatively, he picked it up.

"Hello?"

"Hello," came the voice back at the other end, copper wires and analogue technology making it seem distant and unreal.

"Who is this?"

"Who is this?" it came back after a moment, mocking him.

There are moments of joy that are common to many people in their lives. The birth of a child, the first kiss, the taste of a favourite meal, a shared joke. There are also moments of profound disappointment, and one of the greatest is when you hear your own voice as other people hear it, rather than as you hear it when you speak.

He laughed, even as he felt the familiar pang in his gut, the sinking feeling he always got when he remembered that his voice wasn't a deep baritone.

"Just an echo on the line." He laughed, hollowly. A brief exhalation.

"...an echo?"

The hairs on the back of his neck prickled up, his breath caught. It was his voice, but...

"I'm lonely," said his stolen voice. "Please, talk to me."

He slammed the door open, the old hinge all but snapping with the force he used in getting out of the damned box. It wedged open, and the cat stared after him like he was mad, resentful that he'd let the rain and the cold in.

The receiver swung like a hanged man behind him, but he turned and ran, not looking back, fleeing out into the welcoming rain.

7. All Things Considered
by erisreg

The cat watched the man dwindle into the darkness. The door to the red phone box shuddered and slid closed with an uncharacteristic silence. A moment later, a woman's dark hand lifted the receiver. Its owner put the phone to her ear, and the voice on the line said "Hello?"

"He's gone," Corellwen replied.

There was a momentary burst of static. "Come home," the phone said, in a different voice. The line clicked off, leaving a rusty sounding dial-tone.

Cory put the receiver back into its waiting cradle reluctantly. She looked around the small space for a moment, as if it held the solution to a problem. Then she sighed, picked up the receiver again, and dialled the six-digit access code. The small panes of the booth frosted over instantly, just in time to mask the bright flash of odd-coloured light from the outside world. A heartbeat later, the panes cleared and the door drifted ajar. The booth was vacant, the phone dangling again.

* * *

Cory emerged into fading daylight and looked around at her exit point – a small meadow surrounded closely by tree-cloaked hills. She didn't recognize the area, but it was never the same place twice. It was too dangerous to have a fixed arrival point. Too predictable.

She was in the open, the feel of the portal still strong. Looking at her feet, she saw a glimmer in the soil. She bent down and picked up a small blue pebble, then placed it in her pouch. She might not need it soon, but having the nexus with her meant an easier time returning to her post.

She looked around. There was no hint of an escort. Odd. Not a good sign. She shielded her eyes from the low-hanging sun, and scanned the distance for anything that would indicate her path. She sucked in her breath as she saw the dark shape of a large flier heading in her direction. Instinct told her it wasn't a friend. Keeping low, she broke into a run toward the closest copse of trees. She moved as quickly as she could without breaking cover. Transformation was out of the question. The flier was probably coming to investigate the surge from her arrival. Any more power spikes would just make her easier to find. Most fliers had good eyes. She made for the forest, a nice dense spot with options to flee in several directions if that became necessary.

As soon as she was past the first trees, she dug her way into a cluster of thick bramble. She watched as the shape closed in. It circled, landing mere inches from her arrival spot.

I was right to run.

The huge, leather-winged creature flickered, shifting into the form of a grey-haired man. He peered around, then fished about in a heavy pouch slung around his neck. Pulling out a set of binoculars, he scanned the tree-line, obviously looking for her. He pulled some implement out of the pouch, knelt down, and slowly swept it over the ground. He quartered the area twice, methodically, before he replaced his tools. Raising his arms, he transformed back into his leonine flying form, leapt into the air and started spiralling out in ever-growing circles.

For what felt like an age, Corellwen kept herself silent and still. She didn't venture out of her thicket until the small wild critters around her resumed their usual noises. The green-tinged sun was almost to the horizon. The chances were that some sort of town or outpost lay in the direction the flier had come from. There was nothing else to go on, so she decided to head in that direction. She couldn't risk the power burst of a shape change. She was just going to have to walk. Dusk was embracing the land as she started out, and shadows were creeping from their hiding places.

She crested a knoll at the end of the meadow, and spotted a mound lying in the grass off to the right a way. There was just enough light to make out that the blood-soaked tangle of limbs had once been a blond man. She rushed to him, her heart in her throat. He was still warm. He moaned feebly at her touch. She gently rolled him over and tried to get him into a more comfortable position. His eyes widened and he started to speak.

"Portal!" he coughed, as if sensing it on her. Blood oozed from the corner of his mouth.

"Shh, it's okay. Rest." She tried to calm him down before his agitation finished him.

"No time," he mumbled. He jerked an elbow towards a ridge, the hand flopping horribly, and moaned again. "Twelve degrees north... Brightest star... Red-haired matron, green scarf. Twenty hours. Hurry." He coughed again, more blood spilling. Then he spasmed sharply. When he stilled again, his breathing had stopped.

She considered hunting for stones and building a cairn, but his last word made her doubt that he'd appreciate it. With a silent apology, she quickly went through his pockets for any other clues. They were empty, and there was no sign of a pack or pouch. She smoothed his clothing, and pulled him into a more dignified final pose, legs out straight, hands folded on his chest.

Twenty hours? It made her wonder how far away civilization must be. With a sad shake of her head she turned in the direction he'd indicated, and gazed up at the stars that were starting to show. Picking out the brightest was easy enough, but without a compass, her direction was guesswork at best. It would have to do. She trudged off into the night.

A short time later, the burble of water caught her attention. She made a bee-line for it, and found a clear, spring-fed pool, a small stream spilling out and away. She washed the escort's blood off her hands at the stream mouth, then went back to the top of the pool and drank. The cool water revived her spirits a bit, although it did little for her hunger. She was painfully aware that she was committed to finding the matron. The nexus stone would take her back to London, but not until she was told the activation code.

She'd been hiking up a hill for a while when she spotted a well-kept road that twisted its way up the steep incline. Mystified, she followed it toward the top. From the other side of the hill, the glow of a large, well-lit township stained the night.

It didn't make sense. She'd only been moving for about three hours. Was this just a way-station to her destination? Why travel so far when this had to be a large enough place to cover a meet up? She followed the road into town, determined to find answers – but not until she'd obtained some food.

She came onto the main street, pleasantly impressed with its tidiness and orderly evening bustle. She caught the eye of a girl carrying a basket and asked her, "Is there a place where I might work for a meal in this town?"

The girl sized her up and down warily, and after a moment of thought, cocked her head down the street. "Ma'm Grisom is a good one to ask, miss. West side of the street, a short way down. You'll find her at the sign of the galley." She backed up a step, and hurried off.

"Thank you," Cory called to the girl's back. Then she looked toward the storefronts the girl had indicated.

As she'd implied, a large sign depicting a common trader ship dominated the façade of a building just a short distance up the street. A board beneath it boasted 'The finest fare and lodging in town.' Cory paused to take in the device, which was finely carved and clearly well-maintained.

Then it struck her. The *Galley*. She looked up at the carving again. The ship had a double course, ten rowers long.

Not *hours*. Oars. Twenty oars. Her spirits soared.

Inside, the main room was filled to bursting with benches and tables. There were plenty of drinkers, mostly heavy-set men with weathered skin and strong hands. They were a boisterous crowd, but there were no suggestions of bad tempers or lurking aggression. The likely reason for their exemplary behaviour leaned patiently against the end of the bar, occasionally speaking to the serving maids as they bustled about. He was very tall, and hugely muscled. His eyes seemed to drink in everything, and his movements were graceful and precise.

She watched him observe her approach impassively. As she got close, she realised that he was even taller than she'd thought. It took no effort to summon up a nervous smile. "I was told it might be possible to trade my work for a meal here. The girl said I should ask for Madame Grisom."

42

The man-tower grinned, and she wondered that she'd ever found him threatening. "Don't call Mam that to her face," he said cheerfully. "She'll not thank you, not in the least. Hold a moment, and she'll be out."

He waved one of the serving lasses over, then bent down and spoke softly to her. The girl scurried off behind the bar and through a curtain.

A few moments later, the girl came back out, shortly followed by a woman who could only be Mam Grisom. She was tall and strongly built, with a cascade of fiery red hair. A green shawl hid beneath it, wrapped around her shoulders. She glanced at Cory, then flicked her eyes around the inn quickly. A faint hint of pain washed over her face. She beckoned Cory, and led her through the kitchen.

Less than a minute later, Corellwen was seated at a rough table, with a generous bowl of hot, tasty stew.

"He's dead, then." It was not a question.

Cory nodded. "He clung on just long enough to point me this way. I'm sorry."

"As am I." Mam fell silent, and stayed that way for several minutes. Cory concentrated on her stew, giving the older woman some time. Finally, Mam continued. "You came from London, yes? Corellwen?"

Cory nodded again.

"You were not called back to make a report."

"Oh?" She fought down a sudden burst of fear.

"The Magus has found new allies. Worse than his shapeshifters. They can traverse the portal."

"Traverse the…" A nasty chill wormed its way down Cory's spine.

"London is no longer safe. You will need to be significantly more careful. We know almost nothing about his new agents, but if they can cross worlds, they can also feel power."

"That's bad."

Mam nodded grimly. "And they knew your arrival here closely enough to catch Jake and finish him."

"I need to get back, then. Warn our tentative allies. Keep watch."

"Yes," said Mam. "You do. We need those alliances confirmed swiftly. It's in their interests. They'll need our help if the Magus decides to use their realm as a power base."

"I understand."

"The nearest Ley is east of town. There's a well, at the corner of three fields. Put your back to it. The activation for that nexus you're carrying is the image of a giant's head, buried inside a hill which has a church on its top."

"Got it," Cory said. "I'll head back right away."

"Take care, girl."

"I will."

It took about half an hour to pick her way unobtrusively through to Eastgate and then get out to the location Mam had given her. Enough light spilled out from the town that she could see her way clearly. She found the well easily, turned away from it, and set the nexus stone down between her feet. She heard a faint rustle in the air, off to the right, and instinctively dropped into a low crouch. A dark, heavy bulk whistled above her, and she heard a growl of frustration. The leathery lion-creature she'd seen earlier wheeled in a tight arc, and came back round for another pass. She turned to face it, keeping low.

At the last moment, she shifted into her cat form. Heavy claws passed harmlessly over her, and she sprang up as the beast went overhead, lodging her own claws firmly into its haunch. The creature snarled, and jerked its leg savagely, trying to dislodge her. Cory ignored the flailing, and carefully climbed her way up towards its back. As soon as she was in range, she used her claws to slice at its genitals. The creature roared in pain, and she used its distraction to dart up its back and grab a firm hold at the base of its wings.

She clung there grimly for a while, slashing at its wings whenever possible, fighting its attempts to throw her off. She couldn't do enough damage to force it down however, and it in turn wasn't able to shake her loose. The creature stopped wheeling and diving, and started to head directly away from the well. If it got her too far from the nexus, she'd be in deep trouble.

Cory started pulling the claws on both front paws through the creature's skin, sacrificing stability for damage. It howled, and went into a crazy, bucking tumble. As it did, she released her hold, shifted into her crow form, and dived silently back towards the well.

It took the creature several seconds to realise what had happened. It was still wheeling to turn back as she landed over the nexus stone and blurred back into her human shape. She concentrated on the activation image, spoke the command, and the world spun.

The stench of old urine welcomed her back to her familiar phone box. Safe. Except for anonymous new horrors stalking her through the city, of course. She bumped the door ajar, blurred down into her feline form, and slunk off into the rainy night.

8. Dementia
by David Church Rodríguez

Down the street from the phone box, the Lion's Head was filled with the aroma of steak and ale pie and the clink of pint glasses.

"Don't say that word, Mark. That's a dirty, dirty word." The old man was slumped over the bar. He turned his head to look up at the younger man on the stool next to him.

Mike took a long swig from his pint before speaking. "What word? Dementia? That's not a dirty word, that's a medical condition." Mr. Ryder was exactly the age his father would have been. Maybe he'd have been the same way.

"It's so dirty," said the old man, looking back down at his lap. His hands were nestled there, palms up, shaking. The fingers were rigid, stuck like claws, like the feet of a dead dove. The old man almost never used them any more. The skin was spotted, wrinkled, uneasy to look at. He seemed as frail as old parchment. "It's the dirtiest word humans have ever created."

Tuesdays were always Mr. Ryder's worst days. Mike had been caring for him for the last two months, and was used to the rituals that he relied on. He couldn't remember his own name half the time, and had no idea about other people's, but he'd always remember that Wednesdays were a visit to Regent's Park, Fridays meant the Storyteller and then Eastenders nights, and Tuesdays involved the Lion's Head Pub and the red phone box.

Just thinking about it, Mike felt himself smile. The phone box was the most important thing in the old man's life. That first Tuesday, Mike's second day, they'd gone to the phone box. Mike had helped the old man inside, waited for him nervously. Then Mr. Ryder had positively leapt back out, managing the door effortlessly, a bounce in his step, his eyes bright and knowing. He still looked around the area uncertainly though, and when Mike asked him if he was feeling better, the old man stared at him for a short age, until finally managing an uncertain "Is that you, Luke?" The strength ebbed as the week ran out, and by Tuesday evening, the man was little more than a husk. Until the phone box, and a new name for the week. Recently, Mike had been Spike, Miles, Ike, Malc... This week he was Mark, and he was mildly curious to see who he would be after tonight's visit to the phone box.

He looked at the old man again. He was studying his pint glass, as if trying to figure out what it was and how it worked. Mike could feel sadness creeping out to stain his expression. If he'd even met his father... He shook himself mentally. "Tell me about the box, Sam."

The old man's face lit up. "The box takes you places," he said, fluent enough that Mike could almost forget his condition. "Never where you're supposed to be, well, almost never... But sometimes you feel that you're that much closer to the right place."

Mike grinned. The man's imagination was a gift. Despite everything he'd been through, despite knowing that his mind was rotting away inside his head, Mr. Ryder had something. Especially on Tuesdays. Mike could see a clear spark of anticipation in his watery eyes.

He downed what was left of his beer and stood up.

"Okay, Sam. Let's go visit the box." He didn't expect an answer.

Mr. Ryder smiled beatifically, and descended from his stool. His movements were slow, deliberate, and just a bit shaky. Mike offered the old man his arm, and Mr. Ryder grabbed it without moving his fingers, making Mike smile. He let go again after a couple of steps, and started walking towards the exit – and the rainy night – with an unusual decisiveness. Maybe there was still some hope for him.

They left the pub, Mike fumbling to get his umbrella up. He did his best to keep the old man dry, but Mr. Ryder didn't seem to care about the rain tonight. Mike wasn't sure if he even noticed it. Maybe he was too enthralled with the idea of the box. He certainly seemed to be as close to running speed as he could get, a nice, comfortable pace for Mike.

Despite the rain, the night was warm, and Mike found he was really enjoying the fresh air. He looked forward to seeing what the box would do for Mr. Ryder tonight, who he would turn into.

Out of nowhere, a crazed man charged past them, running like the hounds of hell were on his path. He clipped Mr. Ryder and continued without even breaking stride. Mike lunged forward to stop the old man from falling. He was far too frail. If he fell, there would be serious consequences. Mike managed to catch his shoulder, support him. The old man gasped wildly, and clung to Mike's shirt.

"Are you okay, Sam?"

Mr. Ryder didn't seem to be listening. He was looking at the ground and breathing heavily. Mike hugged the old man, to make him feel safe. He let him go slowly, making sure he had regained his footing. He turned his head, looking for the attacker, but saw only rain.

"Wanker!" The guy might be out of earshot, but it was the best Mike could do. He turned back to Mr. Ryder, still concerned, but the old man was simply looking ahead to where the box was. Mike realized he had dropped his umbrella, which lay open on the pavement beside a puddle, like a marooned boat. He picked it up and flicked it open and closed a few times, then a few times more.

When he looked up, Mr. Ryder was already a short distance ahead. He went after the old man, cursing himself quietly. Everything was starting to seem like a really bad idea. The rain was getting worse, and the wind was picking up, too. He'd never forgive himself if the old man got sick because of his thoughtlessness. The very opposite of care. However, Mr. Ryder seemed fitter than ever, and he hadn't even been into the box. The old man was actually picking up speed. Mike started jogging. Impossibly, the old man continued to pull away from him.

Mike could see the box now. The door was open, and the receiver was off its hook, swinging on its cord like a hanged man. The wind had begun to howl, blasting into Mike, slowing him down. Not Mr. Ryder, though. The old man walked into the box easily, closed the door, and picked up the receiver.

Exhaustion threatened to drag Mike down. Even breathing and walking were becoming difficult. It was like being trapped in the wrong sort of nightmare, where the closer he got to the box, the harder everything became. Finally, he made it. He clung to the handle for a moment, marshalling his strength, and then tried to open the door. It didn't move. It didn't even tremble. A flash of lightning ripped the London night open. As Mike's sight cleared, he realised that Mr. Ryder was looking straight at him through the closed door.

"Mike?" asked the old man.

Mike stared at him. There was a new, powerful awareness in the eyes of the man he had been looking after for the last two months. The forbidden thought at the back of his head, the fairytale what-if, came back hard. Certain. Mike's jaw fell open, and he could feel tears streaming down his face, the first time since childhood.

"Mike?"

"Dad?" Mike tugged at the door again, feeling more like his usual self. It still wouldn't move. "Open the door, Dad!" He kicked at the box, to no effect.

The old man was watching Mike with wide-open eyes, his lips trembling. He looked terrified.

"Dad!" Mike kept on screaming.

"No, no, I can't." The old man shivered and picked the phone back up. "Mike, I'm sorry. I'm so sorry. I can't be here. It doesn't work like that." He moved the receiver to his ear.

Mike started banging the box with his closed fists. He watched helplessly as the old man spoke softly into the phone. He couldn't hear his words, but he could see his eyes, staring straight at him. Another flash of lightning wiped the night away, and when Mike's eyes re-adjusted to the darkness, he was totally alone.

9. All Fall Down
by Peter Dawes

The scents of power, blood and fury pulled him through the deep night. He allowed the call to drag him on, ghosting past hamlets and small farm communities, to within sight of a fair-sized town. It led him to a lonely well, at the corner of three fields. He could feel the last traces of a portal, fading but still vibrant. The other side smelled interesting. Spicy. He released a trickle of stolen life, feeling it coil around the rip. A moment of strain, a blurring rush, and then he was through, into a tiny red chamber punctuated with columns of windows. London. This was London. He grinned, and slipped out into the night. It was good to be back.

* * *

The wind whipped through the trees, shivering the branches, apparently desperate to steal every drop of heat. It was long past sunset, but the crowd of children in the park had yet to retreat. Their coats were clutched tight in youthful defiance of the weather. Laughter ebbed and flowed with the wind's gusts, vanishing one moment, echoing up eerily the next. Mason watched them, smiling, his arms draped across the back of a bench. He quietly kept half an eye on the red phone box a short way down the road.

Until something else intruded, carried on the wind.

Ring-a-ring-a-roses
A pocket full of posies
Atishoo! Atishoo!
We all fall down.

The rhyme snatched him and flung him back, deep into old thoughts and memories. Reality splintered, and for a moment the children wore tattered cloth, and the park was dirt and cobblestone. A young boy wove carefully through a crowd of pedestrians, mindful of the horses clopping past. The air was heavy with dust and the stench of shit. The vision was so dense, he could have drowned in it. Mason blinked repeatedly, trying to erase the vision.

The dull stink of car exhaust returned, the people back to haring along at their usual frantic pace. Somewhere off in the distance, a dog howled. One woman in particular leapt out at him as the embodiment of modern life: harassed, impatient, self-obsessed. She was marching along, blind to the world's promise, thumping irritably at a phone's touch-screen.

"Bollocks." She jerked to a sudden halt in front of the phone box. A couple of the children glanced over in her direction.

She looked up at the heavens, her mouth pulled into a tight, resentful line, and then yanked the phone box door open. She recoiled for a moment as the air inside hit her, holding the door open whilst she rifled through her purse. Mason felt himself begin to smile, and continued to watch her, thoughtful as much as curious.

The woman stepped into the box, using one foot to keep the door open a bit, and picked up the receiver. Unwilling to press it against her head, she held it gingerly at a discreet distance. It was barely visible against the chocolate brown of her hair. Once she was satisfied that the thing seemed to work, she started feeding coins into the slot, and dialled.

A moment later, she started screeching into the telephone, even though the receiver was barely further from her head that it normally would have been. It was loud and strident enough to make Mason think of nails and blackboards.

"Annie... Hey love, I won't be coming over tonight." She paused, then huffed. Mason could imagine her rolling her eyes in disgust. "Yes, I know this isn't my sodding number. My mobile's acting up... No, no bloody signal. David and I broke up, sweetie... Yeah, another smashing night all right. He told me he wanted more space, so I told him to piss off. The bloody idiot. So anyway, now I have to take the tube home instead of getting a ride."

Mason casually uncrossed his legs, allowing himself a moment to study the woman. Her skin was pale, but smooth and creamy, her cheeks lightly blushed. Black eyeliner, applied in thick, gracious lines, brought out the colour in her eyes. Her figure was impeccable too, under a cheerfully bright red raincoat. Mason sat perfectly still until the moment she glanced up, then licked his lips and ostentatiously darted his gaze back to the children, who were beginning to disperse.

He saw her smile from the corner of his eye. "Okay, I'll call you tomorrow after work. Maybe we can work on getting slaughtered. See ya, love." She hung up the phone and fiddled a little, continuing to cast glances in his direction. Then something dragged her reluctant attention back to her surroundings. She wrinkled her nose, giving him a good idea what the distraction was.

She recovered quickly, and flipped her hair casually as she walked out of the phone box. She shot Mason a last, lingering glance before starting off across the street.

Ring-a-ring-a-roses...

The wind gusted again, and the woman shook off a shiver, but she didn't miss a step until one of the children almost ran straight into her. She lifted a hand and swore at him. Mason smirked and stood up, moving closer to the red phone box. He noticed that she'd left the receiver hanging from its hook. *I suppose that makes this one mine.*

"... get back in your bloody house before you kill somebody!" Her words echoed eerily. The boy's response sounded distant, as though the wind itself had spirited his retort away. She lifted her chin slowly and stole a glance over her shoulder, clearly disappointed that Mason wasn't on the bench any more. The wind blasted her again, and she turned back around. "Yeah, off with you," she murmured. She might just have been talking to the boy, but it was a long moment before she resumed her journey.

Mason grinned, savouring the moment. He slipped from one side of the street to the other, and headed in the same direction. Another young boy was standing by the bus stop, next to his mother, who was absorbed in a trashy magazine. Mason freed a hand, and tousled the kid's hair as he passed. The boy stared in wonder, and Mason could feel his gaze on the back of his neck until he rounded the corner and moved from sight. The distinctive red raincoat was a short way ahead.

Mason saw the woman straighten her posture as she approached a group of bored teenagers. She ignored their cat-calls and whistles as she walked past, slumping back to a more comfortable pose once they were ignoring her again. Mason followed softly. It looked as if her heels were stopping her from speeding up her pace. She fumbled with the clasp of her purse for a moment, knocking it open as the wind tried to lift the folds of her skirt. She reached down automatically to hold the pleats in place, uncomfortably juggling the bag to produce a small bottle of perfume. She spritzed it twice before slipping it back inside the handbag.

... A pocket full of posies...

Mason stepped into the shadows as she spun around urgently. Her breath caught, her eyes darting from one landmark to another. The rise and fall of her chest steadied, and when she failed to spot anything out of the ordinary, she turned and continued on. Mason's grin broadened.

She didn't hear the scuff of his shoes, because it wasn't there to be heard, but she was clearly still feeling nervous, because she started talking again.

"You're losing it, Lexi." Her free hand clutched at the lapels of her raincoat. "Off your trolley. All 'cos of some loser. Goodbye and good riddance." Her next breath was shaky, and she stiffened uncomfortably. She rubbed her upper arm and rounded a corner. Mason watched her realise, fifteen feet later, that she'd made the wrong turn. She spat the word "Fuck," teeth gritted, but continued on anyway as though compelled.

The sound of a sneeze off to one side made her jump.

... Atishoo! Atishoo! ...

She spun toward the sound, but there was nothing there to see except endless shadows distorting the urban landscape. Her breath was starting to get frantic, and she had a wild glint in her eyes. The hand clutching her lapels laid flat against her heart, and she stumbled dizzily before regaining her footing.

"All right," she said, her gaze not certain where it should settle. "This isn't fucking funny. Whoever you are, I do *not* appreciate this. I've had a long fucking day." She backed up slowly. Her skin had to be prickling, and Mason saw the hair on the back of her neck stand up. A tear curled round the side of one cheek, but she didn't appear to notice it. She bumped into something solid, something cold and unyielding and wall-like, and stopped. "Safe." The word was barely audible, more of a prayer than a declaration.

Mason cupped his hand over her mouth, sealing it tight.

"Wrong way to the tube, my dear," Mason whispered. His free hand slid across her abdomen, pressing against her stomach. She trembled in his rock-solid grip, and he leaned close enough to graze her skin with his breath.

He paused to study her goose bumps, and nodded in satisfaction. "I knew that you wanted me alone, but this is rather forward, don't you think?"

She squeezed her eyes shut. "I haven't much in my purse." Her voice was a hollow whisper.

"That'd be a shame, if I sought your money. As it is, you seem well supplied with what I'm looking for." His hand slid down from her stomach, slipping between her thighs. He could feel the lines of her through the cotton, and pressed. She moaned into his hand, a light trace of involuntary arousal mixed in with the terror.

Mason took a breath, and chuckled, still caressing her. "Such a long day, and you're already tired of games." He nipped her ear roughly, ignoring her wince. His tongue lapped at the cut, catching the coppery tang of blood, and he suppressed a shiver. "You need to get off your feet," he murmured. "Before you catch your death out here." Her terrified, jumbled pleas echoed in his mind. He ignored them, and pressed his lips against her neck. The delicious scents of fear and lust swirled around him, drowning him. He bit down, into her flesh, and started the river flowing.

He lived a hundred lifetimes in that moment. The taste of copper became the taste of life. Her pleas became a chorus of faces, from age to age. He felt the spray of sea water and the rush of wind. He heard the rainbow crowds of Charis and the bells of Rome, watched horses become carriages, and then trains and automobiles. By the time the woman in the red raincoat slumped against him, he felt just as youthful as he had when the roads were cart tracks, and children sang their innocent rhymes.

... *We all fall down.*

The dead woman crumpled to the ground, knees buckling, her skirt ruffling on the pavement while her arms fell limply to her sides. She settled against a garbage bin as naturally as though she'd decided to take a quick nap. Mason stepped away, not concerned about the crimson streaks running down her cleavage from the holes in her neck. This world was incurious. He wiped his mouth clean with the back of his hand, and strolled away.

By the time he returned to the bench, the children had all gone, off to their homes. He shrugged to himself. A pity. He could come back to the bench tomorrow, though. He took his memories of youth and locked them firmly away, out of mind, where they wouldn't get in the way. All he had left now was the night. He glanced over at the red phone box thoughtfully. The night, and a silent partnership with an entity he hadn't yet figured out.

10. Past Tense
by Salomé Jones

As soon as she opened the door of Café McLaughlin, Amber noticed the smell. It blended into the aromas of coffee and caramelized sugar, but it was undeniably there. Cigarette smoke. That was odd. She remembered the smoking ban being passed, a year ago. But maybe she was wrong about that, too. Maybe that had never happened. It felt like her head was about to explode. Either way, the café held only the girl behind the bar and a woman sitting at a table in the back. Neither of them were smoking.

Amber went to the counter, aware that she was scowling.

"Can I help you?" asked the girl. She had an accent of some sort. Everyone did, in London. She was wearing a name-tag, but her hair had fallen over it. N something. Nancy? Nadine?

"A white Americano, please." Amber glanced over at the cabinet full of pastries. "And a croissant."

The girl pressed buttons on the register, murmuring Amber's order to herself. She looked at Amber and smiled. "Four pounds twenty."

Amber handed her a five pound note and waited for her change. "It kind of smells like smoke in here."

"Sorry about that," Nancy-Nadine said. She didn't sound – or look – sorry. Was the smoke even really there? The girl dropped the change into Amber's hand. "I'll bring your order over to you."

Amber nodded and turned to look for a seat. She was drawn to the light, and moved automatically to a table by the window. She set her handbag on the table, sat down and shrugged out of her jacket, letting it drape over the back of the chair.

Out the window she could see the wide open gates to the park, and the red phone box. It looked different in the light of day. Ordinary. Not like that night. That impossible night. She rested her chin on her hand, stroking her thumb over the hard ridge of her jaw.

56

She wanted to believe that night had never happened at all. But if it hadn't happened, then the previous year of her life hadn't happened either. There *had* been someone named Jon. He *had* moved into her flat. He'd left the flat one morning and not come back. But where were all his things? Why did the answer-phone message say Stuart and not Jon?

"Miss?"

Amber looked up to see the waitress holding a saucer in each hand. "Oh, let me move this." Amber pulled out the extra chair at her table and dropped her handbag into it.

Nancy-Nadine placed the coffee and croissant in front of her. "I believe you dropped your pen." She bent down, picked the pen up, and offered it to Amber.

"Oh, that's –" She was going to tell her that the pen wasn't hers. But then she noticed the notebook in the chair under her handbag. "– nice of you." She felt self-conscious. Had she sat in someone's seat? She thanked Nancy-Nadine and the girl went back to the counter.

Amber glanced around the café again. Maybe the owner of the notebook had gone to the loo. She replaced the pen in the chair.

She took a sip of her coffee and stared out the window. It would have been so much easier if she hadn't, quite by accident, slept with Stuart. It was so familiar, from start to finish. As if they'd been lovers for, well, for as long as she could remember. And they must have been, mustn't they? Because Stuart's things were everywhere. His handwriting was on notes stuck on the fridge: 'Love you, pussycat' and 'See you when I get home, Amb.' His clothes hung in the closet. His collection of Star Wars figures stood in a line on one of the shelves in the lounge.

Worse yet, she'd started to vaguely remember the things they'd done together, months before. Things they couldn't have done if she'd been with Jon.

More than once, she'd almost given in to the idea that she was completely mad. But then, there was the jacket. It still glowed faintly in the dark. Not just the jacket, but the toes of her black ankle boots, where they stuck out past the hem of her jeans. That was proof she wasn't insane, right? Providing it was real...

This was the point she always got to. There were just too many things to accept. Her head was spinning. Her hand shook as she picked up the cup and took another sip of her Americano. Why had she bought the croissant? She was never hungry any more.

She peered over the edge of the table at the notebook and pen. She needed to get this all out of her head. Maybe it would help to write it down. It had been ten minutes or more, and no-one had come to claim them. With a sidelong glance at Nancy-Nadine behind the counter, Amber reached down into the chair and picked up the notebook. It was medium-sized, spiral bound. Small enough to fit in her handbag, but big enough to write something substantial on each page.

She opened the cover, prepared to flip through until she came to a blank page. The careful, even, perfectly legible writing inside caught her eye. Today's date. Before she could stop herself, she'd read, 'The ash on the end of her cigarette is just about to fall. That's what I think when I look at the woman sitting across from me in the café.'

So someone was *smoking*. Amber felt herself relax just a little, and looked up toward where she'd seen the woman sitting at the back of the room. She was gone now. Amber hadn't noticed her leave. She turned back to the notebook. Her eyes slid over the precise, lovely script. Whoever wrote this had been waiting for a man who'd never shown up. She knew the feeling. How many times had she waited for Jon only to end up walking home by herself? She turned the pages one after another, engrossed in the text. When she reached the last line, she looked out at the red phone box. Could this be true?

She got up and put her jacket on, stuck the notebook and pen inside her handbag, and left through the front door without looking at Nancy-Nadine. She went straight to the phone box and pressed her nose to the glass. She couldn't see anything from out here.

She pulled open the glass-paned door, and grimaced at the smell that poured out of the box. How had she not noticed that before? Holding her breath, she stepped inside. There it was, just as the notebook had said. A mobile phone lying on a shelf under the box's own phone. She picked the cell phone up and smoothed her thumb over the dark screen. She pressed a button and the screen lit up.

What had happened to the phone's owner? Amber looked at the icons on the small screen. She wondered if she could tell who the phone belonged to. She scrolled through the list of contacts. Maybe she could call someone and ask whose number it was. Say she'd found her phone.

Riiiiing! Riiiiing!

She jumped at the sound, her heart thumping uncomfortably against her ribs.

"Stupid phone box." She stared at the receiver. Her mind flashed back to the night she'd used the phone to call home. The way the phone had felt in her hand, against her ear. The way that until she'd stepped into that phone box to make the call, Jon had been gone and she'd been alone. She took a step back and pushed the door open with her foot. She wrestled past the door's old, squeaky hinges and out onto the pavement. The phone kept ringing. She took a few steps back, spun around and began walking toward her flat.

Riiiiiing! Riiiiiing! She could hear it all the way to the corner. As she stood waiting for the light to change at the intersection, she began to feel anxious. She wasn't sure why. Guilt, maybe. But about what? The light turned green and as she crossed over the road, she thought about the notebook again.

Jon was a terrible boyfriend.

That's what was making her feel guilty. She'd dared to think that sad little truth. Alice, Gloria, some other nameless woman, something impossible – whichever one it was, Jon was gone, like he'd never existed, and his replacement was far superior. She slowed down, keeping one eye on the pavement ahead of her. Unzipping her bag, she dropped the found phone inside, took out her own mobile phone and pressed 1 on the speed dial.

"Hey, what are you up to?" she said when the familiar voice answered.

"Just finishing up some work," Stuart said. She could hear him smiling.

"Want to get some lunch with me?"

11. Future Imperfect
by Remittance Girl

Friday 23rd. Café McLaughlin.

The ash on the end of her cigarette is just about to fall. That's what I think when I look at the woman sitting across from me in the café. She hasn't taken a drag from it in ages, as if she's forgotten it, but now it's burned down so low, it's going to singe her fingers. I'm waiting for that. For her to notice when it does.

It falls like one of those empty office buildings they demolish, in a controlled manner, and the ash detonates on impact in a trail of little grey flowers along her black skirt. She doesn't notice. She's waiting for someone.

I know that feeling. When you're so caught up in imagining how the whole meeting will play out, you move into a parallel universe where time doesn't run evenly. Parts of the scenario speed by like cars on the highway: a blue one, a silver one, a red one, the one where you meet and smile, the one where you meet and cry, the one where you wait and wait, but the person you're waiting for never arrives. Other parts of the scenario crawl along: the blue car changes lanes and passes the silver one, only just avoiding its bumper, or two almost identical cars pull up beside each other and the world almost freezes as the drivers glance at each other while keeping pace, wondering if they're driving by enormous mirrors. Those slow moments where you pull me down to you and kiss me. Where your bare back slides against white hotel sheets. Where you look at me just before you enter me. Then time flips, speeds and races again. The hand that cups my chin. The arch of a spine. The gratifying rustling sound of a disposable toothbrush wrapper.

The woman is old. She's been careful with her appearance, but she can't fool me. There are lines at the base of her neck where her skin has decided not to cling to the meat beneath it anymore. Her mouth is turned downward at the sides, as if the life she's eaten

60

disappointed her and she's allowed it to drool out the corners because she's too polite to just spit it out.

Just then, she notices the burnt out filter between her fingers. She drops it into the glassy black ashtray beside her chair and, after methodically searching through her purse, which is perched like a pet cat in her lap, she lights another cigarette and gets lost again.

I'm a little shocked she doesn't take the opportunity to check the time and grumble about the lateness of the person she's meeting. Only in the absence of that set of reactions do I wonder just how long she's been there waiting. You only stop looking at the time once it ceases to matter. Once the waiting stops being anticipation of something else and becomes a state of being.

She scares me a little, with her legs crossed just so, and her shiny black high heels twined to the side in a long-lost gesture of femininity. We are wearing almost the exact same shade of nail polish. Her fingers are not pretty either, and they shake a little as she brings the cigarette to her mouth and takes a puff that emphasizes the wrinkles around her lips. For all her neatness, she's a woman without dignity now. A woman who has turned waiting into a profession and has a trail of grey ash on her nice black suit. I consider going over to her and brushing the ash away, but I realize she knows the person is not coming, and so the ash no longer matters. How long, I wonder, has it been since the ash ceased to matter?

Stranger still, I'm overcome with the certainty that if I were to talk to her, to touch her, the world would snuff out like a candle. Because I think perhaps she might be a future version of me. And you know what the rules of time are like – if you make contact with your future self, the universe explodes and gets sucked down an enormous black hole.

Perhaps she's waiting for you. Like I'm waiting for you. She's me having waited a lot longer, having turned into a middle-aged mouse with good posture and a bad nicotine habit. I look for dust on her side of the coffee shop. As if the space between us is time-space. But of course, that's silly. The invisible dust banishers will have been diligently keeping this sterile café dust-free as the future becomes the present.

'I don't want to be you,' I think, glaring at the woman. 'Get out of here. No one is coming for you, you idiot. And I'm not going to let you trap me in your sad inevitability.'

That's when I get up and leave the café. I know you're not coming. I always knew you wouldn't. I knew it before I met you. Perhaps I knew it before I was born. The bright red paint on the phone box reminds me to take out my mobile and SMS you to say that you're a shit. But I don't want to look at it. I'm positive it will contain a message from you with some incredibly understandable and valid excuse.

And if I read that, I'll turn into her. With that realisation, I'm convinced there's only one way to disrupt the horrific future I have seen. I open the door to the telephone box and leave my mobile phone on the little metal ledge.

12. Death's Dateless Night
by Joe Silber

Richard made lists. They helped him pass the time between calls.

Operas he had seen: Rigoletto, Otello, Nixon In China, Madame Butterfly, Einstein on the Beach, Don Giovanni.

Makes of car: Yugo, Trabant, Toyota, Skoda, Mercedes, Mazda, Honda, Cadillac, Bentley.

Lovers: Tina, Simon, Sam, Robin, Quentin, Paul, Meredith, Lawrence, Kevin, Joel, Georgie, Frank, David, Charlie, Carl, Ambrose.

The words to a sonnet he'd once known.

foregone friend friends from grievances grieve heavily hid

He'd been in the parking lot – at the centre of a huge roundabout – for longer than he could account for. He used to be superb at calculating values in his head, but not any more. He simply didn't recall arriving here, anyway.

Five roads approached the roundabout. Six cars were parked in front of the three shops that made up the small arcade at its centre. There wasn't anyone else. He hadn't seen any other person since his arrival. Cars approached, and drove around the circle. Sometimes they drove off, but they always came back. Just like he did. He had stopped looking into them soon after his arrival. When the drivers no longer appeared to be people, probably.

He had stopped looking, just as he had stopped walking up the five roads that approached the roundabout.

The shops had once been a hardware shop, a market, and 'Bombay House Indian Food to go'. Most of the letters had dropped off, visible now just as ghosts of their old presence. Only the last of the takeaway's letters were still in place. Indi ... go. The cars in the small parking area had likewise possessed makes and models once. They were parked head to head, at an angle. Pairs of them made chevrons, each of which was about a Richard-length from the phone box. Once, a cat had sidled between the wheels of the cars, keeping out of the heat. Richard still admired its casual fearlessness.

Had another car pulled in since his arrival? He searched his memory, making sure to take special care. No. There were these cars, and the cars on the roundabout. These were the only cars.

account afresh all an and are as at before

The tyres had been inflated, early on, but Richard no longer recalled when they had flattened, or when the last bits of rubber flaked away.

The shops must have done business, once upon a time. They would have been shuttered and perhaps falling down, Richard believed, if not for *them*. No one ever got out of the cars driving around the roundabout, but Richard was no longer sure anyone had ever been inside them. He couldn't recall ever having ridden in one.

but can cancelled dateless dear death's drown

The clang of a reversing lorry occasionally broke the roar of the traffic behind him, but the traffic always moved in the same direction, and he had never managed to spot a lorry when he turned around to look.

And the phone rang. It always rang when he started to sit down. It rang, loud enough to drown the sounds of the cars. But the red phone box was the only thing to lean on. He did not go near the shops anymore. Even though they provided no shade from the heat of the phone box, the walls used to invite him to lean against them. Then he had peeked inside, and a sea of insects looked up at him from devouring the newspapers and bags of kindling. In unison. He backed away, but they remained still, staring at him, until he had turned his head away.

end expense eye flow

At least, he'd thought he'd seen them move again, in his peripheral vision.

Richard didn't go up to the shops any more.

In what might have been the beginning, he had tried to walk away. He walked each of the roads that approached the roundabout's cars and phone box and takeaway and hardware store. The deepening blue of the sky, no matter which direction he chose, was relieving – that of a desert with the sunset of a hot, exciting day behind him. Each time, a little ball of hope had formed as the deep blue enveloped him. It had dried up each time, horribly, as he walked around a bend or a swerve and found himself back on the path to his roundabout.

Normal English roads bore normal English road signs. One that he had tried to recall carried a faded red train station logo somewhere on its expanse. All lanes lead to London eventually, don't they? He thought maybe someone said that to him once. He recalled the names that once adorned the other signs, and listed them alphabetically in his head:

Bluewater, Chertsey, Dartford, Erith, Harrow, Leatherhead, Maidstone, Potters, Redhill, Swanley, Thurrock, Woking.

Harrow. Potter's Bar. Red Hill. Woke.

The phone box stood midway between the parked cars. They'd been sinking deeper onto their sagging rims lately, the shop windows emptied of hammers, takeout boxes, cartons of spoiled milk. He scratched at his scraggly hair, and sat again against the heat of the red phone box. And the phone rang again, as he expected it to. It only stopped a ring or two after he lifted the receiver, numbly curious as to what it would be this time.

"I'm not doing anything, Daddy. Stop yelling at me. Stop it. Let go. What do you want?"

Had he ever really sounded like that? He looked at the phone again, and put it back on its hook. The questions demanded of his five year-old self came back to him, in his father's shriek. *'Ricky, you lazy brat. What do you always think about in that idle, scheming head of yours? Get up, you shit, and do some work around here.'* He could see the vein popping from below his father's grey flattop, his mother unfocused in a pink flowered apron behind.

The phone had other things to tell him.

Screaming – a woman and a small boy – followed by gun shots. That was the first one. He wondered, later, if he had been involved in that, but eventually decided it had been a mix-up. Should have come through to someone else's phone box. That first time, he'd still had his briefcase. Took it in and tried to balance it on the phone box's tilted shelf. Too narrow. It slid down. The phone screaming to be answered, he finally put the case between his feet. He used to do that every time.

Another version of himself, almost whining, "Ambrose, what can I do to make you come back? I only want to be with you." And the reply, in his head, *'Richie, you're a fine fuck, but that's all you are, and all I want. I won't give you any more and you won't take any less. Goodbye.'*

if in lack long losses love's many moan

Or when a teacher asked him at age twelve to read one of his test answers. The teacher's reply from his head, *'Have you ever heard a more stupid test answer? Any of you? No. I haven't either.'*

The dread finally left him, maybe with the last of the tyres' flaking rubber. His own voice, those of the woman and boy, they no longer belonged to anyone he could help. They didn't wound him.

Except when it was that plea to Ambrose.

Amidst the fumes of the cars and the decay of the shops, Richard could smell the oil Ambrose always rubbed into his bald scalp. The smell brought up the whole man, from his sandals and habitual white linen outfits to his two metres of thin muscle. The sheen of his skin, which always seemed polished, a sharp contrast to Richard's own near-fluorescent glow.

Sometimes a whole memory came flooding through. The voice that growled, "God, Richard, you're beautiful," that he could feel down in his chest. And when he got up to pee in the middle of the night, Richard remembered sitting up under blackout curtains, looking at his outline gleaming against the door.

He'd scan the roads sometimes, then. And sometimes a figure walked towards him from one of the approaches. Sometimes the figure was clean-shaven, with a new briefcase, determined to get somewhere. Sometimes there was some facial hair – three or four days of stubble beneath under-focused eyes. Each time, Richard skulked back towards the red phone box. Just earlier versions of himself. From before his comb broke, before the razor he'd kept in the briefcase dulled to uselessness. Before they must have scuttled off with his briefcase.

And he sometimes thought that even if he'd stopped using the four-bladed contraption when it was sharp, they wouldn't have stood for him destroying the razor in order to get the blades out.

He was pretty sure they would have been too flimsy to slit his wrists or his throat anyway, even when new.

silent since sorrows sought summon sweet tell

Sometimes he tried for his reflection in the glass of the phone box. How long was his beard now, his hair? It was always too bright, too hot to show his reflection anyway. It occurred to him that his suit should have disintegrated some time ago, and he wondered how long it took a suit to tatter. His hair was somewhere below his shoulders. He brought it round in front of his face and looked at it, between reciting to himself the possible voices on the phone, or the lovers he had. Ambrose was number thirteen, probably. Whether there were three or four after him, he couldn't recall. Pale imitations, all of them, the longer preceding sequence and the shorter succeeding.

Between calls, he made his lists. Sometimes he calculated the number of instances of each letter in that sonnet, but rarely got beyond C or D before the phone rang. *I must find the discipline to do it backwards.*

Was there ever a dear friend like the one addressed, the mere thought of whom cancels all sorrow? Richard listed all the people he knew (had once known?) and alphabetized them. The list either started or ended with Ambrose. Hadn't he ever know an Allen or an Abner? But no face, scent or voice attached itself to any such name. If they had existed, Ambrose must have swallowed them up.

Once he had successfully managed to recite all of the sonnet's words in order of length, but it hurt his brain, and then the phone rang anyway.

unused up vanish'd

After he hung up, he had wondered why it had kept silent long enough for him to arrange the words.

of old on paid past pay precious remembrance restored

Precious remembrance restored? In his dreams. Of old past paid? All the time.

Later, surveying the arms of the starfish, those approaching roads, he almost discounted a figure walking into his eternal day, out of the night. Clean shaven or bearded? No Richard ever approached with the long hair and scraggly beard he had now, because he had stopped venturing from his little haven long before that point. When he recognised that the figure approaching was not himself, hope of seeing Ambrose's bald head surged up so fiercely that it dripped from him. The hope shrivelled up, strangled by fear, when he spotted the figure's insectile gleam, and its metallic gait.

13. The Go-Between
by J.F. Lawrence

Kelly turned from the whiteboard to face her students. "Okay, that's all for today. Thank you all, and I'll see you on Monday. Have a good weekend." She stifled a yawn, and shifted her aching feet. Home beckoned powerfully, despite all that clandestine Project Blueprint crap piled on the kitchen table.

Goddamn NSA.

'It has to be you, Professor David.' 'You're our leading expert in several critical areas.' 'It's a matter of national security, Professor.'

She should have thrown plates at them, and damn their *'generous stipend.'* Supernatural powers. Extraterrestrial visits. Elder tech buried under Antarctica. What right did they have to destroy her reality like that?

"Professor David?" A young woman with bright red hair was gazing into Kelly's eyes, apparently trying to see straight through into her brain.

Kelly shook herself mentally. The lecture. Right, Anglesey. "Good afternoon," she said. "I don't think I know you, do I? I'm sure you haven't appeared at one of my lectures or seminars yet. Your hair is too lovely to miss." The girl really was intense.

"Gloria Vandenbussche. I am not a student, Professor David. I was eager to hear your lecture on the Anglesey massacre." Her voice was as dark as her eyes, quiet but firm, a musical blend of British and Spanish accents. "It is a subject that interests my father greatly. He would like to discuss it with you, and has some relevant information which he believes would be of great interest to you."

Kelly blinked at her. "As a general rule, university lectures are not open for members of the public to simply wander in on. In the future, it would be best if you arranged a visit in advance."

Gloria nodded, absolutely no hint of contrition anywhere on her smooth face.

"Anyway. Your father is a Celtic historian? He's welcome to contact me directly. Would I know his name?"

"No," Gloria said. "He is quite reclusive, not an academic. He does not venture away from home often, and has little comfort with computers. I am his link to the outside world."

Great, thought Kelly to herself. *Another technophobic hermit.*

Gloria fiddled around in her bag for a moment, then pulled out an envelope and handed it to her. "My father's invitation. He hopes very much to see you, at his expense. He really admires your authority on this subject."

"Well..."

"Good day, Professor." Gloria smiled brightly at her, turned around, and stalked out.

Free from the pinion of her stare at last, Kelly felt herself sagging with exhaustion. She couldn't leave yet, though. Her staff seemed to genuinely believe that the world would grind to a halt if she ignored her emails for an afternoon.

* * *

Kelly made a strong cup of coffee and settled in to go through the day's administration. If she'd known how much paperwork there was in heading up a department, she'd have run screaming from archaeology. From academia altogether.

She browsed through the endless stream. On the plus side, none of it was urgent enough to bother with today. But there was still no word from Henry. Where the hell was he? She needed him to cover his damned classes. More importantly, she needed a good, strong dose of TLC.

A flash of red caught her eye. She looked out of the window. The hermit's fiery daughter was crossing the parking lot, her motions oddly deliberate. Kelly wouldn't have been surprised to discover that she was hunting small, fluffy creatures rather than just making her way to a car.

The hermit. Kelly groaned quietly, and opened the envelope. The paper inside was thick and creamy, a delight to the touch. The man had money, that was for sure. His note was written with fountain pen, the penmanship immaculate, just a touch ornate. Exactly what she'd expected from the paper.

Dear Professor David,

My daughter Gloria should have told you of my admiration for your work. I am merely an amateur alas, an enthusiastic collector with enough disposable time and income to indulge his passion for the beautiful and esoteric material culture of ancient times. I truly hope you can spare a day or two to visit me in England, so that we can discuss the matter of the Anglesey Deer. I have recently come across a document germane to the story of the Deer and its ritual functions. It may well date from Elizabethan times. I shall say no more on this, but will mention that there is a possible connection to the notorious Dr. John Dee.

I am certain that we will enjoy a mutually beneficial conversation, and I keenly anticipate meeting you in person. I will of course provide air tickets befitting your station, for such dates as you care to nominate.

Please contact me to make arrangements, at your convenience, via my daughter's electronic mail address. She informs me that it is GloriaV666@ demon.co.uk.

Yours respectfully,
Horace Vandenbussche

She stared at the letter, not really seeing it. The Anglesey Deer. Again. The Blueprint file on the Deer weighed more than a large cat, and never once came within spitting distance of getting to a point. They seemed obsessed with the damn thing. Having it come up again was an odd coincidence. The spooks had hammered home the importance of disbelief in happenstance. *'Look for meaning,'* they'd said. *'Messages from the Weird.'*

In other words, if she didn't go, they'd probably drag her off into the woods and suicide her. Like that Brit.

This guy was obviously a bit cracked, but even a flat-out lunatic might actually have stumbled onto something that finally placed the Deer as a genuine historical artifact, rather than just mist and shadows. If so, it would be a huge coup, for the department and for Blueprint both.

She had to see. Besides, London was always lovely. It was time for a visit to the Old Country.

14. A Brief Transaction
by Tamsyn H. Kennedy

Gloria slammed her foot down on the accelerator, her long red hair whipped into a frenzy by the wind. Back in dreary old England, with another errand completed. Every day, some stupid new chore. Never any explanation. Rarely any apparent meaning. At least she'd escaped the country for a couple of days this time, and the hotel had made for a diverting night. But she was tired of being Daddy's damned gofer. She should...

Well yes, she should, but then there was the luxury. First-class lounges. The Merc. Maybe it was time to buy another stupidly expensive something on his Amex Centurion. She'd given the last one to Oxfam, hadn't she? That meant Cancer Research was next. An original Fountainhead monograph, maybe. He wouldn't notice, of course. He never did. After all, his damn bill wasn't written in a dead language, wasn't about bloody perfect bloody Alyssa.

Winding through a leafy bit of west London, she spotted the twinkling lights of a bar. She desperately wanted a drink. A drink, and a pair of strong hands moving over her. She parked the car near the pub – the Lion's Head – pleased to see that her vehicle didn't stand out too much from the others around it. The area was obviously a good one. She shrugged off her jacket, decided that the silky cami top worked well with the severe suit skirt, and slinked out of the car. The city sounded remote, a susurrus of traffic and far-off sirens. Somewhere off in the distance, a dog howled.

The early evening dark was bright compared to the pub's husky gloom. She stalked into the old place, her nose full of the scents of melted wax, rich ale, her own perfume. Her heels clicked loudly on the old wood floor. She had all their eyes, the women too, and loved it, drawing on their power. There was a good vantage point at the bar, and she hopped onto the stool, crossing her legs demurely in just the right way to make her skirt hitch a couple of inches.

Gloria ordered three tequila shots, straight up, from an awed bar-lad. He was cute enough, but way too much of a puppy. She dismissed him, and looked around the bar. A professional couple were sharing an over-priced bottle of wine. They looked stodgy. A girls' night out were sitting round with bottles of weak American piss, but they seemed decidedly low-rent, and besides, groups were an annoyance.

That left a scattering of ancient, decrepit locals, a group of bearded guys earnestly talking nerdy bollocks, and a lone man, all in black, who'd gone back to staring into his whisky. No contest at all. Mysterious won every time. It wasn't as if she wanted him for a damned relationship, after all. Concentrating on him, she started downing the shots, licking her lips after each one.

His eyes flicked up to meet hers. He had presence, no doubt about it. She returned his look with an arched eyebrow and slow smile. The stranger's face lightened, the impassivity giving way to curiosity. Gloria shifted sinuously, allowing one leg to rub against the other, keeping her gaze on his. In response, the man leant forward, ruffling his deliberately messy hair without breaking eye contact. She felt the hormones rush, dancing, through her blood. She could see his interest building, leaving him powerless to resist her influence over him. Powerless to stop her from claiming him. She fiddled with the neck of her camisole, drawing attention to her cleavage, demanding that he come closer.

Moments later, he was by her side. *Good boy.* A few exchanges of quiet, meaningless words. He was already hers. His hand moved up from the small of her back to the skin of her neck. His closeness made Gloria's lips tingle, and she felt a delicious shiver cascade down from his touch. It built into a quiver in the pit of her stomach, and started pooling between her thighs. She grabbed his hand and led him to the door, his sly smile agreeing to her unspoken intention. His skin was smooth and unyielding, his grip powerful and perfect. She glanced back, drinking in the desolate expressions of the barman, the bearded guys. One of the beer-swilling girls, too. She flashed them a grin, and sashayed out, slow and deliberate. She could afford to be generous to the unworthy.

Outside, she looked around for a suitable location. Up the
road, she spotted an old red phone box, at the entrance to a park.
Confinement, exhibitionism, a touch of the genuinely seedy. Perfect.
She guided him up to the box, her hand exploring his deliciously tight
arse. The door shrieked as she wrenched it open. The stranger almost
shoved her inside, wonderfully impatient, pushing her up against the
black plastic and grey metal telephone.

Gloria braced her feet and arms against the walls of the box,
parting her legs temptingly in the process and sticking her bum out.
He pressed his groin against her, and kissed the back of her neck.
His fingers were burning a trail across her body, up to her breasts. He
enfolded them in his hands, pinching her nipples through the cloth,
and she cried out, a moan of pleasure. *This* was her heaven, her true
defiance. She pushed back against him, grinding herself over his
tight, hard lines. His hand dropped down, slid under the silk to trace a
wonderfully rough fingertip around her navel, and then lower, slipping
under the band of her skirt. Then his hands were running down her
hips, past the bottom of her skirt, and back up like fire against the
flesh of her thighs. He hooked his thumbs into her thong, and pulled
it tight for a blinding instant. She gasped, felt it turn into a moan as
he yanked down, relieving the pressure. Cool air caressed her as she
kicked the thong off impatiently.

She ached to have him touch her hot wetness, to feel those
delicious fingers running over her. Instead, he teased the skin inside
her thigh, denying her, making the most of her delighted whimpers
of frustration. Then he plunged his fingers inside her, deep, almost
violent, lighting her up. She threw her head back, groaning loudly. His
other hand came round to caress her, and now she was blazing. *I never
wanted anything but this. Never wanted...*

She hissed as he withdrew his hands, used them to pull her hair
aside, to tug away the strap of her cami. He sucked at her earlobe,
then slowly kissed his way down her neck, lingering longer each time.
His breath was strangely cool, like a whisper of night. She ground
herself back against him again, pleased to feel him thick beneath her,
rock-hard. She sighed happily, and felt him pause at her collarbone.
He took a deep breath.

A savage, eerie wail snapped her out of the moment. A black cat was staring at her from the other side of the glass, crouched, hackles up, ready to pounce. It reminded her strongly of the statues on the mantelpiece of her childhood. The ones that Daddy had never let her *or* Alyssa touch. Guardians, he'd said.

The stranger's icy breath on her skin felt frightening now. His tight grip on her waist, too. She needed to get away. Escape. She yelled wildly, and stabbed a narrow heel down into his foot. He gasped, more in surprise than pain. *His teeth. What was it with his teeth?* She threw herself backwards, knocking them both out of the box. Then she was gone, fumbling through the night to safety.

She thanked the universe for remote-activated ignitions as she leapt into the passenger seat, breath catching in her throat. She sped off, the Merc's wheels squealing, not even bothering with the automatic canopy.

* * *

Back at the phone box, Mason watched the woman run, hurdle into the car, screech off. He laughed. Intuition was a funny thing. He didn't begrudge her a bit of a head start though, even if it had taken that cat to wake her up. He'd have her yet, in both senses. Simultaneously. He picked her discarded knickers up from the floor, and popped them in his pocket.

The hunt had begun.

15. Elsewhere
by Thadeus E. Suggs

Too much had happened in D.C. Too many memories. Consequently, Maz tried to avoid it if he could. Unfortunately power attracted power, whether it was the same type or not, and several heavyweights had set up office there.

Just having to be in the bloody place was irritating. Factor in that it was late and that Maz had no idea where he was, and it was no wonder his mood had gone sharply south. Then, of course, it had started raining. A bloody deluge pouring down on him, in fact. The awning he was now sheltering under didn't provide any extra warmth, but it was better than ambling aimlessly through the downpour.

"Fuck Amow, fuck Blueprint, fuck Crofton, and fuck that fucking wooden deer," he said, to nobody in particular. He pulled a cigarette from one of the pockets in his jacket, and lit it with the tip of his finger. He scowled out at the tedious street, taking short, hard puffs of his cigarette, looking for any clue as to where he was. A soft presence rubbing against his leg startled him out of his reverie. Looking down, he saw a black cat staring up at him.

"Here's the cavalry, eh?" Maz took a last drag and then flicked his cigarette into the street, where the rain quickly extinguished it.

The cat meowed and trotted away down the block.

"What do you expect me to do, just follow blindly?"

It turned back to stare at him, and hissed unpleasantly. Its tail twitched.

That's how it is, then. Maz sighed, and let himself relax a bit, sagging his awareness out of the world just a little. Like slipping on a comfy sweater. To the south and east, several hard knots tugged at him, spike-filled little points of murderous rage. Bully Boys, quartering the city. Heading this way.

"Fair enough," he said to the cat. "I see your point." He weaselled himself back into reality and followed after it, slipping into a steady pace. It led him through a maze of primly-trimmed townhouses, towering federal offices, and urbanely predatory shops. There were moments when Maz doubted the cat knew where it was going, or if it was an envoy at all, but if he fell even a little behind, it would stop and stare at him balefully until he caught up. He trusted its self-interest enough for it to be avoiding Bully Boys, at least.

At long last, they emerged onto the National Mall. The rain had slackened a bit, but that was too little, too late – Maz's feet were sore from the long walk. He knew that they were close, though. He kept plodding on until he realised the cat had stopped in front of the locked doors of the Hirshhorn Smithsonian Gallery. It sat down, its tail curling around its body, and stared at Maz.

He nodded to it pleasantly. "Thank you – Max, isn't it?" He gripped the handle of the locked door, and felt a tingle of static prickle the hairs on his hand. The lock clicked, the door opened, and man and cat stepped inside.

The cat led him up the stationary escalators, all the way to the bloody top floor. A painting of a janitor hung in front of the last escalator, all straight, bold lines and garish colours, but its eyes seemed to be alive. There was a small blue nexus stone buried in the top left corner of the frame, too. Maz jumped at its unexpected appearance, and rubbed the sudden goose-bumps on the back of his neck. The damned thing appeared to be staring right through him. He shivered, and followed the cat down the hallway to a red phone box, which was barricaded off by felt ropes slung between waist-high metal poles. The cat shook the water off its glossy black coat pointedly, sat down, and began to lick itself dry.

As soon as Maz gripped the handle of the phone box, something grabbed his collar, yanking him back hard enough to throw him about ten feet away. He groaned as he landed with a thud, and slid up against the pedestal of a sculpture. Looking towards the phone box, he saw the dark outline of the janitor standing where he'd been moments before.

"What business have you with Lord Amow?" The shape spoke in a rigid voice, making Maz think of multicoloured cubes stacked against each other.

"Should've known," murmured Maz, more to himself than to the janitor. He got up slowly, his ribs tender where the corner of the pedestal had caught him. There was a thin cut in his hand, too. "Delivery for Lord Amow," he said, loudly. "Sorry for not clearing myself first, but this is my first time in this particular gaff."

"We all make mistakes," said the janitor. It didn't sound sympathetic, but at least it didn't start swinging again. As Maz stepped closer, he noticed that it was completely flat and two-dimensional, like a cardboard cut-out. "What's the password?"

"Romulus egg brick."

"Clearance accepted," said the janitor. "Do not forget again. Next time I will rip your head from your shoulders, no matter whom your escort." It rocked from side-to-side as it walked, balancing its feet forward, going back to its painting.

Maz sighed, rubbed his side, and walked to the red phone box. He glanced at the cat, who was still cleaning itself. "Thanks for all your help," he muttered. It ignored him loftily.

Maz opened the red phone box, stepped inside, closed it, and picked up the phone.

There was a voice on the other end of the line. "Maz Fishbein?"

"Yes. Delivery for Lord Amow."

"Come in."

Maz hung up, and opened the door again, stepping back out and into Lord Amow's antechamber. A statue of a huge, powerfully muscled man with a lion's head dominated the small room and its heavy wooden door. It was a new addition. Amow himself, most likely. *Bloody Lords.* He forced a sigh down, and waited, shifting uncomfortably from one foot to the other.

'He pulled a cigarette from one of the pockets in his jacket,
and lit it with the tip of his finger.'

16. Reverb
by James 'Grim' Desborough

The office seemed strange and alien to Talbot today, the low cubicles ridiculous. Why was the office divided up if it didn't hide anything? The constant bleep of the phones was an odd background hum, underlying the constant buzz of conversation, but nobody in the office was talking to anyone else there. The headsets they wore, the computer screens they stared at, they were far more isolating than the pathetic excuses for cubicles.

His headset bleeped, and he hit the phone's 'accept' button wearily, dragging his hands into place over the keyboard. Ready to work. Allegedly.

"Are you happy there?" It was his voice again, the one he'd heard – the one he'd *thought* he heard – in the phone box. His stolen voice.

"Leave me alone," he whispered. He darted looks left and right, terrified that someone would see him. He brought his head down low, covered the headset with his hands.

"You're not happy, are you? This isn't what you longed for from your life."

"Go *away*."

"What happened to the dreams? What happened to who you wanted to be?"

"Real life," he growled. He ripped the headset from his ears and stared at the screen, panting, panicked, hammering the end-call button until his finger hurt.

* * *

Emily was wittering away at him. He hadn't told her that he'd been fired. Not yet. He'd gone into work for a fortnight, sitting there and staring at the machine, afraid to pick up the phone. It took them a week for them to notice that he wasn't working, and another week to

81

fire him. He didn't know what to say to her. They needed his money just to get by. London was so bloody expensive, and it wasn't like he could go back to living in squats and busking, like when he was a student. You couldn't live like that any more, and what would you do without television and heating, internet and a proper kitchen anyway?

What was she even talking about? Something about her job, the inconsequential and soul-grinding tedium of office politics. She worked reception, and he couldn't even remember where any more. What happened to the girl who danced in the rain and threw tampons at MPs?

Blissfully, her tale of the affair between Brian from upstairs and Susan from accounts was cut short by the brisk ring of the home phone. That meant parents, grandparents, or telesales robots. Everyone else used mobiles.

Emily answered with her usual, over-chipper "Hello!" and then went quiet.

He looked up, trying to summon some interest, and saw that her brow was furrowed with confusion.

"It's for you," she said quietly, and held the phone out towards him.

He took it, the unfamiliar plastic oddly heavy in his hand as he pressed it to his ear.

"Hello again." His voice. He blanched, nearly falling from his chair. He took a moment to steady himself and got up quickly, moving to the other room with the phone.

"What do you want? Losing my job wasn't enough for you? You want to destroy my home as well?"

"Your home? Is this what you wanted? Is this what we wanted?"

"I'm happy," he snapped, hunching over the handset.

"No, you're not. You weren't happy at work, you're not happy here."

"I can't hurt her. Don't do this to me." He was almost sobbing now, out of his mind. He had to be out of his mind.

"Hurt her? When did she last treat you to something nice? When did you last make love? When did she last ask about what you did or how you felt? Why are you even with her?"

"Love."

"Nonsense. You can't lie to me. I'm you."

He wavered, bit his lip and tossed the phone across the room with a crash. "Duty," he mumbled, though the phone had been smashed to uncaring pieces.

17. The Storyteller
by Uri Kurlianchik

The boys wanted to know where the storyteller went after the story was over.

They knew he had lots of story circles all over the city, and that he drove a crumbling white Fiat with a many-eyed monster called a beholder drawn on the bonnet, dragons glued to the doors, and a leering rat on the boot. Once a boy peered inside through an incredibly dusty window and saw enough fantasy books, miniatures of monsters, heroes and houses, colourful gaming dice, magic cards, board games, graphic novels and foam swords to last a lifetime. One could only wonder what treasure was hidden inside the rusty boot beneath its scary rat guardian.

They knew he spoke on his mobile, a shameful 2005 affair, in a language they didn't understand. They knew he was funny – he always had one black sock and one white sock. He had long hair, a shaggy beard and glittering eyes. They knew everything was an adventure for him; he could talk about going to the store to get some sugar with more excitement than their history teacher could about a secret commando raid in Iraq.

But most of all, they knew every single word that ever left his mouth was a lie.

It was okay. Their parents paid him to lie. It was nice to live a lie for a couple of hours each week – to fight the evil wizard who sucked the lifeblood of the earth to fuel a monstrous transformation, to be an animated garbage article looking for love and recognition, to venture forth into the place where seasons are made and bring the summer to rainy London.

Right now they were investigating a hobbit who was sucked into the earth in the middle of the day. Ron thought it was land sharks. Lenny suggested it was dark magic, though nobody cared what he suggested. The general consensus within the group was that it would probably have been best for everyone involved if Lenny simply hadn't ever existed.

The stories were nice, but the boys wanted to know the truth.

Then one day, a golden opportunity arose. The storyteller came late to class.

"Terribly sorry for being late, I —" he started, hastily spilling the contents of his backpack on the table and handing out character sheets with sweaty hands. His hair, usually a puffy, mane-like affair, was glued to his face in thick tendrils.

"Don't be sorry!" Ron interjected with a cunning smile. "Give us experience points!"

The storyteller chuckled in a manner which made it clear that while he would gladly shower the group with apologies, he had no intention of handing out free points.

"What happened?" William asked. The storyteller being late wasn't inconceivable — he was very absent-minded — but neither was it usual.

"Well you see, as I drove to work this morn-, well, this afternoon, I was unlucky enough to drive into an iceberg, which eviscerated my car." He chuckled bitterly. "Just like the Titanic. Not knowing the car was bleeding oil all over the road, I continued to drive until the poor thing bled to death. And this is why I was late, so let's not waste one more second on this rubbish. Gentlemen — you have a hobbit to rescue, do you not? You ought to hurry or something quite awful will happen to the poor wretch!"

This story didn't make any sense. Icebergs in London?!

Of course, it was always lies. He never told the truth. They had asked him many questions:

"How old are you?"

"Doesn't matter, I've been dead for 13 years!"

"Do you have brothers and sisters?"

"Only for breakfast."

"Where do you live?"

"Live? I just told you I've been dead for 13 years. You ought to pay closer attention, young sir..."

"What language do you speak on the phone?"

"The Black Tongue of Mordor, with a slight cockney accent."

"Are you married? Do you have kids?"

"I'm married to the job, kids."

"Are you making up these stories or does someone write them for you? What is your real name – could you tell us at least that?!"

"Name... name... Remind me to make one up later today. You'll love it! Regarding the stories – they're all true, every word. I don't make up anything."

No matter how hard they stressed they were serious this time and that the game was over and they were not playing right now – he *always* lied to them.

Today they would find out the truth!

The conspiracy was hatched while the storyteller had his back to the class, drawing dungeons and traps on the whiteboard with colourful markers. Bits of paper changed hands under tables, and behind raised books.

He was so distracted, following him would be the easiest thing in the world.

John was given the job of making up an excuse why the kids would return late from school that day. William, whose father was a lawyer, was charged with financing the expedition in case the group had to follow the storyteller into buses or trains. Ron didn't have to do anything, because he was the ringleader. Lenny was left out because, well, because he was Lenny and in every group of boys, someone always has to be ostracized.

They waited in the schoolyard afterwards, hiding behind the paper recycling bin. The storyteller wasn't quick to leave the premises, like teachers usually were. If anything, he seemed to be going slowly on purpose. He placed all the chairs on the tables, wiped today's victories and discoveries off the whiteboard, turned off the lights and locked the door behind him. Finally, when the boys were just about ready to burst, he walked out at a leisurely pace, whistling some Eastern sounding tune.

The hunt was afoot!

The first thirty minutes were quite boring. The storyteller just walked down the street, quick but not rushing, perilously dodging street lights and passers-by as he constantly texted on his prehistoric mobile.

Then he made his first stop – a food stand by Tate Modern. He ate a jumbo hot dog, and announced to all around that this was by far the greatest work of art in or out of the museum. Then he sat by the river bank for an hour or so and threw breadcrumbs at pigeons while reading, and occasionally making notes in his class notebook. This was followed by a rather shameless nap on a bench.

As the nap dragged on and on, the boys started considering trying to snatch his backpack while he slept. Eventually they decided against it because... well, it just wasn't right, was it? He woke up with a start and a wild exhalation when his archaic phone sang the most shrill and unpleasant ringtone imaginable.

He answered it. After listening for a few seconds, he shouted, "Oh no, not *our* peacock. I'm very angry. Yes! Very angry! Coming right away!" He jumped off the bench awkwardly, and started running along the river, vanishing in the crowds. He was gone before the kids even had a chance to start chasing him. What a mighty disappointment... but wait! What was that on the bench?

Oh boy! He forgot his backpack on the bench! No experience points for this encounter, but at least there was loot! Victory! Hooray!

The kids stormed the storyteller's backpack just like the pigeons had stormed his bread, or their imaginary alter egos had stormed his treasure hoards. Unlike the pigeons and the characters however, the boys' victory was a hollow one. Inside the backpack, they found a plastic bag full of stale bread, a bottle of water that didn't smell very good, a broken umbrella in three parts and a notepad with a summary of their story so far, plus some comments on their next session:

Introduce sophie?

Consider peacock

Goblins steal farmer's son by pit, sell it to dark elf teen who travels in tunnels with boy and mute monk guard, turns out drow and son in love, consider bad ending, too early?

D-load energy spiders, lvl 3 traps (consult peacock), ogre stalkers

Tell mike I will be late next week, inform charles huntingdon-smythe

Call insurance company, ask about carter

If they were out to cheat in the game, it would have been a potent discovery. A fantastic discovery! But they wanted to cheat in real life. The storyteller had won again. Just like in the game, the storyteller was always one step ahead of them. Well, at least they knew what challenges they would face next week and had time to research and prepare... Then again, the story was kind of spoiled now. Some victory.

They walked home, cold, hungry and disappointed. It was dark, and their mothers would be cross. The best John had been able to come up with was a surprise school trip. Even an ogre wouldn't have believed *that* stupid lie!

As they were discussing how to kill energy spiders, whether or not they should push Lenny into the level 3 trap, and what the best way to outsmart the ogres was, a phone rang. It was the same horribly annoying ringtone the storyteller had, only louder. *Much* louder. It was coming from a red phone box, something any person born in the 21st century had learned to unsee by now. William and John froze in their tracks, scared of the thing that had seemingly appeared out of nowhere, but Ron mentally applauded the skill of the storyteller. What a master! What a genius! He had even managed to turn their boyish trick into an exciting adventure with this surprise ending! It was one of his best stunts yet. He ran across to the phone and picked up the receiver.

"Hey teacher, how do you do!" Ron greeted the storyteller.

"Listen I, eh," the storyteller sounded apologetic and embarrassed, like a student making up an excuse for an unimpressed teacher. "I was called for, eh, an emergency storyteller convention in, eh, Norfolk. I won't be able to complete the campaign with you guys. I e-mailed Lenny the story–"

"Lenny? That stupid arse?!"

"Yes. He was the closest to... it. He can help you, maybe. Only he can do it."

"Help us with what?"

"Finding Sophie! Listen Ron, I gotta run. Tell the others it's been a whole lot of fun telling stories and playing games with them and I hope to see you all of you guys next year. Heh, it will be awesome.

You'll go on a quest against the giants. It's a classic really, but I'm adding this great twist... Well, I gotta run. Bye!"

"Wait!" Ron shouted.

"ooooooooooooooooo," the phone answered.

It was over.

18. Here, Kitty!
by Cvetomir Yonchev

Maz Fishbein stared at the heavy wooden door in front of him. The steady drip, drip, drip of water falling from his jacket sleeve was annoying him. So were his feet, which seemed determined to throb in an unpleasant counterpoint to the drops of former rainwater. The blood oozing from the savage paper-thin slash didn't help, either. He shivered, a long, juddering tremor that left him exhausted, and glared at the door. *Come on, you...*

There was a faint click, and the door swung open. Maz wrenched his face into something resembling an acceptable expression, and walked through into Lord Amow's impressive office. Richly-stained oak, deep green carpets, a whole wall of expensive-looking books, an impressive gold-and-lapis statue of Bast, a desk the size of Wales. Maz was in no mood to be impressed, however.

He walked up to the edge of the desk, and shook Amow's hand.

"You look like a wet cur," Amow said. His grip was just like the hand itself, hugely strong, but held in check – a far more effective statement of power than trying to crush Maz's fingers would have been. "Dry yourself by the fireplace, if you wish."

Maz met Amow's eyes. They were solid amber, broken by a small pupil. No white whatsoever. The Lord met his gaze, wrinkling his muzzle a little, fangs glittering. Maz quickly dropped his eyes again, before things turned nasty. *Never challenge a lion in his lair. Or anywhere else, for that matter.*

"Not to worry," Maz said, forcing some cheer into his voice. "I think they've pretty much got the treatment for pneumonia down pat nowadays." He stepped back to the lavish wingback chair facing Amow's seat, and plonked himself down. There was a loud squelching noise as his clothes settled.

To his credit, Amow didn't even wince. He just plucked the gold silk handkerchief from his jacket pocket, and dabbed at an

90

imaginary spot on his tie. "Perhaps I could offer you a warm drink, Mr. Fishbein?"

"I could murder a cuppa actually," Maz said. "Thanks."

"Doris!" Amow followed the bellow with an enormous roar. It sounded like the universe ripping. Maz jumped, and squelched again.

The door opened again, and a little, half-hunched old dear came into the room. She tottered her way over towards the desk, right hand clutching her upper left arm. She was muttering something to herself, but it was impossible to make out. Maz watched her excruciating progress.

She finally ground to a halt by Amow's desk.

"Bring my guest a cup of tea," he told her.

Doris nodded. "Of course, sir." She turned around, and hobbled her way back out again. Amow watched her leave as if it were the most compelling sight in the world. Maz reminded himself not to grind his teeth.

The door finally closed behind her. Amow turned his attention back to Maz. "How are things in London, Mr. Fishbein?"

Maz flinched, caught himself, and tried to turn the motion into a shrug. Things were... harrowing. "Sweet as a nut," he said. *Yeah. A nut made out of human ribcages that had to be snapped open, so the beating hearts inside could be ripped out.*

Amow snorted. "I find that unlikely. But you're right of course, I couldn't care less. To business, then. What is it you're delivering this time? If you're wasting my time with another of the Cockerel's pranks, I'll flay your hide from your living body and use it to refurbish the chair you're busy ruining."

"No pranks, my Lord. I'm here to deliver myself and my services for a change. It's been a while. I was getting a bit lonesome for your regal companionship. A little melancholic, if you know what I mean."

Amow tossed his mane irritably. If he'd had a tail, it would probably have been twitching. "You? What use do I have of you, Mr. Fishbein?"

Maz grinned. "Henry Bannister. I know where to find him. Anyone on your staff able to boast the same, my Lord?"

Amow stared at him, but his right ear flicked, betraying his sudden interest. Then he exhaled, a long, loud sigh. "Very well, Mr. Fishbein. You have a captivated audience."

"This Bannister fellow's been a busy little bee," Maz said. "I've been keeping a few eyes on him. Watching him running around after various pieces of claptrap. It seems he's laid his hands on a rather specific wooden deer. Celtic, of course. Ancient. As far as I'm concerned, he can shove the bloody thing antlers-first up his own arse. But Vandenbussche seems to believe that the deer should have come to him instead, and I have a very strong intuition that you'd have your own interests in the matter."

An unholy clattering brought Maz to a halt. It got louder and louder, building until Doris appeared at his side with a cup of tea on a silver salver. He and Amow both stared at her.

"Your tea, sir." Doris handed Maz the teacup and saucer.

"Thanks," he said, at a loss for anything better.

Doris turned, and meandered away again. Maz took a long swig of his tea. It was hot and delicious. He sighed appreciatively.

Amow coughed quietly, a deep, hollow sound. His hand was a polite fist in front of his muzzle. If he'd had human eyebrows, Maz was fairly sure one would have been arched.

"Where was I? Oh, yes. Vandenbussche. The bloke has enough dosh lying around to buy his mum's rotten soul back from Satan himself. He was the one set me on Bannister – in a certain sense. Money's all the silly bastard has to give though, and I'm not that interested in money any more. Which is why I'm here, my Lord, if you catch my meaning."

Amow leaned forward, and tugged thoughtfully at a whisker. "I believe we may be able to do business after all, Mr. Fishbein."

Poor old Bannister, Maz thought. *Silly bastard would shit himself both before* and *after his heart gave out if he had even the slightest idea of what was coming his way. And all for a little wooden figurine...*

19. Now is Here, Here is Now
by Steven Sautter

It was cold and dark. Henry groaned, and opened his eyes. It didn't get much brighter. He appeared to be on a very basic cot, pressed against chilly stone bricks. "Oh, a dungeon," he muttered to himself. "Been ages since I've been in a dungeon."

He tried shaking his limbs cautiously, and discovered that he was not in fact shackled to the cot, the wall, or anything else. That was nice. His head felt fuzzy though, as if it had been wrapped in thick linen before being thumped repeatedly with a stick.

He pulled his anorak tighter around himself. He did his best to survey the room, but it was impossible to make out anything more than a foot away. A lock clanked somewhere off in the darkness, and then there was a creak as a heavy door opened.

Pale blue light flittered into his cell. A thin man walked in, his features in shadow. "Henry Bannister. You are well," he said. It was not a question.

"No, I'm not bloody well," Henry snapped.

The man turned around and walked out. "In the interregnum, the situation has grown more dire. Come. There is much to be heard and much to be learned."

"I will not," Henry said, getting up to follow him. "I'm not going anywhere until you explain what's going on."

"Is that so?" The man looked back at Henry and smiled.

Henry sighed, and followed the green-suited old chap up a flight of stone steps and along a corridor to a large room, great tapestries hanging from the walls.

"Hm, how medieval," said Henry. "Where's the jester?"

The man positioned Henry in the dead centre of the room. "Stay." He then took out a pouch from the pocket of his baggy green suit. Henry watched, bemused, as the man began to draw a salt circle around them, muttering something that sounded like Welsh under his breath. He traced around them three times, then clasped his hand on Henry's shoulder. "We are now shielded in this circle. A useful innovation. It is good to see you, my son."

"My father lives in Market Foxborough. I've never seen you before in my life."

"Not this one, no." The flatness was gone from his voice, replaced with bubbling humour. "You have hunted the Deer. You have read Frotte. You know me, child. I am the Hunter, and you are my son."

Henry looked into the old man's eyes. They flashed green for a split second, and then faded to grey once more.

"There are forces abroad that would have the Deer. They seek to unbalance the accords. For over a thousand generations we have been at peace with one another. But Amow and his ilk are newer arrivals to the game. They care nothing for the wellbeing of humanity, just for power, wealth. Temporal concerns. Human concerns, for powers graven in the human image. You must try to escape," said the Hunter, gravely.

Henry paused for a long moment. "You're going to hunt me down and kill me, aren't you?"

The Hunter smiled again, the warmest smile Henry had ever seen. Waves of love seemed to radiate from him. "After I've just found you? Your death may be in my cause, my son, but it shall never be at my hand."

"That's not very reassuring."

"In all truth, it was not supposed to be."

"Fair enough."

The Hunter reached into another of his great green pockets and pulled out the Anglesey Deer. He put it firmly into Henry's hand. "The Deer is my symbol. It is awake now. It shall protect you as best it can. I wish I could offer you more. Sadly, the other totems have long since been lost. In time, you shall quest for the arrow and for Wayland's blade, but first you must do this."

Henry held the tiny wooden carving. He felt... not stronger, but sleeker. Faster. "I understand," he said, although he didn't really.

"Turn thrice widdershins."

Henry slipped the deer into the pocket of his anorak and pulled up his hood. He turned anticlockwise in the circle three times, and faded slowly from sight. The Hunter raised his hand in a gesture of farewell. He broke the circle, and was quickly swallowed by the shadows as he walked away.

20. Turn About is Fair Play
by Peter Dawes

Possessing a heightened sense of smell could be a significant advantage. A human might consider it a curse, but for their betters, it often decided matters of hunger and survival. Mason placed it somewhere between a toy and a favoured possession – a valuable, entertaining item in his arsenal. Chases exhilarated him.

She'd left him with the lingering taste of her skin, and the aroma of dirty sex laced with perfume. Memorizing her car's license plate as she fled had been a natural reflex. The thong he considered a gift.

"She left you her knickers?" Maz pinched the article of clothing between his index finger and his thumb. The question hung in the air as the pair of underwear was discarded onto the table. Pockmarks and burns gave the wood its own character, one which matched the rest of the dimly-lit pub. The man shifted to meet Mason's gaze.

Mason was not above outsourcing aspects of a hunt for the sake of expediency. In the days since his return, he had encountered one familiar face in a pub and another near the park and its red phone box. Nothing served better as currency than old debts, which made Maz very... profitable.

Grinning smugly, Mason scooped up his souvenir, lids half-shut as he brought it near his face. "You can still smell her arousal," he said, savouring the delicious scent. He put the underwear back into his pocket. "I want her."

"You and half of England, mate." Maz's hand shifted from the table to half-finished pint. "What does this have to do with me?"

"I want you to find her."

"She's your hunt, find her your own damn self."

In one swift motion, Mason enclosed Maz's wrist in a crushing grip. The man barely avoided tipping his drink onto the floor. He swallowed hard, eyes widening in discomfort. "Care to let go, Mason?" he managed.

"Perhaps." Mason gave the joint a nasty twist. "Perhaps not."

96

Maz grabbed for Mason's forearm. "I know how you bloody creatures view the world, and while I hate having to inform you that you're not the centre of the fucking universe, I do actually have more important things on my plate."

"Such as?"

"None of your business."

Mason applied more pressure, provoking a grunt of protest. "I am going to say this as simply as possible so you can actually understand it," he said. "I. Don't. Fucking. Care. You owe me your life. I'm either going to collect that, or this favour. Should I tell you how long it's been since my last meal?"

Maz shuddered. "You *are* looking a tad paler than normal, mate." Mason turned the wrist a bit further, and Maz's eyes clenched shut. "Bollocks! All right," he said. "I'll look for the poor bitch. Just let go."

Mason released his hold. A wave of relief shivered through Maz, who lifted his hand from Mason's arm to massage his hurt wrist. "Fucking bloodsucker." He scowled at Mason, taking a moment to recover. Then he procured a pen from their waitress, and jotted what Mason remembered down on the ripped-up insides of a cigarette packet.

"Redhead," Maz said afterwards, reading the list back. "Business attire. Comes from money; drives a Merc. License plate LA15 blah blah blah. Give me two days. Meet me at Eros, facing the tube entrance on Piccadilly. Nine p.m."

"Why not here?"

Pocketing the torn cigarette packet, Maz rose from his chair and crushed the remnant of the fallen cigarette with his foot. "I want our future dealings to be someplace your fangs can't get itchy."

Mason scoffed, but allowed Maz to depart.

Two days later, Mason stood in Piccadilly Circus, hands in his pockets while his eyes traced over the surrounding thoroughfare. Neon lights shimmered off the blacktop and a light drizzle accompanied the chilled air. Pedestrians passed him blindly on their way down to the tube. Rain collected on his coat, but he ignored it. Finally, a pair of footsteps closed in on him, slowed, and stopped.

A puff of cigarette smoke drifted past his line of sight. He didn't bother turning toward the figure. "I trust you solved my problem."

Maz huffed and leaned against an adjacent railing. "Wasted valuable time which would've been better spent elsewhere, you mean." He sighed, and his voice turned serious. "You don't want any part of this."

"Any part of what?"

"I can't tell you."

Mason finally turned his head to regard Maz. "I didn't wait out here to be spoken to like a child."

"In this context, mate, you almost are." Maz shook his head. "If you're absolutely sure, though, I'll give you a name. I'll tell you she likes expensive things, and that Carnaby Street is right around the corner. I'll even let you know which shop her father's credit card gets used in on the most regular basis, but I'll give you a bit of advice with all of that."

Mason raised an eyebrow. "And what is it?"

"Leave well enough alone."

"Noted." Mason looked away. "The name."

Maz sighed. "I tried, all right? Gloria Vandenbussche. And that shop is Andromeda." Mason watched the still-lit cigarette sail into a puddle, extinguishing on impact. "This clears our debt?"

"When I find her, it does."

"Well, give her a kiss from me, then." Grit skidded beneath his shoes as Maz turned away. "I'll be on my way. There's bigger fish frying than one crazy vampire deciding to go swimming with sharks."

Mason barely acknowledged the departure. His thoughts already focussed on the prospect of the hunt. As eager as he was to pursue the lead, Mason knew better than to think serendipity would favour him. He walked away from the tube entrance, heading north. Eventually, he picked an empty flat in Soho to hole up in for the day.

The next night, he immersed himself within the streams of humans travelling Carnaby Street. Neither the affluent women with low-cut dresses nor men with trim bodies beneath tailored suits were permitted to grab his attention. Strolling up and down the alley, the collection of shops, tourists, and natives formed a comfortable space of increasing familiarity. It could have been any trendy little street.

That might have been why her car stood out the following night, when he passed it on his way to Carnaby Street. Or perhaps it was the fact that he had been searching for her scent so diligently. He smirked as he strolled into the press of pedestrians, knowing his prey was amongst the crowd. He wove around a conservative-looking couple, careful not to draw attention to himself, and paused. A mane of red was visible from the entrance to the store Maz had named.

Mason fought the urge to run his tongue across his aching fangs as his gaze settled on her. Gloria was browsing the goods, blind to his presence. He stepped away from the door, grinning, shifting his focus to the ground. Fantasies overtook the plots within his mind, envisioning her eyes wide with panic, her body writhing. By the time she emerged from inside the shop, longing had turned into need, and patience had been traded for expediency.

She headed back in the direction of her silver Mercedes Benz, two streets over. Mason kept enough distance between them that she would never notice she was being followed. *You thought you had me in the palm of your hand the other evening, child. Tonight I will play you like a fiddle.* When the Merc was in sight, Gloria dredged the remote ignition from her purse. Before her thumb could settle on the button, Mason closed the gap. He grabbed her hand, twisting it behind her back. He pulled her up against his chest.

Gloria gasped. Mason smirked, fangs already exposed. "Miss me?" he whispered into her ear. His voice sounded like a rasp in his ears. The bags in her free hand dropped to the ground as Mason ran his nose along her neck. "You and I are going for a walk. Follow along, and it will be pleasant. Resist, and I will kill you in that same instant. That includes starting to call for help."

Keeping the pressure on her arm tight, he led Gloria away swiftly, towards a car park further down the street. The few pedestrians in the area who noticed something not-quite-right looked away the moment their eyes met Mason's. None tried to interfere.

Meanwhile, Gloria quivered, making half-hearted attempts at wriggling away from Mason. He twisted her wrist in much the same way he had Maz's, and she responded just as obediently. The fluorescent lights of the car park left certain areas in shadow, providing Mason with all the cover he needed. Spinning Gloria around, he threw her against a concrete pillar, and thrust himself against her before she could run.

"Now," he said. "Where were we?"

She managed a high-pitched squeak as his lips found her neck. Mason jammed his knee between her legs. There would be no stiletto-heeled nonsense tonight. Her fear was overpowering her perfume delightfully. He wrenched her head to the side, exposing her gloriously sculpted neck. One taste first, then he would have her on the ground, her skirt pushed up and body ready for him. Just one taste.

A flash of black darted across the edge of his vision.

Mason glanced up in time to see a ball of fur and fury spring from the ground toward his face. He pushed Gloria down, hard, as claws jabbed for his eyes and teeth plunged into his neck. Yelling his outrage, Mason batted at the cat which had attached itself to his throat. He finally found the scruff of its neck, pulled it off him, and slung it violently to the side. "Fucking piece of shit." He stumbled backward.

Gloria gazed up at him from the ground, shock all over her face. He scowled and wiped away a trickle of blood ebbing from his wounds. "Be right with you, dear," he said. "Don't move. I have a cat's head to collect first."

Gloria didn't answer. She might have fainted dead away for all he knew. The scratches across his face had yet to mend themselves, and his vision was unusually blurred. Mason gritted his teeth, busying himself with crouching on the ground and glancing underneath each car he encountered. *Might have to do this someplace more secluded if that damned cat is going to keep interfering.*

Mason twitched as the sound of shattering glass echoed through the car park. He turned towards the spot where the sound had originated. Heading toward it, he swept around a corner, and came to a halt. There was a car with its windows broken, and the scent of blood leading away from the scene.

He also caught the reflection of a dark girl in one of the unbroken windows.

Mason crouched. Something sailed over his head. He looked

up in time to see a cricket bat hurtle past and connect with a nearby concrete pillar. The wood cracked, and splintered into two pieces, half the bat falling to the ground. Mason spun around. Another blow, better timed, crushed his nose.

The vampire reeled. He turned and stumbled toward a car. He tried to brace himself against the side, fresh blood pouring down his lips and chin. A bolt of pain rocketed through his chest. He moaned at the discomfort, then again at the sight of jagged wood jutting from his chest. The world spun. His grip on the car slackened, fingers sliding, and he crumpled to the ground.

"Maz warned you," the dark girl said. "I didn't want him to, but he insisted. *'I owe him, Cory my love. It's not his fault, what he is.'* I'm glad you didn't listen, you arrogant piece of shit. I'd send you back home with a message, but you know what? I think both our worlds are better off without you in them."

She watched him, back in cat form, as death stole him away piece by piece. Police came and went as the world faded. His last moments of awareness were of approaching feet and voices, the cat's deep eyes, and the sharp scent of her hate.

21. Max
by James 'Grim' Desborough and Salomé Jones

"They've found a way through," Corellwen said into the storyteller's ear. "Meet me at the phone box."

Safran Alef half-shouted down the phone at her. "Oh no, not *our* peacock. I'm very angry. Yes! Very angry! Furious! Coming right away!" The line clicked dead.

Cory grimaced and shook her head slightly. The storyteller often blurted out the first nonsense that came into his head. She looked out through the glass panes of the phone box as she put the phone back in its cradle. *No-one watching.* She let herself shrink down, taking refuge in the form of the black cat. It often felt safer in this world to be an eight-pound, four legged creature than to be a dark-skinned girl.

* * *

Safran Alef got into his car, panting from the unwelcome little run. The kids called it the 'Fiat of Doom', and with good reason. A way through, the girl had said. He hoped she wasn't trying to get the demiurge involved. The Peacock Angel didn't take sides.

He glanced into his rear-view mirror as he prepared to pull out into traffic. A black cat was sitting on the pavement. He frowned. How could she have gotten here so fast?

Bleeeeeep. A horn blared from in front of him.

"Yeah, yeah. Keep your trousers on." He waved and nodded to the other driver, a smile plastered on his face. "It's been a pleasure doing business with you."

When he looked in the mirror again, the cat was gone. Probably a coincidence. Or a hallucination. You did this job long enough, you started to occasionally see things that were really there.

Safran pulled out and drove up through the city. Cars tooted, and every kid he passed beamed at him, some running out into the road in spite of their mothers' shrieks. There was nothing strange about this to the storyteller. When you had a beholder, dragons and more besides on your car, you got used to that sort of reaction. That and angry abuse.

Some time later, he pulled up to the metal gate that marked the entrance to the park. A black, furry ball slid down his windscreen from above. The cat turned and looked in through the glass.

Safran laughed and opened the door. "I was expecting a Cory and I got a Max. You do so love being furry, don't you?"

Max wasn't listening. Something had her attention over by the phone box. Safran got out of the car and shut the door. "So what's the big emergency?" Safran followed the cat's gaze.

She was staring at the red phone box. The door was stuck open. Inside the box, twitching its tail, was another black cat.

"Holy Aziz," said Safran.

The call had come from the box, so the cat on the roof wasn't his Max. From inside the box, Max stared out at... Not Max. Tawny eyes narrowed to tiny slits. Back and tail flexed like a whip. She pulled herself tall on her twenty pink toes. They looked like baked beans set in a black, velvet-lined jewellery box. Her hackles raised and her tail fluffed out, standing straight, the tip flicking left and right in furious agitation.

She slipped out of the box, slow as molasses as Not Max – Nax – flowed down the car like oil onto the pavement, mirroring her every move. They were twins separated by a few feet of grey concrete and, obviously, a yawning gulf of loyalties.

The two crept in circles, slowly drawing closer to each other while Safran Alef, experienced with cats – and women – slunk back into his car to keep out of the way. Around and around they stalked, ears back, slitted eyes fixed upon each other, baring their bright white fangs and hissing. Deep from one throat came an unnatural sound, part of the reason cats had been called the devil's own and burned for so many centuries. A primal yowl of anger and distress. It was instantly answered by the other as they wound ever closer.

Safran Alef watched the stand-off through the car windscreen as they circled. The cats seemed to be competing to get lowest to the ground, belly fur rubbing the pavement, tails twitching. Each yowl was louder than the last as they tried to one-up each other. Safran clutched his steering wheel, white knuckled, not entirely sure what was going on. He was desperately spinning lies inside his own mind to try and make sense of it all when his thoughts – and their stand-off – were abruptly interrupted.

"FUCKING CATS! GO FUCK SOMEWHERE ELSE!" The shout blasted from a nearby flat, followed by a hurled, half-empty can of Special Brew. It landed between the cats and exploded, foaming beer everywhere. That was the signal.

Max and Nax sprang as one and hit each other in mid air, a yowling, hissing ball of fur. They seemed to hang above the ground for a moment, and then landed again in a tangled heap, two identical cats tearing into each other, claws and teeth, spit and hate, rolling around in a twisted coil while shreds of fur formed a cloud around them. They broke apart and flew back together again. One bit deep into the other's haunch and threw her onto her side. Rear paws smacked into the grounded cat's belly, claws extended, thumping and thumping like a manic rabbit. The other managed to wrench free, blood dripping onto the pavement. She gave a huff and shook her head, circling back around behind the phone box. The first cat sprang after her to press the advantage.

Safran Alef couldn't see, still didn't even know who was who. He leapt out of his car to try and follow the fight better. As he slid out, Cory fell into view, banging her head on the concrete. Her hair was a ruin. Her shredded, bleeding hands held a ball of feline fury above her that twisted, bit and scratched.

"You bitch!" Cory snarled. She threw Nax back and sat up, her T-shirt ripped and torn, a painful-looking bite in her bottom staining her jeans scarlet down her hip. Nax flowed back into human form as Cory scrambled to her feet.

Another moment, and the two women were locked in a struggling embrace, spilling away from the phone box and back out into the street. Nax's leather cat suit was the worse for wear, too. A minicab swerved to avoid them, its horn bleating away into the night like a panicked sheep.

"A bitch is a dog, you arrogant slag!"

"At least I'm not a traitor!" Cory shoved Nax back and snatched a fistful of her hair, making her hiss, then scream. She raked her nails across the paler girl's face, and left red, bleeding lines down her cheek.

Nax braced and shoved, forcing Cory back and then twisting and kicking her right in the belly. Her leg snapped out hard enough to throw Cory down onto the pavement in a wheezing heap, blinded by tears. Nax stood over her.

"I'm no bloody traitor. *You* are talking from far off neutrality." She stabbed her thumb at her chest. "*I* chose a side." Nax drew her foot back, preparing to give Cory a hard penalty-kick, but as she swung out Cory grunted and grabbed her leg. Nax was forced to hop as Cory scrambled to her feet, refusing to let go.

Nax yanked her foot out of her boot, leaving Cory blinking at it stupidly. They struck each other again, grappling, pulling, clawing, spitting obscenities and yanking at each other's hair.

Cory's T-shirt was torn to pieces, a ragged shred held together by hem, collar and sleeves. She was bleeding beneath it, but so was Nax. They shoved against each other again and parted. Nax's face and neck were wet with blood now from her torn cheek. They were both looking tired. Cory backed away, hauling her bloodied and ragged shirt up over her head. Her eyes were pinpricks, focused on Nax, and she swayed, weak and clearly fading fast.

Nax smiled a predatory smile and lashed out with her hand, fingers hooked. Long, painted nails raked for Cory's face. The exhaustion immediately faded. Cory whipped the ragged T-shirt around Nax's wrist and yanked, pulling her off balance and throwing her face-down to the ground.

Cory yowled savagely and leapt onto Nax's back. She bit down on the back of the other woman's neck, eyes feral and near-mindless. She held the grip as Nax thrashed and wailed in agony.

Nax wasn't a mouse, though.

Safran heard the crackle of bones, and saw the blurring of reality as Nax shifted form. Cory fell forward onto her hands and knees, a mouthful of fur visible between her teeth. A black and bloodied streak vanished into the alleyways with its tail between its legs.

He watched as Cory tried to spit out the fur. It took several tries. She croaked to herself as he approached her and hunkered down beside her. She turned to watch the fleeing cat, eyes following the trail of blood. "I chose a side, too, Elwyn."

"I know you did." He took his jacket off and tucked it around her shoulders. "Did you just call her Elwyn?"

Cory nodded. "We grew up together." She tugged the jacket around closed and got to her feet. "She used to be... a friend." She took a deep breath and turned toward Safran. "The Magus has found a way through the nexus. London isn't safe any more."

Safran groaned. *Eagle-winged things in the streets.* "When?"

"No telling. Could be any time." Cory looked into his eyes. "She followed you here?"

"You could say that. Come on. We need to get you some better clothes." Safran opened the passenger door of the Fiat, inviting her in.

Cory stood inside the door facing Safran, eyes wide. "You know what the Magus's discovery means, don't you?"

"I've got a pretty good idea. Come on. Get in." Safran motioned to the open door.

"The Peacock Angel is going to have to choose a side, Safran." Her green eyes were pleading with him. "And so are you, otherwise–"

Otherwise, the chaos would make two bloodied girls look like a romantic picnic. "Get in the car, Corellwen. I have to make a phone call."

Safran shut the door behind her and pulled the mobile phone out of his pocket. He clicked the contact list, typed 'P' into the search box, and scrolled through the list: Phone box 13, Phone box, Phone box on the river...

That was it. He clicked the contact and waited while the phone rang.

It was Ron who answered. "Hey teacher, how do you do!"

"Listen I, eh," Safran said. "I was called for, eh, an emergency storyteller convention in, eh, Norfolk. I won't be able to complete the campaign with you guys. I e-mailed Lenny the story –" Not exactly true, but he'd do it the first chance he got.

"Lenny? That stupid arse?!" Just the response he'd expected.

"Yes. He was the closest to... it. He can help you, maybe. Only he can."

"Help us with what?"

"Finding Sophie! Listen Ron, I gotta run. Tell the others it's been a whole lot of fun telling stories and playing games with them and I hope to see you all of you guys next year. Heh, it will be awesome. You'll go on a quest against the giants. It's a classic really, but I'm adding this great twist... Well, I gotta run. Bye!"

A disappointed wail came through the phone. Safran pressed the End button.

"It's for your own good, kid," he said, and opened the driver's side door.

'Another moment, and the two women were locked in a struggling embrace.'

22. The Boxed God
by Kate Harrad

How red the box was. Redder than the sun, redder than splashes of rust on the ground, redder than Ravi's blood. How beautiful it was. They worshipped its beauty. They chanted from sunrise to sunset, surrounding it in a circle of praise, raising their hands towards it, committing every feature to memory: the clouded glass, the dusty handle, the mysterious word sprawled across the top, TELEPHONE. They had never seen anything like it.

It was new, but it had always been there. Ravi knew both things were true, though she did not know how. She only knew that it blazed in the sunlight like a flower, and they, the children, were the bees drawn to its vital, vivid energy. How they loved it, how they loved it.

And how they loved the god who lived inside the box. For the box was not merely a box; it was a container, a glass cabinet designed to display the god in all her pale glory. How beautiful she was. They worshipped her for all they were worth. The god in the box represented the living spirit in the body, the soul inside the flesh. She was life itself, and everything she did was symbolic of the divine.

Ravi liked it especially when she slept, her body hunched in the corner of her narrow red cell like a broken insect caught in a jar. She could watch the god for hours like that, even when everyone else had left. She was the god's most fervent devotee, she knew. Her biggest fan. The god called her that sometimes, when it was the middle of the night and she woke up to find Ravi still watching her. "You're my biggest fan," she would say. And usually she would add, "Please let me out. Please. Do you understand?" And Ravi would bow down to her. But she would not approach the box. Neither she nor any of the children would dare touch the box or reply to the god. That wasn't what they were for.

The best thing of all was when the god sang to them. That happened more in the early days, before she grew weak. She made other noises too, early on – loud noises, sometimes, but they didn't like those much. They had heard screaming before. What they liked was the singing. *Sing to us*, they begged, and the god sometimes obliged. Ravi suspected, secretly, that the god's singing voice was not that good, but she wanted her to sing as much as the others did. More. The songs were like the sound of love. Although the words meant almost nothing to her, she committed them all to memory.

Once, the god stopped after the first line of the song, and began to shout instead of singing. *This is not where I belong! Where am I? Please, please let me out!* The children recognised this as the eternal cry of the god. They knew that eventually the cries would stop, so they merely kneeled and praised the god's suffering, enduring spirit. After a while, she began to sing again.

But that was in the early days, when the god was still going strong. Now she was near the end of her span, and Ravi knew it, for this was not their first sacrifice. She mourned, but she was grateful too, to have experienced such a transforming, glorious thing as the boxed god.

No more sounds came from inside, now. As the god began to die, the children gathered in their dozens, waiting at a respectful distance for the miracle of death to occur, to thrill them with the profound, necessary knowledge that they were still alive.

Ravi was the closest to the red box. And after the miracle occurred, and the god's eyes finally closed, and gradually everyone drifted away, she stepped through the invisible circle around the box and finally she opened it. She lifted the thin body and took it out to the air and held her close, and they watched the sun go down together, and she sang her goodbyes.

But she was happy as well as sad – soon, the box would create another god for them to love, and the singing would begin again.

'For the box was not merely a box; it was a container,
a glass cabinet designed to display the god in all her pale glory.'

23. Still Life
by Tim Dedopulos

The clouds seethed and boiled impossibly, an eternal time-lapse of gold and burnt orange. The sun didn't sink however, it just hovered on the horizon, frozen against the accelerated sky. The breeze was warm, and carried scents of grass and corn and honey. Alice smiled, enjoying the dream's beauty.

A path stretched ahead of her, pale with crushed stone and dust. It curled between crop-heavy fields, tired telegraph poles slouching along beside it. The need to know where it went was like a wound. She resisted for a moment, savouring the tension, and then started walking, whistling happily to herself.

She wandered along for a while, time uncertain and unimportant. There were little flowers growing amidst the grass that bordered the path, most of them red, some white. Somewhere in the distance, a rooster crowed. Maybe this was a halted sunrise, then.

A whiff of smoke caught her attention, heavy and pungent. A cigar. There was some alcohol mixed in there, too. She looked around, curious as to where a bar might have come from, out here. Instead, ahead, the path opened out into a crossroads. An old man was standing just before it, white hair and chocolate skin, dustbowl clothes and a friendly smile.

"Hello," she said.

"Hello, Alice." He nodded to her. Despite his smile, his eyes looked sad.

"Are you all right?"

The smile – and the sadness – deepened. "Bless you, child. I'm as well as I can be, in these times. But the crossroads... Ah, the crossroads is deadly sick."

She followed his gesture. Where the two paths met, the ground was shimmering. Oily colours seemed to play over it. The effect was hypnotic, and quite lovely, but somehow unsettling.

112

"That's... strange," Alice said.

"It's worse than that," he said. He opened his eyes wide, wider, wider still, until they seemed to be filling the horizon, pulling her in, pulling her down. His voice was like steel-mills now, full of iron and fire. "It's oozing."

Alice shrieked and sat bolt-upright, bed-covers falling away. She was reaching for her dream diary even before she was really aware of the soft London night spilling into her bedroom. She flipped the book open, and started writing, pinning the dream down, like a butterfly, before it dissolved into mist and shadow.

* * *

When she awoke again later that morning, at a more civilised time, Alice let herself drift back into the world slowly. The earlier dream was as strong in her mind as it had been before, a sure omen that there was a delicious mystery to chase down. She washed and dressed quickly, comfortably, ignoring the usual minor stab of disappointment at the increasingly unfamiliar reflection in the mirror. *I'll fight Time later*, she thought to herself. *The game is afoot!* She was out of the door in less than ten minutes.

Outside, the air smelled of car fumes, and buildings hemmed her in, but the sun was a welcome warmth on her face, and a light breeze ruffled her hair fondly. She glanced down at the pavement, remembering the dusty path from the dream. All right, then. She set off walking, and after a moment, started whistling defiantly as well. At the end of the street, she let her feet decide which way to turn.

A few minutes later, she was heading along a parade of shops. Familiar territory, in a casual sort of way. The windows held few surprises, but she peered in anyway as she went by. A curious new stack of magazines from the '20s in the flea-market doorway. Some tempting artichokes outside the cramped grocery. An ancient beggar croaked something from near the cash machine, his eyes wrapped around with layers of gauze cloth to emphasise his blindness. As she walked by the deli, a couple caught her eye. The guy looked vaguely familiar, the girl more so, but Alice couldn't quite put her finger on it.

They were buying olives. Looking happy. She puzzled over them for a moment, and then started walking again. *Bigger fish, today.*

There was a crossroads ahead. Common enough, in this part of town. For a moment, she thought maybe... But it wasn't quite right. The sweep of the roads was out of place. There was something about it that made the back of her neck tingle, however. She took the right-hand spur, pulled along by the merest hint of honey in the air.

She passed a row of pleasant terraces, the opening to a grand old mews, some more homes, and then stopped dead. A path split the row of buildings, leading off into leafy greenness. On both sides of the street. Her memory overlapped it, melded with it, the click so clear she could almost have sworn it was audible. At the corner of the crossroads, where the old man had been, a phone box reached up towards the sky. It was defiantly red, proud despite – or because of – its age, but for a moment, just a moment, it shimmered with a slick of colour.

Alice allowed herself a triumphant grin. A café waited just ahead, and she decided to conduct some observation of her quarry over a latte.

Inside, the coffee shop was surprisingly cosy, all soft wood-glow and shining copper. The girl at the counter looked to be deep in conversation with a black cat, which was perched on a stool beside her. She looked up as Alice entered, and smiled.

"Hi. How can I help?" A badge on the girl's apron read 'Hello, my name is: Nadia'.

The cat twitched its tail, then jumped off the stool and out of sight.

"A latte, please," Alice said. A note on a board leapt out at her. "A bacon roll as well, if I can."

"Of course," said Hello-my-name-is-Nadia. "Take a seat. I'll bring that over for you."

Alice smiled her thanks, and sat at a little round table by the window. It was a perfect vantage point for studying the red phone box. The poor thing had clearly seen better days, but it was still there. As she relaxed, and let the impressions begin to seep in, she became aware of an unexpected edge to the box. Melancholy, yes, that was always going to be the case. Strength, too. But beneath that, something jarring. A hint of turbulence, chaos even, and a sense of vastness unfolding...

A clatter startled her back into the café. She blinked, momentarily woozy.

"Sorry," said Hello-my-name-is-Nadia, putting the bacon roll next to the coffee.

Alice summoned a smile for her.

"Admiring the Old Man?"

Ice tickled down Alice's spine. "What did you say?"

"The phone box," the girl replied. "You don't see many of them any more."

"You called it the Old Man," said Alice.

"Oh, yes." Hello-my-name-is-Nadia grinned apologetically. "It's just what I call him. He's so patient there, don't you think?" She bustled off.

Patient? Not the word I'd have chosen. Alice turned her attention to breakfast, which proved to be excellent. Even in the throes of bacon however, she couldn't quite shake the impression of the titanic void lurking behind the box. Whatever it was, it definitely wasn't her old man, the one from the dream. He had been full to the brim with laughter and mischief and sadness, raging fires of life. Sick, he'd called the crossroads. She could see his point.

Alice finished her coffee, paid Hello-my-name-is-Nadia distractedly, and crossed the road. Up close, the chaos of the phone box was almost brutally strong. It felt like winds trying to tear through her, rip her down bit by bit, scatter her to the four corners of the Earth.

Unease welled up inside her, and lay siege to her curiosity. She wouldn't give in to her nerves of course, she never gave in, except this time, the voice that normally whispered delicious questions was starting to scream for her to run, run and not look back. For the first time Alice could remember, she decided it might be best not to poke her nose in.

She tried to take a step back, but nothing happened. Alarmed, she tried again, willing herself to move backward. Instead, her hand pulled the phone box door open. She whimpered, turned around, fled, horrified that her body was continuing to ignore her, was stepping into the box.

The door shut behind her, and as it did so, the phone started to ring.

Don't answer it, Alice commanded herself desperately. *I'm NOT doing this. Don't answer.*

Her hand moved to the receiver, lifted it from the cradle.

She couldn't even scream.

The receiver pressed against her ear, and a tidal wave of sound rolled out, smashed into her. Howling chaos pressed through every cell in her body. There was a flare of impossible colour, and then she was dwindling, dwindling...

Gone.

24. A Taste of Bitter Gold
by Gábor Csigás

Reality was a bad dream. At least, some realities were. Alexander's reality had been exactly that ever since he'd arrived in London a year ago. A bad dream. Not just poorly written and directed here and there, but actively twisted and evil, seriously bad. The worst thing was that he wasn't sure whether he was the protagonist or merely some walk-on. Although it was more like a run-on at the moment.

The street, irritated by Alexander's noisy stumbling, tried to shake him off. It threw people right into his path. He was too tired to dodge them, too slow, so he crashed into them. Some of them pushed him backwards. Or sideways. Muttering. Shouting. Shaking fists. At other moments, the street opened unexpected doors that he had to dodge. It loosened cobblestones that tried to trip him. Worse still, the street granted his pursuers freedom of movement – and they were catching up with him, in their black suits, with their gunmetal hands and foreign curses. The street, under increasingly doubtful skies, wanted to get rid of him. Quickly.

They wanted the vial back. They wanted him too, of course, but the thief was much less important to them than the treasure. For a moment, he considered throwing them back their precious vial, buying a better chance at saving his own hide. But there were no guarantees of safety, and he'd never have a chance like this again.

The Phrygian had been obsessed with the vial for years. He'd manipulated, lied, ruined lives, killed in his quest for it. Alexander's family had been casually destroyed in the process, their ancient vineyards stolen out from under them by banks clutched in the Phrygian's fist. They'd been forced out of Samos, out of Greece entirely, and swirled into this immense melting pot of a city. The vial was, for Alexander, both renewal and revenge – it would sell for an unbelievable sum here in London, and be denied to the Phrygian forever. So Alexander tightened his grip, and tried to force extra speed from his screaming muscles, to make himself faster than the Phrygian's thugs.

The next corner that Alexander turned sliced a maliciously hidden signpost straight at his face. He ducked on instinct, rolled, scraping his hands, his shoulders, his knees. The back of his jacket ripped as he stood up. He had to sprint right then, but dizziness swept over him, his breath finally escaping him. He desperately needed a moment to catch it. The Phrygian's men were closing in on him, their footsteps louder and louder, and he just stood there, staring down this next street. It seemed perhaps even more crowded and menacing than the one he'd just turned off. He looked for an escape, urgently, but there wasn't one.

That was when a girl stepped into an old phone box further down the street. The box was red, like the blood trickling around the unbroken vial, seeping from his torn fingers. Or... was it? For a moment, the box seemed oddly uncertain. The girl was maybe thirty, like Alexander's sister – young, with a cloud of dark, wavy hair. What kind of life did she have, this stranger, this girl? Who was she going to call from that red (yes, definitely red) box? She looked concerned. Alexander watched her enter the rusty metal and glass cage as if hypnotized. He felt trapped, pinned in place by the box. Maybe she was, too. A small, screaming part of his mind tried to snap him out of it. It had no chance, though: his gaze was fixed upon the girl as surely as if he were tied to a chair with his eyelids pinned open. The street shimmered for an instant. There was a flare of impossible colour, and then the girl was gone, completely, as though she had never been. Alexander discovered he could move again, and he started pelting towards the red phone box. And the street, strangely, made way for him this time.

"Come on," he said, panting, slipping into the box and closing the door. "Ring me, ring me, ring me, get me out of here too."

Outside, the Phrygian's thugs had spotted him. They weren't running now, aware that their prey had just trapped himself.

"They probably think I've gone mad," Alexander said, to the memory of the girl who had been there a few moments before. "Sadly, they might be right." There was no-one here. No Trinity disconnecting from an artificial reality, no Dorothy taken out of Kansas, no strange Alice falling into a weird rabbit hole. Only oxygen deprivation.

He had just about decided to tear open the door and try to pull a Solo on the Phrygian's men – charge at them screaming, scare them, perhaps get past them, gaining a few precious seconds – when the phone started ringing. Alexander stared at it, then picked up the receiver.

"Bad idea," a deep, rough voice said. Was there a faint aroma of good wine in the box? "Tricks like that work only in adventure flicks. Those guys would catch you."

"What?" Alexander couldn't think of anything else to say.

"Confusing them by charging them. It's a bad idea. They'll hurt you."

"Who is this?"

"You wouldn't believe me. Let's just focus on your problems."

"Was it you who took her out?"

"Who? Oh, I see. The girl who looked like your Helen. No, I'm afraid that wasn't me. Not my style. Besides, I'm trying to keep a low profile nowadays."

The Phrygian's people were about ten steps away from the phone box. They were discreetly concealing weapons, now that they could see for sure that Alexander was unarmed.

"If you want to punish the Phrygian," said the voice in the receiver, "give them the vial."

"How do you know about that?" Alexander said, watching the suits closing in. "Wait, don't answer that. You're reading my mind, so you must be my... my superego, or something. I've gone nuts. Or the vial is leaking, and it's poisoned me, drugged me, whatever. It's all over now, anyway. They're coming to get me. It was nice talking to you."

"Wrong." At the other end of the line, liquid glugged out of a container, sploshed into a vessel. The man took a big, noisy swallow, and finished it off with an appreciative *mmmm*. "You're neither mad nor intoxicated. You can trust me on that."

The Phrygian's men reached the phone box and spread out,

circling it like wolves. One of them, a well-dressed colossus of a man, stepped up to the door and reached out to open it.

"That was a nice little race, mate," he said. "Now get out."

"I wouldn't, if I were you," said the voice on the phone.

The giant gave the door a pull. It didn't budge.

"What the hell is going on?" Alexander stared at the door.

The man outside was clearly confused. His mouth formed words, but now there was no sound. He gave the door a savage tug. Nothing.

"Do you know what you've stolen?" the voice asked. "That's water. Normal spring water, chemically speaking. But it's enchanted. Has been for thousands of years. That vial, boy, was filled from the exact spot where King Midas washed off Dionysus's curse. The source of the Pactolus."

"Midas? Curse? What are you talking about?" Confused as Alexander felt, the thugs outside were clearly every bit as baffled. They had given up on the handle, and one was trying to smash in a window with a piece of pipe whilst others were trying to prise the door open with a crowbar. One was even trying to push the box over. Several looked as if they were shouting, although inside the box, the entire performance was silent pantomime.

"Oh, Alex," said the voice. "You of all people should know this stuff. Midas was kind to Dionysus's mentor, so the god granted him a wish. Midas, in a fit of sudden greed, asked for his touch to turn everything to gold. So Dionysus gave him what he wanted. Everything turned to gold. *Everything*. Midas couldn't eat, make love or even drink. Eventually, he begged the god to have pity, and take the gift back. Dionysus was in a good mood, so he sent Midas to the Pactolus to wash off the curse. Midas got saved, and the river's sands were, from then on, rather rich in gold."

"Okay, yes, I remember the myth," said Alexander. "But so what?"

"The exact spot where Midas washed himself held onto most of the magic. Hardly anyone knew that, and fewer still knew the precise location. Your Phrygian paid a huge sum to find it, to find the one moment each century when it can be captured, to find the vial that could contain it. He exiled my people – your family included – he

120

ruined my secret vineyards, he desecrated my hidden temples. Bad move, hurting my dear old Greece. The fool craves the gold he hopes his magic touch will bring him once he drinks the water. He thinks the curse will be weaker by now, and that if he drinks small sips, carefully resisting the taste of gold, the effect will only last a short time. The Phrygian, who's even taken his nickname from Midas, resisting the taste of gold! Give me a break."

The voice broke apart into laughter, a wild, merry whirlwind of sound that threatened to collapse into hysteria at any moment.

Alexander just nodded, eyes wide, mind spinning. He realized he was shivering. "I..." He didn't know what to say.

The voice reined in its terrifying hilarity. "You're running out of time, boy. You have a choice. Do you keep the vial for yourself, try to sell it to someone else if you've got even a single brain cell in your head, and, ah – go for the riches, restore your family... or do you let the Phrygian have it, both literally and metaphorically?"

"If I give back the vial, we'll stay poor," Alexander said. The leader of the thugs was talking on his phone, eyeing the small crowd that had gathered round him and his men. The wolves had been circled themselves, and Alexander was sure that London's near-infinite security cameras were taking notice of the commotion as well.

"Yes, you probably would. And if you sell it, you'd all have to flee, and the Phrygian will be annoyed, but he'll prosper. You can't have the revenge and the gold both. Despite rumours to the contrary, greed is not good."

"I have to decide now, I assume."

"Indeed. Quickly, too. I won't keep them out forever, you know. Our conversation's already being noticed – not just by your lot, either."

Alexander looked at the blood-stained vial. The water seemed cleaner than anything he had ever seen. The vial itself was cold to the touch, and covered with tiny, ornate engravings. He had no idea what purpose they served. Protection? Warning?

With a start, he realised that faint noises were starting to leak in from the outside world.

"Okay, okay," Alexander said. "He can have it."

"A wise choice." There was a clear note of anger in the voice now, and strange overtones. "You do have some potential. Learn your damn lessons though, manling. Mythology, history, everything. Stop repeating the same damned dramas. I'm growing tired of them, and you should be, too. You people should wake up from this recurring bloody nightmare, and start living for real."

With that, the line went dead, and the door of the red phone box flew open entirely unaided.

For a long moment, everyone just stared at it, dumbfounded.

Alexander put the phone back on the hook, and stepped out, holding up the vial.

"Here," he said, to the huge leader of the thugs. "Take it. Just let me go. Please. Leave me my freedom. The Phrygian knows I'm not important. And besides, the city is watching us."

The crowd backed away, startled, but Alexander was sure he could hear the security cameras clicking into tighter focus.

The giant looked around at the reluctant crowd, then nodded, plastering on a slightly sickly-looking smirk.

"Sure. Thanks." He took the vial carefully, wrapped it in a piece of white silk, then laid it in a case and slipped that into his pocket. "Catch you later, mate."

"I hope not," Alexander said, and set off on the long trek home.

25. Can I Drown an Eye?
by Joe Silber

Nadia paused in the café doorway, and ran through her check-list. Chairs up, floor swept, machines primed, cash locked away, back door double-bolted, windows shuttered. She nodded, satisfied. There was still a lingering hint of smoke from the rude woman that lunchtime, but she'd done all she could. Cigarettes. She didn't miss them. She forced herself to believe it.

She looked over the empty display cabinet – thoroughly cleaned – and daily specials chalkboard, already updated for tomorrow. *Enough of that already, Nadia. There's a shot of vodka and a soft bed waiting just over the hill.* She locked the front door and pulled the gate down on its steel tracks, cringing at its rusty squeal. An old brass padlock secured it in place, although she was pretty sure that it wouldn't actually stop anyone these days.

She zipped the key-ring into a pocket inside her worn burgundy handbag. *Drop them to the bottom, you will never find them again.*

Max the black cat was stretched out in front of the red phone box over the road. The cat had kept her company in the café for most of the afternoon, indulging in occasional bowls of warm milk. She looked up and stared at Nadia as if she knew something the human didn't.

"Nothing is going to stop you either, eh Max?" She wanted to believe the cat smirked at her.

Clutching the leather handbag to her side, she started off with grim, exhausted determination for her flat. The stretch of London between the café and her flat had been bombed to smithereens in the Blitz. *Smithereens*, she thought. *Ambrose might have used that word. What happened to him? No-one else used words like that these days.* Her grandfather had told her about London's fate in the war, had found and shown her photos of this area once he knew she was going to come here.

They rebuilt it all of course, back in the '60s. So much ugly development. The area started to become popular twenty years later. Now they were demolishing it again.

Those old, ungainly sawdust-and-steel buildings came down with alarming regularity at the moment. She wished they would send out warnings. *Announcements*, she thought. *That's what I mean.* There was something compelling about controlled destruction. Something wonderful. So many people seemed unable to destroy in anything but the nastiest, sloppiest ways.

This person and that come in, and leave again, and no-one leaves any real impression. Nothing but crumpled napkins, and that sense that everything is just dissolving.

She hated this part of her walk home the most. It was desolate on top of the hill – a whole kilometre of nothing. Just the one path, and property that no one had figured out how to re-gentrify.

Uncontrolled destruction, that's all we have. Well, I suppose the Germans thought they had the Blitz under control, but it's not the same.

In her grandfather's old photos, there had been another road at a right angle to this path. It had been built over, some time later. Then they tore some things down, so a year ago it had been all rubble. Later – in the dead of winter probably – some 'they' or other cleared the rubble away. But they left behind a stretch of rust, flecks and nothingness.

Then, two days ago, at some time during her shift, three cranes had gone up. Their bright yellow surprised her, as nothing seemed to be illuminating them. She would have expected an arc light at least. One crane had a banner near the top that might have announced their common purpose to her, but from underneath, she couldn't read it.

The bright yellow towers kept drawing her attention as she crested the hill beneath them and continued down towards her own flat. What had seemed a banner a few minutes before, twenty or thirty metres over her head, now looked like a swaying body when she looked again. All clothed in white.

No. It's just a banner. She was too far down to really tell. The breeze was strong enough to possibly make a flag sway that way. She tried to calm herself into believing that was the case. The bottom of the hill was just a half-kilometre from her flat. *Just walk it quick and calm. There's a drink waiting there, to ease your nerves.* But a strange scent of spring blossoms on the evening breeze worried her, too, so far out of season.

She pulled her handbag off her shoulder and hugged it to her chest. After a hundred metres or so she looked around, nervous now.

"Screw it," she mumbled. She burst into a sprint, away from the hill, right past the phone box on her corner.

As she reached her building, she heard the door buzzing. She saw the doorman look straight at her and nod pleasantly. As she entered, the buzzing of the lock merged with a sudden loud ring from the phone box.

She didn't wait for the elevator. She just ran up the three flights, still operating on the adrenaline that those cranes, that swaying banner, had given her. She unzipped the pocket in her bag as she climbed the stairs, but couldn't run and fumble out the keys at the same time.

She got to her floor and ran down the hall – her flat was at the end with the clearest view of that rubbled hill – and finally pulled out the ring of keys.

Then she was in, and onto her couch to catch her breath. For a second.

In the corner of her small living room stood a dusty telescope. A birthday gift, some years before. 'You talk about the stars so much,' her mother had said. Nadia hadn't the heart to explain that London was no place for stargazing.

Forgetting about the vodka, she took up the telescope and walked to the window. Before she could put it to her eye, the phone rang.

"Nadia. It's Ambrose. Put down the phone, and go back to the box on the corner. That was me calling as you passed."

How could he have known she was passing? "I just got inside. We're talking now."

"No. The phone box, please. You're not safe where you are." Cool, clear Ambrose. Even when he was carrying warnings, he had silk in his voice.

"Right. Okay."

"Go. Now." The voice was harsh now, almost not Ambrose at all.

She hung up. But before she left, she focused the telescope on those cranes, and saw Ambrose's bald pate and white linen suit swaying in the breeze.

The phone rang again. She stared down at it, transfixed, as it got louder and louder. Finally she reluctantly decided to answer it, before neighbours came round to complain.

"I thought I told you" – Ambrose's voice fell into silence, which gave way to static and then turned into his voice again – "to go."

"You're dead. I can see you. Hanging."

"You don't see me dying, dear girl. You see me..." silence, white noise, "...getting information. Now *go*."

Nadia was running almost before she reached the door.

26. Rebound
by James 'Grim' Desborough

It was hard to remake a life, but Talbot was doing his best. Jane and her partner Sue had been kind enough to let him sleep on their couch, even though it had been years since he'd last talked to them. They'd never grown up, still went out pubbing and clubbing every other night. Fuck knows where they got the money for it, but they seemed to manage.

Emily had thought he was having an affair. The endless phone calls, the way he'd refused to answer them while she was there – he wasn't answering them at all, but she couldn't buy that. There *was* no affair of course, but once she'd filed for divorce it was strangely freeing, and now he was ready to rebuild.

New suit, new attitude, time for a new job and then a new life. All his experience in the call centre had paid off. There was an opening for a management position in a rival firm, and he'd been able to convince them that he'd left his previous job due to dissatisfaction and lack of promotion. There was a good chance, a damn good chance, that he'd get this job.

There was even a smile on his face as he bounded up the steps from the underground, twisting around the people coming the other way with practised ease. His pocket hummed as he lifted his hand for a taxi. He fished out his mobile as he slid into the back seat and started the serious business of ignoring the driver.

"Seriously? You're going to make the same mistake all over again?" His voice, strangely crackly and quiet, strangely... analogue, coming from the mobile.

"You cost me everything I had. You begrudge me trying to get it back?"

"I *am* you. The real you. The you that you always wanted to be."

"You cost me my job, my wife, my home."

"*You* did. You freed yourself and here you are charging straight

127

back into prison. This isn't what you wanted. This isn't where you should be. This isn't what you should be."

"Stop the car!" he barked, fumbling as he turned the phone off.

The taxi came to a halt and he chucked some of his dwindling funds at the driver. He stumbled out onto the pavement and tossed his mobile, the last vestige of his former life, down onto the concrete. Then he stamped and stamped and stamped until it was little more than dust. He collapsed to his knees in tears, to the studied indifference of the Londoners who flowed around him, like water around a stone.

* * *

Gone. It was all gone. Nothing left. No money, no wife, no job, no home. He was ruined. Stripped back to the bare bone. Just a man on the street with nothing but the filthy clothes on his back. The last of his money had gone on cheap vodka to try and drown out the doubts, the fears, the creeping insanity of being haunted by his own ghost.

He had nowhere left to go.

Except back to the beginning.

Back to the box.

27. Rude Awakenings
by Tim Dedopulos

Consciousness came slowly, reluctantly. Vague unease gave way to a sharp sting. His face. It was his face that hurt.

"Wake up, shithead." The voice was flat, heavy, British, the sort of thing you heard in cheap movies.

Jarreth opened his eyes as a hand descended and smacked him, hard, across his mouth and jaw. He groaned in protest, and failed to raise a protective arm. "Fu' oth!"

"What was that, sunshine?" A bull-necked thug leaned in close. He had a cap of soft, curly hair and the blankly chubby face of a moronic five-year-old. The kind that pulled the legs off of puppies and old women. "What did you fucking call me?"

"Leave it, Mickey." The new speaker was obviously from the same part of town, but it sounded like this one gargled broken glass for a hobby. Jarreth looked around. They were outside, in a copse of trees, in twilight. Mickey's companion was gangly, with muscles like rope and a jaw almost as long as his forehead. "Wonderboy's awake, ain't he?" He turned to Jarreth. "Stop flailing around like that, son. You're strapped up, and we don't want you doing yourself a mischief."

Mickey backed away, unperturbed.

The other man raised his voice. "Mr. Dixon? He's ready."

There was some rustling behind Jarreth, and the sound of footsteps approaching. He couldn't turn. They had him tied to something vertical. In his imagination, it looked like a Hannibal Lecter gurney. Now that he'd had a minute, he realized he could hear traffic in the background, a low but constant hum. A row of bushes off some distance away could have been the English Gardens in Regent's Park. Not that it made much difference.

A few moments later, a heavy-set man in a black trench coat appeared on the edge of Jarreth's vision. He was carrying a briefcase, and ignored Jarreth completely.

"Steve, if you would?" The boss sounded better educated than his minions, but there was a ragged edge to his voice.

"Yes, boss." Long-jaw stepped forward and held his forearms out, like a forklift. Dixon rested the briefcase on them and popped it open. He rummaged around for a minute, and took out several items. Brandishing a small, gleaming scalpel, he turned to Jarreth, leaving Steve to just stand there. Dixon had a thick old scar across his neck. Someone'd obviously try to slit his throat some years before.

Jarreth swallowed. "Whoa, whoa!" A sudden blaze of white pain in his ear made him break off.

Mickey leaned round to stare at him. "One more word and I'll have your fucking eye." His voice was curious rather than aggressive, as if he was interested to see what might happen.

"He will," Steve said, trying – and failing – to sound pleasant. "He likes eyes."

Fresh pain erupted in the left side of Jarreth's chest, swift and sharp. He could smell his own blood, and moaned. Dixon wiped his scalpel on a piece of cloth, and put it into the briefcase. When he turned back round, he was holding a paintbrush. *A fucking paintbrush!*

Before he could even move his lips, Mickey's fingers dug tighter into his ear. "One. Word."

Jarreth tried to force himself to relax, tried to pretend this wasn't happening. Dixon stepped up and tore the new wound open with thick fingers. It felt like fire engulfing him. He screamed. And then the paintbrush was scraping into him, burrowing for his heart, ripping him apart.

Darkness closed in swiftly, and as he sank into it, he was sure he heard Dixon saying "Kafh Ph'wugn'thah."

* * *

Consciousness came slowly, reluctantly. Vague unease gave way to a sharp sting. His chest, his eyes, his belly – just about all of him hurt, one way or another. He blinked, dazzled by a bright light shining into his eyes. *Was he lying down?* He wriggled around as best he could. *Yes. Definitely horizontal.*

"Get up, 101." The voice was educated, but fractured, with a nasty rasp. It was familiar, somehow.

Jarreth blinked, aware that he very much wanted to do as he was told. He swung himself up off the gurney, and stood as smoothly as he could.

His master stood in front of him, radiant in his power. "How do you feel?"

This was no time for petty moaning. Jarreth tested his limbs swiftly, taking stock. "Fully functional, Mr. Dixon."

"Do you recognize this woman?" He passed Jarreth a photograph of an attractive, dark-haired woman in her twenties.

"Yes, sir. She works at Café McLaughlin."

"Her name is Nadia Zahradnikova. Her home address is on the back of the photo. Kill her, and then anyone with her, and return here – unless the police seem likely to apprehend you, in which case, kill yourself."

"Yes, sir."

"Any questions?"

Jarreth thought about it. Nothing came to mind. "No, sir."

His master nodded. "There is a coat for you on that table, with a gun in its pocket, and a small sum of money."

"Thank you, sir."

"That will be all."

"Yes, sir."

* * *

The woman's apartment block was brutalist in design, faced with square balcony hatches and cast out of light colored concrete. Vintage 1960s, a piece that even Ernő Goldfinger would have been proud of. The place looked familiar, but then so did the rest of the area. Jarreth shrugged to himself. Maybe he'd walked past there once. The memory was elusive, but also unimportant.

It was dark, but traffic suggested mid-evening rather than the small hours. He stood outside the building for maybe twenty minutes, until someone walked up towards the entrance. He darted up close behind the grey-haired old dude, and thanked him when he held the door open behind them. As they went into the lobby, the porter greeted the man, who stopped to exchange a few words. Jarreth slipped past them, and around to the waiting elevator. A few moments later, he was on the third floor, standing outside her door.

The best line of approach was to aim for normality. He knocked on the door. Thirty seconds later, he knocked again, and called out, "Ms. Zahradnikova?" There was no reply, no sound of movement inside the apartment, no TV on in the background. He gave the door an optimistic try, but it was locked. Still, he had to get in there.

Jarreth tightened his grip on the door knob and twisted. Somehow, he felt that he ought to be able to do this. He focused on his hand, dredged up his concentration, and forced himself to twist harder. Hot blood rushed to his arm, inflating it, increasing the pressure, on and on and on. The heat and power built, strength upon strength, until it felt as if his skin would burst. He ground his teeth together, ignoring the pain. His flesh was not ripping. It was *not* ripping.

With a sharp crack, the lock broke, and the handle twisted free.

Jarreth gasped, the horrible pressure fading from his muscles. He gave himself a moment to recover, pulled the pistol out of his coat, and slipped through the door.

Inside, a tiny hallway with pale walls and carpet was barely big enough to contain him and a few coats on a rack. There was a small kitchen ahead of him, wide enough for one person. It was dark, but unless she was contorted into a cupboard, she wasn't in there. To the left, a partly-open door showed a cheerfully-lit living room. Jarreth slowly swung the door open, gun ready. Nothing. Just some cheap furnishings, and an expensive computer, TV and game console set-up. A telescope was set up on a tripod in the back corner. The walls were covered in partly-framed watercolors, not good enough to be purchases, but not that far off. One in particular caught his eye – a study of columns, Ionic, Corinthian, both Dorics, Tuscan, even a Caryatid or two. Nicely executed.

Through the living room, another micro-hall opened onto a cramped bathroom and a reasonably-sized bedroom. He approached the bathroom cautiously, twitching the shower curtain aside at the last moment, ready to shoot. The bathtub was empty, not even a witch. *Huh. Where the fuck did that come from?*

He backed out of the bathroom, and darted into the bedroom. The bed was against the far wall, too low to hide under. Two large cupboards set into the wall were possibilities, though. He wrenched them open, first one, then the other. Clothes, cheap but stylish, along with some art supplies, an ironing board, and lots and lots of lingerie. No woman.

He went back to the start and double-checked the apartment, more carefully this time. By the time he'd finished looking under the sink however, he was forced to admit she wasn't there. *Fuck.*

In the back of his mind, Jarreth heard a memory of a voice. *'Just be still, my love,'* it seemed to say. He shrugged, and let his body relax. Quieting the chatter of his mind was trickier. He breathed in slowly and deeply, forcing himself to concentrate on that breath to the exclusion of all else. Into the tiny silent moment that his focus opened, he fed the tension and desire and narration, holding his attention on the air flowing through his throat and into his lungs. The moment stretched.

Then he felt it. A faint gliding sensation under his feet, a smoothness not unlike the moving walkways you found in airports. As if the city had a current. He submerged himself into it, holding himself always in his breath, and surrendered. His last fully conscious action was to tuck the pistol away again and pull the ruined door closed behind him as he left.

Time fractured, like diving for dreams on the edge of sleep. The world was places, faces, moments that had been teased apart and flashed in front of him. He made himself ignore it, lost in the city's tender whispers. He'd heard people describe London as a book, with every street a story. Psychogeographers. He'd never expected to experience it literally.

Jarreth eased back into himself, spun out of the city's current into an eddy of calm. He looked around as normal consciousness returned, and found himself a short way down the street from the café. A red phone box stood opposite it, keeping guard.

She was there. Of course she was. Where else would she be?

He approached the café door cautiously. The place looked closed, but there were no shutters down, and someone had left a faint light on in the back. Looking cautiously through the glass of the door, he could see the outline of a figure in the kitchenette area. A woman.

Opening the door as slowly and silently as possible, Jarreth crept into the café. The tables, piled up with chairs, provided a certain amount of cover. He moved slowly from one to the next, drawing his gun. He could smell coffee now, and a hint of perfume. The woman shifted slightly, turning her head away.

As he got to the counter, Jarreth dropped into a crouch, using the wood to steady his arm. He took careful aim at the woman in the kitchen, breathed in slowly, and fired.

The bang was deafening, compounded by glass shattering and pans falling over. Jarreth blinked. She *couldn't* have been a pile of cookware. A moment ago, she'd been *moving*.

He flinched at a wild screech beside his ear, and then his entire head erupted in burning agony as someone dumped boiling liquid all over him. He heard himself screaming as he flailed at his face, trying to wipe off the coffee. He couldn't see, and his eyes felt like they were being melted out of their sockets. He shrieked again, and then there was nothing.

* * *

Consciousness came slowly, reluctantly. Vague unease gave way to burning pain and disorientation. His face seethed with pain, and there was a horrible stabbing sensation in his temple.

"Shut up, pig." The speaker was female. With a sinking feeling, he realized that she was dragging him over tarmac, feet first. His arms were pinioned, and the back of his head grated unpleasantly over the road. He wanted to struggle, but it was just too much work.

"You don't deserve this. I should cut your fucking heart out. It's your lucky night. Maybe. But I will tell you now that if you somehow find your way back, and I see you again, I'm cutting your balls off."

He groaned. "Nadia?"

"No, the fucking tooth fairy." A door creaked open, and he was forced into a small cubicle. He could tell it was bright, but nothing else. A phone started ringing. The tooth fairy grunted. There was a clatter, and then something jammed against his ear.

"It's for you," she said.

A moment later, the door closed. A moment after that, the world exploded in a twist of spirals.

Jarreth hung in darkness, soft, absolute, silent. It could have been an instant or an eon. The first change was a soft voice reaching out to caress him. *'I'm always with you, my love. They've done terrible things to your mind, but I can fix you. Come back to me.'*

The voice was as familiar as his face in the mirror. *How...?*
"Alyssa!"

Everything went white.

28. Dear Time's Waste
by Joe Silber

Slowly, methodically, Ambrose climbed a crane just outside the centre of London, bearing a coil of rope with which to sacrifice himself. Traditionally, one performed this ritual from a branch of the World Tree, but a bunch of Norwegian kids had incinerated what remained of Yggdrasil twenty-some years ago. *Hanging myself from the beams of a Protestant church probably wouldn't have worked the same magic anyway, even if it* had *contained the last remnants of Odin's old tree.* And it was London's wisdom he sought, not that of the woods of Midgard.

He'd tracked down the highest point in the open air that he'd been able to find. A construction site, bereft of funds, its equipment fully extended and rusting in the breeze. The location pleased him for many reasons. The road up the hill and down was crossed by an older, hidden road. *Should Old Scratch be carrying what I need, at what better place than a Robert Johnson-style crossroads to wait?*

And those three cranes, towering overhead. *Orbis, Wingwalker, and Huntingdon-Smythe?* He shuddered at the image. *God's teeth. Three from the Bible instead, maybe. Shadrach, Meshach, Abednego? Caspar, Melchior, and Balthazar? No. Let's say Titus, Dumachus, and Jesus.* So Ambrose climbed the middle crane, and thought of that other one who had sacrificed himself to Himself. There was a certain poetry in joining Odin and Christ in giving themselves to get wisdom for others.

Climbing, he thought on other places of sacrifice. *This one bears no resemblance to the old cliff where Prometheus gave up — gives up? How long is 'forever'? — his liver daily. The time may come when birds eating my internal organs for eternity seems like an easy hell.*

But it's my fault Richard is wherever he is. Is it altruism if I want to correct misdeeds for the benefit of my own soul? Assuming I still have one, of course.

Richard has disappeared from this world, but he isn't dead. Not yet. Yes, I gave the man away, in a sense, but only so he could get himself, not so others could take him.

The wind high over London snaked through his loose linen garments, chilled his bald scalp, carried his scent away as the rungs fell below him.

On top of the crane finally, he sat, his legs hanging over the edge. *I should have brought lunch, like the bridge builders in that old photo. Bridge building? I suppose. But that's not it. No pontiff, I.*

He took the coil of rope off his shoulder and wrapped it about his waist, chest, and neck, testing each knot, chanting phrases from rituals he'd never practised, hoping the right something was listening. *A full rope binding? No. As long as I don't quite strangle myself, I'll be okay. Should be okay.*

Rope arranged to his satisfaction, Ambrose dropped himself off the edge, dangling himself in the wind over London, and started feeling for lines of information. He recalled someone saying that information was an idea, a relationship, an action, an area of shared mind, but not a *thing*. The old forms of sharing and dispersing knowledge – speech and its handwritten analogues – had given way to electronic signals. Telegraph, television, telephone. Far users at either end of a signal. The transportation of information, rather than its actual content.

Ambrose forced his mind to filter out the television broadcasts. The amount of shared mind in them was low, the noise and repetition high. A day and a night passed as Ambrose let it all pour through him, creating a sieve of himself.

As the television filtered out, he discovered the bombardment of other signals beneath it. He ignored the radio – too much like television, lots of repetition. No use. What was it that information carried? He tested the streams in his mind. There was an impression of... weight? *So be it. Thresh away the chaff.*

Camera signals. So many camera signals. Why did this vast new network surprise him? The whole city was wired up, but there were very few watching, for so many cameras. Transit hub video walls, football stadium security rooms, thousands of little home video networks, and everywhere, everywhere, police and security service monitors. When had London become so fearful? How *long* had he been away?

Slowly, he gravitated towards copper line communications. Individuals at either end of a line. There was little or no interference, not any more. They had the weight Ambrose sought. People who wanted to communicate used physical means. Phidippides at Marathon. The Greeks had known how to exchange information. *Did it even when it killed them. Us.*

He worked himself into the network, feeling for lines in buildings, under the streets, pulled up into the phone boxes. Sterility repulsed him. Soulless office lines. Those new open phone boxes. Useless. No room there for a person to leave a piece of himself to exchange. The old red ones were strong, though. All sorts of shared relationships in those, layered beneath the good time call stickers, oiled into the rust.

Time wavered, uncertain in the London winds. He spread his filaments, his confidence building. When he noticed the threat to Nadia, he tested himself, warning her of what was to come. He was close to gaining dominance over Chiswick when a savage pulse from a red phone box close to his body seized hold of his attention. The phone inside it rang, and a young woman answered, and disappeared. He could feel her both absent and present, like he could feel Richard. He extended tendrils of his own energy into the box's hinges, scratched glass, dangling handset, and empty cradle trying to find the girl, trace her. The box gave up nothing for a long stretch of his search, until it yielded him a boy.

Breathlessness, fear, and need. The information in the bottle the boy carried, the desire of the bravos surrounding him, these things overwhelmed Ambrose's determination to find the girl. This was a chunk of his old world, sharing itself with London. A piece of glass older than anything human-made in England. And the boy was a child of the vine. There were obligations...

He wound a strong tendril around the telephone – a good, firm grasp – and reached out in a very different direction. It took all he had, pushing further and further, thinner and thinner. He doggedly concentrated on his link to the telephone, maintaining a thumbnail grip. It wouldn't do to get lost out here, between London and the Deep Blue Sea. He continued stretching himself outwards, and even

138

the fear started to fade. What did it matter, if he fragmented into mindless shards?

A clink of glasses, toasts shared over a Peloponnese phone line, consummated in thick, red wine. Unwatered, of course. Modern drinkers had no fear of barbarian madnesses. He infused himself into the moment, seeking.

The response was immediate. "Good, my son. Good." The words rolled through him like butter, full of love and approval. Ambrose immediately found himself safely back together, over London.

In the box, the phone rang for the boy. Ambrose let what followed wash through him, seeking the girl's shreds before they were blown away. The conversation's message echoed his own quest. *Give to get.*

The boy exited, and Ambrose discovered that he'd been left a reward of his own. A route, from the phone box in London to a phone box *behind* London.

And then he heard Richard's voice. "What can I do to make you come back?"

Startled, delighted, Ambrose tried to push his own voice back down the wire. A precise metallic voice like well-oiled machinery cut in, walling him off. "We are sorry, but you have lost your connection to Richard. Do not worry. He is ours now."

There was neither silence nor static in the link as it broke.

29. Pushing Forward Back
by Dan Wickline

Brandon weaved his way through the crowd to his usual table by the window at Café McLaughlin. The English seemed abuzz with talk of the Queen's address to Parliament two days prior, but he didn't have any interest in local politics. He was in London to work on his master's degree. While he unpacked his laptop, the counter girl brought over his cup of Darjeeling, his scone, and a little pot of clotted cream. It was the only indulgence he'd been allowing himself since his big mistake.

A couple of months earlier he'd met a young lady named Connie – 'the whore,' as his dad now called her. After some two weeks of passion and distraction, he'd reluctantly given her his ATM card to get some cash for a nice dinner she was going to cook. Instead she cleared his account of everything but fourteen pounds six pence. With all his student loan money gone, he had to contact his father back in Boston for a series of 'I told you so' sessions and some grudging financial help.

So Brandon now spent his days at the coffee shop, using their free wi-fi. He couldn't afford internet in his apartment any more, and he had to get his paper done. He stirred three packets of sugar into the tea, wrapped his hands around the heavy ceramic tea pot, and let the heat warm them for a moment.

He liked to watch the people go past as he worked. Today it was raining, and everyone walked with the same sense of purpose –'avoid getting wet'. He glanced out at the red phone box across the street. It had never occurred to him, before the first time he'd sat at this table, what an interesting place a phone box could be. He spread the clotted cream on his scone and took a bite. Right now, a woman stood in the box having a very animated conversation. This wasn't the first time he had seen her. She'd been in there before, talking for hours on end, making one call after another. He remembered her not because of the flailing arms, but because she wasn't alone. A small girl was invariably in there with her, sitting on what looked like a red suitcase.

The little girl would pass the time by drawing, sometimes on paper and sometimes, if they were in there for long enough, on the fogged up glass panes that covered three of the box's sides. At that moment, the little girl was drawing on paper. She apparently finished just as the woman hung up the phone. The drawing was handed up for approval and the woman nodded as she looked. Then she turned the paper over and all the color drained from her face.

The woman frantically looked around, then grabbed several plastic bags filled near to bursting with loose papers. She collected them together in one hand, seized the little girl with the other, and dashed out of the phone box. She stumbled to a halt in the doorway, for a moment, trying to avoid a black cat. This gave the little girl enough time to grab her own suitcase before she was pulled off out of sight. Idly, Brandon wondered what had been on the piece of paper to cause such a reaction.

He'd seen people leave the box in tears, or fleeing from it with looks of terror on their faces. Sometimes they came out in different clothes from the ones they went in with, carrying things they hadn't had when they'd arrived. Once, in the middle of the night, he'd been hooked into the café's wi-fi from the sidewalk out front. That time, he'd seen a woman giving off a ghostly glow, like someone had dipped her in fluorescent soup. She'd seemed sad until she got in the phone box, but she'd left in a hurry smiling like she'd won the lottery. He'd even seen several people go in and not come out again, but had just about convinced himself that it was just his short attention span.

After the first pot of tea, he got a refill of hot water from the sympathetic counter girl, and headed off to use the restroom. He stepped away for only a moment, but when he returned, he found a yellow post-it note stuck to the screen of his laptop. On the note, written out in block letters with green ink, were the words 'ANSWER THE PHONE'. Brandon looked around and realized he was alone in the shop. Even the woman running the counter must have stepped in the back. He walked over to the door and leaned his head out, looking for the person who had left the note. The streets were empty. Not even a few people running to get out of the rain. He was about to step back in when he heard it.

Rinnnng rinnnnng.

The sound was coming from the red phone box.

Rinnnng rinnnnng.

He looked around intently, trying to find anyone else inside a shop window or even a passing car. Not a single soul.

Rinnnng rinnnnng.

Brandon stepped out into the rain and crossed the water-logged street. His hair and jacket drank in the cold wetness as he walked towards the phone.

Rinnnng rinnnnng.

He stopped inches from the door. Deep down he hoped the phone would quit ringing. Then he could walk away and not look back.

Rinnnng rinnnnng.

He was lying to himself. He had to pick it up. There was just something about it. He slid the door open and stepped inside, closing it after him to keep the rain out.

Rinnnng rin–

"Hello?"

"Oh, thank God you answered." A male voice crackled through the line.

"Who is this?"

"I don't have time to explain. I need you to deliver a message for me."

"A message? To who?"

"I need you to reach Kelly David at McMurtry University. Tell her it's not safe. Tell her Henry says…"

A long crackle and loud pop obscured the last of the message. Brandon was about to ask the caller to repeat it when he noticed the black cat outside the window of the box. It was staring at him disturbingly. Then it darted off down the sidewalk. The motion made Brandon look up just in time to see a large, black delivery truck headed straight toward him. He dropped the receiver and struggled with the door until he got it to slam open. He threw himself out of the box and down onto the wet concrete sidewalk. The van's hood blasted its way straight through the phone box, sending glass and metal debris flying in all directions. He rolled over, covering his head while splinters and shards pelted his back. He could feel each piece of jagged shrapnel as it ripped through his coat and into his skin.

When he felt nothing else falling on him but the rain, he lifted his head. He expected to see the lorry parked a few feet away, with people running to help. But he saw nothing of the sort. Instead, he watched as the scattered debris began to move. Just slightly at first, but then it was undeniable, the lumps sliding across the ground to find connecting pieces. More and more, the remains merged to form larger chunks. Even the bits stuck in his back dislodged themselves, and took their places among their fellows. The glass and metal were merging together seamlessly, like a 3-D puzzle being built by invisible hands. He just lay there, speechless, as he saw the whole heap straightening, the last few pieces clicking into place. Then the red phone box stood before him again, every bit as solid and sturdy as when he'd first approached it.

Confused and sore, he forced himself to his feet. He looked around again at the completely empty streets, and realised it was late. After midnight, if he had to guess. Where did the lorry go? Where were all the people? Who had been on the phone? How did so much time pass so quickly?

Home. He needed to go home and sleep. He'd figure it all out in the morning. He began to walk. He knew he was going the right way, but none of the streets seemed to be familiar. *Just shaken up.* He kept going. When he passed an all night corner shop, a headline jumped out at him from the Evening Standard board. Something about the Queen planning an unprecedented address to Parliament in a week's time. That was odd, wasn't it? Well, of course it was odd, but with the financial crisis... He forced it out of his mind. He had too many questions to answer as it was.

"Come on, old son. Keep it together. You're almost home, Bran... Br..." That wasn't right. All right, talking to yourself was never great, but... His name felt wrong in his mouth. He couldn't remember what he was supposed to say. The incident at the red phone box must have shaken him up more than he thought. *It isn't every day you're nearly killed.* He thought about it again. Had he nearly been *killed?* Surely not. His body felt sore, but he didn't know why. He pushed the thought aside, and made for a door ahead of him. As he stepped inside he was greeted by a cheerful-looking man, seated behind a desk, a bank of CCTV monitors off to one side.

"Are you okay, Stuart?" The man's voice sounded concerned.

He looked at the guard, running the name 'Stuart' through his mind. It felt like he was trying on someone else's coat, but it seemed to fit him. He could've been Stuart.

"Where am…"

"Amber?" The guard smiled at him. "Yeah. She just went out for a walk. Said she'd be back soon."

"Thank you… James."

Stuart headed for the lift. A check of his front right pocket revealed a key he'd never seen before. The key to his flat. He pressed his floor number out of habit, and waited for the doors to close.

"Indigo Starfish," James called after him.

Stuart put his hand out and stopped the doors. *What is he on about this time?* He shook his head ruefully. "What did you say?"

James smiled again. "I just said have a good night, Stuart."

30. Phone Boxes Taste Bad
by Francesca Burgon

Margaret licked her finger again, and grimaced. She felt herself shudder, and had to just let it stop on its own. She wished it was less horrible, but she wanted to draw on the windows. Even if they smelled of pee and smoke and other things she didn't want to think about.

She moved to a clear spot, careful not to disturb Mother's feet, pushing some of the rubbish out of her way. The glass was nice and thick, and it made an excellent drawing board, especially on evenings like this, when it was raining and they'd been in the box for a while. Margaret giggled as the drops of water chased each other in tiny rivulets down the outside of the window. She couldn't see them very well in the twilight, but that didn't matter.

Mother reached down and grabbed Margaret's hair, yanking her head sideways. She didn't even stop talking. "No, you don't understand. The bully boy will come and kill us. Kill us all. We're victims of the filthy peeds. Hate them all, hate them all, hate the long and the short and the tall."

The tug on the hair was easy to translate. It meant, "Shut the fuck up you disgusting little brat who ruined my entire life. You don't deserve to have a mother who loves you as much as I do. Now keep your mouth closed before I pinch it shut for you."

Margaret understood that it was vital nobody knew she was there. The Phone People mustn't hear her, but she had to be there. Mother was very careful to make sure that they were never apart, so that she couldn't get snatched and taken away by the bully boys. She breathed on one of the panes of glass and drew another picture, a cruelly-taloned hand hovering over her own head. The frown on her picture-face wobbled.

Grandma didn't believe in Them. But They were real. Un-named monsters, They lived everywhere, and Mother was terrified of Them.

She had bags of The Evidence that had to be protected. It would put Them away for a long time, so that they could live somewhere nice and be happy again. Margaret was supposed to stay sitting on her bright red suitcase wherever they went, so that she couldn't disturb The Evidence.

"I can show you. Show you all. Prince Charles knows, you just ask him. He knows, he does. How? I got Evidence on you. I'll bring you down, just wait and see. Make you suffer. Make you live in the parks. Filthy Peed."

With a howl of pure anger, Mother smashed the receiver into the cradle. She rocked there on her feet for a little while, muttering in a guttural tone. Margaret curled into herself, flinching each time Mother's shadow touched her, sure that the hand would grab her and pull her from the warmth of the box. Mother calmed slightly, and started flipping through the worn pages of an ancient phonebook, seeking another person, any other person, to explain herself to. A change of tone, and she became the Smart One. Another moment and she was growling in a thick Irish accent. A beat, a voice and a twist of the mind. Mother was many people, some days. Finally, she found a number that she could call. Her yellow-stained fingers stabbed at the buttons.

In her most secret moments, Margaret wished that one of the Phone People *would* hear her. Rescue her from the rescuing that had wrenched her from the other world and into this one. Rescue her from being filthy and tired and always so hungry.

Another sixty pence got fed in to the ravenous grey machine. Every night they came here, so that Mother could warn people about Them, talk to them about the places she wanted to escape to. Mother was important, she had important secrets. She needed to share them with the people who answered her calls. There were always berries to find on hedges, anyway.

Margaret moved to another spot on the floor, hoping to find a place where she hadn't been drawing on the windows. She'd used up all of the ones she could reach, and had drawn on the backs of all the bank slips that she'd nicked from the post office yesterday. While Mother waited for someone to answer the call, she opened

146

her suitcase, and took out a pen. Her battered doll and the other dress stared up at her mournfully from amidst the crumpled papers and scraps of memory hidden inside. Mother carried paper, The Evidence, in battered plastic carrier bags. It had to come with them everywhere they went. So Margaret felt she should probably have some as well.

Wonder if I'm crazy, too. Bet I am. Best not to let anyone in. Margaret closed her eyes hard, to trap any other ideas like that one from escaping. She clicked the case's clasps shut, and wriggled until she was sitting on the case again. Other people's rubbish lay in small heaps around her on the floor. She reached into the nearest pile, hunting for something to draw on. A fizzy drink can with a drizzle of something sweet, a crisp bag, a soggy receipt... Victory! She picked up a slip of paper with an empty back perfect for drawing.

Margaret turned over the paper and shrugged. It was some kind of bank slip. She recognized the look from the ones she used instead of drawing paper. Maybe she'd dropped it yesterday. It wasn't the same colour though, so maybe it wasn't hers after all. With a slow finger, she sounded out the words printed on the front, whispering them to herself so that she didn't disturb Mother.

"Ho.. ra.. k. Horak.. Horak V.. Vee.. a n Van. Horak Van." The second word was very long, so she decided to try figuring out the numbers instead. There were an awful lot of ohs at the end of the two four. It didn't matter.

What to draw, what to draw? Margaret looked up at Mother, towering above her. What would make Mother happy? Ballet dancers always seemed to work. If Mother was happy one evening, she might give Margaret some food as a reward. She bent her head over the slip of paper. The slightly wobbly lines of a dancer began to spin across it with each careful pencil-stroke.

There was nothing now but the drawing, and the phone box. The stinky floor, the glowing yellow light up in the ceiling, the ancient web cities build up between the light and the corners. The cities were ruled over by fat, old spiders. Margaret decided to draw one of them over the dancer. Around her, the glass panes became frosted again, Mother's voice rising and falling with the drumming of the rain.

Margaret stopped from her drawing for a moment, and leaned against the wall of the old phone box, idly rubbing the nearest window. There was a cat crouched under the hedge outside. Cats were funny. This one just looked wet. It stared at her, and then squirmed back to the hidden insides of the bushes. She licked her finger again.

Yes. Phone boxes tasted bad.

31. Bad Dreams
by Lacie Grayson

Amber clutched the knife ferociously, her arm outstretched. It was a very big knife indeed, bigger than the last time she'd looked at it, with serrated notches down the spine now, and a wicked little curve to the tip. She wasn't entirely sure where it had come from. Outside the kitchen window, the clouds were churning in a most peculiar way. She probably should have been worried about that, but Stuart was staring at her, pinioned somewhere between confusion and pain. She discovered that she was shaking, hard enough that it was tricky to keep from falling over. She braced herself back against the countertop.

Her head hurt like fire. She could remember the life she'd had with Jon. She could also remember the life she'd had with Stuart. The memories ran side by side, impossible, undeniable. Realisation hit like a hammer. *Stuart was her boyfriend.*

She half-dropped the knife down on the counter, and did her best to summon up a sweet smile. None of it made a drop of sense. "Sorry, babe," she said, smoothing her hands over the front of her dress. "I had a terrible night."

He smiled, all his confusion melting away, replaced with sympathy. "You go sit, I'll fix the tea. Let me take that." He smiled and put his hand out palm up. She looked down at the knife still in her hand. Her left eye wouldn't stop twitching. She handed the knife to him, and found herself in the lounge with her fingers pressed to her eyelid, holding it in place. The room was the same as in the Jon-memories, sort of. The big bookshelf full of Jon's dumb mementoes had been replaced by Stuart's DJ kit – decks, monitors, box after box of dead vinyl.

She could remember the night she'd met Stuart. She hadn't wanted to be there, but she went anyway. A low-rent house party in Bristol. Friends had dragged her along, but she managed to keep to herself, focussing her attentions on a single pint so she wouldn't drink too much. That was when she noticed Stuart. His green eyes had been difficult to ignore.

She began to feel a little woozy as the clips of memory flooded into place, pushing away what she thought she knew about the past year. Memories of meeting Stuart, staying in Bristol for a week, then heading back to London. When she met Jon, she'd already been dating Stuart. They'd become friends. *But Jon had lived here with her, hadn't he?* It was as if he never left her, as if the hurt never happened, as if the shoe never dropped.

She smiled. They had plans, she remembered now. Stuart was doing a gig, so Jon was going to come over and keep her company. They'd just hang out, watch a video, drink some wine.

Stuart snapped her back to herself with a cup of tea and a smile. He had two-day stubble, his uniform for nights on duty. The gigs. And it wasn't just the gigs, but the girls at work, too. The way he flirted with them. The way he sometimes more than flirted. *Just like Jon had.*

Was he even a DJ? She looked over at the wall, saw his rack of guitars where Jon's mementoes had been. *Guitarist. Of course.* Silly slip to make.

Her heart beat faster as she studied him. Her memory knew every inch of his lean body, but she couldn't just recall the sensations of him at will. It was like she knew, but didn't know at the same time. It was how she rationalized the cheating. As long as he came home to her. That was the sign of love.

"So, you and Jon going to stay in and watch telly then?" Stuart asked, sounding tired.

"Yeah, maybe pop open a bottle." Her voice shook a little.

Stuart just smiled. "Sounds about right," he said.

He spent the afternoon thumbing through an old Fountainhead novel, and texting with someone. He had someone else. She was sure he did. He had to have. It was evening now, right?

She was secretly excited to see Jon again. She almost pushed Stuart out the door just to make the time go by faster. Luckily, he seemed preoccupied, not even noticing how it was all making her feel.

The less responsive he became, the more she started to wonder just what could be taking up his time.

She was stuck with uncertainty. Were these memories hers? Maybe she had stolen the life of another girl, one who looked exactly like her. When Stuart leaned in to kiss her goodbye, she almost screamed.

After the door closed behind him, she went over to the couch and started to curl up, trying to process the chaos. While she fought with herself the buzzer rang. She opened the door, knowing that it would be Jon on the other side. He looked good, though a little more gaunt than she remembered. Pale, too.

"Amber, are you okay?" He was holding a bottle of wine. The sense of how things were supposed to be was just too much. They touched fingers, and the room crackled with electricity, making her dizzy. His fingers lingered just a moment too long.

She could feel it, but could she tell him? Tell Jon. But Jon had...

Her body twitched violently, and her eyes sprang open. She heard herself yelp. She'd been dreaming. It was only a dream. Cold sweat was matting her hair. She reached out to the form next to her.

"Are you awake?" she asked, shaking his shoulder.

"I wasn't..." the voice next to her groaned. "What's wrong, hon?"

The familiar, different, familiar voice echoed in her ears. "Stuart?"

"Last I checked. Are you okay?"

"I... I'm not sure. I think so. I dreamed you were a cheating asshole musician. And there was..." She lay frozen next to him. *Was she awake yet?*

He lifted his arm and tried to encourage her to move up against him. She slid as far away from him as she could without falling off the bed. He frowned and put his arm back down to his side. "Amber, you haven't been yourself lately. Is there something wrong?"

Without looking at him, she took a deep breath. "This is going to sound weird, but... I think I need some help."

"That's sort of random. What do you mean by 'help'?"

"Well, you know how it is when you're just getting to know someone?" She glanced at him out of the corner of her eye.

"Yeah?" A look of concern spread over his face.

Amber swallowed. "I feel like we're in that place." She fixed her eyes on the wall on the other side of the room as she talked. "As if the first time I met you was a week ago." A little black spider was making his way down the wall in stops and starts. It gave her something to focus on. "I mean, I remember things, sort of, but this doesn't seem real. If that makes any sense."

"Not really, but go on."

"It's just really hard to explain." She glanced over at Stuart. He seemed to be watching the spider, too. "I don't understand it. It's just like one minute everything was different, and now things are the way they are, but they've always been the way they are. I know that's insane, we have proof of our time together... but it's wrong. Something isn't right."

"So when you say you need help, you mean... a doctor?" Stuart blinked at her.

"I guess so." Amber bit the inside of her lip. "I don't know. Maybe not. Maybe just some coffee."

Stuart chuckled.

"But, seriously. Keep an eye on me. Okay?"

32. The Old Barge
by Chuck Walker

The Thames had a life of its own, the poets said. It was true. The old barge Cornish lived on had been tied to the creosote-stained dock for twenty years, and the only time it ever moved was when he hoisted it out of the water to scrape the bottom and repaint it. Years had passed since the last paint job, and the barge looked ready to sink. The coal tar wharf was the only thing keeping it afloat.

Cornish loved the boat. Its rocking eased his restlessness. It was home, and riding the tides of the Thames, he could escape the ache of his failures. He told himself that he wasn't lonely, but it wasn't true. He had chosen his self-imposed exile, and loneliness became his solace.

Robin had found someone else. He wore the wasted years he'd invested in her like a yoke around his neck. The faint odour of her perfume lingered in the cabin, and in the closet, the sweater he'd given her draped over a hook – hung, discarded, along with his love. The last picture he owned of her lay face down on a desk in the salon but it didn't matter – her image was burned into his memory.

He climbed the ladder to the deck, shaking his head, trying to push the memories away. There was no escape. His gaze fell upon the "Robin" carved into the gunwale. While waiting for her one evening, he had cut into the wood with his penknife – etching her name into his heart. His past was the power that kept him on the barge.

The dark waters of the Thames often called his name, but he was not ready for the big deep yet. A nagging hope kept him isolated and apprehensive.

Cornish often gazed into the water, its little white caps lapping at the side of his barge. He looked down into the river, and saw the body, floating effortlessly towards him. Face down in a swirl of bubbles, it bobbed in and out of the current.

"My God," he muttered.

He gawked at it, stunned, not sure what to do. It occurred to him that if he wasn't quick, it would be caught in an eddy and the river would carry it beyond his reach. For a moment, he forgot about everything and grabbed a pole to hook onto the corpse.

The rush of the water tugged at the body, intent on washing it out to sea. Cornish struggled to pull it closer, managing to draw it alongside the hull. He held the pole with one arm. With the other hand, he grabbed a coil of rope and tied it around the arm of the bloated body. He made sure it was secure before he loosened his grip. His hands were icy cold and painful. Shaking them, trying to regain feeling, he looked down at the corpse. The short hair and the suit told Cornish it was a man.

Cornish reached into the water again to retrieve the dead man's wallet. It was slippery from the slime of the river, but he managed to get a firm grip on the leather. Water dripped from it as he pulled it open. There was nothing inside – no money, no identification, just an old snapshot of a girl Cornish didn't recognise. He dropped it on the deck, his hands stiff from the cold.

"Going to have to call the Fuzz," he muttered under his breath. His mobile wasn't working. He'd been meaning to take it in for service. There was no hurry, really. The man couldn't get any more dead, and the rope would hold for now. Still, he couldn't just ignore it. He could call from the coffee shop. Cornish hurried along the length of the dock and across the parking lot. He was almost through the park when he saw the phone box. Funny that he'd never noticed it before. He passed here every day to get his morning coffee, and never once had he noticed the phone box. The glass was cracked in places, the red paint was faded... There was nothing spectacular about it, but it still struck Cornish as odd. He went in.

He dialled 999 and a woman answered the phone.

"Emergency services."

"I've just found a body in the river. I've got it tied up to my boat." He sounded breathless and twitchy, to his own ear.

"Sir, where are you calling from?" she asked coolly.

"I'm in a phone box across from the park."

"What's the address, sir?"

Cornish gave her the address and directions to his barge.

"An officer will be there soon, sir. In the meantime, can you make sure the body doesn't float away?"

"I'll do my best," Cornish said.

Cornish didn't love the idea of waiting for the police. He didn't like the thought of watching the body, or of accepting responsibility for making sure it stayed put. It was just more trouble, and his life didn't need to be further complicated. But what choice was there? He placed the receiver back into the cradle and leaned against the side, feeling a little calmer. He looked around the phone box. Names had been scribbled everywhere, too many to count. He looked closer at one particular name, surprised that it was the same as his own. Underneath it was a crude drawing of a bird. It was odd, and he didn't understand.

"That's quite a coincidence," he said tracing his finger along the letters, but it was too much to think about now. Wiping his hand on his trousers, he shoved it into his pocket and left the box.

As he walked back to the barge, thoughts of Robin swarmed back into his head. He wondered how the Arsehole was treating her. He'd told her not to trust him. Any man who cheated lost the right to be trusted. The Arsehole was exactly the type to avoid, but Robin couldn't see that, oblivious to what his faithlessness meant.

As Cornish reached the dock, he heard the sirens of the approaching police. The first police car stopped ten yards from him, and a detective climbed out of it. The man wore a surprisingly disreputable old tweed jacket. He pulled a cigarette out of his pocket and lit up, then looked over at Cornish.

"Are you the man who found the body?"

"I am."

"Where is it?"

"This way," Cornish led the guy to his barge, unable to stop his hands from shaking.

The detective noticed his nervousness. "Are you all right, sir?"

"Not really, officer. It's not like I find bodies floating in the river all the time. I mean, I see lots of stuff floating by, but most of it's rubbish."

Cornish climbed onto the barge and pointed to the rope that tied the body to the side.

"I have to ask," the officer said. "Do you know who it is?"

"No, sir."

The detective reached down and picked up the wallet. "Did this come from the deceased?"

"Yes." Cornish's nerves were shot.

"You shouldn't have touched it."

"Sorry, sir."

The detective slipped the wallet into a plastic bag, then bent over the gunwale, and began to search the body. He rummaged through the pockets and found a plastic identity card.

"Who is it?" Cornish asked. He was sure the detective wouldn't tell him.

The detective frowned. "Have you ever heard of a Jon Sutton? Does the name ring any bells?"

Cornish fought down the sudden urge to grin wildly. He looked over at the detective. "No, sir," he lied. "Never heard of him."

Lapping waves bumped the Arsehole against the barge. Cornish watched, fascinated, as the lifeless corpse bobbed up and down with the river. He hid his smile. Hope had returned.

33. Bullet Time
by Hollis Dorian

"I'll be damned," Jon Sutton whispered to himself. He was balanced on a pair of stacked shipping containers that reeked of weeks-old produce. Together, they were tall enough to allow him to spy on the events in the oddly-lit warehouse below. The window was cracked and grimy, shrouded in cobwebs, but he could see enough.

The bastards are just sitting there, waiting for it, he thought. *Just like the guy said.*

He braced himself, and strained to get a wider view around the warehouse. A group of black-suited, vinyl-coated men were huddled in the centre, under a set of hanging lights. Their faces were shockingly pale, but some trick of the shadows made it look as if their eyeballs were completely black. The men were in the middle of a card game. It looked like they were killing time. But until what? Or were they just holding the fort, keeping the warehouse secure?

Then he saw her. A pretty girl with raven hair was suspended in an iron cage, some eight feet or so off the ground. She was wearing a spray-on leather cat-suit which hid almost nothing. She looked meek. And scared.

She called out to the men. "I'm hungry."

They ignored her, as if she wasn't even there.

"I'm thirsty," she called out again. Her voice was pinched, staccato. Her hands looked tiny, curled around the metal bars. She looked lost. A bird in a cage.

"Fuckers," Jon whispered. *What kind of sick fucks are these?*

He had to rescue her, and off these guys for good.

A few hours ago, his sister Penelope had phoned up, in hysterics. Bernard had been shot. Murdered, she had said. His mind blazing, Jon left the apartment and... That was when things started to get fuzzy. His apartment refused to come into focus. Hadn't he had a flatmate? A girlfriend, perhaps?

He'd bolted down to the pub Penny mentioned. He knew the Lion's Head well. He'd gone drinking with Bernard there over a dozen times. Sirens. Lights. A crowd was gathered around, watching. They seemed festive. Police were everywhere, of course. They were already loading Bernard's body into an ambulance. His dead body. Penelope spotted Jon, and fell to pieces. She crumpled into his arms, and he held onto her tightly. After a little while, he pushed her away and commanded her to look into his eyes.

"You know who did this?" He could feel the intensity flooding his voice.

"Yeah," she said. "Yeah, I'm pretty sure I do. It's those bloody bastards Bernard has been working for the last couple months. At first it seemed it was going well. Then it wasn't going so well. Obviously."

"Sons of bitches." Jon could hear his teeth grinding together.

"Can you get them, Jon?" she asked. "Can you make them pay for what they did to my husband? I know you don't really do that kind of thing any more, but..."

"You're my little sister, Penny." He feigned something that might have passed for a smile at a better time. "I'll make them pay, all right. But I'm going to need the right tools."

Penny's eyes lifted. "Bernard had guns. It was part of the reason they were after him, I think. Something to do with the guns."

"Let's go have a look, then," Jon said. "The sooner I start, the closer they're likely to be."

They walked back to Penny's flat. At that time of night, the neighbourhood was fairly quiet, just drunkards staggering home. They entered the hall and went up the stairs. Bernard and Penny's son was asleep in bed.

Jon glanced at his room. "You going to tell him?"

"Just one more night's sleep," she replied, her voice whipcord-tight.

Probably better that way, Jon thought. They went into Bernard's study, and she pulled a wooden box from a panel beneath the floor under the desk. She opened it. It contained an ordinary looking automatic pistol and a strange little red case with a silver inlayed design on it. Inside the case, there were a set of crimson bullets, apparently made of wood, carved with intricate symbols.

Jon held the case as she handed it to him. "What the hell are these supposed to be?"

"I don't know," Penny said. "But they wanted them. When Bernard told them he wouldn't deliver them, that was it. That hairy Scottish fucker turned on him and then... this." She slumped into the beaten, green leather desk chair. Tears streamed down her cheeks.

Jon stared at the little nuggets of crimson and swallowed, hard. He felt, for a moment, as if they were singing to him. Or talking, maybe. He blinked, and shook his head. He'd need it clear for what had to be done.

"Where can I find these bastards?" Jon stashed the revolver and the bullet case into his long, grey coat.

"I don't know exactly where, but I know they used to contact him using a telephone box. They'd leave drops there or make calls to give him instructions." She quivered, and her shoulders fell. "What am I doing? I can't let you do this, Jonny. I mean, what about Amber?"

"Who?" Jon looked at her, confused.

"Amber," she said again, "You guys are still together, right?"

"I don't know," Jon said in a ghostly whisper.

Penny frowned. "What are you –"

"Listen, Penny, we don't have time for this. We're blood. As far as I'm concerned, Bernard was blood, too. That little boy sleeping in the other room is going to look at both of us one day and want to know what we did about his father's death, yeah?"

She looked up at Jon, hope and fear fighting over control of her face.

"Yeah?" he repeated.

She gave in, nodded. "Kill them all."

Eventually, Jon managed to identify what had to be the correct red phone box. He propped himself up in an alleyway, occasionally stealing glances at the box. It might take days, weeks even. It was almost certain that the men who'd killed Bernard wouldn't be showing up in person that night, but who knew who else was in on the hit? Jon was rather taken with the wan glow coming from the lonely cubicle, however. He didn't want to leave. He wanted to go inside. He reached down to his coat pocket and touched the fabric. The bullet case was warm, maybe getting warmer.

Could it all have something to do with the phone box? He shrugged off the idea. It didn't make any sense.

Then the phone rang.

He could almost feel the bell, deeply, viscerally. Each time it rang, he took a step closer to the box. It was as if he wasn't truly in control. In a handful of seconds, he found himself lifting the receiver.

He shrugged to himself. "Yeah?"

"Mister Sutton." The voice was refined, with a rich roll to it, but there was something ragged about it, too. Something savage. "I note that you have retrieved my bullets and found your way to the telephone box."

"Who the fuck are you, mate?"

"I know where you can locate the men who killed your brother-in-law. Right this very instant, as a matter of fact. Are you interested?"

* * *

Jon looked down again at the goons and their caged captive. *Right where he said they'd be.* He loaded the red bullets into the gun, savouring their lovely inscriptions. He felt as if he was almost able to understand them. The meaning remained just out of his grasp though, as if the words were dancing before him, shrouded by filmy wisps of gauze. 'My bullets', the man had called them. He'd insisted that they were all that was needed to do the job. Jon wanted to use them so very much, and they wanted to be used. He could feel them, their force just waiting to be released with a squeeze of his finger.

He couldn't wait any longer. He carefully inched the rickety window open, rolling easily onto the first-floor catwalk. He leapt from that to a stack of crates, spreading his weight to land nearly silently. The girl in the cage heard him though, or saw him. She turned to look up at him, eyes hopeful. He held a finger to his lips to let her know to keep quiet. She nodded, looking weak. *Maybe beaten. Certainly abused.* The sight of a human in a cage was making him very angry. He jumped down a level, to a pair of crates which would provide some cover. It would be enough. Hopefully.

He aimed, and pulled the trigger.

The first red bullet left the gun, whistling a sweet tune. It ripped through the arm of one of the men below, catching him mid-yawn. The arm exploded, sending meat spattering in all directions. The man's face contorted with agony and confusion. The bullet didn't pass through the arm, however. It seemed to hover, crackling with red sparks. It was consuming the man somehow, feeding on his essence. His body dwindled and he managed one final, fading scream before the little red devil had completely eaten him away.

The other five leapt up from the table. Cards tumbled to the floor as they upended it, and then drew their own weapons and began firing.

"He's up there!" The speaker aimed in Jon's direction and unleashed a volley of bullets.

Jon felt a warm, syrupy glow ooze over him as he fired the second bullet. Its release was almost orgasmic, a lightning high that flashed through his veins, nearly overwhelming him with pleasure. He knew he should take cover amongst the crates, but he kept his head up despite the bullets shrieking past his face. He wanted to see the second bullet hit its target in the heart.

Somehow, watching made it even better. The second victim, pale with a mouthful of jagged teeth, stumbled backwards. The gun fell from his hand as he frantically tugged at the front of his trench coat. He shrieked and yanked harder, finally crying out in despair. Then his eyes flashed with red light and he, too, vanished into bloody nothingness.

The one who'd spoken before swayed violently, then visibly rallied himself. He waved at the others. "Move in! Move in! Swarm that motherfucker!"

Pieces of shrapnel and wood were flying all around Jon now. There were four more men, two of them advancing cautiously. He had enough bullets, he knew, but that didn't seem good enough. To waste one on each of these men, these mere hired hands, felt... demeaning.

"Three," he said, as he squeezed the trigger again. His eyes rolled back in his head as delight consumed him. He opened his eyes again to see the red sliver dissolve the closest man. Then it turned in mid-air and stabbed into another, sucking him into itself. Finally, it found its way into the chest of the third, and absorbed him slowly, almost as if it were savouring the experience. It was beautiful.

The last man, the one who had been barking orders, backpedalled into the warehouse's shadows. As he did so, he yelled "Come and get me then! You'll run out eventually!"

But Jon knew he didn't need to. He casually aimed the gun, firing one last time. The elegant weapon howled, exploding several links of the chain which held the girl's cage off the floor. As it dropped, the bullet curved round and into the darkened corner, the scarlet light blazing off it illuminating its prey. It caught the final man, ripping into his left arm, passing through his torso, and exiting his right arm. Then it stopped, hanging there to drink him all the way down in a flickering bolt of blood-red lightning.

Jon hopped down from his perch. There was a strong smell of cinnamon in the air. He went over to the cage. The girl was balled up on the floor, head tucked in. He stomped his boot hard on the lock, and it shattered.

"It's okay," he said. He pulled the cage door open and offered her his hand.

She took it, finally glancing up with what might have been fear as she climbed out.

"Don't worry, darling, I'm going to get you out of here." Jon turned to look for the exit.

Pain exploded through the back of his right calf. He went down hard, cracking his knee on the concrete floor, the bone shattering like china. He heard the pop of a silenced pistol as something stabbed through his lower spine. He twisted in agony, and fell. He landed on his side, blood sputtering up from his mouth. The gun clattered away from his grip. He tried to look up at the girl, who seemed a lot less timid all of a sudden. He clutched at his chest, but he couldn't seem to locate the bullet case. Not that it would have mattered. The gun was too far away, and he knew he was already paralyzed.

The girl produced a cell phone and clicked a couple buttons before putting it to her ear. "It's Elwyn." She planted one booted foot on Jon's back.

A shrill voice answered. "Well?"

"Got him," the girl said.

"Does he have the bullets?"

"He did indeed. The boys here are all dead."

"Good. Check for stragglers, eh?"

"I'm not brain-dead."

"Good work," the voice said. "Make sure he's clean, then dump him in the river and get back here."

Jon felt his eyes closing. He had a nasty suspicion that it might be forever.

*   *   *

The first thing Jon noticed, as his eyes snapped open, was that he smelled like a wet dog. One that had been rolling in rotting filth. Then he noticed the stark fluorescent light above him. He was lying on his back in the most uncomfortable bed he'd ever been in. He felt numb, and the world seemed muffled. Then he heard voices, getting more pronounced. He struggled to sit up for a moment. Arms appeared on either side, to help him. He tried focusing his eyes and, after a few moments, they actually acquiesced to his commands.

"Pleasant nap, was it?" The voice was the same one that had spoken to him in the phone box.

"I thought I was dead," Jon said. His voice was shockingly hoarse, his throat dry and inflamed.

"You were," the man said.

Jon turned in the direction of the voice, and realised that he was sitting on a slab. The kind of slab where they put dead bodies.

"What the fuck?"

The man laughed. Jon looked up and stared at him as he approached. It felt as if the world was draining out through the soles of his feet.

"Do enlighten me, Mr. Sutton. Was that 'what the fuck, I'm in

163

a morgue', or 'what the fuck, there's a lion-headed god talking to me'? Or perhaps it was a little of both?" The man was huge, tall and massively muscled. His head was magnificent, animate, real, and not even slightly human.

Yeah, a lion man. Right. "I am dead, aren't I?"

"Not any more," said the lion man. "I am Lord Amow. You have me – me, personally – to thank for your marvellous resurrection. For the bullets, too. Speaking of which..."

Amow handed Jon the red ammo case.

Questions threatened to overwhelm him, but the bullets seemed to have priority. "How did you get them back?"

"That is something of a trade secret, I'm afraid." Amow said. "But I'm assuming that you rather enjoyed using them, yes?"

Jon felt terrible. Everything blazed with pain. But the marvellous feeling of firing the bullets – whatever they were – was strong and fresh, and made him smile. "Yeah, I did."

"Want another... hit?" Amow smiled.

"Yeah. I do."

"Good," Amow said. "I have another target for you to use them upon."

"I'm not in that business any more, Mister Amow." Jon made a point of saying the name.

"So you aren't interested, then?"

"I didn't say that," Jon answered quickly. He could feel the red bullets humming in his hand. Singing.

"Well, Mr. Sutton, which is it? Are you interested in the job or not?"

"Who's the target?" Jon tried to make it sound like that might make a difference.

"An American woman, around your age," Amow said. "She is an academic, used to pleasant treatment on account of her looks and status. An easy kill. But she has been something of a thorn in my paw, and now she has happened upon a little something that belongs to me. A little wooden deer. Kill her and bring it back to me, and I'll keep you endlessly supplied with those little trinkets you seem so fond of. Do we have a deal?"

Jon wanted to resist. He didn't want to kill some poor woman. He wanted to run. He wanted to tell the man, this creature, this demon, to go to hell. But he couldn't. The morgue didn't matter. His resurrection didn't matter. He couldn't remember if he had anything or anyone in his life who did. And he didn't care. The only thing he wanted was to be able to send those little slices of nirvana ripping through the air again, to feast.

"Just this one job," he finally managed to croak out. "I decide whether to play after this. Got it?"

"But of course." Amow grinned like a crack pusher handing over a free sample.

"Just give me the name," Jon said. His hands were turning the ammo case over and over.

"Professor Kelly David," Amow said.

34. Convergence
by Chris Bissette

Wind howled through the crossroads. Shadows slid like oil slicks through the crop fields that bordered the lanes. The air was thick with impending rain. The old man stood on the corner, a pocket of stillness in the chaos. The wind didn't touch him. It didn't dare.

He watched the storm building, his face impassive. Max circled his legs, rubbing lazily against his calves. She didn't seem to mind that he wasn't paying her any attention.

Finally, he shook his head wearily. "This is not good."

He raised his hand and placed it over his face, casting his left eye into darkness. Then he looked through, to the worlds beyond, and focussed on London. The rolling fields and potholed dirt tracks vanished, replaced with roads and cars, the grey of the city. He had a soft spot for London. All those roads and pathways, with all their crossroads. So much communication. Made a man feel alive. Vibrant.

The wind screamed through the city too, whistling around the buildings and through standing traffic. Leaves and crisp packets kicked up small riots in the gutters. The sky threatened to burst. The phone box stood tall in its corner, its warm light spilling out onto the pavement.

"Not good at all."

He dropped his hand, let the fields around him come back into focus. He could feel the village to the south. They were concerned, all of them. Almost all. There was fury and fire to the north, of course, and in the east, the Old Snake was as unreadable as ever. Only the Boneyard felt cheerful, up the western hill. The Barons and their dead weren't going to let anything get in the way of a good party, not even disaster. If worst came to worst, they'd go down with a sword in one hand and a bottle in the other, swapping filthy jokes all the way.

He could feel the Thing in the gibbet like a furnace. The cage was forged from cold iron and ancient pain, and it swung from a

166

heavy temple pillar just behind him. Keeping it at the crossroads was the wiser play, but it was bad enough that it forced itself on his awareness so unpleasantly. He didn't want to have to look at it as well. It was positioned to line up with the red London phone box he'd just been looking at.

Even so, the thing inside it was getting stronger every day. The Egyptian cub had no idea how stupid he was being. Soon, the thing would stand, and tear at the bars. Then it would break free. He could keep it from escape for a while after that, but he wouldn't be able to hold it for long if he was alone. It had already begun to touch the world on the other side, around the phone box. It was still afraid, but soon his presence would be no deterrent.

"Stop," he said, his voice barely a tired whisper.

The wind died in an instant, the clouds melting away. The sunshine was a pleasant reflection of the phone box's light. If only the Thing wasn't so damned hot.

"We have to do something, Max," he said.

The cat looked up at him, her eyes like gold pools.

He reached into his inside pocket. When his hand reappeared it was clutching four frosted glass vials, each sealed with red wax. Max stiffened at his feet, her fur standing on end, tail puffed to twice its normal size. A low growl rippled through her body.

"We have to," the old man said. "It can't wait any longer."

He whistled, the sound low and pure, and something small scurried out of the barley and across the path. Max spat and hissed, dropped her shoulders and raised her puffed-up tail.

"Stop, my child," he said, and the cat fell still. "You know this has to be done."

The rat clambered onto his foot. He reached down, grasped it by the scruff of its neck and raised it up to his face.

With his teeth he pulled the stopper from the first vial. The old man blew across the top of the vial, and light swelled out, cascading over the slim glass neck and settling into the rat. Its eyes seemed to glow as the light enveloped it, though only for an instant. Two other vials followed. The old man paused thoughtfully, and set the rat back on the ground.

"Go to the mountains," he said, and it vanished into the night. Max watched unhappily as it fled. "Don't let me down," the old man said, though the rat was already gone. He dropped the empty vials to the ground. They shattered, almost musically.

He played with the final vial, rolling it over the back of his fingers. Finally he came to a decision, and put it on the ground. He crouched down, bringing his face near to the cat's, and gave her a sympathetic smile.

"You know where the weak spot will be, and what you need to do," he said. "While you're over there, take that last vial to the Scotsman. Think of it as a long play against Blueprint and its child to come."

The cat opened her mouth wide, her long tongue slipping out to lick her upper lip. She picked up the glass vial in her teeth, a gentle motion, then she turned. She formed an angle with the shadows that shouldn't have been possible, and faded out of sight.

Papa Legba covered his eye again, and watched as Max darted out of the phone back and through the London traffic. Opposite the box was a café, its walls sporadically decorated with spray-paint. Max headed straight for it. When she reached the pavement, she pounced. Her paws pressed onto the wall, landing on a stencilled starfish done in indigo paint. The world folded, and Max was gone.

"Good," he said, dropping his hand again. "It is done."

The Thing in the cage was still there, of course. The wheels were turning now, and only time would tell what results they would yield. The Thing was watching him – he could feel its eyes, although they were not visible in the many-angled darkness.

"Soon," he told it. "Soon enough, you and I will dance."

* * *

The world folded, and Max appeared on a heavy wooden counter. Less than a foot away, the apartment block's night porter was staring at her, his TV forgotten.

"He sent you?" James swung his feet off the desk and down onto the ground.

Max purred gently, and nuzzled her head against his outstretched hand.

"It's time, then," James said. "I'll take you to her."

He went to the doors at the front of the entrance hall.

After a quick look down the road to check he wasn't being watched, he turned his key in the door. The lock snapped shut. He returned to the foyer.

"Come on then," he said to the cat, striding toward the lifts. "We haven't got long."

Outside, the clouds swelled over London. They would break soon, and then the downpour would begin.

'He watched the storm building, his face impassive.
Max circled his legs, rubbing lazily against his calves.'

35. Long Distance
by Warren Ellis

Alice rammed her thumbs into her ears, and pushed her fingers into her eyes, and clamped her mouth shut and held her breath, but she knew none of it would do any good. She knew she was going to die in the next few moments. Hot tears crept across her fingertips. She felt them cool quickly, becoming hard frost on her fingernails.

The sound was like a million broken radios broadcasting a million dying shrieks through a million waves of alien static. The movement of the phone box seemed downward in one second, and sideways in the next, as if it were being blasted through wild surf.

She knew she was going to die, and the most horrible, absurd thing was that her life refused to flash before her eyes. Her subconscious, in this ultimate moment of existence, had decided there was nothing worth playing back. There was just the shrieking and the cold and the plummeting, and all that was far more interesting than anything she'd ever done in her life.

Alice experienced a brief, deeply bizarre sense of being *folded*, somehow. It was almost like the perceptual flatness she experienced when she had a depressive episode, one of the flavourless month-long disappointments she'd slogged through every couple of years since her thirteenth birthday. For a second she was no more than a drawing slipped under a door, a 2-D thing in a 3-D world.

The screaming stopped. The ice in her hair began to thaw, and the snow on her skin evanesced. There was sunlight on her face. She prised her fingers out of her eyes, looking up, blinking. There was the sun, warm and fat in the early afternoon. There was also no roof on the red phone box, which was, she realised, how she could see the sun.

She was standing in a small enclosure made of what looked like dried reeds, daubed with red paste. It possessed the basic dimensions of the red phone box, but, clearly, *wasn't* the red phone box. There

ELLIS, DEDOPULOS, WICKLINE et al.

was a gap behind her, which she guessed should have been the door. This was all wrong. But she wasn't dead. And, with that thought, she decided that she could get back to where she started by repeating the action that changed everything. Without thinking or even looking, she reached for the phone handset, and touched something thick and dead.

The handset and housing of the phone had been replaced by the skin of a dead man's face, strung over a wicker frame. Alice screamed, jerked away from it, fell back and out of the booth.

The pavement wriggled under her back. She saw but did not understand the flurry of lights across the pavements and trails around her, harvesting the energy from her fall and distributing it across the locality. She heard but did not understand the language barked at her by the dead face lashed to the wicker frame in what she still thought of as the bloody red phone box. When the local people – short, hairy, dressed simply and sparely – came to her and carried her up, she did not understand them either, but was soothed by the gentle drone of their speech, possessed as it was of a musical lilt that reminded her of Welsh accents. They carried her, carefully and tenderly, along a short trail to a beautiful glade watched over by a great oak tree. Alice, despite herself, was comforted. Working out what had happened to her could wait, for a few minutes. Right now, she felt, she could concentrate on recovering her faculties and getting over the shock. She was going to live. As they laid her in the soft grass, she looked up at the sky and told herself that, whatever happened next, she was going to live.

And then the people split her chest with a sharp spade, dug out her heart and burned it in front of the great oak tree.

'Alice experienced a brief, deeply bizarre sense of being folded, somehow.'

36. Kicking Off
by Joff Brown

The 155 ground to a halt, and the driver's voice crackled over the speaker. "Ladies and gentlemen, this bus terminates here. Health and safety," he added apologetically. "Got some trouble up ahead. These riots. I'm not allowed to go any further, so I'm going to have to let you off."

Agnes Cornish got off the bus. The bag full of Iceland's finest frozen stuff was already cutting into her hand. Three-quarters of the way back to Balham, and chucked off, just like that. In the dark too, for shame, no matter that it was half six.

Some way past Clapham North, by the looks of it. She hadn't been paying attention. *Well, you don't, do you?* She'd been mulling over whether to do chops or steak & kidney pie for Mum and Dad's tea, and whether it was worth going back to Eastenders after six months, now she'd got the box that recorded it for you. *Wossname. Tivo.*

Now, here she was, two miles from home, in an empty Clapham High Street. That was just wrong, for a start. Clapham High Street was never empty.

The other travellers had already scattered. The driver was walking away from his bus, just abandoning it. Nobody wanted to meet her eye, it seemed.

Agnes could hear shouting up the road. Kids. Lots of them. She'd seen it on the news, of course. "Some of the worst violence in London for a generation," Alastair Stewart had said sternly on News at Ten, almost cross-eyed with indignation. "Londoners fear that the worst is yet to come." She'd heard the sirens over the past two nights, seen the local kids shouting and sprinting off to where the trouble was, miles up the road. They thought they were gangsters or something. *All kicking off*, that was the phrase everyone was using.

"Blowed if they're going to stop me going to work tomorrow," she'd told the TV. "Little toerags." It hadn't seemed real. Not in *her*

174

city. So she went up to clean the offices in Moorgate, like she'd done every day for the past three years since Don had died – this year, the money was as important as the something-to-do.

That had felt pleasantly defiant this morning, when there were only a few broken panes of glass around. Blitz spirit, as Mum would say. *Not such a good idea now, was it old girl?*

The early evening was eerily silent, apart from the kids. No sirens, that was the worst of it. Something big was inching towards Agnes from far down the road. Like a slow quake or a summer storm, but made of people. Youngsters, most of them anyway. None of them running, exactly. Some jogging, some sauntering along, some staggering along under the weight of bags and boxes, but moving all the same.

These are rioters. In the flesh. They'd be down her end of the street in minutes. Where were the bloody police?

She could hear laughter as they came. Sounds of smashing glass.

Right. *Sort yourself out, love.* She fished in her bag for her mobile, and wasn't surprised to find it was dead. Darren was always telling her to charge it, "... in case there's an emergency, Mum." *Chalk one up to him.*

Someone whizzed past her on a BMX, far too close. *No respect, that's what Mum would say.*

Agnes looked around. Phone box, that's what she needed. When was the last time she'd noticed them? But there one was, just a couple of doors down. One of the old red ones, thick with paint. A museum piece.

She levered the door open and slipped inside. It stank about as badly as she expected. Not a bad place to be, though. Her own personal tank. *Don't think about them seeing her, coming in.* Greggs and Subway were visible through the grimy glass, the logos cheerily bright. Much good it would do them, she supposed.

She checked for change, knowing she'd already paid for Mum and Dad's chops with the exact money. Seven pence. Great. Agnes stared balefully at the 'MINIMUM FEE 60p' sign. Taking the mickey, they were.

Someone ran past outside, whooping. They were already here.

175

Okay, then. *Stay calm.* Reverse charges to Darren to come and pick her up. Mum and Dad would get worried, otherwise. Darren was big enough and ugly enough to get her out safely. He'd found a body near that canal boat of his the other day, and he hadn't even batted an eyelid. Take more than some estate kids to stop him.

Street arabs, Don would have called them, not meaning anything by it, and she'd have had to tell him off. Not that they *were* arabs, of course. A right old rainbow mix. *Political correctness, eat your bloody heart out.*

Her fingers ached as she stabbed the cold metal numbers. Bloody arthritis. It wasn't like she was old. Not *old* old. She'd read it in *Take A Break*: 60 was the new 40, or something. Lot of blimmin' rubbish of course, but you've got to have something to keep you smiling. You're fine and normal and your kids grow up and you still like a dance, you still listen to the hit parade – the *charts* – but you're 61 and your hands are aching and people are talking about you like you're about to jump in a grave. Her mum *and* dad were still alive! Not a lot of people could say that.

Not at her age. Hmm.

The phone buzzed to life. "I'm sorry," a woman's voice smiled, "there is no connection. Please say the place you would like to reach."

One of these automated services. Bane of everyone's life. "The operator," Agnes said, realising how archaic it sounded. How small her voice was.

"I'm sorry," the smooth voice shot back, "I don't recognise that option. Please select from Greggs, Currys, Snappy Snaps, or Subway."

"What?"

"I said, you can choose to smash up Greggs, Currys, Snappy Snaps, or Subway."

Agnes slammed the phone down. Stress. That's all. Hearing things. Shock of the wossname. Situation. She peered past the prossies' cards, to the street. Gingerly, she picked it up again and jabbed 999.

"It's Greggs, Currys, Snappy Snaps, or Subway," the woman's voice said again, pleasantly. "We recommend that you make your choice quickly."

A noise outside almost made her drop the receiver. Voices. Kids shouting. A boy pressed his pale face against the glass, *aaarghed* at her, laughed.

"Some old dear," she heard them say. More mean-spirited laughter.

Was Connor out there? Her own grandson, Connor. Sixteen, he was. *Surely he'd never do anything like this.* And Jackie, two years younger, but these days that was more like 21, and no questions asked. They wouldn't get involved in all this, she told herself, but she wasn't stupid. She'd seen the old Adam dancing in Connor's eyes. Always up for trouble at his age, and this – this was the Big Top of Trouble. The main event.

One of the thick glass panes cracked violently, the sound making her jump. Someone had whacked it with something. A baseball bat? Bloody hell.

Agnes picked up the receiver. "Greggs," she breathed.

"Thank you for your choice!" said the woman's voice brightly, and Agnes knew that the voice could understand her, whether it was a woman, a computer, or who the hell knew. All three, maybe.

Outside, the tide turned. The knocking stopped.

Agnes peered out of the red-rimmed frame. The toerags had all run over to Greggs, and were kicking at the windows. Someone smacked at its window with the bat. The window bowed in. The bat-wielder swung again. It shattered.

Couldn't be. Nothing to do with me.

At least the kids were ignoring her now, thank God. *Think, Agnes.* Frantically, she stabbed 999, 100, every number she could remember. No sound from the phone. Not even a dial-tone.

The door of Greggs broke, and a few of the kids went inside. The rest were already looking bored. Not much to loot, in a Greggs. Not even pies, once they closed.

"Don't blame me," Agnes said out loud. "I didn't... I couldn't have..."

The kids were sauntering back over. Talking among themselves. Someone said something that sounded like 'Get her out.' Can't jam the door, she thought, they open bloody outwards.

The computer-woman-thing was back. "Please select your next option. Currys, Snappy Snaps, Subway, or Ladbrokes?"

One of the kids pressed his face up against the glass again. He stuck his tongue out at her. *He's fourteen, no older than Jackie. She doesn't have a bloody clue, that one.* She could remember Darren at that age. Just the same.

Whoever the little toerag gurning in at her was, he had a mum. Never mind her. *He* didn't deserve this. That was when something clicked in her head.

"Listen," Agnes hissed into the receiver. "It's not right. I see what you're trying to do, and I'm not playing. I don't know if this is Dom Joly or Phonejacker or Christ alone knows what, but it's in very poor taste, I tell you that. This is serious, out here," she finished, a bit lamely.

Agnes risked a glance outside. The toerags had backed off a bit. Were they waiting?

"Mrs. Cornish? You're through to an advisor." A deep, unctuous man's voice, all of a sudden. In the background, could she hear the screams of the computer-woman? Surely not. "There seems to be some trouble. All you need to do is select another option. It's for your own safety."

She was hardly surprised that he knew her name.

"We deliberately offered you corporate targets, Mrs. Cornish. So as not to cause offence. A victimless crime. Especially compared to the alternative."

My friend Jeeta works in that Subway, you knob, she thought. *What's she going to serve tomorrow? Broken glass sub, footlong a pound extra?*

Her voice trembled. "No choice, thank you very much."

The man's voice was almost a growl. Upper-middle class. Used to being obeyed. "I guarantee you this: thousands of people, many just like you, have made this choice before, with no physical effects. It's completely normal, Mrs. Cornish. Even your son's spoken to us, you know."

The kids moved in a little. She looked out to where Greggs had been smashed, and felt a hot flash of shame. She was genuinely angry. At herself. At the toerags. Most of all, at the man her Mum would have called *his Nibs*, smooth as you like on the end of the phone. *Wanker, more like,* she thought. Now he'd threatened Darren somehow.

The low voice purred back. "Mrs. Cornish, I assure you that your life is in very real danger if you do not give me a name right now."

Who were they, these voices? She thought of what her husband Don would have said, if he'd still been around.

And said it. *"You people."*

She heard an intake of breath on the other end of the phone, and a short, honest-to-goodness growl. A growl! He hadn't been expecting that, had he?

The smooth-voiced man began to talk, but she didn't listen. "You. You're always trying something, you lot. Taking advantage. Well, you listen to me. Just because I'm scared, it don't mean I have to put other people down. You think you can put us in this situation and use it, don't you?"

The kids were battering at the box now, from all sides. But Agnes was too hot with anger to care. Let them come in. She'd give them a piece of her mind, oh yes she bloody would.

She was almost shouting into the receiver. "Spin doctors. Advisors. Financiers. Marketers. Politicians. Wossname, middle men, ain't you? I wouldn't put it past *you people* to have started all this... rubbish, all this trouble on the streets. You promise the world, and you scare people until they haven't got a choice, and then you have your bully boys lock 'em up and throw away the key. And then you steal everything and have your little laugh. *I know your sort.* Scum, you are. Parasites. Well, we're bigger than that here, thank you very much. We're Londoners."

There was a click from the other end of the line. Silence. The kids had scattered. How long had she been in here? Then she heard the sirens behind her.

The door opened, and a policeman's concerned-looking, everyday, blessedly ugly face appeared. "Let's get you home, love."

Where were you five minutes ago, when they were cold-calling for my soul, eh, sonny Jim? Agnes just smiled though. She let herself be led outside, past the shoddy barriers where the police were standing, watching the riots with polite interest.

37. We Will Respect
by Joe Silber

Ambrose had enough time, before the line died, to locate the source of the sound. It was in one of those parts of London that man couldn't usually find, and people like Ambrose assiduously avoided. He realised he knew the place – a sentience gone wrong – when it said to him, "He is ours now."

As the connection broke, Ambrose mumbled, "The hell he is." He also knew he'd been baited.

He withdrew from his trance, and climbed up the ropes that bound him to the crane. Looking about, he wished he had time to appreciate the light drizzle in the ensuing dusk. He uncoiled the rope from about his body and rubbed the bruised skin. A day to recover would be nice, but he didn't think he'd wait that long. (*Which he?* Ambrose thought. *Himself? Richard? Both, probably.*)

For each step down the crane, the foot holding him up returned a flash of pain as the blood flowed from it to the surrounding tissue. A light rain carried his gasps down and away. By the time he touched the earth, his feet could almost bear his weight.

Once on the ground, he put the coil of rope to one side, took three deep breaths and opened his arms to the sky before kneeling and placing both palms on the ground. He then stood and bowed to the west, east, south, and north, mumbling words of gratitude. Finally he stretched out his right arm, pointing, and turned a full counterclockwise circle.

What was it that boy on the tree had said? It is finished?

No, old Son, it's just beginning.

* * *

As he walked slowly down the barren hill bearing his coil of rope, Ambrose heard a growl in his belly and wondered if he had a calorie in his body left to burn. The civilisation of pedestrians, cafés, and open shops usually repelled him, but it was pleasing now. He entered the first market he saw, a jammed corner-shop with three of those little cameras up by the ceiling. Oh, fearful London.

He looked at the shelves and felt... *What did we call it? The pain of return. Nostalgia. They still use that word. Wasn't there a time when we'd return from a ritual to the odours of burning sacrifice? I'm sure there was.* He paid for a packet of sliced ham, a soft roll and a bottle of bright blue liquid that promised renewal.

Unwilling to wait, he sat on a kerbstone and drained most of his drink before ripping the roll in half and stuffing the ham between the two pieces. *This is why we never did these things alone. This should be part of the ritual. But,* he argued to himself, *back then we were just learning what the world had to offer. So few now know how churlish the world is with her secrets. And no one wants to learn them anymore.*

A dull, thin spider crawled around Ambrose's thigh towards a crumb. Lifting the creature gently, Ambrose placed the voice he had heard. Surveillance drones. There was a story about a colony that had gone missing, before the researchers switched from insects to metal pigeons. Surveillance bugs, they'd vanished out from a research facility just inside the M25.

So much time, but never enough to give each headline proper consideration.

Having fed, he walked with more purpose towards the flat he'd taken after the failures at Salonika. Its large windows overlooked the river, but they were the only large thing about it. To have any space at all to stretch (or to summons), Ambrose had to fold the bed back into the wall.

Bed, he thought. *I could just go to bed. Forget.*
Could. But won't.

As he walked past a red phone box, he knew neither he nor Richard would wait.

Ambrose stepped into the box and put his rope on the shelf next to a mildewed phone book and took the receiver off its cradle. More urinal than communication device, no? Ambrose closed his eyes and recalled Richard as thoroughly as Richard would recall himself.

Wingtips, underpressed trousers, ill-fitting tops, carelessly brushed hair that fell over eyes that were never quite in focus. To the look, Ambrose added the scent of his toothpaste and the feel of his skin, and all the sounds of his voice.

And then he stopped to wonder what it was that was putting out the bait for him. An obsolete surveillance drone colony? Really? *That would be something new, anyway,* Ambrose mused as he made his way across the void.

A flash ensued that bore neither light nor heat, and he found himself standing on overheated asphalt in another phone box. It was noontime bright, with no shadows. Outside the phone box he saw six hunks of steel – a piece of metal's dream of an automobile. They stood on hubs, but kept no shadow underneath. There, beside them, was Richard, crouching in the glare of the box.

Richard with a hangover extrapolated a hundred times over.

His hair hung raggedly below his shoulders and his trousers dangled tattered from his waist. His white shirt was stained with the sweat he no longer exuded, the neck of it almost as wide as his shoulders. The skin of his face seemed leathered from the sun, stretched over his cheeks.

Richard looked up at Ambrose's gasp and stood to look at him. Ambrose pulled him into his arms. As Richard relaxed, Ambrose cooed, "Ftoho agori mou. Oh my poor boy."

For several minutes, a gasping came from behind the scraggle of hair, resolving into words. "Boy, Ambrose? I'm–" On the third word, his unused voice rose above a croak. "–older than you've ever been."

Looking about, Ambrose wondered if that might be true. He continued over the din of static that came from the motorway behind them. "I never saw your despair, poor boy. I never thought you'd leave the world. I never saw your will to walk away. So many nevers. I would never have been so hard. I'm so sorry."

Richard felt at Ambrose's dirty linen clothes, cool still and smelling of the breeze that blew through London. "Can you take me back, Ambrose?"

Ambrose couldn't say which meaning Richard had in mind, and didn't answer for a moment. There was a rusted screech as several dozen cars long bereft of rubber came to a halt. Eyes like those of spiders glared at the two men through the cars' scratched window panes.

A sound of aluminium shards shaken in a jar came from shop doorways several meters from the phone box, breaking the silence. "Don't worry about them, Richard. Don't worry." *I have enough worry for both of us.*

He tried to pay the noise no heed as he held Richard and repeated. "I'll bring you home. I'll bring you back to London. I'll hold you tight. I'll heal you."

The jars stopped shaking and the door of the left-most shop opened, dangling on a last corroded hinge. A coterie of (it seemed to Ambrose) many-legged mechanical toys skittered through and under it. He pulled Richard into the phone box.

The voice Ambrose had heard from atop the crane vibrated from all of them as if only one spoke.

"We told you, young man, when you called, that he is." The voice stopped and the creatures turned their heads to each other on rusting vertebrae. It continued after a moment. "Ours. You may try to take him, this Richard, but know..."

Ambrose stared them down through their hesitation, murmuring spells of escape.

"Know that we will follow."

38. Hell Hath No Fury
by Salomé Jones

The piercing doorbell always made Amber think of a fire alarm, like the ones she remembered from fire drills at school. The porters usually called from downstairs to say there was someone on their way up. She'd always try to open the front door before they got down the hall from the lift, just to avoid the damned thing's loud clanging. Sometimes it was unavoidable though, if the porters let someone slip through unnoticed. Like now.

"I wonder who it is," Stuart said from his desk.

"Postman, maybe." Amber sighed and went to the door, mobile phone clutched in one hand. She pulled the door open.

"Amber." The porter stood outside the door.

"James." Amber blinked. It was very rare for him to make a trip upstairs without calling. "Is everything all right?"

"Yeah, I was just wondering if you knew whose –" He broke off as a black cat ran through his legs into the flat. "Uh – cat…"

"Max?" Amber turned her head to follow the cat's progress into the lounge.

"Whoa, cat in the hole." Stuart got up and moved to catch the small visitor, who dodged him neatly and made for the sofa.

"It's okay, Stu. He's friendly." She turned back to James. "Where did he come from?"

"She," said James.

"What?"

"I think it's a girl cat." James motioned toward the sofa where the cat now sat looking as if it belonged there. "So you know her?"

Amber stepped away from the door. "Yes, we've met. She lives in a terrace around the corner from St. John's Wood High Street."

The mobile in her hand started ringing. She glanced at the screen. 'Penelope.' She frowned. The name was familiar, but she couldn't quite place it. It seemed important though, somehow.

"Hold on, James."

James nodded as Amber pressed the phone button. "Hello?"

"Amber? It's Penny." The voice on the line wasn't familiar.

"I'm sorry. Who is this?"

"It's Penelope Martin. Jon's sister."

"Can you hold on a minute?" Amber pressed the phone to her chest. "I'm sorry. I need to take this, James."

"So you'll take care of her?" James whispered.

"What? Oh, the cat. Yeah, I can take her home."

"Great. Stuart, nice to see you, man." James waved.

"Bye, James." Amber closed the door. "Baby, can you keep an eye on our little guest? I need to take this call."

"Absolutely." Stuart eyed the cat, who appeared not to notice.

Amber went into the bedroom and closed the door. She put the phone to her ear. "Did you say you were Jon's sister Penny?" Jon... It rang a bell. But who was Jon? Someone she'd known at uni?

"That's right. Amber? What's wrong? Did you and Jon break up?"

Amber pulled the phone away from her ear. The voice was getting annoying. "I'm sorry, but Jon who?"

"Oh, this is unbelievable. I asked Jon about you this morning and he said the same thing. 'Who's Amber?' So you had a fight, then." The woman paused. Amber could hear her breathing. "Fine. I'll play your silly game. Jon Sutton."

"Oh my god." She remembered. Jon Sutton. Her boyfriend. "There really is a Jon Sutton?"

"All right. I knew Jonny was an occasional toker, but you? You're little Miss Clean. You practically squeak. What's going on?"

"Oh, Penny. It's been like a horrible nightmare. I thought I was —" Amber glanced at the bedroom door. She could hear Stuart's voice from the lounge.

"Hey, Max. How's it going, mate?"

She heard the thump of Stuart sitting on the leather sofa. She smiled and took a breath. "Jon left, Penny. Took off, without a word."

"What? When?"

"About a month ago. I think he left me for someone else."

"Well, he hasn't mentioned anything like that to me. I just saw him this afternoon."

"Just like him, isn't it?"

"Amber," Stuart called from the lounge. "I think Max is hungry. What do you think we can feed her?"

"Um, Penny. I need to go. There's something I have to take care of. If Jon wants to talk to me, he knows where to find me."

A frustrated huff came through the phone, but Amber ignored it and hung up. She plugged the phone into the charger on her nightstand. *Really? 'Who's Amber?' He'd better hope I never catch up with him. Bastard.*

When she went back to the lounge, Stuart was sitting on the sofa, and Max was standing on his lap.

"She seems very interested in your handbag." Stuart let Max go and she trotted over to the table where Amber's bag sat, jumped up next to it and pawed at it, looking over at Amber. "Do you have something edible in there?"

"I don't think so." Amber frowned and crossed the room to the bag. "Let's see what you're after." She unzipped the bag and looked inside.

Max watched her intently.

"I don't see anything." Amber shook her head. "Let's just get you something to eat. I think there's some chicken in the fridge." She put the purse down on the table and went into the kitchen.

While she was poking about in the refrigerator, she heard a soft crash.

"I don't think you convinced her, sweetie," Stuart called.

Amber closed the fridge and stepped back into the lounge. Max sat on the floor next to the handbag, its contents strewn on the floor around it. The cat looked up at her and meowed. Stuart laughed.

Amber shook her head and bent to pick up the spilled items. "Bad luck," she murmured, "to put your purse on the floor." She pointed a finger at Max. "Now I'll lose money." As she scooped up the items, she noticed the phone she'd found in the phone box. "Oh, I totally forgot about this. I suppose I should look into it."

"What is it?" Stuart peered at her.

"A mobile. I found it in the phone box by the café." She held it up.

"In the phone box?" Stuart raised one eyebrow at her, his expression going all serious.

"What makes you say it like that?" Amber turned to face him.

"I don't know. Just something about that phone box. Bit strange."

"Huh. Interesting." Amber plucked the notebook out of her bag, opened it and held it out to him. "Here's some fuel for that fire."

Stuart took the notebook, a curious look overtaking his face.

"I found it in one of the chairs inside the café. That's what made me look in the phone box." She motioned for him to open it.

When he began flipping through the pages, she stared at the found mobile. She pressed a few buttons, looking for the place where the owner's name was stored.

After some shuffling through the handwritten pages, Stuart looked up. "So you think that's her phone? I mean, the same person who wrote this?"

"Colette Wilson." Amber held the phone up so Stuart could see the screen. "That's her name, apparently. I don't know if it's the same person who wrote that, but it seems likely. The café even smelled of smoke when I went in."

"Ah well." Stuart raised his shoulders and let them drop. "Bad boyfriends abound."

"Don't they just." Amber stared out the glass balcony doors.

"Not me, I hope."

Amber smiled. "No, not you." She took a step toward him and bent to give him a kiss. "Okay, I need to return Max to her terrace. I wonder if she didn't follow me home and get lost. Come on, Max. Will you let me carry you?" She leaned forward and held out her hands. Max stood up on her hind legs and jumped lightly into Amber's arms.

"Good girl." Amber grinned and rubbed the cat's back.

"That was easier than I expected." Stuart laughed.

"Me, too. All right. It's just over by the park. I'll be back in twenty minutes or so."

Stuart gave her a serious look. "Be careful out there. City's still unsettled."

"If the riots make it into this neighbourhood, nowhere in England will be safe. I'll be fine." She smiled to reassure him. "Back in a few. Then I'll start trying to find Colette Wilson."

"Okay. See you in a bit. Oh, speaking of phones, who was that call from?"

Amber slipped her handbag over her shoulder. "No-one. Spammer."

* * *

It was after she'd dropped Max off – and watched her slink back towards the terrace – that Amber heard the sound. It was a peculiar, high-pitched ping, like the peal of a single glass chime. It was coming from her handbag.

Must be that other mobile. She dug into the bag and found the mobile phone, unlocked it and studied the screen. There was a new text. Feeling slightly guilty, she opened the text message box. There didn't appear to be any sender. That was weird.

'Come to the phone box at midnight. Bring a cigar, some rum, and a dark-chocolate Bounty.'

Something felt off about the whole situation, though she couldn't place it. The oddness intrigued her. She had an irrational feeling that the message was for her, even though no-one knew she had the phone except Stuart and he didn't know the number.

What time was it anyway? Hadn't it been early afternoon when she left home? But the street lights were on already. She must have been out for longer than she'd thought. She looked at the phone again, saw that the time was 23:45. What on Earth could she have been doing for eight hours? There was no time to think about it now. She'd just make it to the phone box by midnight.

She ran into a corner store and bought a Bounty bar, cheerful in its red and white livery, and a single cigar. It was too late to buy alcohol, but the man behind the counter let her purchase a quarter-bottle of rum anyway. He seemed a bit out of it, moving woodenly.

When she got outside with the stuff, she couldn't remember having paid. She must have though, since he hadn't stopped her.

The phone box came into view, and she studied the yellow glow its interior lighting gave off as she approached it. It reminded her of something, though she couldn't think what it was. She went in and closed the door and as she touched the phone handset, she realised that everything had changed. It was almost like she was watching herself from a short distance away, though she remained aware of her own thoughts and feelings.

She was standing at a broad dirt crossroads. The paths wound away between rolling cornfields, bordered with green verges. The breeze made the crops rustle, their tops rippling like the surface of a great lake. Tall wooden phone poles strung with simple wires stood along the path either side. She could see the dusty ground under her feet, but she had the sensation that she was falling through a vast empty space. It took a great effort for her to keep standing straight.

The pinging sound came again, and she struggled to turn toward it, without flipping end over end. She caught sight of an old man standing at the corner of the crossroads. His white beard stood out against his dark skin. He looked like he had stepped out of time. Or maybe she was the intruder, skipping back to the '30s.

"Hello, Amber. Did you bring my cigar?" He smiled at her, and the sensation of falling diminished somewhat. She moved toward him as though she had too many balloons tied to her shoulders, her feet threatening to lift off the ground with every step.

"I did. And dark rum, and your coconut chocolate bar." She handed the offerings to him.

"Bless you, hon." He ran the cigar under his nose and breathed in the scent of it. "You're very kind to an old man. You're looking well today."

"So are you, Papa Legba." Where had that name come from?

"That's good, Amber." Legba smiled. "I asked you here to tell you something." He opened one of his hands to show her a small red and white ball.

I feel like I can fly. Amber looked at the ball. 'Take it,' Legba seemed to whisper, though his lips didn't move.

189

"The future is uncertain. You're going to be called on." The old man looked down at the ball.

The fields around her wavered. "To do what?" Amber lifted her arm to reach for the ball. She could see herself from just above. Her arm stuck there and didn't move.

"When you get there, you'll know." Legba smiled again.

The ball rose a few inches into the air. She looked at it very hard. Her eyes ached with the effort, and an odd sensation pressed down on the point between her eyebrows. The ball floated toward her, the way it might have floated on a slow current of water. It was glowing. She noticed how much brighter the crossroads was than it had been on the way to the phone box. "Is it morning?" she asked. She looked away from the ball, and it fell to the ground.

* * *

The sound of her own voice woke her. She groaned. Her alarm clock said six a.m.

"Amber." Stuart stroked her arm. "You okay?"

"Mmmm," she mumbled. "Bizarre dream."

He moved his arm, making a space next to him. She slipped into it, and he folded his arm around her.

"What was it about?" Stuart squeezed her shoulder.

"Some man I've never seen before. In the dream, I knew him."

"Was it scary?" Stuart murmured.

No. Had she said the word out loud? So warm and cosy. "Sleepy," she whispered.

39. Heat and Rust
by Kate Harrad

There was a shuddering haze in front of London's grey streets and tall buildings, as if the city were a mirage, an illusion hallucinated by heat-crazed dreamers. Nobody even knew what the temperature was any more. Nobody wanted to know. Nobody wanted to speak at all.

In August, the thought of September was all that kept Colette going. Then September came and went, and so did October, and the city burned on and on under the scarlet sun, and Colette understood that in this London, the heat was never going to stop. The inhabitants weren't waiting for summer to end. They weren't waiting for anything. They were just going on, no longer remembering what it was like not to feel that all-consuming warmth.

Colette remembered. She remembered the café, the woman who'd been waiting forever, the sense that she had to escape before she became that person, the shock of the phone box consuming her and spitting her out again into this stifling, unfamiliar London. But as the weeks passed, those memories grew vaguer and faded, like a film seen once long ago. She had been in this other London for a while now, living in the corners of alleyways, eating whatever she could steal, desperate to find out what was happening to her. Desperate to know whether this was a future London or a past London or an alternate reality, or something else that she couldn't even envisage. Mainly, she was desperate to find the way back.

But it wasn't that easy. When she had first stumbled out – disoriented and faint, transparent like a pencil drawing – her only desire had been to get away from the phone box. Solidifying as she went, she had stumbled across pavements and down alleyways, panicking, lost. When she became herself again, she discovered something.

In this London, there was a red phone box on every corner of every street. All old, all rusty, all identical.

And she didn't know which one led home.

So she walked. Street after street, corner after corner, looking for a sign, anything to tell her she could escape. All she found were concrete pavements and strangers whose eyes avoided hers. Why did nobody want to speak to her? She knew they could see her. Sometimes people handed her food, or clothes, but always hurriedly and with their faces averted, and they moved away immediately afterwards. She didn't speak any of the languages they used, anyway. She pored over stray newspapers, but the words meant nothing and the pictures were ambiguous.

In her loneliness, she began to feel almost fond of the rusted phone boxes. They were the nearest thing she had to home. Then, later, she began to hate them. After a while, she began to vandalise them, so she'd know which ones she'd visited. But mostly they were already vandalised, and anyway, she didn't know if the right box was always right, or only became a portal some of the time. So finally she stopped damaging them, and just tried the phones at random, when she felt like it. Nothing ever happened.

Once, and once only, there was some life to the line, a sense of connection. She became certain that someone was on the other end of the phone, someone who could understand. "You have to help me," she begged. She looked around urgently. "Find me. I'm at the corner of Frith Street and Bateman Street." There was no reply. No-one ever came. She was the only person who ever tried to use the phones. She'd had some funny looks. Nobody thought of the phone boxes as methods of communication any more. Instead they were mainly used to hide from the dragons.

Maybe they weren't dragons. Colette wasn't certain of the taxonomy. But that's how she thought of them whenever she saw a flock, flapping above a tower block, red bellies on show, making a high-pitched noise like an old whistling kettle. She also suspected that they were part of the reason why alt-London was so unbearably hot: their breath, their bodies emitted heat so intense that their touch could kill. She'd seen it happen once, to a fellow street dweller who had drunkenly tried to pet one. The sight kept her awake at night for some time afterwards.

They used the phone boxes too, as nests. Often at night she would pass by a street corner and see a beast hanging upside-down inside one, its huge eagle-wings furled around itself like a very confused bat. Nobody disturbed them, though she didn't know why. It was possible that they were sacred to the people. It was possible that the bodies she occasionally saw lying on rooftops were sacrifices. Each to their own, she thought. The relationship between the people and the beasts was intriguing, but she'd been rubbing for too long against the endless, dulling strangeness of everything. She was on the verge of losing the will to go on. She was becoming tempted just to pick a doorway and live in it, begging to survive, trying to forget she had ever had a home.

But then the dragons started to stalk her.

She had been noticing for a while that wherever she went, there they seemed to be. More and more phone boxes contained a beast – sometimes sleeping, sometimes watching her with hot, hungry eyes. More than once she woke up to find one of them crouching nearby, not moving, just looking at her.

Colette began to suffer from the extra heat caused by the beasts' constant presence. She drifted through the squares and alleyways of alt-Soho with an increasingly blank look in her eyes, waiting for something to happen, something to break. She started having heat hallucinations: horses made of silver liquid flying over the rooftops, ridden by giant silver fish with open, sharp-toothed mouths; seven-foot-tall snowmen stalking the streets freezing all who touched them; buildings previously stone metamorphosing into diamond-sharp glaciers. She could see it all so clearly. She drank warm water from public fountains, rubbed her aching, sweating body with it, and dreamed of ice.

She became convinced that somewhere there was cold water. Drinkable and swimmable. A long, clear pool into which she could dive. But when she dreamed of it, just as she felt the shock of its surface hitting her skin, a beast would appear behind her and the water would dissolve in the fire of its breath. She came to, shaking.

One night she walked for hours around and around the centre, Leicester Square to Charing Cross to Piccadilly to Chinatown, searching and searching for the pool. By dawn she was ready to collapse.

It was then that she saw an alleyway, a new one. London was full of those kinds of surprises, you turned a corner and there was a street you'd never noticed before. It was a tiny space off St Martin's Lane, just wide enough for one. She was looking at it, wondering if she should try to sleep there, when she felt a breath like a volcano on her back.

The beast stood right behind her. Forelegs planted solidly on the concrete, belly dragging, eyes wide, mouth open. She'd never seen one so close before, but she'd seen what happened when they breathed on you. Fire. Consuming. Its nostrils flared. Colette turned and ran into the alleyway.

The beast didn't follow. It couldn't. But it exhaled, and the burning air billowed after her as she ran, forcing her to move just that little bit faster, aware of the burns already developing on her arms. At the end of the alleyway there was, of course, a red phone box. Colette reached it panting, too dazed to notice the rainbow slick on its sides.

But where the alleyway ended, in the road, another dragon was waiting for her, larger than the first. Its eyes were wide, almost shocked. Looking into hers, those eyes startled her into a memory. *The ash detonates on impact...*

Never mind that, she thought immediately, *I'm going to die*. The dragon opened its mouth for the final fire. Colette threw herself backwards, wrenched the door of the phone box open, fell inside. As the door closed, shutting her in, the world outside the box began to grow paler. The dragon stared at her with those surely-not-familiar eyes. She stood up, holding on to the side for support, and picked up the receiver.

Shakily, she said, *"Home."*

Everything spiralled like water down a plughole. She dived into the cool fluidity, the blessed cold of the pool, transported. She was gone.

And then there was concrete, and a voice saying "Welcome to the future, Colette," and a new world happened.

40. Nothing Happens, Endlessly
by Robert Bal

Once upon a time there was a red phone box by the name of Bernard. Bernard was old in the world of red phone boxes, which by human standards is relatively young – about as young as a wooden park bench, all green and mouldy and covered in bird-crap, of which Bernard had his fair share. He was situated under the waving branches of an oak tree named Persephone, who was old in the world of oak trees, which by human standards is very old indeed. And it was from Persephone that the birds, of whom there were too many to name, dropped their crap onto the cracked red dome which Bernard called his hat.

Except Bernard didn't call it anything, because Bernard was just a red phone box. Phone boxes don't give names to things.

The namer of things was called Drinking in Cakewalk Kennington, a middle-aged man by human standards, but a mere dust mote in the eye-blink of eternity. Kennington was lonely, and he drank, although whether he drank because he was lonely, or he was lonely because he drank, it was hard to tell. The fact that he frequently urinated in his trousers, that was not so hard to tell. It didn't solve the loneliness, that was sure.

Kennington had travelled all over the world, and discovered that it was disappointingly small. So he returned to London – the city of his birth – in order to make it as small as he possibly could, to pull the covers of this tiny little world up around himself, tight to his chin, and get some sleep. He was tired. Tired of walking, and looking, and seeing, tired of all the selves and their business transactions, tired of all the what-can-you-do-for-me and all the what-do-I-have-to-do-for-you-to-get-it, tired of the way the world turned and the people bent each other out of shape and used themselves all up in the process.

He lay against a tree near the borders of the park after which he was named, next to Bernard, and he drank, and urinated in his

195

trousers. Mothers and their baby strollers walked by, glaring at him and curling their lips. A mysterious elder statesman in a bright green suit wandered past occasionally. Small children threw stones at him while he slept. Dogs sniffed at his feet. The days passed by, and the world got smaller, just like he planned.

As it got smaller, the things around him began to take on greater significance to him, until they were like the panicked faces of loved ones peering down distraught at him in his sickness. He named them all, his small family that worried so sweetly for him.

But after a time, the world got so small that he could no longer see them, could no longer hear the whispers and taunts, until finally one day, the children and the police officers and the cruellest young men all dissolved into shadows flickering at the foot of his bed. Kennington realised that the world was shrinking at a rate which suggested imminent disappearance, that only these two remained – stout, stoical Bernard, and tall, elegant Persephone – and that they were to be his final companions.

It was then the birds started crapping on Kennington, too.

"Fucking birds!" he yelled at them. But they kept on crapping away. He looked up into the darkness of Persephone's branches, and saw nothing, but he heard them, a giggling gaggle of little beaks. He knew that they were tiny little things, with frail hollow little bones, and that if he could reach them he could crush them in his hands, one by one, with a muted crack and pop, and toss the little mussed up feather-ball corpses to the ground, and no-one would crap on his head again. Once they had been dinosaurs, which would have made them actually dangerous, but now, to crush them would be nothing at all – to a man, which Kennington still was.

But he couldn't reach them – even if he had been able to stand, he wouldn't have been able to reach them – and he knew this, and the birds knew this, too. So he was filled with impotent rage, a familiar feeling. He rolled about in Persephone's shadow, ground his teeth, and wailed, while the birds sang their metallic songs and crapped on his head, and apparently took great satisfaction in doing so. Eventually his head was covered in bird-crap, and he was still, like a statue, because his fury had burnt itself all out.

"I am a man!" he tried to shout. His voice came out garbled and weak however, like the last drops of dishwater draining away into a sink.

The birds stopped crapping on him, frozen for a moment, because what was coming from him now was not cursing, nor wailing, but bubbles – bubbles of laughter. The laughter came quietly at first, a low chuckle from the back of his dirty and lined throat, which became a rolling chortle from his round scarred belly, until tears sprang from his eyes and washed trails of skin clean upon his cheeks.

In the shadows of Persephone's branches, the birds were silent.

Kennington stopped laughing, although still trembling, and wiped his wet, gooey face. He had a drink from his bottle. There were no more than a couple of mouthfuls left. He stared at the bottle, and a longing gripped his heart, a yearning for a life he had never known, a world he had barely touched, a mystery the scope of which he had hardly begun to guess at.

Kennington sighed, and had another drink. It was then that Bernard spoke to him.

"Ring ring," said Bernard. "Ring ring."

Kennington looked up at the red phone box. This was the first time since Pigeon Man, long ago, under the Westway, that anyone had spoken to him. And for a moment in time, Kennington felt something in his heart lift right up.

"Ring ring," Bernard went on. "Ring ring." His tone was fairly noncommittal, as if he didn't really mind one way or another whether Kennington replied to him or not, as if he would go on talking to Kennington regardless.

Kennington crawled over to the foot of Bernard's door on his knees and knuckles, gripping the neck of his near-empty bottle in his fist, and paused. He was gasping for air, for as the world shrinks, so do its oxygen reserves. He looked across to Persephone, wanting both to seek her approval and to thumb his nose at the birds one last time, but there was nothing there save a shadow, a flickering phantom. The world was too small for Persephone to fit her awesome limbs into now. Kennington hung his head a moment, there on his hands and knees, to mourn her passing.

197

And then he no longer remembered who or what it was that he was mourning.

Bernard was still speaking. "Ring ring," he said. "Ring ring." His voice seemed to enter Kennington's head via his crown, course through his spine, and come out at his tail. It felt as though he were skewered, kept up on his hands and knees by the sound.

He reached a filthy hand up to Bernard's door handle and pulled it toward him. His arm and his thighs trembled with the exertion. Bernard's door opened just wide enough to allow Kennington to hook his other arm around it. The bottle rolled out of his hand and spun in a small circle on Bernard's floor. Leaning back on his knees he pulled, grunting, and the door opened further. He stuck his head and shoulders into the space, but he was tired now, and he let the door swing painfully back against his ribs.

"Ring ring. Ring ring."

Kennington's breath was coming in short, ragged bursts now. He couldn't say whether it was the pressure of the door on his ribs, or whether it was the disappearing world finally running out of air, but he felt as though he were breathing in through a balloon, deflating its finite capacity, which was not enough to fill his lungs. He felt the pinprick of panic on the skein of his self, felt it finally begin to unravel.

He leaned against the door wearily. His bones felt hollow, like those of a bird, but the door gave. He rolled forward into Bernard's floor-space, and pulled his legs up to his chest. The door swung shut behind him.

He lay there with his eyes closed, hugging his legs, for a moment. The cool bottle pressed against the side of his head, and he reached for it, sat up slightly, and opened his eyes. Kennington looked out of Bernard's glass panes as he drank his last mouthful, making the most of the little that remained.

There was nothing out there.

He looked at the bottle. There was nothing in there, either.

It hit him like a series of cellular explosions, a chain reaction from somewhere deep within the chemistry of his tired body. This was it. For real, this time.

"Ring ring," came the endless call. "Ring ring."

"I'm coming," Kennington said, and reached up over his head, fumbling blindly with his fingers for the receiver. They found what they were looking for.

"Ring –"

It was heavy, and his arm shook, so he cradled it to his ear with both hands, as if it were a newborn child.

He cleared his throat. It was the Alpha and Omega of human endeavour, and it echoed weakly in the sudden silence.

"Hello, Bernard," he said, his voice tremulous, his eyes squeezed shut.

"Hello?" The voice was close, husky, and measured.

Kennington listened, and could hear the sound of even breathing. "I'm here, Bernard."

"Hello?" said the voice. "Is that you?"

"It's me, Bernard," he replied, "It's me."

Kennington heard a sigh. "Where have you been?"

"I been all round the world, Bernard. I walked and walked and walked, and everywhere I goes I heard the same song. Everyone's singing it, Bernard. Ain't something you can learn overnight, like raindrops keep fallin' on ma head, or singin' in the rain. It takes real commitment."

Kennington paused, and his lower lip trembled. He swallowed a sob. "There ain't no way out, Bernard. You just haveta accept it. These fucking selves, they're hard-wired to sing this song. Everyone's the same, Bernard. All over the damned world, all the same. There ain't no escape."

There was a void of silence on the line. Kennington listened to it. The speaker on the other end seemed to be holding his breath.

"Are you coming soon?" said the voice.

"Will it change anything, Bernard?" he cried.

"When are you coming?"

Kennington sighed, a long, wheezing sigh, and it was as if the world inside him had reached critical mass, and was collapsing in on itself, too.

"Now, Bernard. I'm comin' now." His hands fell loosely to his sides, his eyes drooped shut, and his head lolled forward onto his chest.

The receiver dangled upon Drinking in Cakewalk Kennington's shoulder.

"Hello?" said the voice. "Hello?"

41. The Anglesey Deer
Part I:
Beasties, and Who the Fuck Knew What Else
by Gethin A. Lynes

A strange mist gathered around Henry, a fog of bright colours that thickened, obscuring the room beyond The Hunter's circle of salt. The last thing he caught was The Hunter's hand raised in farewell, before the sickening Technicolor swirl stole all sense of place, of space and direction from him. His stomach lurched, his head spun, and in a nauseous swoon, he passed out.

When he came to, he seemed to be surrounded by a fog in truth, its cold, damp fingers clinging to his skin. He was lying on a stone floor, moist and cracked and covered in lichen.

He sat up, and almost without thinking, felt for the deer in his pocket. There was a faint, sullen light filtering through the mist. Not knowing what else to do, he took the deer out of his pocket and ran his fingers over its surface. It felt warm and comforting to the touch.

It seemed as though he was still in the room where The Hunter had cast his spell over him. The circle of salt surrounded him still, one edge misshapen but unbroken where perhaps his foot had kicked at it while he was unconscious. The edges of the room were faint through the fog. At one end Henry could just make out the closed door through which he'd come, following the old man. It looked half rotten, but he couldn't remember whether it had looked like that before. At the other end, an iron door stood open. It hung from one hinge, twisted and broken, and the mist curled in from outside.

Henry got to his feet, and was about to step forward to see what was beyond the door, when he noticed huge gouges in the stone around it, and across its rusted surface. They reminded him instantly of the rips his cat made in its little wooden scratching post. He looked down at the unbroken circle of salt around his feet, and decided to stay exactly where he was for the moment.

He tried to remember exactly what the old man had said to him before he'd passed out, but all he could recall was something about there being things to learn, and that the Deer was awake. He held the thing up to his face, peering at it in the gloom. It certainly didn't look like it was awake. Oh, and didn't he say something about Wayland? He could only assume he was talking about Wayland the Smith.

It sounded like a bunch of claptrap, the sort of pseudo-pagan Celtic nonsense the campus Wiccan Society went on about. *Mind you*, he thought, *he clearly cast some sort of spell on me. Well, either that or he slipped me some acid while I was asleep.* He wondered if he could trust anything the old bastard had said. *I mean who the hell is he anyway? The Hunter? Looks more like a fucking leprechaun in that ridiculous suit.* Now that he thought about it, it had seemed a bit like he was being swallowed by a rainbow at the end there. But somehow the idea didn't really work. Perhaps it was the old man's Welsh accent. *I wonder if there's such a thing as a Welsh leprechaun.*

There was no point in dwelling on it, though. The man wasn't here, wherever here was, and Henry was — with nothing more than a supposedly magical wooden deer to help him. Who even knew if it was the real Anglesey Deer, or if the Anglesey Deer was even real in the first place. Perhaps it was only another legend, handed down in the Welsh imagination since the Roman sacking of the island.

Sitting here wasn't going to make it any clearer though, salt circle or no salt circle. Henry shoved the little carving away in his pocket again, and stepped out of the circle. He did his best to ignore the enormous scratches around the door, and walked through.

He was in a wood, the great hulking shapes of trees in the mist all around him. He turned around, but could see no sign of the doorway, nor anything that suggested he'd just walked from a building. Not having any idea where he was, and so no idea of where to go, he set off in the direction he was facing.

Grey light, as of a feeble sun far off, washed through the fog around him, leaving his feet shrouded in gloom. The going was slow, the forest floor thick with stones and fallen branches, decaying leaves masking the uneven ground. Massive roots spread out from the trees, forcing him to tread carefully. He got steadily wetter in the heavy mist.

Henry wasn't much of a woodsman at the best of times, and certainly not in the cold and wet. He was shivering. He told himself it was just the cold.

After a long while he came to the top of a rise and emerged from the fog and gloom into broad daylight. He stood on the edge of a long, steep slope, with high, thick clouds above, and a wide valley spread out below him. At the foot of the hill lay the smouldering ruins of a village. It was surrounded by earthen ramparts, and the charred, broken remains of a wooden wall. There looked to be little more than a single street of low shacks, small patches of thatch still clinging to their eaves. The muddy road was filled with broken bodies and slaughtered livestock. Here and there were the burnt and gutted shells of old cars, and where the gate once stood at the far end of the street, a truck lay on its side.

Instinctively Henry stepped back into the shelter of the trees. There was something very wrong here. He peered out from the gloom beneath the thick canopy. Beyond the village, lay a vast carpet of trees, and in the distance rising above them, a knot of high-rise buildings. Henry stared at them. *That's bloody London!* There was no mistaking it, and he could just make out the top of the London Eye to one side. Where the hell was he? What London was that? He wondered again if the old man had doped him up, if this was some sort of drug-fuelled nightmare.

Whatever was going on, Henry reckoned, he'd be better off there in the city than out here in the forest with fog, and beasties, and who the fuck knew what else. He started down the hillside at an angle, giving the village a wide berth. He didn't really fancy crossing open ground, but the valley was much longer than it was wide, and he was more concerned with getting to that distant London as soon as possible.

His fears of violent death in the open proved unfounded. He reached the tree line on the far side unmolested, not to mention a good deal warmer, after some time walking in the open.

To begin with he made better progress than he had through the trees above the village. There was no fog, and there was a well-trod path leading in mostly the right direction. For all his caution about crossing the valley, Henry didn't once question the wisdom of following an established path away from the scene of obviously recent slaughter.

His good speed did not last that long however. The sun began to go down, an inky gloom creeping in amongst the trees. After an hour or so, he was in pitch blackness, and was forced to stop. He hunched down between the roots of a tree and tried to relax. The night was cold, and it was not long before he was shivering once more.

* * *

He was lost in deep thoughts of pints and fish suppers when the sound of voices brought him to. A full moon had risen while he dozed, and the forest was bathed in a pale, cold light. He sat silent, listening. The voices were chanting, a low murmur coming closer, and he caught the flicker of flame through the trees.

His heart stuttered, pulse hammering in his ears at the thought that whoever had razed the village he had passed was coming here, to burn him.

But it was momentary. The fire was that of torches twinkling, he saw, as a procession came in sight of his hiding place. They were druids, even Henry could see that. Or, at least, they were a white-robed, beardy, druid cliché. He wondered again if they were conjured by his imagination, and he was having a rather lengthy hallucination. As they passed, Henry saw that behind the man in front, who carried one of several torches, was an ancient druid, bent shouldered and shrouded in long wisps of white hair. On open palms, he carried a wooden carving of a deer.

Henry watched as they passed, thirteen of them, and then he followed.

* * *

The druids stood in a circle, the old one with the deer in their centre. They were in the middle of an open glade, the moonlight full and bright. Half-hidden in the trees at the far side of the glade, a gibbet held a cage full of roiling darkness. The druids ignored it, their attention turned inside their circle. In their midst stood a squat standing stone, and Henry watched from the shadow of the trees as the deer was placed gently on its top. The chanting, which had fallen to a murmur, rose again to a crescendo, and then ceased. The old man opened his mouth as if to speak, but stopped short. He was looking straight at Henry.

A wry smile twisted one side of the ancient druid's mouth, and Henry thought he caught a quick flash of green from beneath his bushy eyebrows. He seemed on the verge of walking toward him, when from off to one side came a sharp twang, and the old man staggered, a long, barbed arrow through his neck.

The glade erupted. Some of the druids rushed to the old one's aid, the others turning outwards and forming a tight circle about them. They gripped staves or torches or pulled wicked looking sickles from their belts. From out of the trees on all sides soldiers rushed into the moonlight.

They were like some strange Roman legion, but the long tunics and the classic helmets – with their long cheek guards and here and there a brilliant red plume – were where the resemblance to history's most vaunted army stopped. They carried an ill-suited mishmash of armour and weapons, with only a few brandishing the javelins, short gladius swords, or tall shields for which they were famous. The rest wielded iron bars, or ball-peen hammers, hatchets, and even a hockey stick or two. And some of them used the metal lids of garbage bins in place of proper shields.

Henry was petrified, huddling in the shadows beneath an enormous oak. Like a motorist passing the site of an accident, he was sickeningly fascinated by the slaughter – and slaughter it was. The soldiers were appallingly efficient. Even with nought but a hockey stick, they dealt swift and bloody death. The druids didn't stand a chance. In a matter of moments only one of them remained standing. He had his back against the standing stone and a sickle in one hand. In a flash as the soldiers closed on him, he dragged the blade of the sickle across the palm of his free hand, and grabbed the wooden deer from atop the stone.

The change in him was immediate. He seemed to increase in size as Henry watched, becoming taller, broader, more solid. He leapt at the nearest soldiers, taking them by surprise. He took the sword arm off one at the elbow, snatching the gladius before it fell, and set about himself on both sides. He seemed untouchable, a blur, leaving a mist of blood and death all about him. Half a dozen soldiers had fallen before they had a chance to react. Others reeled away, desperate to escape the reach of this giant, bearded lunatic.

One soldier with a broad, crosswise plume on his helmet, stepped up, one arm raised, and there came the thunder of a shotgun blast. The last of the druids fell.

Henry heard the snap of a twig, and spun around. He felt a searing pain in his chest and looked down to see the broad blade of a gladius protruding from his chest, just below his left collarbone. He looked up to see a soldier in a plumed helm at the other end of it. The man turned toward the glade.

'Croftus,' he called. The one with the sawn-off shotgun turned away from the gibbet cage and strode over, doffing his helm and holding it under one arm.

As he approached, the first soldier pulled his sword from Henry's chest and shoved it under his chin, the point in his throat, forcing him backwards into the glade. The blood welled from beneath his collarbone and Henry could feel it hot and wet, running down his chest beneath his anorak.

The two soldiers spoke to one another. They were speaking in Latin. Henry had been a shit Latin scholar at his best, and that was twenty years ago. He was feeling a little light headed, but he did manage to catch *Mona* and *Nemeta* and *Londinium*. Not that it helped him any.

Stupidly, he was reminded of Mr. Batton, leaning over his shoulder explaining the perfect tense '*-i, -isti, -it, -imus –istis, -erunt.*' He didn't know whether it was Batton's heavy breathing in his ear, the stench of booze and cigarettes, or the blood flowing out of his chest, but his knees buckled.

The soldier pulled his sword away and whipped out a hand, grabbing him by the front of his jacket, holding him up. His head was swimming, and part of him wished they'd just spit him and be done with it. And then three things happened, almost at once.

The blood running down the inside of Henry's anorak reached the pocket where he had the Deer, and he felt a fire running back up the leaking blood, and into his chest. The dizziness passed, clarity returned, and strength flowed back into his legs, stronger than ever. Just as he was about to whip out a hand, without even thinking, and take the soldier's sword, the second thing came: a siren, a long *woot woot woot*, sounded through the trees, and went quiet. And then the third: in a split second, without a word, he was released and the soldiers fled.

Henry stood there, not knowing quite what to do, as a tall figure emerged from the trees. He was wearing a black shell suit, with yellow stripes down the sides of the legs and arms. On his head was a baseball cap and a set of furry reindeer antlers of the sort that tacky retailers force their staff to wear at Christmas. In one hand he had a megaphone.

Henry was flabbergasted. *A fucking chav? Out here in the woods?* This was the last sort of person he wanted to see. He was on the verge of turning and following the soldiers into the trees, when the chav lifted his megaphone and sounded the siren again. *Woot woot woot.*

And then a great horde of chavs emerged from the trees. The first dozen gathered about the megaphone wielder's feet, squatting on their haunches like dogs. They wore white shell suits, with the hoods pulled up, their sides slashed with red. The rest spread out to either side. They carried knives, and bottles, and the odd newspaper, rolled up hard into a club.

The chavs in white growled, leering at him. Inside their hoods Henry saw the gleam of teeth. There seemed to be too many of them, long and sharp, and overlapping each other at crooked angles. In fact, he couldn't see how there was room for anything but teeth in those hoods. He realised there was something wrong with the entire horde, their hands ending in great curved claws, or long tapered tongues, forked at the end, lolling from their mouths. And then it dawned on him. *White, with ears of red.* These chavs were the hounds. This was some kind of fucked up Wild Hunt, its antlered

207

leader sounding the charge with a megaphone instead of a horn. Henry began to back toward the trees. He saw the leader raise the megaphone once more and, like the soldiers, he fled.

* * *

Henry had no idea how long he'd been running. Hours, at least. He could still hear the Hunt behind him, the baying and snarling of the chav-hounds almost on his heels at times. The Deer had given him a strength he'd never before known, a sharpness to his senses far beyond that of an ordinary man. But even so, he was beginning to tire, the megaphone's siren sounding closer each time now, branches whipping at his face where earlier he had dodged them, or simply batted them aside.

Now and then, he came across patches of bitumen, old roads cracked and peeling away into the forest at their edges. Once, he passed a petrol station, the buildings gone, nothing left but a steel canopy broken by the trees, and a lone pump, missing its hose.

He caught his toes on a snaking root and went down. As he scrambled to his feet, he heard a savage snarl behind him. He spun just in time to see one of the chav-hounds launch itself at him, clawed hands going for his throat, jaws spread wide and dripping with saliva. Henry ducked, and the beast clawed at him as it flew past, raking his shoulder.

Not bothering to see where the thing landed, Henry took to his feet again, fear spurring him on, a deer making a last ditch effort to outrun the wolf pack. As he ran he saw lights ahead through the trees. At first he thought they were the fireflies of exhaustion, dancing before his flagging brain, but soon they grew more solid, becoming a brilliant orange glow against the darkness of the woods.

He burst into a clearing, and saw an old woman standing before a hole in the air. She was bent-backed, and struggling to lift suitcases from a sizable pile through the hole. On the other side, Henry saw the familiar sight of street lights, and heard the noise of traffic. He took this in almost instantly. Without slowing his pace in the slightest, he hurtled for the portal.

Tottering beneath a suitcase almost half her size, the old woman didn't even see Henry as he barrelled into her, knocking the suitcase aside, and carrying both of them through the portal.

Pulling himself to his feet, Henry looked about, momentarily bewildered. He was standing on Lambeth Bridge, Westminster and the London Eye in the distance. Surrounding him was a haphazard collection of suitcases, and in the middle of the road sat the old lady, scowling. He was about to step off the curb to help her up, when he heard a snarl behind him. Whirling around, he saw the portal was still open, the darkened woods on the other side. One of the chav-hounds was racing for it, the baying of the others not far behind.

Henry stood in mute shock, feeling drained of the spirit of the Deer. The chav-hound was upon the opening. It leapt, rows of jagged teeth glinting orange in the light of the street lamps. And then the portal closed with a crack, and the chav-hound's head was on the wrong side of it. It fell to the pavement, where it crumbled to ash, and blew away on the gentle breeze.

Henry turned back to see the old woman dusting off her hands. She glared at him, and wagging a finger at him, opened her mouth to speak.

'Shit,' said Henry, and legged it.

42. Like the River Itself
by Chuck Walker

The barge rested on wooden blocks. High and dry, it waited for a final coat of paint before Cornish launched it into the Thames again. His despair had given way to the burning desire to rid himself of his past. Memories, once thick as honey, had tied him to the barge. They were slowly dissolving, as if dunked in hot tea. Hints of happiness touched him. At first, he didn't understand the feelings, and took guilt in the pleasure he'd experienced watching a corpse slap against his barge. There was no other word to explain the sound, now etched in his memory, of a body against wood. It felt wrong to describe such a sad sound as a mere slap, however. He derived some further guilt from his lack of compassion.

The police had removed the body, lifting it onto his deck and placing it in a black plastic bag. Cornish had fought the urge to smile, but he had believed – hoped – that he would finally be happy. He'd watched the police haul away the body, observing, utterly unconcerned by the death of another human being.

Indifference was new. His existence had been passive and pliable. He passed through life invisible to others, hurt by the lack of deep connection, repeatedly discarded by women like Robin. He had little to look forward to, but he wasn't used to emptiness.

He hoped that restoring the barge and painting the hull would help him put Robin behind him and start over. He even contemplated ripping out the gunwale which had her name carved into it, but he decided to keep it as a reminder. He never wanted to experience the pain of abandoned love again – maybe seeing it would prevent him from falling into the same trap with someone else.

Finding the body had changed his life.

Cornish wanted to be rid of the dependence he felt towards his partners. He wanted to be secure in himself. Fixing the barge was the first of many changes he'd imagined. He hoped others would follow.

Crossing the gravel drive, Cornish stopped to look at the men applying the last coat of paint to the hull. It glowed in the work-lights, bright and glossy. Too bad, Cornish thought, that no one would see it once it was under water.

"Hey, guv," the boatyard foreman called. He was standing on the deck of the barge. "Come on up and see what she looks like."

Cornish walked under the hull and climbed the ladder. The first thing he noticed was Robin's carved name. Maybe he was wrong to leave it.

"She's a lovely boat." The foreman slid his hand along the deck railing.

"You've done a great job fixing her up for me – thanks."

"It's been a treat working on her." The foreman looked down at the gunwale. "Sure you don't want to replace the wood here?"

Cornish glanced down at the name and slowly shook his head. "No, it's okay. It's a badge of my own stupidity."

"I can understand that." The foreman laughed and placed his hand on Cornish's shoulder as if they shared a private joke. "When do you want to put her back in the water?"

"You tell me. Whenever the paint has had enough time to cure."

"Give it until the day after tomorrow. That'll be long enough."

Cornish nodded and shook the man's outstretched hand. "See you in a couple of days."

* * *

Cornish moved back onto the barge. Comfortable, knowing he was home, he sat in the dark, dreaming. He loved the smell of the new wood lining overhead, and the feel of the refurbished leather cushions under his fingers. The boat rocked gently with the current again, and Cornish was happy. He watched the sun set over the Thames as if it was the first time he'd seen it. The city skyline shone a colourful red with edges of pink against a dark blue sky.

He sighed, sipped wine, enjoying the pleasant English night.

When his mobile rang, Cornish answered without looking. "Hello," he said calmly.

There was silence for a moment. Cornish could hear soft breathing.

"Hello?" He could feel himself tensing.

"I'm sorry," a breathy voice said.

Cornish squeezed his eyes shut. Blood rushed to his head as his pulse raced. "Robin." His voice broke as he said it.

"Yes." Her reply was nearly a sob. "I need to talk to someone."

He wanted to hang up.

"Are you there?" Robin sounded distraught.

"Where are you?" He didn't recognize his own voice. Emotions he thought gone tore back into his head. *Funny how something as simple as a voice has the power to screw you up.*

"I'm in the phone box at the edge of the park. Can I come see you?"

Two paths appeared before him, and he saw the consequences of taking either one.

"Darren," Robin pleaded.

He had to decide. "Yes. I'm on board. You can come over." He hung up, already regretting his decision.

* * *

Stepping onto the barge, Robin looked around. "You've had the boat fixed." She tried to smile.

"Yeah, it needed it." Cornish studied Robin as she admired the boat's new look. There were ugly shadows in the hollows under her eyes.

"I was sure you were going to sink with this old tub before you fixed it."

Cornish didn't buy her tease. As much as he had loved her, he feared the hold she had on him. "Why are you here?"

She bit her lip. "I had to see where you found him." She moved to the side of the barge. "Is this where he was?"

"Yes," he said. He was startled when Robin began to cry. *She still loves the Arsehole. She hasn't come to see me. She's come to commune with a ghost.*

Cornish climbed down the ladder into the lounge and closed the hatch, leaving Robin to her grief. The love he'd felt for her was gone. He didn't feel happy, or crushed, or avenged, and he didn't feel her sadness.

He felt free.

43. When the Phone Rings
by Francesca Burgon

Margaret's mother hung the phone up again. She'd worked her way
through several pages of the phone book tonight, and she seemed
happy at the way the evening had gone. Margaret had been very
careful to keep quiet for the last hour or so.

Mother looked down at her, sitting on her suitcase, and smiled.
She reached down slowly, and tucked a strand of Margaret's hair
back behind her ear, her fingers warm and gentle. "One day you'll
understand," she said. "You'll know everything was done in your
name. We'll be safe and away and... Well."

Margaret had the spider-ballerina clutched in her hand. It was the
best of the things she'd drawn in the last few days. She held it up, and
Mother took it, smoothed it out so she could see. Once upon a time,
Mother had taught art. She looked at the drawing, and smiled again.
Then the smile wavered into a frown. Mother turned the piece of
paper over, and her eyes got all big and goggly, and Margaret saw the
fear set in.

"Where did you get this?" Mother waved the bank slip in front
of Margaret's face. "Where?"

"It was on the floor of the box, Mummy. I didn't take anything
from your bags. I didn't!" Margaret cringed back, hiding her face
behind her arm quickly. Not that it ever made any difference. Mother
never hesitated to make her anger felt when they were alone.

"We have to find this person. We have to explain to him how you
– YOU – ended up with his money! He'll think you stole it. They'll
take you away from me. Do you know what happens in those places
when they take a kiddie away from her mummy?"

Mother's voice was rising. Margaret felt tears prickling. She
backed even further into the corner of the box.

"They hurt kiddies and make them sorry," Margaret whispered.
"Then they turn you into a look-a-like and kill you, so that mummies

don't know if you're real or not. Mummy, I found it on the floor. Please, Mummy. I didn't take it. Don't hit me. Please, don't tell."

Mother grabbed Margaret's arm and twisted it until she could see the birthmark hidden on the inside of her upper arm. She let go again. "Lucky for you, I know when you're real and when you are a look-a-like. Going to kill the look-a-like. Where. Did. You. Steal. This?"

Margaret shook her head desperately. Mother lunged for her, one big fist already clenched.

The phone began to ring. Mother immediately spun around, her mouth pursed in a sharp line. She snatched up the receiver.

"Hello?" she snapped, her voice full of suspicion. "Who is this?"

Margaret watched from her position by the door. The phone never rang. Not *ever*. It wasn't the right way of things. It was... frightening.

"I see," said Mother, to the phone. "You're Vandenbussche, are you? Mm. Where? There had better be a reward for this."

Margaret picked up her suitcase and decided to wait outside so she could dodge better if Mother was still upset. Mother replaced the handset on the cradle, and turned to stare at Margaret through the thick panes of glass. Then she bent down to retrieve The Evidence and backed out of the phone box, making sure that she had every single piece of paper in her bags.

"We have to take that piece of Evidence to the rightful place. Show the filthy Peed that the bully boys can't hurt you and me. It's not too far. We'll be there in a bit." Mother began to walk away, her bags twisted together and tied with pieces of string, some digging into the skin on her wrists. Margaret followed, holding her red suitcase beside her and the one bag of Evidence that Mother allowed her to carry. Every time she picked it up, she remembered how proud she'd felt the day that she was given it.

When they finally arrived at the rightful place, Margaret was ready to rest. She found a spot by the hedge that was fairly dry, sat down on her suitcase, and waited.

Mother marched up to the imposing door and rapped on it sharply. She waited for a moment, then rang the doorbell. Whoever was inside wasn't moving quickly enough for her liking. Her lips tightened, and the lines around her mouth deepened. Margaret moved her suitcase a little further away, clutching her evidence bag to her tightly.

"Not in," snapped Mother. "Bleedin' bully boys been here already. Come on. We're going." She turned around quickly, carrier bags rustling against each other, threatening to break at the handles. Margaret got up. Her summer dress was soaked through, and she felt like crying. They'd missed the overnight shelter by some hours.

Behind them, the door opened slowly and a man looked out into the night.

"Yes?" he asked, his voice ringingly clear. "What do you want?"

Mother turned around, putting on the Schoolteacher Smile.

"Yes, hello. We found something that we thought was yours, if you're Horace Vandenbussche. If you aren't, where might he be, please?" She swayed slightly from side to side as she spoke.

The man tracked her movement with his eyes.

Margaret could see that he wasn't coming out from behind the door. Hesitating, she moved into his line of sight.

"S-Sir?," she began, trying to keep her voice under some sort of control. "I found this piece of paper on the floor, and Mummy says it belongs to you." She walked forward, holding out the bank slip for him to take.

He plucked it from her hand and glanced at it to ensure it was everything he was expecting.

Then he simply shut the door.

Mother stood there, her mouth open, no sound coming out. Margaret hurried away, wanting to get away and find somewhere warm for the night. Mother had different ideas. She marched up to the door and knocked on it again.

"Me an' my girl came here in good faith to bring that back. Least you could do, filthy Peed, is feed us. Fascist bully boy. Hate 'em all, hate 'em all, hate the long and the short and the tall. They'll hurt us and beat us, and pretend not to see us, but really we only hates them all." Mother began to sing and dance on the large white steps leading up to the house.

Her cracked voice rose into a shriek, and she rapped sharply on the door again in time with her song.

Margaret was never sure exactly what happened next. She was standing there, waiting for Mother to come, when the door opened again. This time the man had a nasty look on his face. He did something to Mother, who crumpled silently to the ground, scattering The Evidence from fallen bags as she collapsed. Papers fluttered down the steps and across the garden on the breeze. He grabbed Mother by the hair and dragged her into the house. Margaret hadn't even had time to move. Not until the door was shut again. Then her chest began to shake.

The shakes spread out over her body, hurting her bones. She started sobbing, the tears forced out by the shaking. She didn't know what to do. Didn't know where to go. The one person with any answers was lost behind a door that she was too afraid to go near.

There was only one place she could go. So she ran, through streets slick with rain, dodging past oblivious people who only muttered about what a kid was doing on the streets this late at night. She ran back towards the dryness of the phone box. As she approached it, strange flashes of light disturbed her, flickering in bands of blue. She paused, concerned that whatever it was, it might be a bully boy.

The door of the phone box was open. One man was leaning against it to keep it wide, while a woman struggled to haul out a long, lumpy looking package. They both wore shiny yellow. As she watched, the two people finally got the package out of the tiny space, and slowly carried it away, towards the flashing lights. It could have been anything. Something wonderful. A princess tucked into a carpet, being taken to a place where she could be warm and safe. Cleopatra in her hiding space.

Maybe it would be her safe place, too. She darted over to the phone box, and nestled up against the back wall. It wasn't very bright in there, and her suitcase might be red enough to help keep her hidden, if the scary man came looking for her. What she really wanted though, with all her heart, was for Mother to come back and make it all safe again.

The light in the phone box flared bright. It made Margaret feel warm and sleepy, and for an instant, she was sure she heard an old man telling her that her Grandma was coming.

Somewhere outside, an unfamiliar woman was speaking. Margaret was too comfy and tired to be concerned.

"Wait up, Dave. Look. In the box..."

44. Game, Sekhmet, and Match
by Steven Sautter

Kelly's flight to Gatwick dragged on and on. Nothing whatsoever happened. It was just eternities of tedium broken by occasional deliveries of something vaguely resembling food. She hadn't heard from Henry for a week. Unprecedented. Vandenbussche was a total blank slate, too. She ground her teeth, glanced down at her book for the 437th time, and went back to watching the seconds crawl.

An eon or two later, she was through customs with most of her luggage, a fresh passport stamp, and what felt like an iron spike pounding into her temple. The car rental people proved competent, fortunately. They took her to a car, pointed out that it was in good shape, and finally left her to get on with the drive to London.

Once she got out onto the road – the wrong side of the road – time seemed to start moving again. A couple of hours of freeway later, she was heading into one of the city's expensive residential districts. The address Vandenbussche had given her turned out to belong to a lavish Victorian house set on impressive grounds. The building was attractive, its brickwork trimmed in dark blues and maroons. The attached gardens stretched on and on, and boasted several topiaries in the shape of cheetahs. In the distance, Kelly could even see a hedge maze. She left her Astra in the parking area, and walked up the gravel path to the front door. When she buzzed the doorbell, it played a cheap, computer-bleep version of 'Cat's in the Cradle.' *No accounting for taste*, Kelly thought.

A little while passed before Gloria Vandenbussche answered the door. She looked distracted, too busy working out the mysteries of the universe to be concerned with door duties. "Father has been expecting you," she said, and moved out of the doorway to allow Kelly in. The door swung shut behind them with a thud.

Gloria ushered Kelly through the house silently. Unlike the stately exterior, the inside of the house was a mélange of styles, each fighting for dominance. Baroque timepieces vied for space next to jukeboxes. A print of Munch's *The Scream* was overshadowed by a poster for an old black and white shlock horror film. There was even a rather-nice looking Greek statue with a ratty old top hat plunked completely over its head.

They stopped in front of a door with an electronic keypad above the handle. Gloria punched in a five digit code and the door creaked open.

"You need to oil that," Kelly joked. Gloria just gestured for Kelly to go inside, and then wandered off elsewhere.

"Professor David." The man was large and lithe, with a deep, booming voice. He rose to greet her from behind a cheap IKEA desk. "I am gratified you came." He was wearing a decidedly odd purple track suit.

She shook his hand. "Horace Vandenbussche?"

"Obviously." He sank back into his plush-looking chair. "I'd hardly be anyone else. Although I'll confess that I do indulge in an alias or two now and again. A certain amount of anonymity is useful, wouldn't you say?"

"I wouldn't know." She sat down across from him in an uncomfortable black inflatable chair.

"Naturally not. The indomitable Professor Kelly David needs headlines to bolster her archaeological fiefdom, not obscurity."

It sounded a lot like he was sneering. *Goddamn Brits.* She suppressed an instinctive retort. His isolation probably stemmed from his social ineptitude. She nodded instead, and kept her voice pleasant. "It's the bane of the academic's life. Publish or perish."

"Hence your eagerness to snatch the crumbs from my palm, I presume? That and a little hint of luxury, of course. Did you enjoy my largesse?"

Kelly blinked, and paused for a breath or two. Poor Gloria. No wonder she was so troubled. "Thank you, yes, the flight was pleasant, but that's definitely not why I came here."

"You are absolutely correct, Professor David. You're interested in the ritual functions of the Anglesey Deer. Its... activation. Yes?"

"Well, yes, I suppose I would be."

"Well, yes, I suppose I would be." Vandenbussche's voice was a ghastly parody of her own. "Are you always so mealy-mouthed, Professor?"

"What?" Kelly stared at him.

"Say what you damned well mean, woman. You are desperate to know how to activate the Deer. SAY IT!" The last words whipped out, an astonishing roar.

Kelly flinched at the fury in his voice, then felt her own rage ignite. She smothered it with her pity. The poor man really was quite profoundly impaired. "I would say so cheerfully, Mr. Vandenbussche, if I had any idea what you were talking about." She kept her voice light, pleasantly reasonable, the tone she saved for drunk students. "I'm here at your specific request, after all. I am eager to understand you, however. The Deer is of immense historical importance, and if there was some sort of associated ritual framework, then of course I'd be fascinated to know more about it. Your contribution would, of course, be fully attributed..." She saw his expression, and trailed off.

Vandenbussche's hands were balling into fists. "Where is the Deer, woman? Did you think I wouldn't notice that you'd sent your little pet to find it, your Henry Bannister? *Tell me where it is.*" There was definite menace in his voice now.

"Henry? Where is he? What are you talking about?"

"Yes, that's another good question. Where is he? ANSWERS! Now, Professor David."

She rocked back in her stupid little chair, scared now. "I have absolutely no idea what you are talking about."

He went very still, and stared at her for a long moment. Some of the anger seemed to drain away, although he still looked like a coiled spring. "I believe you, Professor. That's a shame."

"It's a relief, as far as I'm concerned."

He sighed. "I can see how you'd feel that way. However, it does mean that you're going to be exactly zero fucking use to me."

"I..."

Vandenbussche seemed to flow up out of his seat, all grace and power, and somehow his purple tracksuit didn't look quite so stupid. He grinned at her, and his skin actually rippled. Right across his face.

It was as if his skull-bones danced. It settled, darker than before. Beige. Then the lines of his face were flowing, the grin widening and widening, teeth sharpening. His mouth slipped outwards, away from his skull, lengthening into a muzzle. A cheetah? His body bulked up too, arms and legs strengthening, shoulders and hips swelling powerfully. The hands had sprouted long, wicked claws.

She stared at him, utterly aghast.

"Professor David." The human voice purred out from the impossible cheetah head, a bit rougher now, but heavy with smug delight. "I'm hungry. If you wish to live for another minute or two, you should probably start running." He crouched for a leap, and flexed his claws at her. Even from several feet away, his breath stank of rotting meat.

Kelly fought back a shriek, and scrambled up out of the chair as Vandenbussche sprang at her. She threw herself out of the way, barely keeping her balance. Behind her, she heard the chair pop and start deflating with a hiss. He let his momentum carry him past, getting between her and the door. He seemed just as comfortable on four legs as on two. He slashed out with a hand, catching her arm with the tip of a claw. It burned like fire.

"First blood."

There was no choice. Kelly wrapped an arm around her face, and launched herself full-tilt at the window. The frame and its glass exploded around her as her shoulder and elbow crunched sickeningly, and then she was rolling across the ground. She snatched a glance around as she lurched to her feet, ignoring the stings of a score of minor cuts. Open lawns. The hedge maze. A gazebo. Back in the house, Vandenbussche was stalking towards the broken window, licking her blood off his claw.

She started running, making a beeline for the hedge maze. It wasn't much, but it was better than open ground. She heard a gentle thump as he cleared the window. She resisted the temptation to look back, instead putting her head down and sprinting as hard as she could. Behind her, she could hear the thuds getting swiftly closer.

Kelly darted into the hedge maze. There were four different paths available, thank the Gods. She picked one without breaking stride, and hurtled along it. After half a dozen junctions, she realized that she could no longer hear Vandenbussche on her heels. She slowed a bit, partly to reduce the amount of noise she was making, but mainly because her lungs felt like they'd been sandpapered, and her legs were screaming blue murder.

The maze was overgrown, the hedges apparently unmaintained, but the paths were hard-packed chalk. That meant her physical trail wasn't too obvious, at least. How was his sense of smell? There was no way to tell. She pressed on as quickly as she could, remembering an old tip that said to always turn away from the centre. In several places, the maze had almost grown together, and there were a couple of times where she had to duck under branches. She kept going though, feeling increasingly disjointed.

She turned a corner and found herself in a circular clearing. In the middle, a tall statue stood on a marble plinth. Sekhmet, the lion-headed Egyptian goddess of warfare and pestilence. Painted limestone, by the looks of it.

"Do you like it?" Vandenbussche's voice startled her.

She turned around, too drained for panic. Too hopeless. "Twelfth Dynasty, I assume. Fine condition. Where's it from?"

"It's not *from* anywhere. It was made for me." He stalked closer. "Thank you for a merry chase. I'll consider making this hurt a little less." He flexed his claws, and reached for her.

An explosion of sound seemed to freeze Vandenbussche in place, a loud snapping noise, followed by a peculiar droning hum overlaid with little spitting crackles. He opened his mouth as if to howl, but no sound came out. Instead, red lightning arced between his jaws. There was light in his chest, too. Then he was dwindling, quickly, until nothing was left but a nasty smear on the chalk, as thick as blood, but the color of bruised bananas.

There was a man at the back of the clearing, in an oddly formal blue velvet jacket. His face was blessedly human. He had some sort of automatic pistol, and she could see it was trained on her.

"Thank..."

"Shh." He cut her off. "Don't spoil it." His voice was dreamy, ecstatic, and Kelly felt the fear returning. "Are you Kelly David?" he asked, eventually. He sounded less out of it now. "The Glaswegian said you'd be Kelly David."

She nodded mutely. She could feel herself shivering. What the hell had happened to Vandenbussche? Was it that gun?

"Give me the Deer."

"I don't have it. That's why the creature you just shot was going to kill me."

"Oh. That's annoying."

"If I had the damned deer, I'd give it to you. I'm through. But I don't. I just want to go home."

"I was told to kill you," the man said. "By someone who looked quite a lot like the chap I just shot, actually. But if you don't have the Deer, I don't think there's any point."

"Uh..."

"I mean, it would feel really good." He waved the gun. "*They* want me to kill you. But I'm not certain. It might make him angry, if he needs you later. All right. I'm not going to kill you. Watch out for the bully boys, eh?"

She gaped at him as he turned around, fondling the gun, and slipped back into the maze.

45. Hidden Truths
by Tamsyn H. Kennedy

Gloria rooted around in her old jewellery box in a panic, fumbling through earrings and necklaces she hadn't worn in years, thinking only of getting away. She hadn't seen Daddy change since she was a child, since he'd raised his claws to her mother, and her mother had left. She'd stood there, helpless, glued to her bedroom window as he stalked the professor, as Jon appeared. Jon had... he had *killed* her father. That wasn't even supposed to be *possible*.

All right, Jon had never much liked Daddy, but he had always been polite, respectful. She would never have thought him capable of killing him, even if he'd known a way. But... She peeked out the window again, and saw him talking to the professor. Were they in on some sort of plan? Jon turned back toward the house, and Gloria panicked.

Her best chance of escape was in the jewellery box, supposedly. She'd tossed it in there long ago, when her mother had left her behind. She'd pressed it into her hand, telling her the words to speak insistently, over and over. Gloria had discarded the damned thing without a second thought, angry at her mother, already certain that she would never use it.

A hint of blue peeked from under a velvet bag and she grasped it, pulling the pebble into the light. The colour reminded her of her father's steely eyes. She'd hated the way he glared at her with them, but now all she could think was that she would never see them again. In her mind she saw his body being devoured by whatever red blood-magic Jon had loosed on him. She saw his silent scream, an indignity so at odds with his controlled existence. She was left with the startling truth that he was gone... and that she was free.

Only two people could know what that meant to her. She looked down at the cold blue pebble in her hand. Only two people, and she was never going to talk to her sister.

She didn't know what to expect of where she was going, but grabbing a leather bag, she filled it with basic necessities – underwear (practical and sexy), makeup, purse, and her little can of pepper spray. Then she changed into a belted shift dress and leather coat.

She heard the sound of a door creaking open downstairs, and sprinted down the hall to the bathroom. She realised as she ran why Daddy'd never oiled any of the hinges. She turned the water on full and locked the bathroom door. While she waited for the bath and sink to fill, she dragged a heavy dresser in front of the door, and sat on the cold bathroom floor holding the pebble with both hands.

Clearing her mind to feel the flow of the nexus, enhanced by the water around her, Gloria whispered the words her mother had taught her. She felt a pull, just as the handle to the door rattled. Her last thought was to wonder how Jon could do this to her, and then she was gone.

* * *

The green tinged sun was setting as she surveyed her new surroundings, the taste of bile lingering in her mouth from the transition. A sparsely gravelled dirt road meandered through the countryside towards a small town in the distance. The sun was already dipping below the horizon, and she set off briskly along the road, not wanting to be caught outside after dark.

She remembered her mother's tales of people taking the shape of animals, and in the fading light, the thought of being watched by sinister birds or foxes or even field mice terrified her. Every twitter in the trees, or rustle in the long grass beside the road made her heart thump wildly, and she hurried on. Only the inn would be safe.

Or so she hoped. She hadn't seen her mother in fifteen years, and who knew what sort of reception she was going to receive.

The fireplace in the Twenty Oars was burning strong. In front of it a dog rested, paws crossed, watchful eyes alert for misplaced morsels of food. Gloria sat and waited for the serving girl. She couldn't remember the last time she'd felt this nervous. It was as if her confidence had died alongside her father.

From the girl she asked for wine, and an audience with the innkeeper. The girl brought a carafe and a goblet, and left her alone. Gloria poured herself a drink, and swallowed it in a single gulp, trying to steady her nerves. A breath after, she poured another. Mam emerged, red hair the same shade as her daughter's. She rushed to Gloria's table, reaching out to touch her, but stopped short, seeming unsure if such closeness was welcome.

"I felt it," she said. "I felt him pass. I hoped you would..." She stopped awkwardly.

Despite the wine, and her determination to hold it together, Gloria felt her defences breaking.

"I have missed you so much, my baby," her mother said.

Tears threatened, but Gloria blinked them away. Seeing this, Mam took her hand and gently led her upstairs to one of the inn's rooms, Gloria shuffling silently in behind her. It was taking all her energy not to collapse into a distraught heap.

"Lie down, darling. Rest," her mother said. Gloria sat down on the edge of the bed, looking down at the floor. She didn't trust herself to meet her mother's eyes.

"No-one can harm you here," Mam said. "You are under my protection. We will talk soon."

Gloria was hardly paying attention now. The pillow was cool and inviting as she lay down. She rolled over to face the wall, and after a moment heard the door open and close as Mam left her alone. She thought of her father and all the words she would never say to him and she let herself cry. She was soon asleep.

* * *

The morning bustle of the town outside the window woke her. She was used to the calming tones of breakfast talk radio, not the clatter of carts and the noise of animals, of goats and cattle and dogs barking.

Downstairs the main hall was empty, the patrons having come and gone. Not knowing what else to do, Gloria sat down at one of the tables beside the constant fire. In a moment, Mam came out of the kitchen carrying a clay cup and fresh bread rolls, almost as if she had been waiting for her.

"Warmed milk for you, my dear. I know it's not the same. No matter how long I spend here I still miss my morning coffee."

Gloria remembered her in their kitchen holding a mug, making breakfast for the family. She quashed the image.

"We need to discuss something." Mam sat down across the table from her.

Gloria's guts tightened, instantly suspicious. It was exactly the tone Daddy took when he had some errand for her to run. Mam opened her mouth to speak but Gloria interrupted. "Why?" she demanded, anger rising inside her.

"You want answers about your father. Believe me I want them, too."

"No," Gloria interrupted again. "Why did you leave?"

Mam's tone remained calm. "I didn't want to, but... your father and I found ourselves heading in different directions. On different sides you might say."

"Bullshit!" Gloria clenched her fists like a toddler demanding a toy.

Mam sighed. "No-one knows the truth of a relationship unless they're in it. We tried for so long to make it work. Perhaps it was not supposed to."

"Don't treat me like a child, Mum. I saw what he did to you."

Her mother nodded. "I couldn't be in the same world with him after that. But I didn't want him killed."

"Who did?" Gloria asked. "I want to know why."

"There are more pressing troubles I must address first. But if you help me I will do everything to find the information you want."

There it was, another parent with a task. But she could sense the anxiety behind her mother's request, the lines on her face created by war, not age.

"What's going on?" she asked.

"A damned fool wants to open a portal to travel to your world and its ring of variants. The nexus is closed to him because of his dark magic, but I am afraid he will find another way. He has opened small cracks through which he can influence your side. There are artefacts... I am sure he will be searching for them. Gods alive, the monsters he would unleash. The suffering. He cannot be allowed to gain access." Her eyes were a prophecy of fear and destruction.

Gloria nodded, though she didn't quite follow. She felt the familiar sense of frustration, of being sent on another errand she didn't understand. But it was her mother asking.

"What do you want me to do?" she asked.

"Oh, my precious girl." Mam's posture relaxed. "The Magus has a dwelling in the mountains. I cannot go – he can feel my every move – but you could."

"Why me? Isn't there someone else here that would be better suited?"

"There *are* others, dear, but this world is becoming more dangerous, and there are many things that need our attention. You used the nexus, you survived your father's service, you are strong. There is no one else I would trust with this."

Gloria took a long sip of her milk, thinking it through. Eventually she spoke. 'What do I need to do?"

Mam took a grey crystal from her skirt pocket. The air around it seemed darker, as if it was sucking in a portion of its light.

"You must go there and seal the rifts for good. Get inside the mountains and smash this. The energy released will fix any nearby tears between the worlds."

"Won't that be dangerous?" Gloria asked.

"I won't lie, my darling. It will be. But you're more than capable. It's lucky that you came when you did."

"When I come back we'll find out what happened to Daddy?"

Mam nodded. "I promise."

Gloria took the crystal. She needed to know what happened to her father, whatever the cost.

"I'll need a map."

Mam pushed back her chair. "Of course! We must hurry and pack for your journey. Soon this nightmare will be over."

* * *

Gloria left the inn, bag laden with food and wine and other things she would need. Her makeup and her sexy underwear had been left behind, but not her can of pepper spray. Her dress was gone, replaced by a belted tunic, practical woollen leggings and comfortable, sturdy boots. Over all she wore an oilskin cloak against the rain that gathered in dark clouds on the horizon.

In the distance she could see the mountains. If only her lovely sports car was here. She could relax into the leather seats, put The White Stripes on the stereo and be back in a couple of hours. Instead she would have to walk. Her mother had offered a horse but she was never the sort of child to take lessons. Checking the crystal was secure in her pocket, she gritted her teeth. She would be back for answers.

* * *

In the shadow of the inn a rat watched her walk away. When she was gone, with a glance around to make sure it was alone, it veered, stretching grotesquely, and a moment later, in its place was a crow. Opening its wings the bird cawed once and took to the sky, heading towards the mountains.

46. In the Dark
by James 'Grim' Desborough

Henry was run ragged. His limbs felt leaden and ached with every movement. He was scraped and sore. Skinned knuckles stung whenever he moved his fingers. His thighs and calves felt a size too small for the rest of him, tight and painful. Every breath was a lungful of fire and every rib felt like a dagger stabbing deep into his chest, yet still he pushed on.

White knuckles bled red, clutching hold of the Deer for dear life, he fought to keep moving. *They* were still behind him, out there, somewhere. He could hear them moving, running, taunting him, hooting and hollering words that weren't really words. He could see shadows against the trees, against the walls, dancing in the orange light that seemed to come from everywhere and nowhere all at once.

The tighter he gripped the Deer the more he seemed to see, to feel, to smell, to hear. The more energy he seemed able to call up from some primal pit deep inside. The closer he held it, the harder his heart beat in his chest. His sweat rose like steam around his body, fogged his glasses and made everything soft-focus, dream-like.

Where was he?

Nothing made sense. There was a hint from the Deer that this was the right direction, but no idea of what that actually meant.

This wasn't the London of streets and asphalt, of parks and gardens. It was something else. There were patches of the city here and there, poking through the dreams like moments of déjà vu. The worn red brick of a century past, the white walls and slate roofs of the century before that. Broken glass glittering on the ground, bombed out buildings.

Over it, around it, reclaiming it, were remnants of an even older London, something more primal. Trees and bushes wormed their roots through gaps in the brick and tore up the ground. One moment he was running down a long, straight street, the next he was wading through the soupy water of a swamp. Always the Deer in his hands pulled him along, past exhaustion into delirium, seeming to lead him.

Through dim and misty vision he plunged on, through a rusting iron gate and into a winding maze of hedges. Stumbling, falling, he barely noticed the light change, the orange twilight becoming true night. Damp grass and dirt underfoot rather than the debris of centuries.

* * *

Kelly didn't know how to get out. The hedges were too high. Turning away from centre seemed to send her further into the maze. She couldn't remember how she'd come through the other way, and although the Vandenbussche... thing... was dead, she didn't even know if she wanted to get out. What if there were more of them? Was the daughter like that?

Fear sweat was cooling on her skin now, making her shiver and shudder, making it hard to move. There were tears stinging in her eyes as much from confusion as anything else. A man sent to kill her had saved her, but why? For what? All this death and destruction, all this strangeness. Whoever was behind all this thought she was important somehow.

She swayed, the branches of the hedge scratching along her side, snagging at her clothes. The she realized just how fucking cold she was. The statue of Sekhmet was no substitute for walls, warmth, company.

She was snapped out of her reverie by the sudden thump of feet on ground, the heaving, panting breath of someone just on the other side of the central space. She steeled herself and thought a moment about just running, but something told her not to. On quivering legs, her heart in her mouth, she crossed the space, and then bit her lip, staring at the figure on the ground.

"Henry?" Was that her voice? So weak and feeble sounding. Was it him? He was dripping with sweat, rasping and gasping, bloodied and bowed – and in his fist was the Deer. The very thing all this mess was about.

"Kelly?" He crawled, *crawled* towards her. "I was trying to get to y..." He could barely speak, dribbling the words out between ragged gasps. There was a strange, feral, gurgling growl from behind him. Something unnatural, something wrong, something predatory in the shadows with glinting teeth standing out against the blackness. It sniffed the air, which still had the tang of that peculiar gun smoke to it, and seemed to think twice. The Vandenbussche-thing had been killed here and even Kelly could still smell the stink of its passing in the air.

Henry scrambled closer to her and slumped at her feet, turning to watch as the blackness withdrew with a rustle of leaves, into the dense growth of the hedge. It seemed to be swallowed up and then, as quickly as it had come there was an absence, rather than a presence, and they were alone.

"Jesus fucking Christ, Henry. What the fuck is going on?" Kelly shoved her hands back through her hair and stared at him as he struggled to his feet like a newborn foal, clinging to her, all but climbing her body as he struggled upward.

"Some bloody white knight I am. You saved me. How very bloody progressive of you." He turned a moment, with a shudder, looking back at the hedge. "Those things that were after me, they were *scared* of you."

Kelly hugged him tight a moment, sagging under his weight as he hung off her, trembling, and then burst into tears against her chest. Her own tears stopped before they could burst forth and she just held him, stroking his sweat-wet hair.

"Not me, Henry. This place. Things have happened. I came to London looking for you." She kissed his forehead and pulled him back from her, taking his hand firmly in hers. "We can't stay here. I know you're tired, but we need to get away."

He nodded and swayed, pulling her, his bloodied, dirty hand a painful death grip on hers, the other wrapped around that damned deer. "I can hear traffic, over this way." From tears to taking charge. Maybe his pride had been stung. She was amazed he still had any reserve energy, but he seemed to surge with it again out of nowhere, pulling her along.

"I don't know the way out!" Those tears came close to the surface again, frustration made her eyes sting, and she stumbled as he dragged her.

"Through then. Not around." He forged into the hedge, forcing through it, snapping branches, scratching himself – and her – as he pulled her after him. How did he have the drive? Despite his exhaustion, there seemed to be an endless source of strength that let him keep pushing on. The need to survive, maybe. They destroyed the maze and swung over a low, mossy wall, out onto the street, hobbling away into the night to put the house behind them. Far behind them.

* * *

Henry sat on the cold metal lid of a recycling bin in an alley. The smell of cooking from the shop was maddening, and every hoot and yell of London's drunks wandering the streets made him think of the things that had hunted him through the other world. It kept him on edge, meant he couldn't relax, kept his adrenalin pumping.

His head hurt, leant back against the wall, and every breath was full of that enticing – and sickening – smell of frying onions and dripping fat. His hands lay upon the Deer in his lap, drawing strength from it. He hoped Kelly was all right. He didn't have any money. She still had her wallet and her cards. They were both wary of being seen, but they had to eat. So here they were.

He pulled his head forward and then slammed it back against the brick, punishing himself. He'd cried all over her when he saw her. He'd been weak, stupid, and she'd come all this way to find *him* as much as anything else. How long had he been gone anyway? He didn't know. She wasn't sure. He'd missed her so much and had fallen apart the moment he saw her. He hated himself for that. He'd wanted to seem strong, for her to see him as the victorious, conquering hero. That wasn't to be.

Kelly came back around the corner, holding a plastic bag out at arm's length as though it were radioactive. They huddled together in the shadow of the bin, tucked back from the street, out of sight. They furtively ate their kebabs and guzzled their cola, both of them needing food, drink, something to ground them. It had been the only place that was open, mercifully denying them the burden of choice. There was barely a word exchanged as they filled their bellies and tossed the packaging aside, huddling in the shadow against the cold and the glare of the world.

"Do you hate me?" His voice sounded pathetic, whiny to him. He put his arm around her waist and tucked his head into her shoulder. Even through the sweat, the fear and the sharp sting of the chilli sauce he could still smell the floral scent of her soap. Comforting, sensual, the very memories he'd been hanging onto to keep on going.

"Hate you? Why the fuck would I hate you?" She was seething, he could tell by the hiss in her voice. She didn't swear that often but they were both on edge.

"Dragging you into this. Disappearing. Getting you nearly killed. You know? Little things like that."

Kelly pulled away and punched him playfully on the arm. "I was worried about you. I'm just glad you're alive. Glad I'm alive. I can get angry at you *later,* once we're safe and all this craziness has stopped. Do you even know what's going on?" She curled against him and he felt her body heat, the softness of her breast and the little belly she had that she hated so much. The Deer seemed to throb under his hand, warm and alive, but maybe that was just his own pulse.

"I don't know that I do. I don't know that anyone does. So many people want this deer for so many reasons. That phone box is a crossroads of some kind…"

"A crossroads of bullshit and bad karma."

"Yeah, sure, you could put it like that." He laughed, a little. It felt good to laugh. "I can't help but feel we're caught up in something important. That we're important in all this somehow. Or will be. I'm not sure what I can say. How much I can say."

"Listen to you with the ego." Kelly reached over and brushed the Deer with her fingertips, touching his hand at the same time. "If I'd had this, I'd be dead now. So you did save me too, you know. Do you know what it does?"

Henry steepled his fingers against hers, intertwining them

together. He was shocked at how rough his nails and fingers had become, barely remembering how that had happened. The heels of their palms rested on the Deer.

"A guide maybe? The legends aren't consistent."

"When are they ever?" They shared a laugh together, that time.

"We're academics. What the hell are we doing?" Henry turned his head to her and squinted through his glasses. She didn't seem to have an answer.

A voice seemed to come out of nowhere, deafeningly loud with the unselfconscious roar of the stinking drunk. "Oh fuck! Schorry, I wash juscht going to have a pish!" Stinking he most certainly was, reeking sweetly of cheap cocktails. It made them both start with fear, wide-eyed in the dark as the drunkard – unbuttoned, untucked and rumpled – swayed back and forth in front of them. "Thought you needed a car to go dogging, eh? I'll leave you lovebirdsch to it, right?" He winked, leered and reeled away, bouncing off the wall on his way, in a sweary, boozy blur.

"Jesus... I thought he was one of those things that were after you." Kelly clutched his hand tighter and shook her head.

"And he thought we were..."

Kelly shoved the Deer aside from his lap and it fell to the ground, the object of all this fuss cast aside. When he turned his head to look to it, not wanting it out of his sight, Kelly grabbed his chin and turned him back to her. Kissing him with sudden intensity, warm and wet and deep.

"Fuck me," she moaned, straddling him, sudden, hot weight in his lap. He groaned and set his painful hands against her hips.

"You know, they say that nearly dying is an aphrodisiac." His hands clutched, gathering a double-handful of her bum and dragging her against him. That same pulse he felt from the Deer was now a warm knot low in his belly, and he could feel himself getting hard.

"Henry. Don't be a gentleman. I need you. Don't think. Don't rationalise. Don't lecture, that's *my* job, just please... give me this." Her voice was a growl now, edged with need. He could feel her, smell her, was hyper-aware of the taste of her lips against his own and he gave in to the inevitable.

Their hands scrambled at each other's clothes but neither of them had much patience for it. She knelt up and dragged her trousers down around her knees, leaning forward over him as he scrabbled at his own clothes. They kissed again and she swallowed his gasp with her hungry mouth as he sprang, hard, from beneath his prison of grubby denim.

He could feel the heat of her skin against his hands and radiating against his bare, hard flesh. His hands grasped, rough nails tracking red marks over her smooth, bare bottom as he thrust his tongue into her mouth, desperate to be close to her, breath hitching in his chest at his sudden eagerness.

Her hand, warm and firm, grasped him and pushed him between her legs. He felt the tickle of hair between her legs and then the exquisite, smooth split as her soft wet lips parted around him and he bucked up into her. He shivered with triumph at the sound of her muffled yelp as he pushed up, deeper, taking her to him with a yank of his hands.

Everything else faded away. She was all there was. Her hips rolled, deep and smooth over him, swallowing him up. Her tangled trousers were tight across him as she rode him, awkwardly. He became forceful, demanding, riding a surge of energy as he yanked that constricting cloth out of the way. He bucked up, hard, almost throwing her from him.

"Yesssss, like that." She was biting, famished. Tears rolled down her cheeks as his hands rode up under her top and pulled her breasts from the cups of her bra. He rolled her rock-hard nipples in his palms and crushed her tender flesh too tightly in his hands, making her hiss for a second time.

They twisted, turned, and then he had her against the wall, undignified, his jeans around his ankles, her nails in his shoulders, mouths on each other biting, licking, kissing as he thrust up into her with abandon. The street was a world away. The only witness the mute deer as they fucked with frantic desire and her feet dug into his back, the short heels of her shoes painful against him, like spurs.

He gave a bullish grunt and shoved into her harder, lifting her against the wall. The brickwork scraped her bare flesh, red scratches appearing as he pressed up and stopped abruptly. A deep shudder seemed to rise through him from the balls of his feet to his scalp, making his hair prickle. The hot knot in his belly snapped apart as he came, hard, deep inside her, kissing her neck, feeling the heat of her flush as she gave a bashful little whimper and clenched herself around him.

* * *

Kelly huddled against him, feeling his warmth. He'd always been a gentle lover before. It was nice to see something more. In such a place as this, such a time as this, perhaps even more so. She wrinkled her nose as she huddled to him, pressing her thighs together at the uncomfortable trickle she felt there. Weirdly, she felt like she should apologize for what had happened, but it seemed like any words now would spoil the moment. At least they had each other.

He broke the silence. That made her smile. He was *always* the one to do so, and yet she was the lecturer, the talker. "We should try to get back to the airport. Get the hell out of here."

There was a fog now, hazing their view of the street. It seemed odd, this far from the river, in this day and age. A real London fog, strange but somehow fitting. It would help hide them.

"That's as good a plan as any. I don't know where else we could go to, or who we could get to help." She reached out to the deer beside them and picked it up, looking into its graven little face as she shifted to sit up. "This is what they all want. It's the only leverage we have, dangerous as that is."

He sniffed and made a grimace. "What's that smell?" He shrugged and furrowed his brow, nodding at her words. "Maybe we should wait until morning. Hardly any cabs around at this time of night, and they won't risk much in front of people."

She shifted the deer to one hand, turned her wrist and looked at her watch. "Only a couple of hours now until the sun comes up. Think we can hide here until then?"

There were footsteps in the roiling fog and a shady figure resolved itself, barely, a glowing coal lighting up a hazy glow like a halo in the mist. Henry shifted and clambered up to his feet, knee joints clicking painfully as he did so. "Hey, we're *not* dogging. Can't you piss somewhere else?"

"Och, and there I was hoping for a quick one off the wrist." The voice was cruel, sarcastic and hard. The coal glowed again and the fog thickened. She realized she knew what that smell was.

Dope.

"Henry..." she called out to him, but the smoke got in her throat, blinded her, made her voice seem small. All she could see was a dim, shadowy outline as the figure with the joint reared back and then smacked its forehead into Henry with a crack like a fairground ball hitting a coconut.

Henry went down with a grunt, clutching his head, crawling around on the ground as the smoke whirled. She picked herself up, panicked, every other discomfort washed away in a rush. Croaking and coughing in the smoke, trying to see the man by the glowing end of his spliff.

"Who are you? What do you want? Why can't you leave us alone?"

His voice came again, close, intimate, his arm around her throat before she could react, his hand at her wrist, thumb pressed between the bones, making them grind painfully. "I'm yer fuckin' minicab, love. I'm the wingman." He laughed at some private joke. "I'm here to take ye somewhere special, an wi'oot yer loverboy there. Y'ken? You've got a pressin' engagement."

He jerked her hand high and dragged a ring across it. There was a sharp pain, a spray of blood and they were gone.

In blackness, she realized to her horror that her hand still clutched the deer, and that Henry was left behind.

47. The Anglesey Deer
Part II:
Kill The Next Person
by Gethin A. Lynes

Henry pulled himself to his feet. His head was pounding where the little Glaswegian had nutted him. He touched the spot gingerly. There was a lump already, and his fingers came away dark with blood.

"Fucking Scots," he muttered, leaning against the wall next to the bin where moments ago he'd had Kelly's legs wrapped around him. *Oh God, Kelly.* He couldn't help thinking that this time she was gone for good. What could he do? He had nothing. No one, and no Deer, to help.

He felt an anger rising inside him. This was all getting beyond a joke. Ancient Welsh druids, leprechauns, feral Romans, wild chavs, mazes, deer, fogs, and now to add insult to injury, Kelly had been stolen by a fucking magical, stoned Scotsman. *Fuck the Anglesey Deer, fuck the Scots, and fuck Kelly for getting me into this shit.*

No more tears, no more frustration, he was done with all of it. He was going back to the College, packing his things and going home, and if anyone got in his way, he was going to fucking kill them.

Who am I kidding? I have to find Kelly. He stood there in the dark alley, with no idea how he was going to do it, only that he would. *But I will fucking kill the next person who tries any shit with me.*

Just as he thought that, a little glow flared in the fog ahead of him, as someone dragged on a cigarette... or a spliff. The anger blazed in him again. He grabbed a bottle that was sitting in the top of the bin at his side and, gripping it by the neck, he smashed the bottom against the wall.

Brandishing the jagged glass, he stepped toward the light. "Come on, you little Scots cunt, I'll fucking do you."

The light came toward him, a tall figure resolving itself from the fog, hands raised in supplication. "Easy there, Hank my lad," the other man said, clearly no Scotsman. "Just want a little chat, okay?"

"It's not fucking Hank, it's Henry – and who the fuck are you?"

"The name's Maz. I can help you."

Henry hesitated, not at all trusting what the man said, but knowing that he needed any and all help he could get. Why did his voice sound slightly familiar? "You can help me get Kelly back?"

The light of the other man's cigarette flared again, and he reached up to take it from the corner of his mouth. He exhaled, smoke drifting out of his nostrils. "There's no coming back from those people, mate. She's dead."

48. Say That Again
by Salomé Jones

Amber picked up a kitchen chair and carried it into the lounge. She put it down next to the one Stuart was sitting in. He was in front of his desk, writing.

"You know I dreamed that you were a DJ the other night. You got a lot of girls." She sat down in the chair and looked over at his screen. His novel.

He grinned and put a hand on her knee. "Maybe I should change careers."

"Before you make that leap I should tell you in the dream I also tried to stab you with a kitchen knife." She put her hand over his where it rested on her leg.

"Good to know. I think I'll stay right here then, boss." He raised an eyebrow at her.

She reached up to stroke the eyebrow, a tiny streak of blond stuck on his forehead like a sleepy caterpillar. "I can't believe I ever thought you looked like him."

"Who?"

She shifted her focus an inch to meet his eyes. "No-one. Old boyfriend." She shook her head. "Hey, if I were to ask you when our anniversary was, what would you say?"

"Is this one of those girl tests?" He squinted at her.

"Ha ha!" *If only it was.* "It's just that there are different ways to look at it."

"I see what you mean. So it could be the eleventh of May, the twenty-second of August or erm… September something. Twenty-seventh."

She smiled. "And why those?"

"Oh yeah." Stuart rolled his eyes. "This is one of those girl tests, right? May. Our first official date. Twenty-two August. And the twenty-seventh of September. The day I moved in here with you."

Oh my god, he remembered all those dates? "Where have you been all my life?" She grinned.

"Or you know…" Stuart was looking at her intently.

"What?" She shook her head again. 'Stop it. You're going to give me the giggles."

"I was just thinking, it could be today." He swivelled his chair around to face her.

"What could be today? Our anniversary?" *Twenty-fourth of April. What could that be?*

Stuart fidgeted with some papers on his desk, opened and closed a drawer without turning his body to the desk.

"No, don't tell me." Amber put a hand on his arm. "I can get this." She stared out the window, her eyes tracking the lights of the cars moving down one of the dark streets far below. *First meeting, first date, he moved in… Well, the only other thing that could be an anniversary would be–* She focussed on him again and saw him watching her.

His hands were open, palm up on his lap. He was holding a little white velvet rabbit with a red bow under its chin. "I was trying to wait to do this 'til the novel was finished."

Amber realised her mouth was open and closed it. "Stuart."

"You should look at it before you say anything." He offered her the rabbit.

"Where did this come from?" She scooped the rabbit up, its velvety fur soft against her fingers. It was lightweight, but it wasn't stuffed. She could feel its hard shape under the velvet.

"I bought it."

"It's adorable." She rubbed the rabbit's little pot belly. There was a ridge in the middle. When she looked more closely she saw a line around it. It dawned on her. "Does this… open?" She pushed back on the rabbit's ears. It split, the top half folding back along the midline. Inside, half submerged in its satiny insides, was a ring, bright with stones. "Oh my god, Stuart."

"I hope it's the right size. J and 1/2, right?"

"How'd you know that?"

"I've been paying attention." He touched her knee. "So this

is where the question goes. I've tried to come up with something original for weeks. I just can't seem to do it justice. Old cliches and all that." Stuart broke off, a soft smile on his face.

Amber closed her eyes and took a deep breath.

"Will you stand on a hilltop in front of a huge crowd of people and promise to live with me forever?" Stuart whispered.

"Say that again," Amber breathed.

Stuart cleared his throat. "Will you—"

Amber laughed and opened her eyes. "Yes. Oh my god, yes." She stood up and threw her arms around his neck.

His muffled voice said something she couldn't understand, and she realised that perhaps he couldn't breathe with his face crushed against her chest like that. She let him go. "What?"

Now it was Stuart's turn to grin. "I said, 'Really?'"

"Yes, really." She kissed him, slowly, her hand against his cheek. "We should celebrate this. Let's have some wine." She went into the kitchen to look, flipping through the cupboard where there was often a spare bottle, and then the fridge. She went back into the lounge. "I guess there's nothing in the flat. But not to worry, I'll just run over the road and grab something. Red for love."

She flung her jacket on and grabbed her purse. "I'll be back in five minutes." She looked at her cell phone. 11:45. That couldn't be right. An odd chill crept up her spine.

"What's wrong?" Stuart asked.

"What time do you have?" Amber blinked at him.

"Erm, quarter to ten."

"I thought for a second it was too late to buy alcohol. The time on my phone is off for some reason." Amber flashed her teeth at him. "See you soon." She shut the door behind her.

Her feet barely seemed to touch the ground as she exited the lift. James sat at his usual post. He nodded to her.

"See you in a minute, James," she said. "I'm just going to—"

"I know," said James.

Amber laughed. "What?"

"Psychic." James tapped his forehead with two fingers.

"Oh, he told you, did he?" She shook her head and waved as she went out the door.

She was standing on the corner waiting for the light to change when she heard the sound. It took a moment for her mind to single it out from the traffic noises. A short, high-pitched ping. It was then that she remembered her dream.

I'm not going to look, she thought. *Not now.*

The light changed and she ran across the street, around the corner and into the little shop. The papers were all screaming about some philanthropist who'd been found dead in Hampstead. Drowned in gold? Was that even possible? A tabloid dream-story, anyway. She pushed it out of her mind. She rarely bought wine in here, given the outrageous markups, but she knew the layout and walked straight to the right section. A bottle of burgundy offered itself to her at the front of the shelf. As anticipated, it was a bit pricey, but she took it anyway. *Special occasion.*

While the man behind the counter rang her up, she glanced around. She seemed to be the only customer in the store. She couldn't remember that ever happening before.

"Cigar and chocolate bar this time?" said the cashier.

She focussed on him. "What?" She felt flushed, for some reason.

"Twenty-one pounds sixty."

Amber gave him the money and took her bag. Obviously she needed to get more sleep.

Just as she got outside, she heard it again. The ping of a text from the other phone in her handbag. She rummaged around inside it, unable to see in the dark.

"Damn it. Do *not* do this to me now. You're spoiling the best moment of my life." She breathed out, a heavy sigh of resignation, and pulled the mobile phone out of her bag.

The screen of the found phone was bright. *You know what to do.*

"Yes," she muttered. "Go home and have a toast with my fiancé, that's what." She dropped the phone back into the bag, but before she could zip it, it pinged again. She peered inside. *He is our gift to you.*

"Okay, *that* is it." She zipped her bag and began walking, picking up speed as she went. "I've had enough. We're going to put an end to this right now."

Within two minutes she was in sight of the phone box. In the yellow interior glow, she could see someone talking on the phone. The door was blocked open. She slowed slightly, watching for signs that the person was nearly done with the call.

When she got closer she could tell it was a man in a blue suit. Some kind of hipster outfit. It reminded her of something. He was deep in conversation and didn't seem to notice her arrival.

She paced around for a couple of minutes before she lost patience and tapped on the door. "Excuse me."

The man turned.

Amber froze. It was *him*. Jon Sutton. "You!"

"Hold on a minute, mate," Jon said into the phone. "I'm nearly done here, darlin'," he told her in a low voice.

"You're done here all right. This was you all along, wasn't it?"

"Hang on." He held the phone against his chest. "Do you mind? This is an important call."

"I don't care. You are going to explain this to me right now."

He lifted the phone to his ear again. "I've got some mad bird trying to get into the phone box, mate. I'll have to call you back. Yeah. Five minutes." Jon put the phone back in its cradle. "Do you need to make an emergency call?"

"I want to know why you've been sending me SMSes." Amber shoved the found phone in Jon's face. "It's not enough that you bloody abandoned me. Now you won't leave me alone."

"Who the hell are you?" Jon cocked his eyebrows at her.

"You *bastard*." Without thinking, Amber drew back her fist and swung. It connected with the middle of Jon's face and he fell backwards, flailing. He grabbed her arm in the process and pulled her back with him, dragging her into the phone box.

The door flopped shut with a bang. There was an odd flash of heat and sound and they were falling, flying through the dark. She screamed and screamed and screamed. When she stopped screaming, she was still falling. She couldn't see Jon anymore, but she could hear him, howling as he fell.

It took a moment for her to realise, but her jacket was lighting up the space around her. She could see the phone still clutched in her hand. She touched the screen and waved it around. She could see Jon now. He was looking straight at her.

"Why'd you do that? I don't even know you," he screeched.

Amber glowered at him. "Say that again."

"I don't *fucking* know you."

Amber lashed out with her foot and missed. "You had better hope I don't survive this."

49. Cat Amongst Your Pigeons?
by Gethin A. Lynes

Lorna stood in the doorway a moment, taking a quick survey of the room and letting the sound of her footsteps on the wooden floor die away. The building was quiet. Enough light came in through the grubby window to show her the solitary trail of footprints she had tracked through the dust on the floor. No one else had come up here in a long time – a good sign.

She walked over to the window and, standing carefully to one side, looked out. Below her, a waterlogged park populated with skeletal trees disappeared beneath the murky water of the Thames. The farther trees were little more than twisted fingers of rotting wood clawing at the surface. Lorna found it amusing that it was still called the river. It was a bloody inland sea.

On the south bank, she could see the crumbling towers of some old castle or palace and, beyond, the islands that used to be part of the city. Nothing moved, apart from the water. Not for the first time, she wondered why they bothered to call it New London. It wasn't *new*, it was a dilapidated shithole. Half of it was under water, and the half that wasn't was pocked with the scars of battle, and clogged with broken bodies and the relics of former glory.

Lorna liked it though, in spite of the state of the place. She sought out those reminders of another age, a different city. The once-moving staircases. Occasional street-side cafés, perfectly preserved markers of a carefree existence. The rust-bitten cars and other dead vehicles that used to run on petrol, in a time when people moved with purpose, not merely because they had to. The crumbling red phone box she'd seen when she arrived still raised in her a longing for a quaint, slow life she had never known, could barely imagine.

It was nothing like Glasgow, with its seething mass of steel and slavery. Up there, it was a constant drone of hammers and machinery, muffled by the concrete walls of heavily guarded factories and compounds. New London was quiet. The silence here was broken only by the rumble of Overwatch patrols passing by, the occasional explosion of fighting, or, here and there, a solitary scream.

Lorna had come here to disappear. Her old Granda's stories made London into a maze, teeming with people. A place to get lost in. But that had been London, and this was New London. The people had gone, or died, or both. There was no one to hide amongst, and there were pigeons, so many pigeons. Lorna knew all about the pigeons. They were surveillance droids, Overwatch's eyes, everywhere, ignored by everyone. Maybe once upon a time they had just been birds, but when was the last time anyone had seen a baby pigeon?

Maybe her Granda didn't know anyway. He'd spent most of his life in Market Foxborough. Before the world had changed. Before her mother and father had disappeared. She shook her head. *Nae use thinking about that.*

Outside, the light was turning, the buildings south of the water becoming indistinct through the grimy window. Lorna didn't come near the water very often – too much chance of getting stuck, or caught by Overwatch – but sometimes she needed to get away from smaller streets, to look over the water and see a distant horizon, the promise of something different.

The buildings here did have the advantage of being mostly empty though, thanks to their proximity to Overwatch. Lorna stepped away from the window, careful even in the growing dusk not to move too quickly. Do nothing that might get noticed. An ancient, tarnished brass bed sat against one wall, its mattress dusty and covered in dark stains. Lorna took off her worn backpack and sat down.

She rummaged in the pack, pulling out a ragged map of the city and her solar torch. She hadn't laid it out to charge in over a week, and its light was dull and grey, but it was enough to see by. Just.

The map showed London before the Overwatch propaganda machine had tacked a New on the front of it. It was covered in the alterations that Lorna had made, showing where streets had changed, where buildings no longer existed, either swallowed by the water or razed by fighting. She studied it carefully, planning her route to tomorrow's Underground stations.

There was rumour of an escape. People who had made a home in the old Tube network, safe from the death and prying eyes of the world above. But no-one knew if it was true, or how to get in. Every station that Lorna had checked was sealed, solid steel doors welded across the entrances. It seemed the sort of thing that Overwatch would do, but she couldn't be sure. Were they keeping whatever was down there in, or was the Underground keeping Overwatch out?

Then there were the inexplicable posters, too. Every Underground door that Lorna had come up against bore the same strange notice, which read:

Cat Amongst Your Pigeons?

Help can be found
at the corner of ******** & ********

Beneath the writing was a photograph of a motley bunch, posed in front of an old red phone box. They seemed ill-suited to each other and were mostly nondescript, though a few stood out. One was a hard-faced man with a flame dancing atop a raised finger. There were a pair of identical men at one end who looked at each other with perturbed expressions. Then there was a sad-seeming young woman in the middle, giving off a ghostly glow that cast a pale light on the others.

Unfortunately, the street names were always obscured, as though someone had gone round to every single Tube station and rubbed them off. Lorna could make no sense of it. Why would anyone rub out just the names? Why not tear down the whole poster?

She stowed her map and torch again, untwisted the old rubber band that tied her knotted hair back, and lay down on the mattress. Her stomach ached, tight with hunger, but she refused to turn to the box that contained her meagre supply of food. Tomorrow was going to be a hard day, and she would be in more need of something to eat come the morning.

Lying there in the dark, Lorna wondered if she even wanted to find her way into the Underground. Did she want to forgo daylight, fresh air and the romantic remnants of old London for the dubious safety of the tunnels? Wasn't she content enough skulking around the streets of the Covent Garden Enclave? She was fascinated by their macabre rituals of looting and burning the dead, by the dance of exchange around Monmouth Street where – against all probability – coffee could still be obtained.

She was astonished at how highly prized it was, when real sustenance was so scarce. But people came for it anyway. The only currency that existed now was submission, and the rulers of the Enclave exacted it, brutally, from the steady supply of caffeine junkies. Even Lorna had enjoyed the occasional cup, though whatever pleasure she'd given to the grizzled Monmouth guard who supplied her, he'd returned her in equal measure.

No, she probably wouldn't give it up for the darkness below. But she had to circle around through the ruins of Buckingham Palace to get back to safer territory anyway, so she might as well check out the Tube stations on the way. Besides, maybe she'd find that red phone box again.

As she drifted off into an uneasy sleep, she wondered if it was the same red phone box as the one in the posters.

* * *

Lorna looked down from the window of a high loft. There was a small park below her, and then the rubble surrounding Victoria Station. She must have been mad to come here. The station was some sort of depot for Overwatch vehicles. All the buildings in a wide circle around it had been torn down, to provide a clear view of anything approaching.

Lorna had been in the loft for hours, unsure of what to do next. She was never going to get near the Tube entrances. That morning, Pimlico had provided the usual results – sealed entrances and posters with the street names removed. It had taken a good part of the day to pick her way warily to Victoria. She had wasted the remaining daylight up here, frozen in indecision.

Floodlights were coming on at the station, but Lorna was

morbidly fascinated by a flock of pigeons in the small park. Heads bobbing, they pecked around in the gloom, amongst the broken bodies that littered the grass. Victims of Victoria Station's soldiery. As she watched, a mangy black cat detached itself from the shadow of a tree, creeping toward the pigeons, belly to the ground. Even from this distance, Lorna could see how ancient and scrawny the beast was, and was surprised at its remaining grace.

Unnoticed, the cat got within a foot of a knot of pigeons, crouched behind some unidentifiable portion of a person. Then it sprang. It landed in the middle of the birds, claws bared, dealing bloody death on all sides. The pigeons, however, took no notice, and went on wandering about, heads bobbing away.

She was right. *Fucking surveillance droids!* As she looked on, the cat sat back on its haunches, uncertain of how to proceed amongst such oblivious victims. Then a flicker of light from the street corner caught her attention. A man in a long black trench coat stood there, the glow of a cigarette bright as he drew on it. He was staring straight at her.

Lorna ducked away from the window, aware that it was already too late. She snatched her backpack from the floor and made for the door of the loft. Booted feet were running up the stairs, intimidatingly urgent.

Without thinking, she sprinted back to the far end of the long room, bunching her backpack around her fist as she ran. At the end of the room, a recessed window looked out over a sharply sloping roof. She rammed the backpack through the glass and quickly climbed out. The next building was not far, and she could see a small balcony a floor down. She took two bounds down the steep tiles and leapt, thrusting the backpack out in front of her.

She hit the balcony slightly too high, her backpack punching through the window above it, and caught her shins painfully on the sill. She collapsed in, across a desk that sat inside, sliding across it to land, hard, on her elbow.

She lay still for a moment, cut and bruised and bleeding, before forcing herself to her feet and bolting out of the room. It was dark in the passageway, but she found her way to a staircase and fled down the stairs, taking them four or five at a time.

When she spilled out into the street, she paused. A few doors down was where the rubble started. The man in the black coat was gone. Lorna bolted across the road and through the park, dodging corpses, kicking unconcerned pigeons from her path. The cat was nowhere to be seen. On the far side, she turned away from the station and ran to the end of the block. She knew that somewhere ahead and to the right was Buckingham, and perhaps cover in the ruins, but the street she was on was wide and open.

She went left, and then ducked right into a narrow arched alley. Somewhere behind her a rifle shot rang out. She ran on through a wilderness of broken buildings and narrow lanes, navigating on blind instinct, the soles of her shoes slapping loudly on stretches of pavement. Eventually she emerged on the far side onto a wide, dark avenue lined with trees. Away to her right she could see the dark mass of the Buckingham Gardens.

After dashing across the road, Lorna slowed to a trot, making her way cautiously along the street in the darkness under the trees. Then up ahead, at the junction of another street, she noticed a red phone box, almost hidden in deep shadow.

Could this be *the* phone box? She ran again. Looking quickly around, and seeing no-one, she pulled open the door. There was someone inside. The pungent smell of piss wafted over her, and pooled about her shoes.

Lorna stepped back. "You fucking schemie bastard. Get tae fuck. G'aun, get."

The ratty wee man inside started in surprise, and quickly did up his fly. He turned around, tugging his coat closed over... a severed arm?

"Aye, doll. Sorry, sorry," he whined, his voice thick and apologetic. Another fucking Glaswegian. He shuffled out. "Sorry, hen," he said again, and scuttled away, hunched and holding his coat closed.

Ignoring the smell, and the puddle, Lorna stepped inside the dark phone box and closed the door.

* * *

Angus walked away, just glad the mad bitch hadnae tried tae get his precious arm away frae him like the others. There was a sudden bright flash in the darkness behind him. A wee bit feared it might be soldiers, Angus turned about.

The street was dark. The red phone box and the mad bird inside it were gone.

'A mangy black cat detached itself from the shadow of a tree, creeping toward the pigeons.'

50. Two Talbots
by James 'Grim' Desborough

Talbot shambled up to the phone box. He stank of musty sweat, and the sour stench of alcohol wafted from his pores. His shoes were a scuffed mess, with only tiny scraps of the original leather clinging to them, the laces tied and re-tied together into a chain of crazy knots. What was left of his cheap suit was worn through, almost transparent at his elbows and knees. He was stained and ragged, his hair grown out to his collar, a tufty beard sprouting in all directions from his chin. His skin had become sallow and stained with dirt from his time on the street.

"Fugginbastah," he muttered, his head smacking against the front of the phone box and squeaking as his skin rubbed down the glass. "S'all your fault... everything... took *everything*."

Talbot swallowed back the bitter bile at the back of his throat and wedged his foot against the door of the phone box, trying to scrabble it open like a cat scratching at a litter box. He scraped off one of those few bits of leather left on his shoe and wedged his toe in the door, trying to prise it open, struggling and swaying as he nearly fell over with the effort. It didn't occur to him to open the door with his hand. Instead he used his foot, his knee and his head to lever it open, painfully slowly, then leaned – off kilter – against the door to keep it open.

For a moment he supported the weight of his hands on the stinking, striped scrap that used to be a tie. The knot pulled so tight it looked like it was about to split the silk atom. Then he fumbled his hands lower, untying his broken belt, unzipping his trousers, fumbling his cock out of the filthy rag that used to be his boxer shorts and clumsily holding it. A grunt and he began to laugh as he pissed into the phone box, a stinking stream as dark as stout and so pungent it was a wonder that the concrete floor of the box didn't start bubbling and melting.

"Ha! How do you like that, you life-stealing bastard? You cunting fuckbucket, huh? How do you like it? How do *you* like being pissed on?"

A couple passed him by and he flipped them the bird, or tried to, somehow getting his fingers muddled up. By the time he'd straightened himself out and found his middle finger they were gone but he was still pissing. He twisted his head back to concentrate and was surprised to see the rancid stream splashing on a pair of boots. The stream became a trickle and then stopped.

"Oh... sorry, didn't know there was anyone in there."

"There wasn't."

The voice was disgusted, edged, strong. Even without the crackle he recognised the sound that had tormented him down to this wretched half-existence.

It was his own.

Talbot looked up into the face of... Talbot. He scrambled back, hurriedly cramming his penis back into his trousers and fumbling with the zip, one hand thrust into the pocket to hold them up. "Get the fuck away from me!"

"I can't." Talbot stepped out of the booth and shut the door gently, shaking the rancid droplets of piss from his shoes. "Do you have *any* idea how hard it is to get decent shoes? No, of course you don't..."

"GET AWAY!" Talbot tumbled back, skinning his palms on the asphalt and scrambling to move away. "We'll explode!"

"What?" Talbot cocked his head to the side in a crow-like gesture.

"Explode! I've seen it in science fiction, two of us in the same place, the same time. We can't touch!" Adrenalin had sobered Talbot up pretty damn quickly, and he scrambled back again as the other Talbot took a step forward, as though he was made of acid.

"Oh, well, no, it doesn't work like that. We're the same but we're not. We have... uh... a different quantum frequency, so we can exist at the same time and the same place without any problems. See?" Talbot leapt forward and grabbed Talbot firmly by the leg as he tried to pull back again.

There was no explosion.

"Oh, oh, thank fuck." Talbot practically shat himself with sudden relaxation when he realised he wasn't going to die, but his relief rapidly turned to anger. He kicked out with his shoe and cracked it against Talbot's shin, sending the other man stumbling back with a hiss of pain.

"What the fuck? Wasn't pissing on my shoes enough?"

"No." Talbot got up onto his feet, shaking with rage. "You destroyed my life. I should bloody well kill you!"

"Bloody? You were swearing up a storm a minute ago. When did you become such a pussy?" Talbot grinned and the two men faced off against each other. "Just wait a minute and hear me out..."

"I guess I owe myself that much." Nastily aware of what a run-down, destitute tramp he'd become, Talbot brushed self-consciously at the remains of his suit and then ran his hand back through his greasy hair.

"We need you."

"Who needs me?"

"We do... Look, it's complicated, but we're what passes for 'the good guys'."

"The good guys? What do you think I am, twelve?" Talbot sneered, fidgeting and stepping back and forth.

"You used to believe in good and bad, didn't you?" Talbot stabbed an accusing finger at him. "What happened to change that?"

"Life isn't good or bad. You have to compromise. You have to see the world in shades of grey because that's what it's like! You just have to cope as best you can." Talbot ground his teeth, the two men facing off closer and closer as though they were about to fight.

"I never compromised." Talbot grunted. "I lived *my* life how I wanted. I went after what I wanted and I fought for what I believed was right."

"Oh yeah? How's that working out for you?" Talbot thrust out his chin and glared accusingly at Talbot, detecting a hint of weakness.

"Not so great," Talbot deflated slightly in admitting it. "A string of failed relationships, some prison time, never any money. There's things I might have done differently – but that's why we need you."

"What, you're jealous of my life?" Talbot scoffed and shoved Talbot back with a grubby hand.

"In a lot of ways, yeah." Talbot sighed and rubbed his temples. "Listen to me. I never took responsibility for a damn thing beyond myself in my life. You learned to be dutiful. You took responsibility. You did a job you hated for the money you needed to get by, to keep a missus you didn't really love happy. You even tried to start a family, for the love of the fuck. That gives me chills. I might have fought the power, but you," he grabbed Talbot by his grubby shoulders and shook him, "you learned to be a functional, thinking adult."

Despite himself, Talbot was flattered – for a moment – but then he bristled and shrugged out of Talbot's grip. "Yeah? Well, you fucked that up the arse, didn't you? I'm alone, jobless and on the street all because of you. I thought I was going mad. Maybe I have gone mad, talking to myself in the street."

"You weren't happy, were you?"

"No," Talbot spat out bitterly. "Neither are you."

Talbot nodded. "You're right."

"So what now then?"

"Between us, we're a whole person. We're different paths on what we could have become when we were younger. I'm the best of the passion, the uncompromising will, the creativity, the moral compass. You're the best of the duty, the determination, the perseverance, the willingness to compromise when it's needed. You know how to get on with people, to make a commitment."

"And we're each the worst of ourselves, too." Talbot ran his hand back through his hair again, remembering how much he stank.

"Yep. That's why we need each other."

"What... are we going to merge into one person or something? I'm not sure that I want to... disappear."

"That's not quite what will happen. We each need to take on the best of each other. We're required, to make a difference to something that really matters, but we have to both be the best of ourselves."

"What makes you think we can make a difference?" Talbot shifted to the side, next to the phone box, sitting on the wall while he gathered his thoughts.

"You know how they say one good man can make a difference?" Talbot sat down next to Talbot and put his arm around him, withdrawing it as the smell gave him second thoughts.

"Yeah."

"It's bullshit. It's not the good man, it's the opportunity, it's the place."

"So then... we're not needed? You're not making any bloody sense."

"We're the ones with the opportunity. We're the ones who can grasp the moment and make a difference."

"Fine. It's not like I have anywhere else to go." Talbot let his head hang, resigned now to his fate, hissing as Talbot tore a clump of hair out of his head. "Christ man! What the fuck?"

"Sorry." Talbot held the little clump of greasy hair in his fingers while he rummaged in his jacket. "You can tear mine out if you want."

"No, that's okay, you crazy bastard." Talbot stared, disbelieving, as Talbot tore out a clump of his own hair, mixing them together and fishing back in his other pocket, taking out a little sack-cloth doll with an unlaced belly. He shoved the hair inside and drew the laces tight. "Right, let's see if this voodoo bullshit works, shall we?"

Talbot frowned and watched as Talbot took out a lighter and set the little sack-doll alight. It caught with surprising swiftness, and sparkled as it burned. The stink was remarkable – burning hair never smelled good, but there was something else about the stench that made it even worse.

Once it was consumed, they both stood up.

"Do you feel any different?" Talbot straightened the scrap of Talbot's tie as he said it, looking at him curiously.

"Yes... I feel stronger somehow. I think the word is... cocksure." Talbot thrust his hands into his pockets and glanced back towards the box. "What about you?"

"I feel like we should get going. I don't want to leave my friends alone. I'm worried about them." Talbot glanced nervously towards the phone box as well. "We shouldn't waste any time."

"I can't go and meet your friends looking like this." Talbot wrinkled his nose and gestured up and down at himself. He didn't really need to say anything at this point.

"My clothes will fit you, and you can have a bath at my place."

"Where is your place?"

Talbot hooked his thumb towards the phone box. Together, they walked to it, crammed inside its stinking interior and shut the door.

51. We Don't Like Cricket
by Gethin A. Lynes

Maz stood at a crook in the path, the collar of his trench coat turned up against the wind and rain. He watched the old man, thin and rugged in the chill twilight, walk up the muddy lane from the village. He flicked the damp end of his cigarette into the gloom, and waited.

The old man looked right at Maz, or right through him, as he turned the bend in the path and continued on. He passed close enough that, standing in the deeper shadows beneath the trees, Maz could see the rain beading his heavy coat, could smell the pub on his breath. Maz stared after him. He walked with a slow, steady pace, followed by the suck of his green wellingtons in the mud. There was something familiar about him, something vague that Maz couldn't put his finger on, but then, it had been an age since he had been here.

When the old fella was out of sight, Maz stepped out from beneath the trees, and made his way down the narrow lane toward the village. He'd loved this lane as a boy, the narrow track between the old rotting fence on one side and the crumbling stone wall on the other. Walking beneath the twisted arch of trees, on his way up to the woods, Maz used to pretend he was entering a different world, somewhere magical, where chalk monsters emerged from the shallow pit of the old quarry, and Old Crow helped him get back the magic arrows he was forever losing in the treetops.

Now as he trudged down through the dark and mud, Maz felt he was coming back from another world, but this one was an altogether different kind of magical – grim and callous.

The last of the light had gone when he reached the bottom of the lane, the muddy rut turning to the soft crunch of gravel underfoot. Where it emerged from between two high-walled houses into the village, Maz stood at the edge of the footpath and looked up and down the dark street. Hambledon on a Saturday night. Dead quiet. He, it appeared, was the only thing that had changed.

He dug another cigarette out of his pocket, and stuck it between his lips. A small flame sprang up on his palm, and he quickly cupped his hands around it. There might be no-one about, but there was no point in drawing undue attention to himself. He lit the cigarette and stepped out into the street.

Even to Maz's preternatural vision, the village was dark. He spent too much time lurking in shadows amid the ubiquitous lights of London and all the other cities he travelled. He'd forgotten just how black the night got, out here where there were no street lights.

The drizzle muted the thud of his boots on the pavement, but even so, he walked quietly, listening. He was confident he'd made it out of London unseen, but in the world he inhabited, there were no certainties. There were a lot of players in this game, and his pretend employer Amow had more eyes than anyone knew. *Old bastard*, Maz thought. *Used to love cats. Now I can't fucking trust a single one of them.* He appeared to be Amow's prized employee, but he still didn't trust him for an instant.

Further into the village, where the houses crept momentarily to the edge of the road, and the blackness was broken by light spilling from their windows, Maz passed The Vine, the old sixteenth century inn. He used to get taken there for Sunday Roast with his friends Nick and Simon Huntingdon-Smythe, their father Charles... *Shit.* Maz stopped, looking back the way he had come, back toward the lane. *That was Charles.*

He stood for a moment, staring back along the road, filled with a flood of memories he'd thought long dried up. And then he realised he was smiling. He shook his head. *Fuck. I shouldn't have come back*, he thought, and turned around. But he'd had to come back, he had to see Charles. He was playing a dangerous game with Amow, and he had to get a better understanding of the stakes.

He walked on, leaving the glow and the muted laughter of the pub behind. The night was soon dark as coal again, dotted here and there with the warm light of windows, once more set a way back from the road.

He'd lied, of course, when he'd told Amow he knew where to find Henry. But finding things was one of Maz's specialties, and

ELLIS, DEDOPULOS, WICKLINE et al.

things included people. Despite the man's supposed evasiveness, he hadn't had much difficulty. But what he found when he collected the bloke was not what he expected.

There was power in the man, though Henry seemed unable, or unwilling, to see it – which suited Maz perfectly. Much easier to keep a man under control if he thought himself a weakling. Holed up in one of his many safe houses in London, there had been plenty of time to question the man, to determine the nature or the source of the power that emanated from him. There was no doubt it had come from or through the Anglesey Deer, but that in itself didn't give him much to go on.

The Deer was gone, and over the time Maz kept Henry hidden away, the residue of its power within him had not seemed to have waned at all. What did that mean exactly? What was that power? And what of the Deer itself? Was its power diminished by what it had poured into Henry?

Old Charles was the only person he could think of that might have some answers – or, at least, who might have some answers without any vested interests that involved staking him to the floor in an industrial cool-room.

Lost in reflection, he had stopped listening to the world around him. He came to the bus stop. As he passed the old wooden shelter, a great phlegmy cough hacked at him out of the blackness. He started violently. An old man sat hunched on the bench. Maz turned to look, almost stopped to ask him if he was all right, and then hurried on.

A few moments later, where the old man had been, a black cat sat watching Maz disappear into the night.

In the heart of the village, he turned off the main road, and walked up to the Church of St. Peter and St. Paul. He stepped past the low gate to the churchyard, and cut across the cemetery. Another of his favourite haunts as a boy. He walked quickly now, unwilling to dredge up any more distractions, any more memories.

At the edge of the graveyard, he turned up the pale line of Church Lane, barely visible beneath the cloudless sky. The farther he went along the lane, the slower he walked, reluctant steps offering his head every chance to change his mind. Eventually he came to a halt.

A low, cast iron fence ran beside the road on his left, twined with ivy and struck through with branches of thick shrubs. Where he'd stopped, the fence was broken by a narrow gravel driveway, the gate left open. To one side of the gate, the fence bore a white sign, its black letters barely discernible in the dark. But Maz could make out enough to know it still read 'Fishbein'.

He shook his head. *Of all the names you could think of,* he thought. *You pick Fishbein. What a shit name.* Of all the fucked up things he'd put up with from his parents, choosing the name Fishbein had pissed him off almost the most. What the fuck was it with parents and names? Did they really not remember how vicious school kids were? They might as well have called him Michael Hunt.

Banishing the past once more, he looked down the driveway to the dark, silent house. He hesitated a moment, and then, with a deep breath, walked past the open gate and down to the front door. He reached up and, hoping he'd be wrong, found the key on the doorsill. He let himself quietly into the house and closed the door behind him.

At the far end of the driveway, two black cats sat and watched the door close. They turned and looked at each other, and then vanished.

* * *

At the creak of movement in the hall, Maz's eyes flicked open. He sat stone still, listening. The slow sound of soft shoes coming down the stairs. He waited, silent, not breathing. The steps reached the bottom, and shuffled into the kitchen. He heard the tap run, the kettle being filled. He let out a long, relieved breath.

He'd fallen asleep by the empty fireplace, after dragging the sheet off his old man's armchair. The bastard used to cry blue murder if anyone sat in his chair, probably still would if he knew, no matter that he had no more use for it. He rubbed his eyes and sniffed. His nose was blocked, his throat dry. He watched a storm of dust motes swirling in the dim morning light that leaked in through the heavy curtains. He was probably the only person that'd been in the room in a decade.

He pushed himself out of the chair, stretched, and wandered out to the kitchen. He stood quietly for a moment and watched his mother laboriously grinding coffee in the old brass Turkish grinder.

"I'd love one," he said.

With a speed that belied her ancient, creaky frame, his mother spun around. She had one hand raised, fingers splayed and pulsing with blue fire.

"Hello, Ma," he said. Her face drained of colour, tears welling in her rheumy eyes. They stood silent, looking at each other, Maz struggling to meet her gaze. "That's a good one," he said, pointing at her blazing hand, trying to break the mood. "Haven't learnt that yet."

She looked down at her hand. The flames sputtered and went out. She looked back at him, and then in two quick steps, crossed the kitchen and slapped him savagely across the cheek. She looked him hard in the eyes. "Not a bloody word," she said. "That's the least of what you deserve." And then she gave him a short, fierce hug, and turned back to the sink.

Maz could see her white-knuckled grip on the coffee grinder, refusing to let her hands shake and staring stubbornly out the back window. He crossed the kitchen and took the grinder from her.

"Sit down, Ma," he said. "I'll do it."

* * *

Lord Amow stood, hands clasped loosely behind his back, staring down at the distant Houses of Parliament. As much as the view from The Tower was quite magnificent, and Amow admitted it was, he hated this cursed city. London had all the arrogance of a long-standing centre of power, instilled over generations into its populace, and none of the charm. And the rain, the incessant curse of this bloody island.

Christ, he thought, *what I'd give for a day in the Egypt of my youth, the smell of the Nile in the air, instead of this stinking Thames they have the gall to call a river.* And then he chuckled at himself, amused by his habit of invoking Christ, as though he were any more than a tawdry prelector, too stupid to keep his mouth shut when it might have kept him alive.

His amusement was cut short, however, when another presence entered the room. He turned from the window glowering. The cat sat on his desk, next to a delicate glass likeness of the Hirshhorn Museum. Amow growled, deep in his throat, his feline eyes narrowing to slits.

"How many times," he said, "do I have to tell you to use the door, Elwyn? Watching you change is repulsive. And get off my desk."

The cat jumped down and veered, stretching grotesquely for an instant before a young woman stood naked before him. Amow snorted, unsure of whether she was goading him, or just stupid.

Hands behind her, the girl leaned back coyly against the edge of his desk, keeping her eyes carefully lowered. Her svelte body was crossed with old scars and the angry red lines of a recent fight. This only increased her allure, and Amow thought briefly about adding a few marks of his own before having his way with her. He kept himself in hand, however.

"Well?" he asked.

"He's in Hampshire, in the village, as you suspected."

Hambledon, Hants. For the life of him Amow couldn't understand why any of these people had chosen to settle in that little backwater. There were plenty of more romantic little hamlets to be found, and the place had hardly changed in the few hundred years since they started on with that cricket nonsense. Perhaps that was the attraction, the 'Cradle of Cricket'. Ridiculous game.

"And the Annalist?" he asked.

The girl looked up at him, and shook her head. "We followed him to a farmhouse, but couldn't pass the gates. It's heavily warded, for now. We assume the Annalist is inside."

"Unlikely," Amow said. "It is not like him to be so overt. You had better go back and oversee things."

The young woman, perhaps disappointed, pushed herself away from his desk.

"Use the door," Amow said, turning back to survey the city. Then, almost as an afterthought, he turned back. "A moment, before you go."

She stopped, a gleam in her feral eyes, and sauntered back toward him. With a massive, open hand, Amow struck her, splitting her lip and sending her sprawling across the floor. She rolled onto her back and looked up at him with a bloody smile. Amow stepped languidly toward her, unbuttoning his shirt.

* * *

The conversation had died some time ago. Maz's mother gazed past him out the window at a flight of black birds against the leaden sky, yet seeing nothing. He couldn't really blame her. He could tell she was happy to see him, as he was her, but he knew what sort of memories his presence would be dragging out of the past, their chains a weight on the soul.

"How's Dad?" he asked, instantly desperate for an excuse to get out, leave her for a while to her thoughts.

"What? Oh, he doesn't talk much these days. I suspect he'll be wanting me to build the pyre before too long."

"Where is he?"

She gestured vaguely toward the garden. "Down on the back wall," she said. "Overlooking the cemetery."

Maz pushed back his chair and stood up. His mother didn't even seem to register the movement. He left her where she was, and wandered down to the bottom of the garden. There he found his old man, propped between two jutting stones in the garden wall, overlooking the cemetery to the south.

Maz leaned on the wall next to him, and turned to look at the desiccated head that was all that remained of his father. The skin was cracked, as patchy as the lank strands of hair that still clung to the scalp. Maz could see thin strips of leathery muscle still holding the jaw to the skull.

"Jesus, Dad, you've seen better days." Silence. The gaping eye sockets, with the hard, unmoving kernels that had once been eyes, gave no indication that he had even been noticed.

You shouldn't have come back, boy. The voice, as familiar as an old song, filled his head.

"Don't start, Dad." Maz turned to stare out over the cemetery, the muscles in his jaw bunching as he clenched his teeth.

You were right to go.

"Yeah, tell that to Ma." He dug a cigarette out of his pocket, and cupped his hand against the wind to light it.

I have, boy. But she always knew. It's why she treated you the way she did.

"Don't, Dad. I had enough of your excuses as a kid. Even then I knew they were bullshit."

Do you think she was given a choice? She woke up to find her mate was no more than a three thousand year old walking corpse, and bore a child she knew would not be hers. She sacrificed—

"Enough. I know. I know all of it. I've heard it from both of you a thousand times in a thousand different ways. It doesn't excuse it, any of it."

Maz turned around, putting his back to the wall. Up at the house, he could see his mother in her morning ritual, sowing the salt circle around the house. He sucked sharply on his cigarette, flicked the butt away into the damp grass.

Why are you here?

"I'm looking for some answers."

There's nothing we can do. And perhaps it's better —

"Better? You mean easier. After all your years, you've still got no clue do you? Who the fuck said I want answers from you."

Don't you?

"I came to see Charles. I gave up thinking or caring about you and your fucking prophesies a long time ago."

Then why come to the house? Why open old wounds?

"Maybe I just really wanted to see my mum, you ever think about that one?"

It's not fair to her, Maz.

"Fair? When did you give a shit about fair? Sitting down here in your own little garden world and thinking about the universe, or whatever the fuck it is you do. You're right, Dad. I shouldn't have come back." He turned and leapt the wall, skirting the cemetery and striking out across the oilseed rape, away from the village, followed by his father's silence.

* * *

Maz climbed the front steps of the Coombe, the grand old house that belonged to Charles Huntington-Smythe. He raised a fist to knock on the door, and then stopped. He wasn't sure what he was doing here. He certainly hadn't intended to come, he'd just followed the old paths he used to run when the rapeseed came up to his shoulders.

He had no idea if Charles would even remember him, let alone recognise him. Nick and Simon had been gone a long time, and it was even longer since Maz had left. He turned away, again wondering what the hell he was doing in Hambledon.

Maz had one foot on the steps when the door creaked behind him. He looked over his shoulder. Charles stood in the doorway.

"Come in, Maz. I've been expecting you."

Maz hesitated. "You saw me on the path yesterday?" he asked.

"I did," Charles replied. "But I've been expecting you for a long time."

Not knowing what to say, Maz allowed himself to be ushered into the house. Charles led him into the kitchen and sat him at the large table.

"Tea?"

"How about a whisky?" Maz replied.

Charles nodded, and put a brass, claw-footed ashtray on the table. Maz raised an eyebrow. "You'll need it," said Charles.

* * *

In the gloam once more, Maz wandered slowly, almost absently along Church Lane, the brilliant yellow of the rapeseed on one side dulled by the burgeoning darkness. The hedgerow that ran the length of the lane on the other side was a chatter of unseen birds, the hum of insects a match to all the information that was buzzing about the inside of his skull.

He felt he stood on the edge of a vast precipice, the urge to throw himself off almost overwhelming. *But is that leap an escape from all this, or do I throw myself into the depths?*

He understood his father's reluctance to speak for all those years, to explain. Gods, rituals, invested carvings, assassination, sacrifice, MI6, MI17, Project Blueprint, phone boxes, cats. And even fucking pigeons now? Oh, he understood now about Henry, about the Anglesey Deer, but the man was only a very small cog in a very big machine – one that had been building for millennia.

He hadn't reckoned on getting quite so many answers from Charles. He'd wanted to know what he had to toy with, how far he could push Amow. What he got was far more. It was a matter of deciding which side to take, or whether to take one at all. Whatever he did, the nature of reality as he knew it was going to change.

He was nearing the house, wondering desperately what the fuck he was going to say to his mother. He stopped, unsure of whether he was ready to go back in there yet. And then he caught a blur of movement in the inky twilight, a scrap of black over the garden wall up ahead.

Maz! His father's warning a roar in his skull. And then Maz was running, without thought, sprinting across the last corner of the rape field. He cleared the shoulder-high garden wall by a foot, landing with hands blazing fire.

From the back door of the house three black cats emerged, enormous, their bulk closer to that of leopards. They veered, and three young women, sleek and powerful fanned out to meet Maz as he stormed toward the house. One stood before him, blocking the door, the other two circled to either side. The two on his flanks leapt at him, their speed making them a blur.

Maz did not slow his pace for an instant. He raised his hands outward, eyes remaining on the door. White hot light leapt to meet his assailants, and they fell away, no more than ash and blackened bones. The third veered again and fled, a black streak across the grass. She almost made it as far as the wall.

Inside, across the wooden floor of the kitchen, a wide streak of blood led into the hall. Maz found her there, his mother. Her clothes scorched by her own fire, she bore countless wounds, the deep, jagged lacerations of massive claws. Sightless eyes stared up at him, a mockery of the blank stare she had worn when he'd left her earlier.

Maz's own fire, still burning hot around his hands, flared, turning blue. Upon his breath the name Amow grew into an anguished scream, his entire body filled with it. The roar of fire filled his mind, blue and cold. It burnt away his confusion, a clear singular purpose now, consuming him until he could contain the conflagration no longer, and it burst from him, searing away all thought. He fell insensate to the ground.

* * *

His father's ethereal voice brought him round. Maz dragged himself to his feet. He stood in the middle of a crater, the bottom half of a perfect sphere where his parent's house used to be. Shattered stone lay everywhere. He climbed to the lip of the crater, and only when the bite of the wind struck him did he realise he was naked.

The flames had flooded the yard, he could see, everything ash and ruin. Thick smoke drifted up from the oilseed rape, where the fire had washed over the garden wall. *Shit, Dad.* He raced over the charred grass to his father's place on the wall.

The skull was a husk of white ash, the edges of it already blowing away in the wind.

They've gone for Charles.

"I'm too late."

Yes.

"Dad, I..."

No, Maz. There is no need. Everything is as it should be. That was a good pyre, boy. You know what you must do.

With no further farewell, the last of Maz's father scattered. He was alone, surrounded by the smouldering remains of the past, his long hair, burnt as white as a distant sun, blowing in the wind that carried his father aloft.

* * *

Maz stopped the car in front of the old phone box and got out. He walked around to the passenger side, opened the door, and dragged

272

Henry out of the seat. The man opened his mouth as if to speak.

"Uh uh," Maz said, sticking a warning finger in his face. "I know what you're going to say. I don't give a fuck about your girlfriend. She's not important. I don't really give a fuck about you either, mate. You've got the Deer in you now though, and that'll be needed."

Without another word, he pushed Henry into the phone box, and squeezed in after him. He pulled the door closed, and a moment later they were gone.

52. A Night in the Court of Sophia
by Uri Kurlianchik

They were driving up the M4 toward whatever strange place Middle-Eastern pretenders to Godhood considered appropriate for meeting their earthly subjects. Cory, hoping conversation would take her mind away from having just been sliced and diced, said, "What are you thinking about?"

After a pause so long it bordered on annoying, Safran replied. "The ones who think they're the most rooted in reality are actually the farthest away from it," he said. "Because reality is a lie."

Awakened from her drowsiness, which was hopefully the result of being tired rather than of losing enough blood to irrigate a small garden, Cory stared at him for a long time. He looked strange, as he always did, constantly making funny expressions, and he was not paying the road half the attention it deserved.

"Is that why you speak nonsense all the time?" she asked without thinking.

"No," Safran said, nonchalant. "It's because there's a little leprechaun driving my tongue and I suspect he got his driver's permit through bribery or sexual favours."

Safran always teased kids with amusingly pointless replies to all inquiries. It looked fun from the sidelines, but being on the receiving end was irritating. Coincidentally, the same could be said for going through a vicious and literal catfight.

"Come on, I'm not a child," she said.

"Do you expect special treatment because of that?" He smiled.

It had been a god-awful day and a patronizing reply – or whatever the hell it was – was the last thing she needed. She almost hissed at him, but remembering how vital his assistance would be, checked her temper. "Listen, I'm in a great deal of pain here. If that rubbish about cats having nine lives were true, one of mine would have soaked into your seat by now."

"That's quite all right," Safran said cheerfully, giving her a look that made her wrap his jacket tightly around her. "I'll tell people that a pretty girl sat in here for a whole hour, dripping blood. Heh. They would be in such a state of shock! 'A pretty girl in a Fiat? Inconceivable!' That's what they–"

"I am *serious*," she said coolly.

"Like the planet Sirius? They are all very serious there. They go about being serious all day long. If you tell them a joke they look at you sternly and say, 'Shhh! I'm being serious!'"

"Sirius is a star, not a planet." She sighed, and coughed up something that should probably have stayed inside. She spat it out the window.

"You certainly sound like a Syrian, only you don't have a moustache." Safran looked amused now.

"I do. I'm a cat, remember? I have long and pretty whiskers." *Or at least I used to.* She wasn't yet ready to face the horror of the mirror.

"Yikes!" Safran said in a way that was not at all sympathetic or comforting.

"I'm serious though, why don't you ever get involved in anything? I know you're powerful. I know you have friends in the highest places. Why don't you care about this city... this world even?"

"It's all a game."

"Huh?"

"This war of yours. Your villains, your heroes, your cities. Your people, landmarks, and roads. Your encounters on the road. It's all a game." For the first time since she'd met him, he didn't look playful or amused. He looked hurt. Good, she had his attention.

"But if the bad guys win, it's for real!"

"Yeah? And if you win in Monopoly you win for fake? Games *are* real, while you're playing them. If they're not, then there's something wrong with you. You're like... like a bigot."

"A *bigot?*" This made so little sense, she couldn't even decide if she should be offended.

"Yes, you discriminate one reality to the point you don't even give other realities a fighting chance. That's racism, my furry friend. Okay, not racism. Realism. Same shit. You see millions of people going to work, returning from work, day in, day out until they die. This is real life. Then you have people who are, you know, astronauts. They're out there. Geeks and freaks, always daydreaming, don't take life seriously, won't amount to anything. They're never here. It's true, they're really not *here*. When you watch a movie, you're also not *here*. Unless you're like, analyzing your failure to perform last night or considering the fate of the universe and everyone in it. What the hell does it have to do with classic British comedy shows, eh?"

"You've stopped making sense. Like–"

"So you have this one life which you hate, but still cling to, because you believe it's the real one. People with imagination sometimes have distractions – they travel, read books. I don't know, they paint their house in mousy grey and attach a nose and a tail to it–"

"Are you high? Seriously, I got punched in the head, but I think your brains are the ones–"

Safran went on raving as if she wasn't there. "When someone is in a better world than this one, they tell him, 'grow up, get a life, settle down' and crap like that. If he's too persistent they find a way to murder him – with bonfire, drugs, a shove off a cliff – each generation has its reality defence mechanisms. But what does it mean? What does it mean to get a life?"

She shrugged. "It means they think you need to go get laid, I guess."

"Maybe. I don't know. I don't care. Maybe getting laid and all that it entails is what roots you to this 'real world'. Your dick is one of the ways they get a hold of you. There are others – faith, ambition, love, fear. Only it's not real. Not more real than all those worlds people frown upon. A Syrian with a wye is no more real than a Sirian with an i. I mean, it's just one bloody letter, one stupid letter and you're going to deny a whole planet the right to exist because of one letter? God with feathers, you're worse than Hitler, do you know that?!"

"SAFRAN!"

"What?" He turned to her, looking genuinely surprised.

"You sound like you a have a record of bullshit turning in your head and the needle goes up and down randomly."

"Told you," Safran said and spoke no more.

They drove on in silence, both pissed off. *Great work, girl, you antagonized the weirdo who could potentially sway the outcome of the war. Played like a true cat. Now, try to be a woman.*

"Are you mad?" she asked, trying to look cute.

"You really can't ask that question without a troll face... Or are you referring to my mental condition? In the case of the latter I assure you, without the slightest hint of a doubt, with signed statements by 99 leading Islamic scholars and Jeff Robinson, who's a very smart guy, that sanity is subjective."

"I meant whether you're still going to help me, us."

Safran bit his lip. "I want to. Even though you're an ignorant defender of the Lies, I like you. Both as a girl and as a house pet, which were the same thing back when I was a kid. Yes, we used to walk girls on leashes. They still do that in some clubs in London. Very fashionable, I hear... but I'm losing myself. I will do all I can for you, but I answer to a higher Truth. *Sancta Sophia.* Exalted Wisdom."

He stopped rather abruptly in the middle of nowhere, and got out of the car. Cory followed him. There weren't any road signs nearby. It was just a stretch of road, so dark that even she had to strain her eyes to see.

"How you can see anything is beyond me," she said.

"I don't have to, I know this place by heart," Safran answered. "It's a border between—Ah!"

He tripped on some roots and fell down awkwardly. "I'm just clumsy, there's nothing wrong with my memory!" he exclaimed, getting up and walking on. Cory shrugged and followed.

Wet branches kept whipping her face, cunningly hitting her along the throbbing red lines left by her enemy's claws. Something was off. It was as if the darkness wasn't darkness, but a veil that shook with the wind. No, not the wind, something else. Somehow, in this place, Safran's nonsense made sense, while everything else didn't.

Cory felt a strange kind of terror. It was like the feeling of falling that startles you just before you fall asleep. It was like the infinitely brief panic of almost tipping off your chair. It was the horror of being swamped by waves at the beach.

Only it was continuous. She started gasping for air as if drowning.

Without looking back, Safran said, "That's the kind of fear you fight – murder – to avoid. That's why I don't tell people the truth. Mostly the not-wanting-to-get-murdered part, but also because they react like that. With children, there's hope, if you do it gently enough. But you old folk, you get scared, flap like fish out of water and then murder like it's 1229. I guess I suck as a messiah but hey, I'm still alive!" He grinned like the Cheshire cat.

She looked around. She saw a burning castle not far away, surrounded by grim crusaders. Huge things like mountains crawled sadly along the dark landscape. A peacock the size of reality flew through the sky and disappeared beyond the black veil.

It was like a dream, only the opposite – like she had woken from a dull dream into a fantastical reality. The air tasted sweet. The trees were no longer trees but people, grey and featureless, so plain she couldn't even tell their sex or age. They walked in the same direction as she and Safran, but weakly, listlessly, purposelessly. Often, one would trip over and shatter like a clay figure, his scattered parts immediately consumed by the earth.

"Don't try to help them!" Safran shouted as Cory instinctively reached out to a person who collapsed near her. The harshness in his voice made her stop. "They are beyond help. They're doomed to be sucked back into the Lies you call reality. There is no hell worse than Earth and there is no heaven higher than Truth. They haven't earned Wisdom yet."

The darkness, the veil, began to recede. It wasn't light shining through it, it was something much... more. There were no words to describe it.

By now, the figures had become scarce, very few people walking among them. These were more distinct, men and women, saturated like badly Photoshopped pictures. Naked and proud, they walked like kings and queens, as if expecting to be greeted.

"Stop!" Safran barked. "Go no further, or you will crumble, and be reborn into the Lies. This is as close as I dare approach. You'll have to talk with him yourself."

"Me?" Cory didn't feel she had the spirit to face a god, nor did she think she looked the part.

"How well do you think I can plead for a reality I hate? You love this world, *you* speak for it."

"But how?"

Safran didn't say anything. Instead he pointed behind her. She turned and saw a red phone box, its banality a scream against the maddening backdrop. She looked at Safran. Like the mundane phone box, he now seemed, even here, so incredibly unimpressive.

He smiled, shrugged, and said, "One must always maintain decorum. Besides, even gods comply with British telecommunication regulations, don't you know?"

The phone rang. All the people and the things that defied description froze. Cory stepped inside and picked up the receiver.

53. The Magus
by Tim Dedopulos

Jarreth glared at the tree. It was a bit like a pine, tall and straight with branches that stayed close to the trunk, but its leaves were oddly broad, and wisp-thin. They caught the wind easily though, and let the light filter through them to lower branches. Dapple trees, Alyssa called them. Unfortunately, this one had crashed right into the middle of her mandrake patch. Dapple wood was relatively light, but thickly fibred, especially when green. It was a great building material, but a real pain to hack up. He sighed, and tried to identify a spot where he might be able to get some good leverage.

"Jarreth, my friend," he said, "not only are you talking to yourself again, but now you're going to try to dead-lift a tree."

It took slightly more effort not to answer himself than he would have liked.

Finally, he decided on one of the thicker branches towards the middle of the trunk. He squatted down beside the tree, tucked his shoulder in below his chosen branch, and lifted.

He braced himself. His heart started pounding like a jackhammer, the blood surging inside him. He could feel its pressure rise, feel the skin tighten around his temples and on the backs of his hands. Forcing himself to focus, he unfolded his legs inch by creaking inch. Pain exploded in his shoulder and both knees. He ignored it, concentrating as hard as he could on his breathing, quick and deep. His skin felt like a drum. He rose further, even though his arm was clearly giving some serious thought to dropping off. A damned tree was not going to beat him. He bellowed, straightening convulsively, his skin thrumming. The tree rose up off the little field.

As Jarreth's vision tinted red, he held himself upright beneath the load, refusing to let his knees wobble. It was easier with the weight of the tree travelling straight down through his locked joints, and he took a couple of long, painful breaths. But getting it lifted was only part of the battle. Fortunately, the uprooted stump of the tree was outside of the mandrake patch. He turned in toward the trunk a little, focused himself, and took a hasty step forward. The tree turned with him, its weight crashing through him to his knee and ankle. He groaned, and straightened himself before it crushed him.

The next step was worse, and left him feeling like his lower back had been set on fire. He ignored it, and took another step, and then another. The tree started slipping, and he desperately twisted his shoulder under it. He could feel muscles tearing in there, and his grip weakened, but he got it back under control. The blood sang inside him like molten steel, lending him the resilience to keep standing. He locked down the pain, and forced himself to keep walking. Finally, after a ten-pace eternity, he'd gone far enough.

Dropping the tree, he leapt backwards. It crashed to the ground, safely off the mandrakes. His arm hung uselessly by his side, so he lay down next to the Dapple, closed his eyes, and let himself breathe. Slowly, as his heart slowed its wild thumping, the pressure in his head and chest decreased. As it did so, the pain in his joints faded. The sensation in his shoulder was horrible, similar to how he imagined a subcutaneous ant colony would feel, all writhing and scurrying around under his skin. The discomfort eased though, and he regained control of his arm.

After a few minutes, his pulse was back to normal and all the twinges were gone. He got up. The mandrake patch looked rough, but the plants seemed salvageable. He grinned. "Gotcha." He set off back towards the cottage, picking his way through the herb beds. Most of them had escaped damage in the storm.

Inside, he was surprised to see Alyssa just sitting there at her worktable, staring across the room at the wall. He studied her face carefully. "Alyssa?"

She looked up at him, and summoned a weak smile. "I'm all right, my love. My mother has been in communication." She tapped her forehead, above the bridge of her nose.

"That doesn't sound good."

"Gloria is here, on a mission for Mam. She needs help."

He frowned. "She'd never accept *your* help, surely?"

"No. But she would yours."

The penny dropped. "Ah. It's time for wonderboy to pay for his rehab, huh?"

Her face fell further. "It's not like that, love."

"It's okay, Allie. I don't mind."

She nodded, reluctant. "Gloria is headed for the Magus's territory. She needs a guide, and a defender. It's dangerous."

Jarreth patted his shoulder.

She glanced at it, looking puzzled.

"Count me in," he said. "When do I leave?"

"An hour ago, if Mam had her way."

He held out his hand to her. As she took it, he pulled her to her feet, and enfolded her in his arms. "Plenty of time for a proper farewell, then."

Alyssa laughed. He wiped a tear from the curve of her cheek, and bent his head to kiss her.

* * *

The mountain road had been well-tended, once. It still served as a handy boundary for farmers and other land-holders. Agricultural traffic in and out of Hatherdon Town kept it weed-free, even a day out. Minimal rutting on its surface suggested it had been built with a dense base layer to accommodate heavy vehicles. To pass the time before Gloria's arrival, Jarreth amused himself by constructing a little mouse-sized hut out of pebbles, twigs and bits of straw. He was working on whittling a tiny picket fence to go around it when he glanced up at the sound of footsteps, and saw a flame-haired girl approaching.

He put his knife away, stood, and smiled at her, making sure to keep his hands visible. "Hey there, Gloria V."

Gloria froze. "Don't take another step, asshole." She sounded like Banderas's girlfriend in the Zorro movies, but she had Alyssa's cheekbones and lush mouth.

"My name's Jarreth Medlin. Your mom sent me."

She stared at him, apparently trying to flay him with her eyes.

282

"Jarreth. Jarreth! *Her* toy." She spat at the ground. "You can just crawl back to my sister and –"

"Mam said you might get huffy. She said to tell you 'this world is becoming more dangerous,' and that I'm one of the 'others,' whatever the fuck that means."

"Is that so?" She sounded unimpressed, but her glare softened a little. "What good are you?"

Jarreth grinned. "I'm an architect."

"Perfect," Gloria said. "I really need a tower-block built *right up your ass.*"

"I've got some tricks up my sleeve, don't you worry. I knew where to wait for you, didn't I?"

"Yeah." She squinted at him, suspicious again.

"I know how to get to the right place. Any right place. That's why Mam sent me."

"We'll see. Where was I born?"

"The Hospital Universitario Virgen Del Rocio in Seville."

She shrugged. "All right, you can tag along. I'm warning you now though, any funny stuff and I'll do more than just tase you, '*bro.*'"

He flashed her his best charming smile. "Don't worry, I'll be a perfect gentleman."

Gloria sniffed. "I've heard that before."

"I can imagine."

She frowned at him.

"We should get moving," Jarreth said, careful to hide his amusement.

The countryside they walked through was pleasant, gently-rolling downs punctuated by copses and occasional streams. Most of the land was being worked one way or another. Small, brownish sheep-like things were common, and watched incuriously as Jarreth and Gloria passed. Little villages were frequent, clusters of stone and timber houses set a short way from the main road. Inns were readily identifiable in each, but there was no clear sign of chapels, town halls or other religious or civic buildings. Some time after lunch, the hamlets thinned out. As they did so, the farm fields got larger and increasingly messy.

The highlight of Jarreth's afternoon was spotting a huge, rambling mansion off across the fields. It had elements of the Federal style about it, as well as bits of Gothic and even some dashes of English country house, all as part of a unified but unfamiliar aesthetic. It had been constructed from an unattractive stone with a distinctly green tinge, but it was in surprisingly good shape for a derelict. What was it even doing out in the middle of nowhere to begin with? He decided, reluctantly, not to go for a closer look. *On the way back, maybe.*

It had been almost two hours since the last village when dusk started to creep up. They decided to make camp just off the road, in a stand of Dapple trees a hundred yards or so from a lively little brook. They both had locally-made tents, basic but sturdy, and bedroll mats – plenty for early summer. Jarreth built up a fire while Gloria got some water from the stream. They ate a simple meal of trail-bread, smoked ham and dried fruit mix, with a pot of Alyssa's "Rest and Restore" tea, her second best-selling product.

"What's that?" Gloria sounded unhappy.

Jarreth looked around. A big rat was watching them from beside a tree root. "It's just a rat," he said.

"Why are its eyes glowing?"

"I'm sure it's just the firelight reflecting."

"They're glowing blue, Jarreth." Gloria's tone of voice suggested she was trying to make a particularly stupid child see sense.

"Maybe its eyes absorb the other wavelengths."

"I thought rat eyes were supposed to be red."

"*Our* rats, yes. Who knows, here."

She thought it over for a moment. "Well, I don't like it."

"I'll add it to the list," Jarreth said quietly.

"What?"

"Nothing."

Gloria sighed. "I hate this primitive bullshit. Shitty tents, walking all day, dry food... God, it's so tedious. No wonder we invented TV."

"It could be worse."

"Yeah, I could have been killed by strangers three days ago, like my father." She pulled her knees up to her chest and wrapped her arms round them.

He flinched. "I'm sorry, Gloria. I didn't know."

"He was an asshole," she said, closing the discussion.

Jarreth nodded. He crawled into his tent a few minutes later, leaving her staring into the fire.

The next day was quiet, save for Gloria's grumbling. Around mid-morning, the ground either side of the road took on an odd lumpy texture. The hummocks stretched out as far as he could see in both directions, closely packed but without discernible pattern. Signs of agriculture dropped off at the same time. The uneven ground persisted for five miles or so, and then switched back to flatter terrain. The farmers and their villages didn't reappear with it, though.

Instead, the land took on a forlorn feel, unkempt, all blurred edges and patchy spaces. It looked unloved and unappealing. There was little evidence of habitation of any sort, except for the road and its detritus – a broken cartwheel here, a long-discarded boot there. Jarreth found it oddly intimidating. If Gloria felt any similar discomfort, she kept it well-hidden beneath her mask of supreme boredom.

Late in the afternoon, he caught the unmistakable tang of a log fire. Unsure of what to expect, he held off saying anything. A short while later, they came around the side of a hill and saw a big flint-work inn, complete with well-kept lawns and a tidy stable yard.

"Fantastic," he said.

Gloria snorted. "You don't get out much, do you?"

"Would you prefer another night of tents and cold bread?"

"At least they'll have a beer, I suppose. Come on then, what are you waiting for?"

He grinned at her back as she stumped off towards the inn, and then hurried to catch up.

The grin lasted all the way into the building. He'd expected the interior to be a simple rustic affair, plain but wholesome. Instead, it looked like someone had looted a small palace – and a century ago, at that. The common room was very large, with a high ceiling. Badly-matched furniture was scattered throughout, ranging from an impressive dark-wood dining table fit for a 20-person banquet down to a few things that looked like dressing tables with the mirrors snapped off. The chairs were just as random, including padded armchairs, wing-backed seats, plain stools and even a crude stone throne in one corner. The walls were covered with thick drapes in a variety of colors. Everything was shabby, faded, scored with use. The place seemed empty.

"Wow," Gloria said.

Jarreth nodded.

"Master. Lady." The speaker was right by Jarreth's ear, and he jerked away, bumping Gloria as he spun round. There was a man just behind him, beside the door. He was tall and thin, with wild hair and unsettling eyes. He wore threadbare finery to match the décor, with a plain-looking apron over the top.

"You startled me," Jarreth said, trying to sound apologetic.

"Ah," said the man.

Gloria scowled. "This is an inn, yes?"

"It is the Bluebell," said the man.

"Then I would like you to bring me a beer and some hot food." She looked at him expectantly.

"Sweet young lamb," said the man.

Gloria stared at him.

"And cool ale," he added, eventually.

"We'll just sit anywhere, shall we?" Jarreth said.

"My name is Ackagee," said the man.

Jarreth forced a smile. "Great. Lamb and ale for two, then."

"Master," said Ackagee. "Lady." He flashed them a sickly-looking smirk, and then tottered off across the room.

Jarreth spotted the doorway the man was headed towards, and picked out a mid-sized table with a couple of sturdy-looking chairs reasonably close to it. Gloria sighed, and followed him, muttering to herself.

Less than a minute later, Ackagee returned, carrying a silver platter piled high with steaming lamb, roughly shredded and served on a bed of roasted whole carrots. The meat was incredible, delicately spiced and so tender it almost melted away in his mouth. Jarreth immediately forgave the man's eccentricities. The ale was almost as good, light and refreshing with a hint of fruit to it.

By the time they'd finished eating, dusk had fallen. They were still the only customers, and if Ackagee had any other staff in the place, they were very well hidden. When the man came to take their empty platter away, Jarreth looked up at him. "Hey Ackagee, it seems quiet tonight."

The man gazed back at him.

"Uh, you get many customers in this place?"

"It is the Bluebell," said Ackagee.

"Okay," Jarreth said. "Great."

Across the table, Gloria rolled her eyes.

Jarreth smiled encouragingly at Ackagee. "So are you alone here?"

"I'm never alone," he said, voice momentarily subdued. "You wish a room, Master, Lady?"

"One room, two beds," Gloria told him.

Ackagee nodded. "Five marks, for this, and tonight, and tomorrow morning."

It was a pittance. Turnip money. Jarreth fished some coins out of his pouch.

"Here, take ten. The food was really great." He held out the money.

Ackagee took five marks, and stepped back.

"No," said Jarreth. "Here, the rest is for you, too."

"Five marks," Ackagee said, and left.

Jarreth shrugged awkwardly at his back, and put the rest of the money away.

They stayed at the table for another half-hour or so, making small-talk and working their way through the pitcher of beer. Still no-one else appeared. Once it was dark outside, Jarreth found the day's exertions catching up with him, and called for the innkeeper's assistance. The man led them up a staircase and along to their bedroom, which matched the chaotic grandeur of the common room downstairs. Gloria discovered an attached washroom, and actually squealed at the presence of a bathtub freshly filled with hot water. Jarreth left her to it, and just flung himself onto a bed. Within moments, he was sound asleep.

In his dreams, a giant rat with glowing blue eyes chased him through an endless graveyard, calling after him in a dark, Creole voice he couldn't quite understand.

When he woke, Gloria was already up. She was standing by the window, looking out. Jarreth watched her in the growing light. There was a lot of Alyssa in her, when she wasn't being defensive.

"I expected to wake up in a meadow, inside a ring of little mushrooms," she said, not turning round.

"Yeah." Jarreth nodded, even though she wasn't looking.

"There are no birds singing, you know. I'm sorry if I have been difficult. The last fortnight has really been shit."

"It's okay."

Gloria turned around to face him. "She has good taste in boys." She smiled lazily. "You should have joined me in the bath."

The heat in her voice made his pulse sing. He swallowed, fought himself under control, and forced a wry smile. "Your sister has some scary abilities. I like my spleen where it is."

"I have some abilities of my own," she said, raising her eyebrow.

"Oh, God. I bet you do."

She grinned. "We'll make a perfect man out of you yet."

"I... Uh..."

"Come along, Mr. Gentleman. Let us see if that strange old beanstalk has anything for breakfast."

Jarreth nodded quickly, and busied himself gathering up his stuff. Ackagee was not in evidence downstairs, but the table they'd sat at the evening before was set with a large pot of tea and a fruit pie, hot from the oven. They put a big dent in it, and when Ackagee still didn't show, Jarreth defiantly left another five marks on the table before they headed out.

As they walked away from the Bluebell, Jarreth couldn't resist looking back. As Gloria had said, somehow it didn't seem possible that the old inn would still be there. It remained in place however, stubbornly visible behind them.

An hour later, they were walking past a patch of gorse when it seemed to Jarreth that the road twitched. His feet became oddly reluctant.

"Wait," he said.

"What's wrong?"

A broad-chested deer walked out onto the road ahead of them. Close behind it came a savage-looking mastiff with a matted coat and something large and dark-pelted that seemed to be an unholy cross between a badger and a boar. The animals stopped and turned to face them, forming an unnerving line.

Jarreth blinked. "What the *fuck*?"

The animals snarled, simultaneously. Even the deer peeled its lips back and made a low, aggressive noise. Jarreth took a step back, and they charged. Time seemed to stutter. Heart raging, he felt his body swelling. His left eye ached. The muscles seemed to spread and tighten in his back and legs, forcing him into a crouch. Gloria gasped. Moments later, the animals reached them.

The deer was in the lead. Jarreth let it come. It closed on him, head down low, aiming for his stomach. He twisted aside, whipped his arm round its neck, and jerked upwards with all his strength. Something crunched. He saw its knees start folding and released his hold. The wild dog leaped at him from behind the deer carcass. He ducked quickly, relying on the deer to cushion his fall. The dog flew over him, jaws wide. Jarreth rolled to the side, putting himself between Gloria and the mutant badger. It hissed, and darted towards him. Even as he was dodging aside, it twisted and leapt at him.

Jarreth flung his arms out to ward it off, catching it at the midriff. He fell backwards with it, desperately trying to keep it off him. The damn thing must have weighed a hundred pounds, and felt like it was made of solid muscle. Its hind-legs came up and clawed at the insides of his arms, raking agonizing gouges into him. He yelped, and it snapped at his face, catching the tip of his nose with a fang. He straightened his arms convulsively, throwing the thing away.

Scrabbling to find his feet, Jarreth started to get up. Something hot and furious barreled into him from behind. Pain blazed in the back of his head as the mastiff tried to gnaw through his skull. He toppled forwards, landing on all fours, dislodging the dog.

Looking up, he found himself face to face with the monstrous badger. It opened its cavernous jaws, breath stinking like a week-old

ELLIS, DEDOPULOS, WICKLINE et al.

corpse. *The damned thing is going to bite my fucking face off.*

Gloria shrieked. He heard the sound of her footsteps, quickly coming up behind him. There was a brief hissing sound and then Gloria half-growled, half-shouted, "RAH!" There was a loud yelp – *the dog* – and then Gloria was right next to him, holding something.

"Cover your face," she yelled.

Before he could move, there was another hissing noise. The giant badger began to walk backwards, shaking its head furiously. And then it hit Jarreth. His lungs started burning. Tears streamed from his eyes. He looked around, trying to locate the mastiff. It had retreated down the road a short distance where it sat whining and pawing at its eyes.

Gloria put her hand on his shoulder. "Are you all right?"

Jarreth coughed, looked over his arms, then felt the back of his head and neck cautiously. "I think so," he croaked. "What the fuck happened?"

Gloria shuffled awkwardly. "Pepper spray. I did tell you to cover your face."

"You didn't get me too bad. Wish I'd known you had that stuff."

She looked at him unhappily. "I got it when I was still in London. You never know when you're going to be attacked these days."

"Well, it was a good time to find out. Thank you. That fucker was about to chew my eyes out."

She offered him a hand. "Fifteen minutes is all it will buy us. I don't want to be standing here when they recover. Can you get up?"

He struggled to take a breath. His lungs felt like they were closing up. "Just give me a minute." He closed his eyes and tried to will his lungs to relax.

"I'm sorry about the pepper spray, but we don't have a minute."

He groaned, but what came out was more like a squeak.

"Jarreth, are you having trouble breathing? Just say yes or no."

He tried to answer, but no sound came out. He nodded and then burst into a violent coughing fit.

Gloria grabbed his arm. "Listen to me, you pathetic Yank. We're in danger. Serious fucking danger. Get yourself on your feet whether you can breathe or not, or I'm going to kick your arse myself and leave you here for dog food."

He let her help him to his feet, and tried not to collapse coughing. "I'm a fast healer," he muttered. Jarreth could feel his feet itching to get off the road, to angle away from the gorse and out into the wilds. "Need to get the hell out of here. That guy we're sneaking up on, your sister says he can sense all kinds of stuff from miles away. We don't want to stay on this road."

"Shit. What are we going to do?"

"Follow me."

Off the track, the next ten minutes felt like something from a bad dream. He followed his feet, speeding up or slowing down as they seemed to urge. His lungs were twitchy, and whenever he sped up, he felt his chest tighten and his throat start to close up. It felt as if they were threading their way through an invisible maze. They moved away from the road for a while, a fast walk the most Jarreth could manage, and turned sharply to push through a bramble hedge and go around a small hill. They'd just dropped down a stream-bank when a huge, broad-winged creature flapped past some distance ahead.

"Fuck," Jarreth muttered. "You might have to run without me."

"Don't be a bloody idiot. Is it going to kill you to run?"

"Maybe," he wheezed.

"That's a better chance than you have if you stay in view."

"Good point."

Moments later, they were back up on the plain and sprinting for a stand of trees. They ducked into some brambles. As they sat silently, Jarreth felt his lungs opening up.

"I think it's gone," Gloria whispered after a little while.

They left the brush and continued on.

On and on it went. Sometimes, they might manage to go as far as two or three miles in a straight line before veering off at some crazy angle. Streams featured heavily in their route, and several times, Jarreth spotted aerial searchers. It was exhausting, but the urge to keep pushing was relentless.

Their path became less tangled as the afternoon progressed. Finally, as the sun got ready to set, Jarreth found himself forcing through a patch of scrub into a half-hidden cave mouth. The place stank, and the floor was unpleasantly clammy, but they set up a crude camp in there. Neither of them suggested lighting a fire. It was a far cry from the withered opulence of the night before. He and Gloria briefly discussed sleeping in shifts, but they were just too wiped out.

As they spread out their bedrolls, Gloria said, "I'm sorry about shouting at you before. I just had to—"

"Not a problem. You saved my ass." He glanced nervously out of the cave mouth. *Now, let's just hope we live through the night.*

Despite his fears, sleep claimed him almost as soon as he lay down on his bedroll.

Light filtering into the dank cave woke him the following morning. He stood up, his body one gigantic ache, and woke Gloria. They barely managed to have a hurried breakfast and get the bed rolls packed before his feet started prickling again, pulling him out into the world.

Progress was simpler this time, to his great relief. He was taken on fewer deviations, and he only spotted one of the big fliers, a mile or more away. Late in the morning, the terrain started getting rougher, and a short while after that they entered the foothills. Their path led them into a rocky area with poor visibility, which set Jarreth's nerves on edge. He could feel their destination drawing nearer though, like an itch he could almost scratch.

The stone shack seemed to appear out of nowhere. Walking along the base of a scree slope, they dodged around a huge, weathered boulder, and there it was in front of them. It was sagging dangerously, the roof collapsed in two sections, but it was the first sign of human habitation Jarreth had seen in two days. As they got closer, he noticed that a path had been hacked out of the rock leading away from it. Further on, other tumbledown buildings were visible, first just a few, then an entire ghost town.

It was an eerie place. His feet led him cautiously through it, past solid, sturdy-looking homes and places of business. A decrepit inn gaped at him blankly, doors long since rotted away. A big guildhall dominated a market square, complete with some sort of clock-tower. There was even something that might have been a schoolhouse. Gloria walked along beside him, treading softly. She seemed reluctant to break the silence.

They picked their way down the side of a large, multi-windowed building that could have been a hotel or a brothel. It came out onto a path that led out the other side of town to a large stockyard space scattered with stone or gravel. A big, squared-off tunnel entrance led back into the cliff, and his feet led him straight towards it.

Gloria elbowed him in the ribs. "Look." She pointed at the corner of the tunnel entry.

A large rat was sitting there on its haunches, watching them approach. Its eyes were clearly glowing with an eerie blue light that had nothing to do with reflecting the afternoon sun.

"Fuck," said Jarreth.

"I told you," Gloria said.

He looked at the rat. "What is it?"

"Ha bloody ha."

The rat nodded to them, and vanished into the tunnel.

Jarreth stared at it as it departed. "I'm still being pulled in that direction. Do we risk it?"

Gloria shrugged. "Do we have a choice?"

"Not really."

"Well, then."

Just inside the tunnel entrance, Jarreth found an open-topped barrel in surprisingly good shape. He peered in, and found a bunch of tar-dipped torches. They looked reasonably fresh. He waved Gloria over. "Here. This area must be in some sort of use still." He realized he was nearly whispering.

"Does that surprise you?" Gloria dropped her voice to match his.

He took a couple of torches, and handed one to her.

"I'll keep this one unlit until yours runs out," she said.

Jarreth nodded. It took a minute or two to find his flint and steel, and get the torch lit. He kept looking around nervously, but there was no sign of guards or workers, just the steady pull of the true path beneath him. When the torch was finally going, he gave in to the urgings, and advanced.

They quickly found themselves inside a network of tunnels. Many of them showed clear signs of mining, but some stretches were natural. Jarreth's internal guide led him through the junctions confidently, long past the point where he'd become totally confused regarding their route. The relentless darkness of the tunnels was as oppressive as the stone engulfing them. He found himself imagining patterns and features in the flickery light, and hearing things that he knew for certain weren't real. Occasionally he thought he caught a flash of the rat's blue eyes ahead, but it was impossible to tell if it was actually there. Gloria followed behind him doggedly, keeping quiet. As he walked, a feeling crept over him that she'd been stolen away, replaced by an audio doppelganger. He found himself scared to look back, to avoid tipping off the thing that had consumed her.

Jarreth gritted his teeth, and glanced over his shoulder.

Gloria stopped. "What?"

He smiled at her. "Nothing."

"Crazy man." She poked him in the shoulder playfully.

He turned to continue, and a writhing darkness rose up before him, smelling of old blood. Tentacles stretched out from a body that seemed to be made of black goo, pulsing and rippling as they reached for him. He shrieked and leaped back, knocking Gloria flying. The abomination chuckled at him, a deep, thick sound of cruel amusement.

"Holy shit!" He waved the torch at it, trying to fend it off.

It deliberately held a tentacle just over the torch flame, moving to keep it in the fire. It flowed forward a pace, and he retreated before it.

Behind him, Gloria was getting up, cursing in disbelief. He focused on his heart-beat, and nothing happened. No surge of pressure, no increased pulse. There was no pull from his feet, either. Not even a faint tingle.

"Pepper spray?" Gloria yelled.

"Are you fucking kidding me? Run," he said, trying to keep it together.

"What?" Gloria sounded confused. "Where?"

"Run!"

The thing lurched forward again, tentacles reaching for his head. He ducked back, spun round, and took to his heels. Gloria got the message finally, and came with him. He glanced back. The abomination was outlined with a faint red glow, just a couple of paces behind them. He rounded a corner, and sped along a straight part. A horrible slurping noise told him that the thing was having no trouble keeping up. Less than a minute later, they burst out into a cavern with several tunnels leading off it.

"Which way?" Gloria sounded totally freaked out.

The thing burst into the cavern behind them.

Jarreth looked around wildly. "I don't know!"

The thing flowed past them, and started advancing from the side. They backed away. It reached towards him again, a whole mass of tentacles groping for him. He jumped back. There was a tunnel behind him, so he darted for it, Gloria close behind.

"Herding. Us," she managed, between gasps of air.

"Shit," Jarreth gasped.

The abomination laughed again, right behind them.

There was nothing they could do, except run. The tunnel careened right and left, probably the path of some old ore vein. When they came to a junction, the thing moved with dizzying speed to cut off their options. It kept chuckling, as if it were enjoying itself immensely. The one time Jarreth tried slowing, it lashed out with a tendril that burned into his shoulder like acid. He immediately sped up again, ignoring the thing's amusement.

He slammed around a corner, lungs burning, and fell down a short drop into dazzling brightness. A moment later, Gloria landed on top of him, making his ribs scream. He braced himself for agonizing death, but it didn't come. Instead, the horrid chuckling receded.

Jarreth took several long, deep breaths as his eyes adjusted, then looked around. He was in a cavern of glittering crystal, seemingly lit from within. The walls were etched with complex geometric designs. Each was enclosed within a double circle. At the heart of every design was a small pool of dark purple radiance, pulsing like a heartbeat. Crystalline megaliths stood around the floor, embedded into the smooth rock surface. Thin channels of golden light ran between them in a tangled network.

A richly-robed man with a thin face was standing in the center of the floor. Four figures stood with him, reptile-headed horrors with the bodies of powerful men. He stared at them.

Gloria disentangled herself groggily, and gasped. "It's him."

The thin-faced man looked at the pair of them, and sighed. "What a let down. Kill them."

Jarreth turned to Gloria. "I got nothing. It's up to you."

The dragon-men were crossing the room towards them.

She looked at him. "I need time!"

He clambered to his feet and started circling around the room away from her. Two of the Magus's servitors peeled off to keep moving towards him. All four of them were drawing long, ugly swords. He glanced over to see Gloria getting to her feet, a shard of crystal in her hand.

Jarreth whooped at the dragon-men, moving further away from Gloria. "Come on, fuckers."

"The girl first," the Magus said wearily.

All four immediately started converging on Gloria, who shrank back towards the wall, eyes wide.

Something jabbed Jarreth painfully in the ankle. He flinched away, and looked down. The blue-eyed rat was sitting there by his foot. It looked up at him and squeaked urgently. He stared for a long moment. The rat made some indecipherable gestures with its paws, then chittered at him again. Finally, it shook its head in disgust.

Jarreth bent down and picked it up. As he did so, he heard a deep voice in his head. *Finalman*. It was the Creole voice from his dream, rich and rolling. *Jete m', moun nan opsyon sa*.

Somehow, he understood the instruction. *Throw me*. He hefted the rat, and flung it at the Magus.

The Magus was concentrating on Gloria and her crystal. The rat flew towards the side of his head. In the last instant, he turned, and the rat vanished in a wild flare of golden light. The Magus shrieked, and clapped his hands to his eyes. At the same moment, the dragon-men dropped to the floor, melting into blobby pools of greenish muck. Their swords clanged as they hit the stone floor. The Magus groaned, and staggered, wiping his eyes.

"Quick," Jarreth yelled.

Gloria stepped forward and lifted one of the swords. She placed the shard on the floor, and hacked the sword down at it savagely. It exploded, and as it did so, the crystal walls of the chamber brightened with a sudden tracery of bright white cracks. There was a sound like a chime. The purple pools swelled, thinning and lightening. Dim scenes became visible through them—a desert, a modern city street, a stretch of parkland, a filthy alley.

The entire room exploded with sparkling shards, bathing Jarreth in soft light. He hung in it for a moment, weightless, and then found himself at a poorly-defined country crossroads. Wheat-fields stretched off in front of him, with a little village in the distance. Gloria was beside him. Across the way, a trampy-looking guy with a massive black beard and totally crazy hair was looking around frantically. Their eyes met. "Oh fuck me," the man said in a very thick, mushy accent. "Crofton, you fucking *shite*." He vanished.

A moment later, the light faded. Jarreth looked around. They were in the Magus's portal room still, ankle-deep in crystal shards. The stone of the cavern walls was visible now, although some chunks of crystal hung on stubbornly. Fading footsteps suggested that the man himself was getting the hell out of Dodge. That struck Jarreth as a really good idea.

"I guess the Magus is okay," Gloria said.

"He certainly sounds it, whatever the fuck it was that just happened. He's going to be pissed at us." Jarreth couldn't help cackling. "'What a let down,' my ass."

Gloria chuckled, but sobered again quickly. "It could make the return journey annoying."

Jarreth felt his feet tingle, and grinned. "Don't worry. If there's a safe path for us, I'll be able to find it."

54. Who the Fuck is Kelly?
by Gethin A. Lynes

Lorna plummeted through painfully bright nothing, eyes squeezed shut against the blazing white. She might have been falling for days. All sense of time had fled, left behind in the grubby, piss-drenched interior of the red phone box. The initial panic, the terror of the sickening crunch when she hit whatever bottom she was hurtling toward, that had faded after a while, too. She felt almost relaxed. Eventually, braving the glaring light, she opened her eyes, and found herself standing inside the phone box.

The sensation of falling stopped instantly. Her stomach twisted, violently. She shoved open the door, leant out, and vomited onto a pair of polished black boots.

She looked up, a long string of drool hanging from her nose. There was someone standing in the boots, holding out a rag.

"It's okay." The voice was nasal, a bit whiny. "Everyone pukes afterward."

She took the rag and wiped the vomit from her nose and lips, and stood up. He was standing a little too close, and she recoiled slightly from the pimpled, pock-scarred face so close to hers.

"It's Lorna, right? I'm Lawrence." He held out his hand. He was wearing black military gear, with a pistol on one hip, doing his best to look manly. Dressing like a black-ops soldier did little to hide how scrawny he was.

Lorna ignored his hand. "Want tae get out o' my way, Lawrence, so I can step out o' this puddle of piss an' vomit?"

"Uh, yeah, sorry," he stammered, stepping to one side. "There's, um, a sink over there." He motioned toward the far end of the dimly lit room. "If you want to rinse off."

She stepped past him and walked unsteadily over to the sink. She felt woozy, but took stock of the room anyway. No windows, bare concrete, single steel door. There was no doubt she was below ground. *Not good if Captain Skinny or his friends – if he has any – turn out not to be so friendly.* Glancing quickly at him in the mirror over the sink, she saw that he looked uncomfortable.

The hot tap *worked!* She ran water into the sink, and just stood there for a moment with her hands in it. She couldn't remember the last time she'd felt hot water. Then she bent over and washed her face, rinsed the acrid taste of vomit out of her mouth.

When she straightened up, the blood rushed from her head, and she staggered. She reached out, grasping at the sink to steady herself, and caught Lawrence in the mirror, staring blatantly at her arse. *There's something not right about that little man,* she thought, as the porcelain basin rushed up to smack her in the temple.

* * *

The static cleared and the monitors flickered back to life. The view panned along the darkened street. The squad crouched in the shadows beside the sergeant, breathing hard.

Algot glared at the screens. "What the fuck happened, Sergeant?"

"Don't know, sir," the Sergeant's voice crackled in his ear. "All comms went down, some kind of interference."

The Sergeant lifted the visor on his helmet, and Algot's primary monitor blacked out.

"I meant, what the fuck happened to the girl, soldier? And put that bloody visor back down. You know the rules."

The view of the other soldiers and the dark street flickered on again, accompanied by the muffled crackling of obscenities in Algot's ear. He ignored it.

"No sign of her, sir," the Sergeant replied.

"How's that, Sergeant? You were right fucking behind her."

"You tell me, Overseer. You've got a better bloody view of the area than I do."

Algot hammered out commands, his fingers a blur over the keys of his old-school keyboard. The peripheral monitors around him, his Pigeon array, scanned back over the last few minutes, searching for another view of the street, for some trace of the girl. Nothing.

Fucking pigeons, he thought. The problem with their innate programming, designed to keep them behaving like actual birds, was that they behaved like actual birds. *It's that bloody cat's fault. If I didn't know any better, I'd say it was there on purpose.*

"Keep looking, Sergeant," Algot ordered. "Let me know if you find anything."

He switched off the monitors and swung his Gravichair round to face Finch. *Oh yeah, Finch's not here is he? Poor bastard. Stone cold up there in that dead satellite.*

Algot missed Finch. He missed the banter. He missed just having someone else in the room. He hadn't seen another person in the flesh down here in at least a month. *Or was it several months?* He didn't notice the days passing much any more, didn't notice his time off go by. He was just locked away and forgotten beneath The Yard, doing the work of at least three people.

Fucking Overwatch. He took a swig of his tea, and picked up the crumby remains of his cheese sandwich. *I half hope that sorry band of fuckers down there actually succeed. Jesus, who am I bloody kidding? More than half.* He took another swig, and then stopped dead. For the first time in a week at least, he had finally succeeded in finishing a cup of tea before it went cold. The last few mouthfuls were tepid, but tepid wasn't cold. Putting down the empty cup in satisfaction, he gave the Gravichair a nudge and let it drift back into the centre of his monitors.

He brought the feed from the sergeant's helmet back up on the primary display. Everything was askew, and it took him a moment to realise the sergeant's head, or at least his helmet, was lying in the middle of the road. He could see the legs of the rest of the squad, standing around, unmoving, weapons dangling limply by their sides.

"Sergeant?" He tried the comms, but his only answer was the crackle of static.

His fingers moved in their habitual spidery dance over his keyboard. He loved the tactile clatter of the keys beneath his fingers. *You just can't beat old-school,* he thought, for the umpteenth time. Even in the early days, when Overwatch was nothing more than an over-zealous police force, and he and Finch were pimple-faced kids, Algot had been forever dodging insults for the outdated gear he used. Even without a Tac-suit and his head shoved in a surround unit though, Algot had been the fastest Op in the Metro.

As quick as thinking, he brought the nearest flock of pigeons online, hoping there were no more fucking cats about. While the flock was en route, he backed the main feed up and let the last several minutes of the squad's activity begin scrolling.

Just as the soldiers began closing in on a small, wiry man in a long coat, Algot's entire array of monitors flickered. Their images gave way to the familiar, shadowy figure of Lord Amow. It was one of those little hypocrisies that really gave Algot the shits. He'd known people that had disappeared for even the most momentary lapse of attention to their work, and yet everyone was expected to drop everything, no matter how urgent, when Amow chose to speak.

"Overseer." The voice was as rich and even as ever.

"Sir," Algot said, never one for platitudes. He'd never actually seen Amow's face, so he couldn't be sure whether his barely perfunctory acknowledgement of the man's status was taken very well. He was still alive however, so he couldn't be pushing things too far.

"I am given to understand that the David girl has found her way to our little friends down below."

"It would appear so, sir."

"There remain no signs that they know we are aware of them, I assume."

"Well, not so far, but I didn't actually witness David's disappearance. Something has gone a bit pear-shaped with the squad that was following her. I didn't manage to get the readings."

"Pear-shaped, Overseer?"

"Yeah, looking into it now, sir."

"Well, I expect —" Amow broke into a sudden fit of coughing that sounded suspiciously like a cat hacking up a fur ball. The screen went blank.

Algot waited for a moment for Amow to come back online. When the screens remained blank, he shrugged to himself and brought his displays back up. He watched as the squad sergeant barked an order to stop and the little man turned around. The moment he faced the sergeant, the image on Algot's monitor distorted, bending in and out of shape, and the audio feed cut out entirely.

Algot tried to follow their muted exchange. The citizen seemed to slump slightly in resignation, and open his coat. He had what looked like a withered human arm held against one side by his elbow. Algot got no chance to puzzle over it however, as the man lifted up his tee-shirt.

A moment or two later, Lord Amow flashed back across the array. "Now, Overseer," Amow began. "I assume you have rectified the problem with the David girl... Overseer?" Algot was slumped in the Gravichair bonelessly, his sightless eyes rolled back in his head. Amow hissed in frustration and the monitors surrounding Algot went black once again.

* * *

Angus stopped beneath the trees and put his back to the street beyond, leaning heavily beside a jagged rent in the iron fence. As with most of the gardens around New London, the fence was now a broken and twisted mockery of its former self. He reached into his coat and pulled out his flask, taking a long swallow, choking on the fiery liquid.

He bent double, pressing his knuckles against his closed eyes in the darkness. A strangled sob escaped his throat. After a while, he drew a long breath and stood up to take another swig from his flask. He really didn't give a fuck about Overwatch, but there were the empty shells of a dozen soldiers back there in the street, and their voices were in his head.

There were always voices in his head now, but most of the time they were little more than whimpers, or the muffled protests of a soul drowning in the black depths of his mind. When they were freshly harvested though, their pain and fear was a cacophony of confusion, filling his head with anguished cries. The only way to shut them up was to numb himself into unconsciousness.

Still, no time to knock himself out right now. The soldiers were very far from the first souls he had taken, and he'd done it much worse in his time. Dragged them clawing and screaming from broken, bloody bodies. From cous... friends.

Angus had a final drink, and put his flask in his coat, pushing himself away from the fence. He turned and stepped through the torn iron bars, emerging from the shadow of the trees into the dirty orange glow of the street lights. He began his long circle back to Westminster Cathedral.

The streets were desolate, cold. He grew steadily more agitated. Eyes were watching him, and he looked around nervously, hunting for observers in every dark window, around every corner. He kept waiting for his footfalls, the muted thud of his heavy boots, to bring more soldiers. More voices, to crowd his thoughts.

He hurried on, hitching up the desiccated arm he carried beneath his jacket. He knew that Wingwalker was somewhat disturbed by the thing, but he was no more able to give it up now than he was to silence the souls entombed within him. The arm had become his one link to the world as it had once been. The sole, tenuous thread that bound him to this miserable appearance of sanity.

Angus just hoped that the macabre old bastard never got it in his head to take it away from him. There was no denying the ancient shit, no refusal, and the arm was a vital piece in his long play for salvation. You didn't spend more than a century in the company of Crofton Wingwalker without learning a thing or two, after all.

* * *

The once-white walls of the tube station were stained by years of dust, and by smoke from skirmishes with Overwatch before the Underground had been sealed. All but one of the fluorescent lights that ran down the centre of the arched roof had been smashed, and the narrow platform faded into blackness.

Halfway down, light spilled into the gloom from the passageway through to the Jubilee Line. Lawrence climbed out of the dark of the tracks and up onto the platform. Maz was sitting in his customary chair at the edge of the light's reach. The far end of the platform was behind him, a jumble of tables, chairs, and shelves. The man watched Lawrence emerge into the light, unblinking, a smoking cigarette dangling from one corner of his mouth.

"What?" Maz asked.

"Um." It was the best Lawrence could do.

"Yeah," Maz said. "That's about what I thought. So where's the new girl?"

"She, uh, she fainted. Cracked her head on the sink in the transport room. She's in the infirmary."

"Do I need to go check on her, Lawrence?"

"Why? So you can work your unshaven charm on her when she wakes up?"

"Do fuck off, mate," Maz said, and went back to smoking his cigarette.

Lawrence turned and walked off to find the others, hoping faintly for a less uncomfortable atmosphere.

Jon Sutton was cleaning his pistols, of course. Everyone was intimately familiar with his daily ritual. Lawrence could barely stand it any more. The obsession with which the man lined up the horrible red bullets on the table, the constipated pace he dismantled the guns with... it all made Lawrence twitch. He wanted to rush over and sweep everything down onto the tracks. Instead, he just ground his teeth. Jon went rigid if anyone else came within a yard of his bloody guns, ready to lash out like a clap of thunder, ready to break bones.

"Where is she?" Jon asked.

Lawrence was almost as uncomfortable with Jon as he was with Maz. "Banged her head," he said. "Fainted. She's sleeping in the infirmary."

Further down the platform, Talbot turned around from his game of cards with Talbot. "You didn't diddle her while she was unconscious did you, Lawrence?"

Lawrence felt the heat in his cheeks, knew he was going bright red, hated it. "Fuck you, Talbot."

"Yeah, fuck you, Talbot," the other Talbot said cheerfully.

Talbot turned back around. "No, fuck *you*, Talbot."

The one piece of luxury furniture Lawrence had managed to scavenge on his surface raids was a high-backed arm chair. He had given it to Amber, and no one else was allowed to use it. It slowly spun to face the Talbots. The sight of Amber's pale, moonlit skin deepened Lawrence's flush.

She raised one eyebrow in disapproval. "Talbot, leave him alone."

"Ooh, do I detect a hint of... something?" Talbot said. "You aren't worried the new girl might take your place in Lawrence's spank bank, surely?"

"Talbot!"

Talbot and Talbot grinned at each other and sniggered.

Trying desperately to will the heat from his cheeks, Lawrence glanced round at the rest of the platform. At the far end, behind Jon, Mr. Ryder and The Bookdealer sat bent over their perpetual game of chess. The orange-tiled wall, with its brown leaf motif, was a bright contrast to their drab attire. In the other direction, beyond Amber's chair, the old rat-eaten sofa and bunk bed were empty.

"Where's Colette?" Lawrence asked.

"Down in the passages somewhere with Bannister," Talbot said without looking up from his cards. "Trying to help the poor boy forget about his darling Kelly."

"Doing a bloody good job of it, too," added the other Talbot. "If what I heard from down there earlier was anything to go by, anyway."

"Well, be that as it may, we all must gather," Lawrence said. "Now that Lorna has arrived, our purpose is upon us."

Talbot looked at Talbot. "Is he serious?"

Talbot shrugged. "Geeks," he said.

Even Amber rolled her eyes.

* * *

Lorna gently rubbed at the side of her head where she'd cracked it on the sink. The lump had gone down a bit, but the pounding in her head was no better. It was making her cranky, and the way the others squabbled continually wasn't helping.

One of the older men, Orbit the Bookdealer or something, came back from the makeshift kitchen at the far end of the platform. He pressed another cup of tea into her hands. She smiled at him, and then let her attention wander away again.

She wasn't sure what she'd expected. She'd been searching for a way into the underground – the fabled resistance, the escape from Overwatch – for as long as she'd been in New London. She'd not expected much. But when Lawrence had led her through to the aged platform with its single fluorescent light, she'd realised that whatever she'd envisioned, it was something more glamorous than this.

There's nae fucking resistance here, she thought, glancing quietly around. Sure, from what she'd seen in the last hour, all of these people had some fancy trick or other up their sleeves. A fat lot of good that was going to do them against the polis. To be fair though, the only person who thought anything else seemed to be skinny Lawrence.

Lorna was silently relieved that the others seemed to think there was something off about Lawrence as well. She couldn't tell if he just desperately wanted to be part of something exciting, or if he was playing some game she couldn't understand. He seemed convinced that Lorna herself was the key to whatever it was they were supposed to do. They were only waiting on the last two, Henry and Colette, to arrive from down below. Then Lawrence was going to reveal everything to them.

The irritation in the room was almost as strong as Lawrence's nervousness. *They'd better not be long,* Lorna thought, *or either Maz or Jon is going to fucking strangle the skinny sod.*

Then, finally, she caught the sound of footsteps and, holding hands, a couple emerged from the passage to the other platform.

The man – Henry – stopped dead. He dropped Colette's hand and stepped away from her guiltily, staring at Lorna. "K-Kelly?" he stammered, voice heavy with disbelief. Then he fainted dead away.

Lorna looked around the others. "Who the fuck is Kelly?"

* * *

306

Crofton Wingwalker sat cross-legged within a wide circle of chalk. Lines of sigils crept outward from it and formed further circles, which in turn spread their own arcane fingers outward to form yet more circles. The vast room, dancing in the light of a multitude of ritually invested candles, looked like a trigonometric mind-fuck. The culmination of centuries of planning.

Each of the circles held the focus of a single thread of his plotting, all of them interwoven like some great, intricate tapestry. Their forms, their origins, their purposes were as diverse as the places and eras from which they'd been gathered. Arrayed closely around Wingwalker's own circle were the Anglesey Deer, a miniature representation of the red phone box, the East India Co. Knife – Kelly David had provided that, along with herself – and an ancient, golden statue of the lion-headed god Maahes.

It was impressive that Maahes, Lord Amow as he currently styled himself, had managed to clutch to life so tightly. Most of his contemporaries had faded from existence millennia before. But whatever tricks the stubborn fool might possess, a second-rate Egyptian backwater god was no match for the encyclopaedic mind of Crofton Wingwalker.

Angus's entry to the sacristy in the Cathedral above was a soft awareness. The faint esoteric scent from Crowley's left arm always told Crofton where the little lunatic went. He clung to it like a whelp to the tit. If it hadn't made for a useful tracker, he'd have taken it away decades ago.

Crofton could feel the slow bleeding of anima from the sepulchral shell that Angus had become. He was overburdened, and in the natural course of events would be dead soon, ripped apart by the souls trapped within. As it was, he wasn't going to get the chance. The ritual would take place first. Angus would end with the knowledge that he had helped kill the last of the true gods.

Rising slowly to his feet, the old man rubbed his sore knees. He might be the greatest surviving power that walked the earth, but it had been nearly a decade since he had last consumed the boiled fat of a virgin boy. His body was once again beginning to feel the strain of its tremendous age.

Whispering obscure words to himself, he stepped out of his circle, careful not to disturb the precise lines of chalk. He picked his way to the focal point of the room where Kelly David was chained within an enormous circle, naked and spread-eagled. Her back was arched tight in throes of continual orgasm. Her fingers were still clutching convulsively, but she was no longer making a sound. The pale silver cord was clearly visible now, starting just below her navel, stretching up to disappear into the darkness above. Perfect.

Beneath Westminster Cathedral, Crofton Wingwalker stood in the centre of his circle, too restless to sit. The air hummed, crackling as the energy built in the massive chamber. His skin prickled, the hair on his neck and arms standing up. Like before a thunderstorm. He was on the cusp of ascendancy, everything in motion at last.

The flow of anima from Kelly David to the daughter she'd never met was growing ever more potent. The silver cord, fuelled by her ecstasy, was like a line of pale fire.

In the nave above, Angus stood within a chalk circle of damnation. His skin was practically bubbling with barely-contained souls. Perfect. In addition, their release would prove a most brutal diversion for the swarm of Overwatch soldiers coming here to attempt to seize Crofton himself.

Oh, Amow knew where he was. He'd made sure of that, made sure the Egyptian fool knew where Lorna David and her "protectors" were. Amow was nothing more than a big kitten chasing the piece of string that Crofton dangled in front of him.

It was unfortunate that the fools in the Underground had to die in the backlash. Wasteful. Some of them might have proven useful as more than just worms on a hook. The nervous boy would have made a good potion, for starters. There was nothing to be done for it, though. The daughter needed to be suitably charged and primed for when Amow got his claws on her. Then the fool would get a *real* surprise.

Crofton raised his arms to begin his final incantation. White-hot pain seared through his back, and to his amazement, it was not words that came to his lips but blood. He staggered around to see Angus standing there. A savage grin was on the little fool's face. He was holding the ritual athame that had taken his cousin so long ago, and it was dripping with Crofton's blood.

How dare he! Little piss-ant. Crofton spat a mouthful of blood over the idiot.

Angus's eyes bulged in sudden pain. The skin of his chest, bared to reveal the sigil, started to roil as the souls within sought escape. Angus moaned, a tracery of cracks appearing on him. It occurred to Crofton that he might just have fucked up.

Angus's chest burst open with a revolting rip. Blood splashed everywhere. Crofton barely had time to open his mouth before the furious spirits found the hole in his back, swarmed in, and ripped his soul apart.

* * *

A short time later, in the nave of Westminster Cathedral, a platoon of Overwatch soldiers stood nervously around a circle of strange symbols chalked on the floor. In the middle of it lay an ancient, withered human arm.

'Arrayed closely around Wingwalker's own circle were the Anglesey Deer,
a miniature representation of the red phone box, the East India Co.
dagger, and an ancient, golden statue of the lion-headed god Maahes.'

55. The Liberating Blade
by J.F. Lawrence

Time froze.

Angus stared at Wingwalker, suspended in dying mid-fall. Everything around him had stopped, fading just a little, catching him outside time. He looked around. The woman, brought here by the old man's awesome magic, was fixed in a tortured position, no longer straining against the silver chains that bound her. Only Angus could move through time, it seemed. There was a cosmic silence.

The knife's handle was glistening with its latest victim's blood. It seemed to Angus that the spatters formed little crimson worms and blobs that scurried to make themselves into a gruesome message:

WHY, ANGUS, WHY? IAIN

Angus howled. "I'm so sorry," he moaned, over and over again, a mantra of agony. His vengeance hadn't changed anything. There was no salvation.

He had been so fucking stupid. Wingwalker had promised the Earth and everything beyond, offered to make him a great adept, seduced him with the headiest visions of knowledge and power, offered him the universe. Instead, he'd made Angus his slave, warped outside of humanity by his glamours. His master had destroyed him, not made him wise – turned him into a pathetic soul-eater, a desperate addict doomed to be just another broken tool.

That had shifted somehow, in the end. A miracle, after the professor and her deer. The glamour started to fall away following a terrible dream, and over the following months – that seemed to last millennia – he became human again. He knew the agony of every soul he had taken, recalled each face with a clarity that almost blinded him. He understood their terror, living each death as if it had been his own. And worst of all was the sacrifice, the murderous ritual that required the fat of a dying virgin male – the hideous torture he and Wingwalker had inflicted on poor Iain and so many others.

311

That spiritual cancer was all gone now, and there was one last thing to do.

"Hey, Angus."

Angus looked up, horrified. "Oh my Christ!"

"No, Angus, it's only me. It's Iain. I've come for you."

Angus fell to his knees, choking on his tears, and begged forgiveness. Iain took his arm and helped him to stand up on his weak, quivering legs. He hugged his cousin in an embrace that felt like total love.

"S'awright, big man, s'all awright, ken? I understood everything. It wasn't you, Angus, okay? It wasn't you."

Angus felt the pain fading. He was crying now with the joy of the unburdening.

"I know, Angus, I know. It's time to go now, big man. Okay?"

Angus knew. Looking at Iain's tranquil face, he nodded. Smiling with a happiness unknowable to those who are not about to die cleansed in spirit, he was released.

Time unfroze.

56. The Light at the End of the World
by Salomé Jones

Light shone out of the holes in the telephone handset. Cory swallowed hard and put the phone to her ear.

"Hello?" *What should I call him?* "Uh… Lord?"

Something was tickling her face. She jerked the handset away from her ear. Light was oozing out of it, like a thick liquid. It dripped down the handset to her arm and fell in bright drops on the phone box floor.

Whatever, she thought, and put the phone back to her ear, ignoring the light as best she could. "Peacock Angel, forgive me. I don't know how to address Your Greatness. I've never talked to a god before."

"WHY HAVE YOU COME?" The voice boomed out of the earpiece.

Cory jumped. From the air inside the phone box, smaller voices murmured.

What do you want, Corellwen? Why do you fight for them? Why have you chosen this side? Why do you fight for the Lies?

The words resonated from the walls. She looked around, ceiling to floor. She noticed the growing pool of white light in the bottom of the phone box. She could see no source for the voices. Was she imagining them?

"Uh. I came to ask for help. A magician has learned some of the old secrets and is attempting to use them to destroy all the old gods. He's changing our world and now he's found a way to pierce –"

"WHAT WOULD YOU HAVE US DO?" The low, great voice came through the phone, followed by the muttered chorus around her. *Why should we help you, Corellwen? This is your chosen path. You chose this fight. You did not choose a victorious path.*

She thought about what Safran had said. *You love this world,* you *speak for it.*

Hesitantly, she said, "H-Help us. Help us defeat this evil." She licked her lips and stared down at the floor. She could no longer see her shoes. The light filled the phone box up to her ankles. She picked up one of her feet. "Um. There's a lot of… light here. Am I…?" The line crackled. "Are you still there?"

"WHY DO YOU LOVE THIS WORLD SO?" *Don't you know it's not real? It's not real, Corellwen. Like you. Just like you, Max. You cannot be two things at once. All is lies.*

"It's a good world, full of good people." She thought about her mother. Her sister. "People are suffering and dying. My own family—"

"THAT IS THE WAY OF WHAT YOU CALL REALITY. BIRTH, SUFFERING, DEATH." *You cannot escape the suffering. You were born to suffer. There is nothing more.*

Tears stung her eyes. "That's not true. People do good deeds. They help each other. I've seen it with my own eyes. People laugh. There's more than suffering. There's also joy. There's love. Do you *see* us from wherever you are? Have you seen the wonder in a new mother's eyes? We've made something good here." She took a breath, heart pounding. Silence answered her. "Please. I beg you to help us."

There was a faint splashing sound as she shifted her feet. When she looked down she found that the light had risen above her knees. It was much lighter than water, so that she barely felt it as it rose higher. She could see the line of it running out of the handset now. More than a trickle. More like a stream of it.

"Are you listening?" Cory looked over her shoulder through the glass panes for Safran. He was watching, his hand covering one of his eyes. She shook her head at him.

"DO YOU KNOW THE CONSEQUENCES?" The voice boomed out. *Do you understand? Do you see?*

Cory gasped. "What consequences?"

"YOURS IS ONLY A SLIVER OF A WORLD. WE SEE BEFORE US HALF A MILLION CORELLWENS, BEGGING FOR AID, A PANOPLY OF CAUSES, LIGHT AND DARK AND ALL SHADES IN BETWEEN. YOU ARE ONLY ONE. WHICH WOULD YOU HAVE US HELP? WHICH WOULD YOU HAVE US LET DIE?" *How do we choose? Why do we choose?*

"Half a million of me? What? I don't–"

"WE USE A NUMBER SO THAT YOU MAY UNDERSTAND. TRUTH IS HALF OF INFINITY. SOME WILL LIVE. SOME WILL NOT." *Death. Life. All is one. One is all. Everything is the same.*

"You mean… all the dimensions. There's… me?" *Of course there is. Why am I so stupid?* "So…" She felt defeated. What was she even fighting for? It was all so hopeless. She tried to imagine the other iterations of her at this moment. *What if we all give up? Will evil win everywhere?*

She took a deep breath. "Give us a hint, then. Clue us in. Just give us a slight advantage. An ally…" Something tickled her underarm. She glanced down. The light was up to her chest and still rising. She looked out at Safran in panic. "Is this light thing some sort of timer? What will happen when it covers my nose and mouth? Can I breathe in this stuff?"

The line crackled again.

"Are you still there?"

"WE ARE ALWAYS HERE." *Always, always. Everywhere. Everywhen.*

"Look, just a small thing. Just… I don't know. Fuck! Something. Anything. Give us…" She looked outside again. Safran had covered both eyes now. *Damn it. No swearing in front of gods.* She chewed her lip. *What if…?* The light had reached her chin. "Make Safran Alef help us, then." She squeezed her eyes shut.

She waited for an answer from the Peacock Angel, but there was only silence.

"Safran Alef. That's what I ask you for. Do you hear me? Are you even there?" Just after she spoke the words, the light rose over her mouth. It was weightless, but forceful. It wanted inside her. She could feel it creeping between her lips, and she knew somehow it would not be a good thing to let happen. She tilted her face back and shouted into the mouthpiece. "You could save us *all* if you chose to. You don't have to help only one."

"SAFRAN ALEF'S WILL IS HIS OWN." *He does what he wants, that Safran Alef. Yes, he does. He's mad as a hatter. Quite, quite mad.*

315

"What? Are you saying he could help us if he wanted to?"

The phone beeped loudly. "Please deposit two pounds forty-five pence for the next three minutes," said a woman's voice.

"I don't think I have any—"

The light had reached her nose now. She let the phone drop from her hand and stood up on her toes, fumbling around in the opaque, bright pool for the door. The front of the box was opposite the phone side, wasn't it? She couldn't remember. Did it open inward or outward?

She pushed against it but nothing happened. It opened on the left, didn't it? Or was it on the right? She hadn't paid attention. She was running out of air now. Her chest ached with the need to breathe. She slid her hands frantically up and down the front wall of the box, but found no handle, nothing to show her the way out.

She couldn't resist the pull of her lungs any longer. She was going to suck the light inside herself. And then she'd be lost, she knew it. She felt dizzy.

I'm going to die here.

There was a noise from outside followed by a *glug, glug*, like the liquid being poured out of a bottle.

"Did it occur to you to get out of there?" Safran's voice.

Cory opened her eyes. The light was spilling out the door. It had dropped down to her chest. She stepped out the gap in the door, sucking in shaky breaths. There was a soft splash as the light poured out of the box after her.

Cory stepped away from the bright puddle. "I thought you said you couldn't come any closer?"

"You're welcome." Safran retreated toward the car. "Are you all right? Is my jacket all right?"

She blinked at him. "He... They wouldn't help us. Couldn't help us. They *said*."

"Is there a Plan B?" Safran rubbed one hand through his beard.

She nodded. "They said you could help us."

Safran looked startled. "In so many words?"

"'Safran Alef's will is his own.' Those were the exact words. Oh, and also some mutterings about you being mad as a hatter."

"Well, that last part is obviously true. Come on." Safran motioned toward the car.

Cory didn't move. "So will you?"

"Will I what?"

"Help us."

"No. Now let's go back to the car."

Cory crossed her arms. "Why not?"

"Why not? What part of everything I've ever said did you not hear? This is your world. I'm just a witness. You can't be a witness and participant at the same time."

"But the Peacock Angel said–"

"The Peacock Angel said what? My will is my own? Well, my will is that you fight your own battles and I stay out of the way. Now come on."

Cory clenched her jaw. "You said you wanted to help before. Now you have permission. What about your friends? Don't you care what happens to them?"

"What friends? I remain aloof." He shrugged.

"What about the kids you teach?"

"What about them? If they don't make it they'll just be sucked down into some other so-called reality. It's all very simple, really." He rubbed his nose. "Will you come on now?"

"What about *me*, then?"

He looked up at the strange, grey sky and shook his head. "You? You just like me for my clothes and the fact that I give you rides when you're bleeding."

Cory felt a growl rattle in her throat. "Fine." She peeled the heavy jacket off her shoulders and held it out. "Take your stupid jacket."

He reached over and pulled the jacket out of her hand. "Hey, I'll have you know I paid eight pounds for this fine jacket at the Salvation–"

Cory held up her palm. "Talk to this right here because I'm done listening to your rubbish." She spun on her heel and began walking back along the road. She felt like crying but she knew she couldn't let herself.

"What are you doing?"

"I'm walking back to London to look for help." She kept walking. It was getting darker with every step. She could barely see the road.

"You're going the wrong way."

She felt Safran's hand on her arm. She whirled around. She couldn't see him but she could hear his breathing. Words tumbled out of her.

"Of course you hate it here. You don't love anyone. How do you think people learn to love? They let themselves get close. But you hold yourself apart from everyone and everything because it makes you uncomfortable. A witness? That's just a wasted life. Why do you think we do this? To fucking feel, Safran. There's no other reason." She slapped at his hand on her arm, the force stinging her palm. "That's what real is. The lie is when you live without feeling." She pushed out with the heel of her hand toward where she thought his chest was. It connected, harder than she'd expected.

"Ow!"

"Now, which way is it to London?"

"Oh, for the love of Aziz and all his minions, you had me at 'take your stupid jacket.'"

"What? What are you saying?"

He grabbed her wrist and started pulling her along. "I'm saying I'll help you."

"You will?" She screamed and tried to throw her arms around him, but he kept walking and she missed.

"I'll help you once. If the future gets taken care of. At a time and place of my choosing."

She had to hurry not to be dragged behind him. "Time and place of your choosing? What does that mean exactly?'

"It means… I don't know what it means! It sounds good. Let's say, when the need is greatest."

The car door opened in front of her and the interior light came on. She could see Safran in the dim glow.

She smiled at him. "Thank you. You won't regret it."

"I regret it already. Now get in."

She punched him in the shoulder.

"Ow! You're too *violent*. Now get in the Fiat of Doom before something worse happens to you."

She wasn't sure what he meant, but she knew she didn't want to find out. She got in.

57. Backlash
by Tim Dedopulos

The Overseer was unkempt, past his prime, and thoroughly dead. The fellow lolled in his chair bonelessly, gawping at static screens. Amow sighed, and prodded the corpse. Stone cold, of course. No rigor mortis, though, which was interesting. He waved his assistant away impatiently, and the girl scurried off to wait outside the door.

Once she was gone, he allowed the fingers of his right hand to extend some decent claws. They felt good. Strong. He tipped the Overseer's head forward a little, and slid one of the claws into the top of the skull. It was a little like slicing through a decent stilton. He made contact with the brain inside, and frowned. *No residual energy. Not even a trace.* The man had only been dead a few hours, so there was no way that his spirit ought to have disengaged so thoroughly.

"Damn it."

There had to be some sort of soul-capture at play. Amow pulled up the room's spare chair, and sat. After a moment to centre himself and gather his essences, he took hold of the Overseer's head again, and tugged it forward into his lap. Held between his hands, it became the focal point of his concentration. A cascade of impressions poured off the corpse, links to other people and other times. There was just a suspicious blankness in the magical frequencies, though. It didn't make any sense... unless someone was deliberately impeding inquiry. *A block? Surely not the ludicrous idiots in the tunnels.*

Amow blasted a gout of energy down the link. Sparks hissed, and long, thin streaks of the corpse's skin cooked instantly, crackling up with an appealing aroma. It was like pounding a brick wall, though. The block was strong, and almost totally invisible. Surprisingly good work. Definitely not that Fishbein fool. Amow took a deep breath, called up all of the energy he could spare, and lashed out. The block held. He kept up the torrent, ignoring the loud sizzle as the body roasted, pouring force upon force. A mere *fraction* of that energy had shattered Carthage, but the block stubbornly refused to yield.

The room exploded as a backlash smacked Amow straight out of his seat. All the monitors burst simultaneously, showering him with a rain of glass shards. He lay there on the floor for a long moment, smirking.

The creator of the block was dead, and the block was gone with him. The trail was clear. He followed it back with just a thought, mildly surprised to find himself in Westminster Cathedral. The entire edifice stank of ritual, stale soul-theft, and the Anglesey Deer. Finally, the Deer. He could feel the fading traces of that crazy old bastard Wingwalker, which explained the block's impermiability. It didn't matter. The ancient pest was dead at last, and long overdue it was, too.

"MARY!" He put a bit of extra force into the roar.

His assistant came running. "Yes, s..." She trailed off when she saw him. "Are you all right, Lord?"

"What? Oh, yes, of course. Get hold of Dixon and the girl and tell them to get to my office immediately." He sprang up from the floor, and brushed the glass from his suit and mane. "Oh, and have this man delivered there as well. Swiftly please, Mary. I don't want it getting cold."

Fifteen minutes later, Amow was in his office, picking the last shreds of lunch from his teeth. A knock at his door announced the arrival of his lieutenants at last. They entered the room, and stood in front of his desk. Dixon at least had the grace to look curious.

"I've found the Deer," Amow said. "I assume you two can mop up our little insurgency problem without my direct assistance?"

Elwyn nodded impatiently.

Dixon glanced at her. "I've checked the reports. It should be fine, Lord Amow."

"Good," Amow said. "Get on with it, then. I'm taking the Bully Boys. You can use as many men as you like."

"Thank you," Dixon said.

Amow snarled at him. "Well? Go on."

As they left the room, he tuned his thoughts to the proper channel and issued a summons. He followed in their wake.

It was going to be a beautiful day.

* * *

After Lawrence had told them what he knew, about the prophesies, about the past, about the future – the *now*, really – Amber sat thinking through all the implications. The world was in ruins, he'd said. Lorna, a child of the changed world, confirmed much of his story. Amber wished they had some wine or beer. Pear cider sounded lovely. It would have helped calm her nerves. Instead she sat watching the others, listening to snatches of conversation.

The expression on Henry's face was finally starting to look somewhat normal. He, Lorna, and Maz of all people had been off to one side for half an hour now. Amber sighed. Another complication. It had come out in the briefing that Lorna was the mythical Kelly's daughter, which made Henry the likely father, and left Colette in a somewhat awkward position. It couldn't have helped that there barely looked to be ten years of age between parent and child. From the bits of shouted conversation she could hear, it seemed both father and daughter had been stunned by the news. Lorna had never met her parents, and Henry had been unaware of her existence until now.

Only Orbis and Mr. Ryder seemed unaffected by the revelations. They were engaged in another of their interminable chess matches. Mr. Ryder always played black, which didn't seem entirely fair. Then again, Amber wasn't sure that she'd seen any of the games start or finish, so perhaps they were just shuffling pieces around as a way of getting the youngsters to leave them alone. If so, it was working. Lawrence was talking at Colette, although she clearly wished he wasn't. Talbot and Talbot meanwhile were trying to wind Jon up, but he wasn't biting. Too busy polishing his bullets. A little pang of regret stabbed her in the side, but she forced it away.

"My knight!" Mr. Ryder's voice cut across the room.

Amber glanced back at the old men. Orbis was holding a black chess-piece, and both he and Mr. Ryder were staring at it as if it had sprouted fangs. She moved over to them. She could have sworn she wasn't nervous, but she couldn't stop shivering in spite of the warmth of the room.

"Is everything okay?"

322

They both looked at her.

"That is an interesting question," Mr. Ryder said eventually. "Wellness can be as troublesome to define as truth or reality. Okay for whom? For me? For my companion?"

"For all of us." Amber shifted her gaze back toward where the others were standing. "You know…"

Mr. Ryder grinned, a surprisingly dark expression that held nothing of amusement in it. "No, Ms. Goodman. Everything is far from being well." He looked across at the piece that Orbis was still holding thoughtfully. "We are going to be under attack very shortly now."

Orbis stood up on his spindly legs, and slipped the chess piece into his pocket. "Yes. It's time we took our little game to the station hall, Rider."

Mr. Ryder nodded. "The crow has fallen, undone by the handyman. At the last, the lion scents the deer, and wakes. Talking of which…"

At the other end of the station, she could hear Henry gabbling, excited and urgent. "I said it's Kelly!" he yelled. "She's there!" Maz said something, but Henry cut him off. "I can feel her, damn you!"

Mr. Ryder gently shook Amber's elbow to get her attention. "Gather them," he said. "Then join my summer friend and me in the great hall. It has begun."

Ten minutes later, Amber had finally managed to get everyone out to the old station hall. Henry was buzzing with impatience, and had made it perfectly clear that he was only in the tunnels still because he didn't know a way up to the surface. Neither Lawrence nor Maz seemed inclined to help him get out in the face of Mr. Ryder's unnerving warning.

The old men were facing each other over a primed chessboard, one that she hadn't seen before. It was big, at least twice the size of the ones they usually used, and polished so that the squares gleamed in the artificial light. The playfield was bordered with bands of golden writing, letters or sigils or something of the sort. The two armies facing each other were very different, as well. White seemed to be drawn from forest imagery, with stout oaks for castles and a druid as king. Black just came across as sinister, with deeply cowled major pieces lurking behind pawns that could have been people – artists, tradesmen, milkmaids, each one very different.

Henry had started tapping his foot irritably by the time the old men looked up from their board.

"My thanks to you for assembling," Mr. Ryder said. "As Lawrence has told you, there are forces arranging themselves against us. They seek all our deaths, in one way or another. This seems a little unreasonable to both my friend and me." He gestured to Orbis.

The other man nodded. "Not sporting at all. Messy, besides. I never could abide ignorance."

"Some of you have earned this death sentence merely because you have set yourselves in opposition to those who would control all. Others are foci, due to be absorbed. Fortunately, we do have certain means to resist such scouring. Our enemy calls himself Amow in this time and place, and at this critical moment, he is distracted. He sees what you have seen, Mr. Bannister. He is divided. You are going to have to divide likewise, in order to work effectively against him."

"Us?" Amber looked at Mr. Ryder curiously. "What are *we* supposed to do? We're just ordinary people. We don't even have any weapons. Well, except him." She nodded to Jon.

"Ms. Goodman, have you asked yourself why you're here?"

She shrugged. "The phone box."

"You're not the only ones who entered the phone box. Many others didn't survive that encounter. You have been chosen."

"I have no idea what you mean."

"Each of you has a patron." He studied the chess board. "I believe you met an elderly gentleman by the name of Legba before you arrived with us. You exchanged gifts."

Amber blinked at him. The others were staring at her. She swallowed, opened her mouth and closed it again without saying anything.

"I see we understand each other." Mr. Ryder nodded.

"What about you?" she asked.

He smiled. "There are certain laws that bind my old friend and me. We may not act at this time, not without permitting undesirable actions on the parts of others. So we are simply going to sit here, and play a little game."

Orbis nodded. "Most regrettable. But unavoidable. So you young folk need to split yourself into a trinity of trinities. Three threes, to answer the call."

"I'm going after Kelly," Henry said, his voice shaky.

"Of course you are, dear boy," said Orbis. "Your daughter will go with you, too."

Lorna shuddered, and then shrugged. "Fuck it. Aye. Let's go drop in on me mam."

"I'll go with you," Colette said quickly. "It only seems right."

Mr. Ryder nodded. "As you wish. Enter the box. It will leave you somewhere near your destination."

Henry immediately darted towards the box, turning in the doorway to glare impatiently at the two women. "Come on!"

"Well," Lorna said, looking round at the rest of the group. "See yous all later." Colette managed a shaky smile. They followed after Henry, ignoring his frown.

"Then there were six," Maz said.

Orbis pointed at the Talbots. "You two. Separate teams. The echoes will be disorientating to the other side."

They looked at each other and grimaced in synchrony. "Fine," they said.

"I'll have him," said one, pointing at Maz.

"Only if I get the Lone Gunman," said the other, cutting over Maz's half-hearted protests to point at Jon.

"Fine," said the first. "I want Amber, too."

"Hey," Amber said.

"Oh, no you don't," said the other Talbot. "You've already got Maz. You can have Larry the lamb. *I'm* getting Amber."

"Hello, I can *hear* you!" She glared at them.

"All right, keep your hair on. I'll let you have her."

"This isn't fucking school sports lessons," Maz said.

"Oh no?" Talbot grinned nastily. "Got any better ideas? Assuming you're happy to go along with the creepy old guard over there. I didn't know they had it in them."

"Yeah, they put on quite the performance," said the other Talbot.

"It doesn't matter," Lawrence said. He sounded down. "Let's just get on with it." He went to stand by one of the Talbots.

"Wrong Talbot, mate," Talbot said.

"Oh." Lawrence moved position.

"They're fucking with you," Maz said. "He's the right one."

"Oh," Lawrence said again. He seemed even more depressed than before.

"Would you two stop it?" Amber's voice sounded harsh, even in her own ears. "It's no time for joking around. We may all be about to die."

The Talbots shared a slightly guilty smirk.

She took Jon by the arm and guided him over to the correct spot. He seemed broadly oblivious to what was going on. She turned to the old men, studying each of them for a few seconds. She realised she'd never actually *seen* them before. There was something odd about them. As if the lines on their faces, the folds of skin on their necks, weren't skin at all, but marble, smooth and radiant. *Old men, but then… not old men.* "What now?" she said.

"Excellent question, my dear," said Orbis, frowning thoughtfully. "Pawn to King's Bishop Four, I think." He moved a piece on the board.

The hall shimmered. Amber sucked in her breath. She heard gasps from one or two of the others as well. For a long, horrible moment they were plunged into total darkness. Vast wings seemed to beat in the air all around her. Then illumination returned, a patchy blend of light and shade that made the room seem far larger than it had before. Tunnel entrances led away from the room to the left and right. The door they had come through from the platform was gone.

"Eh?" Lawrence seemed confused.

"Your move, Rider," said Orbis.

The Talbots nodded, and exchanged grim looks.

"Come on then," Amber's Talbot said, and led her and Jon towards the right hand side of the room.

* * *

"Get down, eejit." Lorna punctuated her furious whisper with a sharp tug on Henry's shirt. He didn't resist, dropping below the windowsill.

"Sorry," he mumbled.

"Look, I ken that this isnae familiar to you, but fae fuck's sake. Keep out of sight, pudding."

He swallowed, and tried to force himself to concentrate on her words – and that voice – rather than her face.

"How far do we have to go?" asked Colette, her voice deliberately soothing.

"Quarter mile, maybe," Lorna said. "It's crawling wi' Overwatch goons, though. They dinnae normally fash much about the auld parliament and Cathedral, but something's got them well narky today."

Ice trickled down Henry's spine. They had to know about Kelly. "It's –"

"Aye, we know, everything's all about me dear auld long-lost mam." Lorna sounded bitter.

Henry's head swam. "Don't you dare –"

"Ha!" Lorna cut him off.

Colette placed a hand on both their shoulders. "Please. I know this is difficult. For both of you. We need to keep calm."

Henry swallowed. "Yeah. Sorry, Lorna."

"Aye, reet," she said. There was a hint of softness in there, though. She shot him a warning glance and darted a look over the windowsill, her hair ruffling in the sour wind. She chewed a lip pensively. "There's a row o' houses we can work through, tae get closer. Shells, again. I've used them before. The Baron had them picked clean years ago, so the Overwatch dinnae pay them much mind nowhen. The two o' yous need to be quiet though, y'ken? Stomp on another chunk o' glass with they great feet o' yours, and we'll be done."

"I get it," Henry said. "Promise. And look –"

Lorna shook her head. "Whatever fucking mushy crap you've got in that noggin o' yours, can it 'til we're safe. Your lady-friend is right. Out here, it's business only. Or death."

"Right," he said.

Lorna nodded once, and slunk out from under the window

to flatten herself against the remains of the wall. From there, she darted to the doorway, beckoned to them to follow, and vanished into shadow. Henry shared an unfathomable look with Colette, and followed.

It took the best part of twenty endless minutes to pick their way through four broken husks. The buildings had once been central London, familiar and safely eternal. Seeing them like this was like coming home to find that your lounge had turned into a haunted asylum. It was deeply unsettling, on a heap of different levels. They were in the future, but not that far – twenty years or so, as near as he could tell from what Lawrence had said. The London he knew held over ten million people. This one would be lucky to support a hundred thousand. In Westminster, the ruins they were creeping through would have been office blocks. It was hard to imagine.

"Look!" Lorna's urgent murmur seized his attention. "There."

Through a doorway, and most of a window beyond it, he could see Westminster Abbey. It was blackened with thick, irregular streaks of soot, and some of the decorative architecture had crumbled, but it was in much better condition than most of the city. Overwatch soldiers were everywhere, menacing in their visored facelessness. They almost could have been robots.

"That's the pigeons," Lorna said.

Henry blinked. "What?"

"Robots. The pigeons are the robots."

Was she reading my mind?

"Ah, stop staring like that, you big nelly. I'm nae mind-reader. You were talking tae yerself."

"Oh. That's not good."

"Damn straight it's not," she said.

"Wait," said Colette. "Did you say that the pigeons are artificial?"

"Aye, but reet realistic like. Mobile cameras, y'ken? Drones didnae catch on. Too noisy. Too obvious."

"Oh. How thoroughly unpleasant."

"Yeah," Henry said. "You could say that." Through the shattered window, the troops were moving. It looked like they were gathering. He pointed at them. "Hey, look."

"Hello," said Lorna thoughtfully. "What's all that?" She looked the way they'd come, back into the heart of the ruined complex. "They'd not usually be so obvious if they'd caught hide nor hair of us."

"Maybe they're moving on," Henry said.

Lorna looked amused. "Aye, and mebbe it's Hogmanay tae boot."

Despite her scepticism, the soldiers mustered into one block, facing up the street towards where the old British parliament had been. A short time later, they started moving off in the same direction. Lorna hissed, and carefully crawled over to the shattered window. Using the bits of side-wall as cover, she made cautious observations both up and down the street. A moment later, she was back with them. "Looks like they've moved off fae now. I don't like it. It stinks of trap."

Henry drew in a sharp breath.

"But," she said forcefully, giving him a baleful stare. "It's all we've got. I just hope the auld bastards back at the station know what they're doing."

"All right," Henry said, trying to keep the relief out of his voice. "Lead on, MacDuff."

She glowered at him. "It's 'lay on.' Also, they wuz about to go at it tae the death, and I'll thank y' not tae quote fucking propaganda at me tae boot."

"Uh." It was all he could think to say.

She grinned at his distress. "Ah, dinnae fash yerself, sassie. Let's do this."

The three of them made their way to the edge of the ruin, and after a long final check on Lorna's part, dashed across the road towards the end of the Cathedral.

The instant that he stepped through the hole, it felt as if every eye in the world was staring down at him. He broke out into a cold sweat, and fought the urge to cower on the tumbled flagstones of the former pavement.

"G'aun!" Lorna's voice was full of urgency.

He gulped, and scuttled out into the road. *Don't look around. Just move.* He forced himself to obey, and drew on all his energy to race across the horrible, open expanse. In his imagination, pigeons watched coldly through laser-eyes, and blank-faced killers trained rifles between his shoulder-blades. Then he was in the building's shadow, tucked up against the wall, head down, heart like a steam-train. Slowly, slowly, he got his breathing back under control.

Then Colette was beside him, panting. "However did you move like that? You were like a dart! It's incredible." She smiled. "I knew you had plenty of stamina, but..."

He tried to answer her smile. "I don't like feeling hunted."

A moment later, Lorna thumped down beside them. "Areet. So far, so good. C'mon."

Henry shook his head at her resilience, and followed her round the end of the building to a doorway. She scouted ahead again, and then waved them through.

The pews had gone, and the whole edifice had been extensively defaced, but the Cathedral still had a certain beauty about it. The ceiling soared above them on majestic arches and buttresses, still intact. The floor and walls had been built to both inspire and last, and the graffiti and filth could only go so far to detract. There was little sense of the divine here any more, but a power did linger. A testament to mankind's sense of spiritual potency, maybe.

"What the howling fuck?" Lorna was a short distance away, looking at something on the floor.

He and Colette hurried over. At Lorna's feet, a wide swathe of the floor had been cleared. Ritual symbols had been carefully painted onto it in red, gold and black, a concentric circle design containing a pentacle, with subsidiary nodes marked at vertices and other advanced flourishes.

"It looks like a circle of containment," Henry said. "Um. For summonings, usually. Demons, spirits, that sort of thing. What's that in the centre?"

"An arm," Colette said. "Nearly mummified, and covered in marks."

"Oh, yes," he said. "I see. Glyphs. A real mix. I can see Sumerian, Ogham, Nahuatl, Norse runes, even some hieroglyphs."

"I've seen that fucking arm," Lorna said.

330

They stared at her.

"The filthy, schemie fucker in the phone box." She blinked back at them. "Dinnae look at me like that. There wuz this nasty weegie shit-heel in the phone box, just before I came down to join yous all. Ratty hair, a long overcoat, and he was cradling this fucking arm like a babbie at the tit."

"Are you sure?"

Lorna looked at him, her expression flat. "Come the fuck on, man. How many fucking dried, severed arms covered in crazy occult bullshit do you think there are in London nowadays? It's nae a boom tourist export."

"Right," he said.

"It disnae matter, any road. Can you feel where our damsel is?"

Now they were inside the walls, she was like a blazing beacon. "Yes. Down."

"The crypts," said Lorna. "Aye, because of *course* the fucking crypts."

They crossed the hall to a set of stairs carved into the floor. Lorna led the way down, muttering to herself about the light. They came out into a corridor.

"Down there." Henry pointed.

"Aye," Lorna said. "The way that's all lit up like a fucking Christmas tree. There's nae suspicious about that." She moved on anyhow, grumbling quietly, her back as tense as steel cables.

Henry followed, mind blazing. *Kelly was alive, but...* He forced himself not to think, to just walk. He barely noticed when Lorna stopped outside a door, just breezing on past her, following the call.

The room inside was large, brightly lit by burning torches and candelabras. Every inch of the surface was covered in ritual markings of incredible delicacy. Off to one side, wrapped in impossible chains of blazing energy, spread-eagled and naked, was Kelly.

It was really her, as he remembered her, flame-haired and smooth-skinned. Behind him, someone cursed. He dashed towards Kelly, skidding to a halt at the edge of the blood circle she was enclosed in. She was writhing and moaning, and he gradually realised that it was ecstasy working on her, not pain.

"Kelly!" She didn't react. "KELLY!" *What have they done to her?*

"Henry, you should look here." Lorna's voice was gentle, but insistent.

"What is it?"

"Come see."

He pulled himself away from Kelly's horrific prison, and went over to where the women were standing. "Don't go near her," he said, as he approached them. "Don't cross the circle. We don't..." He trailed off.

There was another large blood circle, set around with vaguely Celtic symbols. Two corpses lay sprawled across it. They looked as if they'd melted together somehow, bubbling into each other. From hair and clothes, one was an old, refined man, and the other was a street tramp.

"That's the arsehole with the arm." Lorna waved toward the tramp.

The man's hair and beard clicked into place in Henry's mind. "Fuck. That's the Scottish cunt who..." He looked over his shoulder. "Oh. Fuck!" He kicked the little bastard hard in the back of the head – then again, and again.

Colette took his hand. "Henry," she said, softly.

"Right." Henry forced himself to stop kicking. The little shit *was* dead, after all.

"Areet, Henry. You're the one wi' the knowledge here. What the fuck is all this?" Lorna's wave took in Kelly, the walls, the corpses, and the selection of ritual items worked into the ritual design.

It was an important question, and Henry tried to focus. He found himself looking back at Kelly and forced his gaze away. "Hm. I should remember that knife in the tramp's hand. As for the rest of it, well, that looks like a miniature of the phone box. That's a votive Egyptian statue there, looks like Maahes, the god of Warfare. I can see a rune-stone, an ankh of some sort, a Cunning Man's crow-staff, a Balinese demon mask... Hang on..." He picked his way through the pattern. Was that the Deer? It was! "And this is the Anglesey Deer. It's an old friend of mine." He snatched it up, and felt a calmness he'd barely been aware of missing settle over him.

"Ahh." The voice was deep, rich, rolling with amusement. "I rather thought you were going to take all afternoon."

Henry spun round to face the door. A tall, powerful man in a Saville Row suit was standing in the doorway. His head was that of a lion, complete with an elegantly flowing mane. Henry stared at him. *Amow.* Somehow, seeing him in the flesh was worse than he'd imagined.

"My dear Mr. Bannister, my sincere thanks for reuniting fully with the Deer. I've been waiting so very long to eat you."

Henry blinked. *Eat* him? "What have you done to Kelly?"

Amow chuckled. "Me? Nothing. You'll have to ask Crofton Wingwalker about her – he's the older of the two corpses, the one with the hole in his back and the soul like confetti."

Deer held tightly in one hand, Henry flowed over to the ornate knife and snatched it up without breaking stride, coming to rest between Amow and the women.

Amow laughed, sounding genuinely amused. "You really have no idea, do you? Child, I was born with a knife in my hand, carved out of Amenti by mother's will and the need of the people. There is nothing you can do. Absolutely nothing." He raised his hands, and clapped twice. "Restrain the male. Kill the females."

From the walls stepped a ring of burly, grey-skinned thugs, half a dozen or more. They looked – no, they were – identical: shaven-headed, pig-eyed, heavy-set, in jeans, white t-shirts and heavy black boots. *Maz's damned bully boys.*

As one, the thugs sniffed the air, grinned and charged.

* * *

The tunnel was white-tiled, strangely bright and clean compared to the station tunnels that Amber had seen so far. Maybe it didn't matter any more, though. She really wasn't sure the tunnel entrance had even been there before. Reality wasn't what it used to be.

Jon and Talbot seemed happy enough to just get on with things anyway, and let reality take care of itself. Well, Talbot did. If she was honest with herself, she wasn't sure that Jon really knew where he was or what was going on. He was totally wrapped up in his little red bullets, crooning to them as he walked.

Talbot twitched. "They've arrived."

"How do you know?" Amber tried to keep the fear from her voice.

"We saw them, myself and I. They're fanning into the tunnels."

"Uh, okay. So what do we do?"

"Shoot them," Jon said, his voice wrapped in bliss.

Talbot shrugged. "Pretty much, yeah. This way." He led them round a corner, and down a sharp curve.

The world rippled for a moment, like a flash of unreasonable heat-haze, and the corridor they were in was now hacked from unfinished stone. It was dark and oppressive, like an old mineshaft from a black and white movie. A small amount of light came from primitive little electric lamps on the floor, powered by thick cables that ran off into the distance. The curve they'd been negotiating was gone.

"Just a moment," said Talbot. "Along here." He turned to the left and blithely trotted off, Jon in tow.

Along here, my arse, Amber thought. She bit back a sarcastic comment, and followed. The dimness lifted slightly, thankfully. It wasn't until she glanced down that she realized she was glowing with the soft, silvery light of a bright moon. Talbot glanced back at her, and nodded. It was all she could do not to scream. For some reason, she had a flash of memory of the black cat, Max, that had come to visit one afternoon. What would the world be like to a cat? At least as inexplicable and randomly dangerous as anything she was experiencing, she guessed. Maybe it really was best to try not to think about it too much.

"They're up ahead." Talbot's voice was quiet. "Back against the wall."

Jon snarled silently, lips peeling back further than she'd have thought he could manage. Then he shook his head, and jumped past Talbot. Shouts erupted down the corridor. He fired off two barely-aimed shots and moaned, a low noise of pleasure that made Amber's skin crawl.

Ahead, someone screamed. Gunfire chattered back towards them. Talbot swore, pulled a pistol of his own from his coat, and dropped to one knee. Jon fired again, and did a dreamy twirl in the middle of the corridor, laughing.

In her mind's eye, Amber saw a figure raise a chunky assault rifle affair and open fire in jerky freeze-frame movements. The bullets zoomed down the corridor, as fast as lightning. They stitched a line of red up Jon's front, bloody little explosions that rose up his stomach and chest to destroy his face. He twitched and collapsed, laughter gurgling from ruined lungs. She shrieked, and the vision popped like a bubble. Jon was still there, dancing. Acting on instinct, she kicked out, catching him behind the knee. He staggered, and fell against the wall, still laughing. Bullets chattered past him, striking sparks off the floor and the wall at the back of the junction. Talbot fired three times, cool and efficient. The gunfire ceased.

"Aww," Jon said. "You took him away. Good thing there's more." He dashed up the corridor.

"Fuck me." Talbot shot her a look. "What a space cadet."

"He's..." she began, defensively. She shrugged. "Well, yeah."

They followed Jon, cautiously. When they got to him, he was caressing one of his horrible little projectiles. Two more were just lying on the ground. There was only one body, cradling the large gun that she'd imagined.

"What the hell?" *Don't think about the vision, Amber. Just don't think about it.*

Talbot looked at Jon and his bullets, and shook his head firmly. "I don't want to know."

She didn't correct him.

He took the assault rifle from the corpse. "This is more like it. Two clips, too. Here, take my pistol."

Amber shook her head.

"Don't be crazy! You can at least put down some covering fire."

"But..."

"Look, don't use it if you don't want to. This is the safety, here. Just switch it off when you need it. Really. Just in case."

She reluctantly took the weapon, and put it in her shining jacket, determined to ditch the horrid thing at the first opportunity.

"Thank you," Talbot said. "Jon, you got all your little darlings?"

"Oh yes. Can you hear them purring?"

Talbot paled a little. "Purring. *Sure.* We've got to move on. The others are up ahead somewhere." He gathered the two of them with a glance, and continued along the corridor.

They moved onwards. Talbot confidently picked a route through a network of tunnels, differing from each other only in size. The mine workings appeared to extend off indefinitely in all directions. There was no suggestion that they were abandoned, but at the same time they were oddly empty. She spent half the time looking over her shoulder or down side-tunnels, terrified that they were about to stumble onto another pocket of armed murderers, but either they were well-dispersed, or Talbot was somehow able to avoid them.

After an uncertain time, she distinctly heard gunfire, and other, less easily identified noises. She flinched, as Talbot stopped dead in his tracks. "Shit," he said. "Something's wrong."

Jon smiled, and caressed his pistol.

What did Talbot mean? Trying to ignore Jon, Amber followed nervously as Talbot sped up a bit. They trotted down the tunnel, and came to a large five-way intersection. Soldiers were ahead of them, facing away.

Jon mewled, and whispered something to his pistol. He turned to her and Talbot, placed a finger against his lips with comic exaggeration, and said, "Shhh!" Then he fired the gun, and went oddly rigid.

One of the men ahead jerked back, and threw his arms wide. A little electrical storm seemed to kick off in the back of his neck, crackling with red lightning. *What the hell?* The lightning was eating away at the soldier's body. He jerked spastically, making wretched noises, diminishing swiftly. It looked like he was being sucked into a black hole from a cheap sci-fi show. Apart from the infernal colour-scheme, that was. His fellows were darting glances his way, but obviously had other things to worry about.

With a horribly final crackle that rang down the tunnel, the soldier vanished. Jon let out a loud groan of pleasure, and relaxed limply. The storm abated for a moment, the red bullet hovering impossibly at its heart. It darted to the next soldier, and slowly burrowed through the side of his helmet and into his ear. Immediately, his helmet started to crumple as his head imploded.

"All of them," Jon crooned. "All of them."

Amber dropped herself to the floor, curled into a little ball with her hands over her ears, and let her mind go away.

There was a period of soft blackness, and then a high-pitched humming noise jolted her. As she tried to figure out what it was, she realized Talbot was shaking her. "Come on, Amber."

She made a sound of protest.

"It's done for now. It's not safe. Come on." He had hold of her wrists.

She reluctantly let him pull her up onto her feet. Maz, Lawrence and the other Talbot had joined them there, presumably from another tunnel.

Lawrence had an assault rife now, as did both Talbots. She glanced at Jon, who was smirking like a cat. She looked away again, unable to ask the question.

Maz noticed, and answered it for her anyway. "They're not bullets. Just look like 'em. They... devour. Mulch down the soul into energy, and feed a bit back to the user, for a hit. Evil little fuckers. No coming back from one of *those* for another try on the wheel."

Another try on the wheel? Amber frowned. "Um, can anyone else hear that ringing sound?"

"Don't be rude about my darlings," Jon said. He sounded light-hearted, but there was a definite undertone of menace to his voice.

Maz shuddered. "Wouldn't dream of it, mate. Bloody useful, right at the moment. Talking of which... Peony, you know what to do."

One of the Talbots sighed. "Yeah, yeah. Talbot, come here. His pearly highness there wants us to have a big old man-hug."

"Peony?" said the other Talbot.

"Gotta have something to call the pair of you," Maz said. "You're Poppy. He's Peony. So much more egalitarian than Alpha and Beta, don't you think?"

"Fuck off," the Talbots said, simultaneously.

Amber pressed her fingers to her ears. "It's nice," she said, trying to be encouraging.

The Talbots gave her a long look.

"Just bloody hug, you muppets," Maz said.

The Talbots approached each other. Amber could see Maz brace himself as they touched. The ringing got much louder, and she felt a faint sense of the world lurching. A moment later, as they were letting go, she dimly heard a very shrill scream.

Maz breathed out. "Ouch. Well done, lads."

"What the hell?" Amber grimaced and rubbed her ears.

"Peony got hit with some sort of resonance spell." Maz looked smug. "Now when they make contact, there's a really hideous blast of feedback, sorta thing would have made Hendrix cream his jeans."

"Won't it hurt them?" Amber studied the two identical men.

"Not as much as it'll hurt what's coming for us. Come on, let's see if we can find that screamer before she gets her fucking breath back."

Lawrence looked like he was about to have a nervous breakdown. He gulped, visibly trying to pull himself together. "Which way?"

"That way will do for a start," Maz said, pointing in a broadly leftwards direction. "Hang on..."

Reality rippled again, shimmering in its fake heat haze. The junction they'd been standing at was gone. Instead, they were in a gently curving corridor. It was entirely metal, with a floor-way made of grating, and pipes of various sorts running along the walls. Lighting was provided by softly-glowing strips in the ceiling. It looked cluttered, particularly after the Spartan mineshafts.

"That'll be the Rider," Maz said. "Bless him."

"Where are we?" asked Lawrence.

Maz snorted. "Still right here, lad. Still somewhere else. Try not to ask meaningless questions, eh?"

Lawrence nodded, cowed.

Amber patted him on the back gently. "I don't like it either."

The look he gave her in return was an unguarded blend of gratitude and worship. She smiled back weakly.

"That way," one of the Talbots said, poking his thumb back over his shoulder.

Maz nodded. "Not bad. Yeah, that's the one."

They set off down the corridor. It split at a gently Y-shaped junction ahead of them, the Talbots confidently taking the left-hand spur. Maybe fifty feet along, they came across some charred corpses.

"You're welcome," said Maz. "But don't stop on my account."

Amber looked away from the bodies.

"At least these poor bastards get to keep their souls. Hopefully when they come back down next time, they'll get easier turns."

"You really mean that?"

"Yeah," he said. "Don't worry about death. That's no worse than waking up from a vivid nightmare." He paused for a moment. "It's the whole soul-shredding thing you want to worry about."

"Oh," she said. "Uh, thanks."

They moved on. At the next T-junction, the Talbots were already turning to the right. Ahead of them, there was a big circular metal door filling the tunnel. Maz raised an eyebrow, and pressed a chunk of metal that could have been a button. There was a clank, and the door whooshed back into the walls. He sighed, and stepped through, the others close on his heels.

They were in a huge metal-plated hangar or warehouse or something, hundreds of feet across, dozens of feet tall. The central section of the floor was completely cut away, opening onto a lightless abyss. The edge had a protective railing, but it was still dizzying just to look at. In the middle of the abyss, a square column of plain steel rose out of the depths, continuing upwards until it was maybe ten feet above the level of the hangar. It couldn't have been larger than six feet on each side. On the top of the column, concentrating on their game, sat Orbis and Ryder.

There was a sound on the other side of the hall, and Amber looked past the column to see soldiers fanning through another circular door. There was someone else with them, as well.

"That's not good," Maz said quietly.

"I challenge." The voice was female, pitched to carry in the large space.

"Very well." Orbis's voice flooded the huge room, soft but perfectly audible. "What precisely is the nature of your challenge?"

"You're interfering, Lords."

"Oh?" Orbis sounded amused.

"You've been altering the terrain to favour your preferred pawns. That's interference, and the laws do not permit it."

"The challenge is accepted for consideration, weighed, and rejected in accordance with the forms," Mr. Ryder said. His voice was politely formal, and as cold as ice.

"There has been no favouritism," Orbis said. "No special considerations. The laws are witness. My old friend and I are simply... playing."

Maz bumped into Talbot, knocking him towards Talbot. Amber clamped her hands over her ears.

"I –" The woman broke off in a shriek as the two Talbots collided.

"Thought so," Maz said, a pained look on his face. "Stay close, you two."

The two identical men stepped apart, eyeing each other with what looked like concern. "All right, mate?" they asked in unison.

There was some movement at the other end of the hall. Amber's spine started tingling, and her stomach jumped. In her mind's eye, she could see Jon falling, falling... "Jon!"

He turned towards her, amiable in his anticipation.

She felt herself swaying. "Come away."

A powerful black figure stepped through the doorway behind him. Jon took a step, and the new arrival casually planted a broad knife through the back of his neck. Jon fell, still smiling, crumpling on the floor like a broken puppet. A puddle of blood oozed out around the blade.

The black-clad man stepped to one side as soldiers boiled out of the door they'd come through. Someone was screaming, raw and horrible. To Amber's shock, she realized the screams were her own. A hand grabbed her jacket and dragged her back, away from Jon's lifeless smile, even as fire blossomed within the doorway and soldiers began howling in pain.

The world shimmered. The metalwork of the room took on a nasty reddish tinge, and was now fiercely scored with deep, unsettling glyphs. A hint of sulphur wafted through the air. Then the gunfire started up.

* * *

Henry darted forwards to intercept the thugs, knife held chest-high, ready to strike. Energy pounded through him, the Deer flooding his senses. In contrast, everyone else was wading through quicksand. He closed with the nearest thug, easily swaying aside from a clumsy punch. Following the movement through, he came alongside the man and slashed at the side of his throat with the dagger.

It was like cutting through toffee. Henry stared as the knife scored through the grey flesh without even a hint of blood. The neck knitted itself back up as the blade passed through it. By the time he'd completed the move and regained balance, the thug was turning towards him again, a very ugly grin on his face. There was no sign that he'd even been scratched.

Henry took a step back, fighting a sudden wave of horror. *What the* –? Pain exploded in his back. He staggered forward, lurching out of the way of the thug in front of him at the very last moment. He dropped into a roll to avoid another blow, and when he sprang back to his feet, glanced over to see three of the attackers closing on him. Lorna and Colette were on the far side of Kelly, edging round to keep the blood circle that contained her between themselves and one of the bullies.

He danced back a few steps, towards the corner, leading the thugs away from the women. His lower back hurt like hell. A fourth thug forced him to cut his retreat. Instead, he stepped forward, hoping they were dumb enough to get in each others' way. Fists and feet pounded out at him. He moved aside from one attack, turning his head to avoid a second punch.

A knee came for him, and he kicked out at it, spinning the thug off balance. The joint should have broken, but he didn't wait to check. He ducked another punch, striking out at a groin with the heel of his palm. The thug staggered back. A meaty hand fell on his shoulder. He grabbed it round the wrist, and dropped onto his side, rolling and kicking out so that its owner went flying into one of his companions.

Henry sprang to his feet again, and looked around. One of the thugs was disentangling himself from another's feet, but they were all grinning identical idiot grins.

Pain blazed in his left temple, and his sight went blurry. His head felt like raw meat. The force of the blow flung him back towards Kelly. He fell, scrabbling away from the thugs. There were five in the group now, all sneering. *How were they all standing, still?* His heart sank. He tried to get up, and failed. The room was spinning too hard.

Footsteps darted up to him. Lorna and Colette. *Oh no.* "Don't," he managed.

"Shh," said Colette. She put her arms round him.

The bully that had been chasing the pair of them started closing on them.

"Nae fucking way," Lorna said, ferocious. She planted herself squarely in the bully's way. "That's my auld man."

The thug stepped forward, and casually swatted Lorna out of the way. She screamed in pain, flung backwards by the blow. Almost before Henry had realized what was happening, she was collapsing back across the containment field and through the horrible chains, to fall on top of Kelly.

There was a sickening sense of depressurisation, a deafening wail of sound, and the world turned mauve.

* * *

Lawrence pulled Amber back, away from the door. He tugged her head down a bit as he did so. "Keep low!"

She nodded. In front of her, Maz flung fire at the door, adding to the smoke and confusion that was already there. The gunfire from that entrance eased, then fell silent. He took some swift steps back, and crouched down beside Lawrence and Amber.

"That should do most of them," he said. "The unshielded ones."

She shared a quick look with Lawrence.

"Listen. I don't want either of you touching that gun of Sutton's. Got it? It's way too fucking risky. If you check out here, at least you'll just end up back in the Real Place. Go playing around with that thing, and... well. Just don't touch it."

She nodded.

"I've got to see a cat about a dog. That Talbot feedback trick won't work forever. Luck."

"You, too." She watched him leave, and looked over at Lawrence.

He shrugged. "No idea." He fiddled with the large gun at his side for a moment. "I should stay with you. Keep you safe."

Amber shook her head. "Thank you. We'll be an easier target together, though."

"Okay then," he said, deflating. "I understand. Take care."

She let him go. *Safer for him.*

He scuttled off, and she shrank back a few more steps, towards the railings and the abyss. She closed her eyes, and took a deep breath. *'You're going to be called on.'* The voice was deep and dark, and echoed to her out of the vaguest pits of memory. *'To do what?'* she'd asked. *'When you get there, you'll know.'*

She exhaled, took another deep breath, tried to calm herself down. She forced the tension out of her shoulders and stomach as best she could. The fear lessened as they relaxed a bit. She took the pistol out of her pocket and looked at it, tried to figure out how to work the safety button. Failed. Her hands were shaking too hard. She could still hear the odd hum, sometimes ratcheting up a notch to give her a small shock.

As she crammed the gun back into her jacket, gunfire chattered somewhere across the room, back and forth. It seemed time to move a little, so she did, creeping along in the same direction as the railing. Metal rang out behind her. She ignored it, and looked around.

To the left, the Talbots were standing side by side in mirror-image poses, fists ready to strike. The man they were facing was heavy-set, wearing a long black trench-coat over dark clothing. *The man that killed Jon!* He had a thick scar on his neck, and he was brandishing a knife.

As he stepped forward, the Talbots split apart. The humming diminished. They were moving in perfect unity, almost as if one mind worked both bodies. They spun, and instantly the three men were locked in an intricate dance. The scarred man lashed out, forcing one Talbot back even as the other blocked the blade's descent. They dropped, legs sweeping for the man's ankles, but he jumped, tucking his feet out of the way and striking down with a heavy fist. It was turned aside by one of the Talbots' shoulders.

The sequence of moves and countermoves became too confusing to follow. Arms, feet, fists, blade, attack after attack, somehow none of them finding their target. The Talbots never quite touched each other, but each time they came close, the world rocked slightly, and the humming stung her ears and sent an odd feeling down the back of her neck. And even though she couldn't see any blows connecting, the Talbots were taking damage. One had a cut over his eyebrow. The other's cheek was bruised, and he was favouring his left leg. If the scarred man was hurt, it didn't show.

A wild yell drew her attention across the room. Maz was standing no more than five feet from a pale woman with long dark hair. She was wearing a black cat-suit, of all things. They were both rigid with tension, muscles straining. Vague hints of flickering energies and sounds played over them.

Why doesn't he use his fire? Amber wondered.

Lawrence charged at the woman, waving his gun like some sort of musical instrument and yelling. Maz's head turned towards him for an instant. The woman's expression twitched just slightly, and blood erupted from Maz's forehead. The humming became a sharp squeal. Lawrence collapsed mid-stride.

Maz grimaced and raised a hand, but the woman was slowly forcing him back now, step by step, towards the railings. Amber still couldn't see the forces she used. Maz was flinching as he gave up ground, like he was being hammered on repeatedly.

Damn it. I need to help him. Her mind whirred, searching for a solution. What she found was a memory. *I feel like I can fly.* There had been something small and red...

Amber looked back towards the door, where Jon's corpse lay, a short distance in front of a pile of charred bodies. His strange gun had dropped from his fingers, the bullets spilling out of it like blood. Those bullets. They'd scared Maz.

She glanced in the direction of the fight. Against the railing, Maz's face was grim. His back was bent over the rail, painfully twisted. Each shudder seemed to force him closer to toppling. The woman's face was a mask of savage glee. She took a step towards Maz, and raised her arms, hands pointing towards him.

Don't touch the gun, Maz had said. *But what if I could…* She concentrated on one of the red bullets, looking at it as hard as she could. To her left, a Talbot bellowed in pain. She felt a wave of nausea wash over her. The universe seemed to scream into her ears. She ignored the noise, staring at the bullet. Her eyes began to ache, and a strange pressure settled between her eyebrows. She breathed deeply, slowly, kept up the focus of her attention. The world contracted, and then the bullet shivered, and floated upwards. It felt like it was reaching towards her somehow, a little tendril, but in her mind's eye, a small white and red ball dropped into the way. The tendril touched the ball, and retracted.

The bullet was in the air above Jon. *It's working!* Amber pictured a stream of water flowing from the door, past Jon, and through the room to where the woman had Maz up against the railings now. The bullet spun slowly, to face the place where the two were fighting, and started flowing towards the woman. Amber deepened the stream a little, pouring herself into it. The water sped up, carrying the bullet with it. She pushed harder and harder, letting herself sink back to a sitting position. Anything, just to keep the flow moving. *Come on, come on!*

Against the railing, Maz didn't seem to have noticed the river flowing past him. Shooting forward on the torrent now, the little red bullet tore into the pale woman's wrist. The woman shrieked, a horrible blend of agony and utter desolation.

Three things happened almost simultaneously. Maz sagged to the floor. Off to Amber's left, someone shouted. She looked round to see the scarred man frozen in mid-swing, staring towards the cat-woman. The Talbots struck instantly, one grabbing the man's head as

345

the other threw himself at his feet. As the man fell forward, Talbot yanked his head back savagely. The neck snapped with a sound like a rifle-shot. The sound seemed to send a cloud across Amber's vision. She watched in her mind's eye as the red bullet hung inside a little red electrical storm before turning and ploughing into Maz's neck. She snapped back to the moment. *Maz!* But he was still there, crumpled next to the railing.

The screams were quietening. The woman staggered back, her face full of horror. Her arm was completely gone, and the monstrous bullet was burying into her shoulder. She jerked and twisted as it burrowed inside her, and then at last she was collapsing in on herself. A moment later, she was gone. The red bullet hung for a moment, in a haze of lightning the colour of blood.

Time seemed to stutter. Amber heard the deep, dark voice again. *You will be called on.* The bullet turned, angling toward where Maz lay. Amber saw herself as if from outside her body. Without thinking, she took two steps and leapt. She was floating, gliding toward Maz, as slow as molasses. Time swirled round her. Voices she couldn't quite make out. Faces flashing past. She thought of Stuart, his green eyes. *Will you stand on a hilltop and promise to live with me forever?*

And then she was in front of Maz, the bullet creeping toward her as if she had all eternity before it arrived. There was the shrill of the universe flailing. She clapped her hands over her ears. The bullet sped toward her.

"Bishop takes queen." Mr. Ryder's soft voice was as clear as a bell.

The white and red ball from her memory hung in the air in front of the bullet. There was a red flash as the two collided. The bullet burst, sending out a spray of electric sparks that burned like fire when they hit her.

Amber crashed to the floor, tumbled into a sitting position and vomited noisily all over her own legs.

* * *

Henry shook his head cautiously. Taking heart from the way it still appeared to be attached to his body, he blinked a few times.

Everything stung, and his back hurt like hell, but he seemed to be okay for the moment.

A ferocious roar scattered his thoughts. *Amow.* The reality of the situation came crashing back. He scrabbled to his feet, glancing around in a panic. Colette was on the floor next to him, looking groggy. Lorna and Kelly were off to the side, trying to disentangle themselves. *Kelly was awake!* The bonds were gone, too. His heart leapt.

In the doorway, Amow threw back his head and howled again. He was hunched over a little, and his body language suggested discomfort. His face looked to have paled as well, although it was difficult to be sure. The thugs had been scattered around the room, but they were busy picking themselves up and dusting themselves off.

Amow stared at Henry for a long moment, snarling. Finally, the lion-headed man pointed a thick, wickedly-clawed finger at him. "Crush this fucker."

The thugs came together swiftly in a cluster. Then, incredibly, they dropped into a huddle like something from an American football timeout. Henry looked around quickly and snatched up his knife, for the little good it had done so far. When he glanced back up, he almost dropped it again.

The Bully Boys were melting.

He stared as their heads sank into one huge blob. Arms and bodies flowed together, clothes vanishing completely. They blurred and faded together into a vile pillar of bubbling flesh, scattered with eyeballs, mouths, clumps of ratty hair.

The towering pillar screamed, as much in triumph as in pain, and contorted. Writhing, it seemed to split under its own impossible mass. Henry almost sighed in relief. But instead of falling, the tower shuddered apart, forming legs. Long, thin arms shot out of its mass, first a few and then a score or more, whipping around like tentacles. Each one ended in a cruel hook. Eyes formed around the top of the pillar, a ring of them, shockingly human-looking. Several maws clustered below them.

It took a thundering step towards Henry. Half a dozen tentacles reached toward him. "Oi, twat." It's voice was an eerie chorus of malice, full of stupidity and hate. The tentacles beckoned, horribly.

"Come on, if you think you're hard enough."

Henry could hear Kelly and Lorna talking quietly, urgently. He swallowed, and took a step back.

The thing laughed. It surged towards him, shockingly fast and smooth. Henry dived to the side, rolling, the power of the Deer surging within him. A bludgeon of tentacles smacked into the floor where he'd been standing.

He came to his feet to see the thing turning towards him, its height shrinking a little as it took a couple of moments to spread itself wider. He glanced around. Lorna was darting across the back of the room, and Amow stepped out of the doorway, caught somewhere between a chuckle and a cough. Kelly had her eyes closed again, and Colette was beside her, helping her to her feet.

The power of the Deer was beating within him, now. He could feel the blood quickening in his ears, pounding like surf. The thing advanced on him, sniggering to itself, backing him towards the corner of the room. He let it herd him, then stepped forwards, slashing as a tentacle reached for him. The knife sliced through it, and the piece dropped to the floor. Henry grinned at the thing's wince.

Pulling on all the power he could draw, he threw himself at one of its legs. He crashed into the creature like a wrecking ball. The leg bowed in. Then it snapped back into place, and he was thrown backwards onto the floor. The creature laughed, low and gurgling.

As he stumbled to his feet again, he noticed that the severed tentacle was flowing back towards the main body of the thing. A moment later, it rejoined the mass. He tried to duck to the right, to get away, but the thing easily shifted to block his way. The creature advanced a little more, ropes of tentacle held out to both sides, hemming him in. "Stupid little geek," it said, its ring of eyes glittering with malice. "You shouldn't fuck with the Bully Boys."

Amow was advancing towards them, grinning a massive, hungry grin. To Henry's amazement, Lorna was creeping up behind him, the votive Maahes statue held over her head like a bludgeon.

Henry forced himself to laugh loudly. "You're as pathetic as that scrawny kitten you work for. Watch this!" He started waving his hands around in what he prayed was a suitably mystic manner.

Amow coughed out a laugh, and Lorna smashed the statue down onto his head. Amow immediately dropped to his knees, mewling. The creature stiffened, tentacles going rigid.

As Lorna lifted the statue up for another bash, Kelly took an unsteady step toward them. "Crofton Wingwalker left you a message," she said, her voice barely audible. Then she called out a guttural phrase in a language Henry had never heard before.

A black circle appeared around the abomination. It roared like the ocean, quickly filling with indigo light. There was a loud sizzling crackle, and a stifling stink of violets, and then it winked out, taking the creature with it.

Lorna smacked Amow with the statue again. He snarled, and swiped at her weakly, forcing her to dance back.

There was nothing between Henry and the lion-headed bastard any more. He sprang forwards, blade flashing in the candle-light, and buried the dagger deeply into Amow's left eye.

The man froze. Waves of sandy colour rippled out from the dagger, washing over him. After a moment, his long whiskers crumbled, dropping to the floor. His mane followed, and an instant later he was collapsing entirely, sagging out, losing all form until all that remained was the East India Company dagger lying neatly on top of a pile of sand.

Henry stared at it for several long seconds. Then he turned to look for Kelly. She was standing, leaning on Colette for support. He took a step toward her, her eyes rolled back in her head and she flickered, as though she were only an illusion. There was a soft pop, and Colette gasped.

Where Kelly had been a moment before, now there was only air, and the scent of flowers.

* * *

It was several days before Orbis and Mr. Ryder pronounced everyone recovered enough to consider leaving. Amber found it difficult to accept the apparently festive atmosphere. Lawrence's wounds had healed amazingly well under Colette's care, but Henry was a shell of his former self. None of them knew for certain what had happened to Kelly, but it was the whispered consensus that she wouldn't be back. All that seemed to keep Henry from complete despair was Lorna's presence. Then there was Maz. She had the impression that he'd changed in some way, but perhaps that was no surprise. He certainly wasn't being communicative about it.

After lunch on the fourth day, Orbis called everyone together to meet up in the station hall. She was relieved to see that it was back to being its old, abyss-free self.

"We must take our leave from this time," Mr. Ryder said.

"Shame," said the Talbots, speaking perfectly as one. "And I was having so much fun here." It was a disturbing effect.

Henry had gone as white as a sheet. "Stop that, you arseholes." They smirked at him. "Whatever you say, Hankyboy."

He shuddered, and Colette put her arm round his shoulders.

"You've all been through a lot, but it's not over yet," Orbis said.

Amber groaned. "Can't we go home?"

"Of course you may," Mr. Ryder said. "But ask yourself this: how did London find herself in the condition in which you see her now? Surely you do not imagine that this occurred in just one night?"

"Well, no, of course not," she said.

"And I assume that you would rather not experience the fall of civilization for yourself, first-hand?"

She kept quiet.

Mr. Ryder grinned at her wolfishly. "Then, Ms. Goodman, there is still work to be done. But not tomorrow. Or yesterday, as it were."

Orbis gestured widely. "Hold hands, please. In a ring."

Lawrence hesitated.

"You, too, young man," said Mr. Ryder. "You have a role in the past, a history to slip into. Everything will become clear in time."

Blushing, Lawrence nodded, and moved into the group.

"Kick back, relax a bit," Orbis said. "Catch up on some reading."

Mr. Ryder smiled, not entirely reassuringly. "When the call comes, you will know."

The room spun, faster and faster, walls blurring. The world jumped horribly. Amber gasped at the torrent of air sucking her up, and up. After a long time, she came to an abrupt stop. Her head pounded queasily. Disoriented, she swiped hair from her face and looked around.

She was in a phone box. Through the glass, she could see the street – dark, but familiar. She shoved the door open and stepped out onto the pavement. She moved away from the box a couple of metres. To her great relief, nothing happened. For a few seconds, she just stood there. Drinking in the sounds and smells of London – *her* London. Then she took off running along the familiar route toward home. Past the terraces, the roundabout with its pub, the corner shop. She ran all the way to the tower of flats where she lived. She slowed at the gate, and caught her breath as she walked through the front garden, up the steps and into the building.

James was at the front desk. He grinned when he saw her. "Indigo," he said.

She laughed. "Starfish."

The lift doors slid open, and she stepped inside. A few seconds later, the lift stopped and Amber darted down the hallway to her flat. She patted her jacket pocket and found the bump of her keys there. She took them out and opened the door, quietly. She kicked off her shoes and slid her jacket off, tossing it onto the sofa. Then she walked quietly into the bedroom and stood in the doorway, staring at the long, broad form under the covers. After a moment she tiptoed around the bed and pulled the curtains open, just a little. A sliver of silvery light stabbed through them, making her eyes ache. The light shone on the face of the sleeping man.

Stuart made a soft noise of protest, and shifted slightly. She took a deep breath and felt herself relax. She reached out to shake him, and froze. There on her finger, bright with stones, was the ring he'd given her. Beside his head, on the pillow, was a large white chess-piece. A bishop.

She went round the bed, undressed, quick and silent, and slid under the covers beside him. She sat back against her pillows. Her head was whirring. *So many questions.* Over Stuart's shoulder, the alarm clock read 2:22. A wry smile crept onto her face. She lay down, pulled the covers up, and snuggled herself up behind him.

Our heroes will return in Book Two.

Coda. Karma's a Bitch
by Sezin Koehler

The door of the red phone box shattered as Mondo Xang crashed through, tumbling in a ball of expletives to the ground. His green cape wrapped itself around him in a bulletproof cocoon, worried by the hint of danger.

Sputtering, Mondo punched the cape. He cursed as he bruised his hand again. "For the love of sex, I'm fucking safe, you idiotic thing!"

The cape shrank to its smallest size.

"Oh, don't tell me I've somehow managed to hurt capey-wapey's little *feelings.*"

The cape somehow got even smaller.

"Jesus Christ throws up! Remind me to ask The Deity for a man's cape next time." Remembering where he was, Mondo jumped to his feet, fists raised, staring into the booth. Waiting.

"Come and get me, Orchis Morio – you sorry excuse for a rat turd!" Mondo counted to ten. The phone box remained nothing more than a broken old piece of street furniture. What was it even doing there? Surely everyone just used mobiles nowadays? Orchis Morio stubbornly failed to turn up. Mondo put his hands down. "Hah! Take that, bootlicker!"

Satisfied, smirking, he turned and walked away, assessing his surroundings. Back in London. Good. Late evening or early morning, a park, a flickering street light. A black cat stalked past, glaring at him before sauntering off.

Picking at the crotch of his grey Kevlar suit, Mondo grimaced. "While I'm complaining to the Deity about you, cape, remind me to tell her to work on my outfit. She really needs to see about putting some goddamn room around my jewels. I can feel the ball-sweat dripping down my leg."

The cape stayed silent, but he knew it was listening. After a

353

moment, he looked left and right frantically. Trees moaned under the weight of the wind. What were they hiding? "Whose ass do I need to kick next?"

A body slammed into him from behind, biting and scratching at his face. Staggering under the unexpected weight, Mondo slammed a sharp elbow backwards. It connected with a meaty thump. There was a grunt as it hit home, followed by a thud as the body fell to the ground, whimpering. Mondo turned to see a naked woman curled into a foetal position, blood oozing from her mouth.

Oh fuck, I just hit a girl. I'm so gonna pay for this. Despite the occasion, his eyes couldn't help roaming over her bare expanse of tightly-toned flesh. "Cape! A blanket."

The cape shivered, and flowed out into a coarse woollen blanket, coloured an ugly brown. Mondo fingered its rough weave.

"This? This is the best you could do, you ineffectual piece of cheese mould?"

The cape shuddered, retracted, and sullenly formed itself into something more like thick brushed cotton, in such a way as to suggest that it heartily wished it had been a better person in its last incarnation so that it could have avoided being stuck serving such an almighty asshole. Mondo glared at it and covered the girl, scowling at the bruise already blossoming in her side from his reinforced elbow. He winced, and apologised to The Deity.

The Voice's response was immediate, and depressingly shrieky. "Don't apologise to me, you moron! Apologise to HER!"

"Okay, all right! Santorum!" Mondo looked down at the naked woman. "Lady, I'm sorry! Why the hell did you attack me like that, though?"

She was out cold however, her breathing shallow. Mondo wrapped the blanket closer around her and picked her up. She weighed just a tad more than a feather. Was she human? He couldn't tell. Too many shapeshifters around these days. They were a plague, like insurance salesmen and politicians. Hell, they probably *were* insurance salesmen and politicians. Easy to take on a human form, appear weak and then BAM! – your nuts are in a sack. That evil bloody child he rescued from slorgs in the Calaris Dimension, for example. Flesh-eating little Andronican shit. Would have been more than just his nuts stuffed into a lunch-box if The Deity hadn't intervened. Mondo shuddered at the memory of tentacles quivering hungrily down his belly towards his pride and joy. Way too close to properly re-earning his 'Dead Man' title. *Never again.*

Mondo walked away from the phone box, towards the flickering street light. The nearer he got, the more resistance seemed to build. It felt as if his feet were encased in cement – as if a rubber band had been stretched across his chest, pulling tighter with every step forward. He tried to press on. *SNAP!* He was jerked backwards, smashing into the red phone box. The impact annihilated what little bits of glass remained in the crumpled door, and further caved in the already-twisted metal.

"Mohammed on a fucking pogo stick!" Mondo's back felt like it was cracking as he pulled up. He couldn't keep hold of the woman. She thumped to the pavement with a dead sound, her skin dotting with blood as she landed in the glass shards. Not even a moan.

The phone rang, and Mondo screamed again. He recovered, and slapped himself across the face. "Buck the fuck up, you fucking Nancy. For the love of orgies!" The phone's peal was unpleasantly strident against the quiet chirping of the night. Insistent. He considered letting it ring, but found himself unable to stop reaching for it. His cape fluttered up and wrapped around him, sensing imminent danger, but Mondo couldn't do anything with the warning. He lifted the glittering black handle from its perch.

"Hello?" Mondo heard his own voice, echoing infinitely. "Hello!?" A more insistent and slightly desperate echo. "HELLO!"

* * *

On the shimmering sidewalk, the woman opened an eye. A cruel smile trickled down to her mouth. *Just you wait,* Morio thought, from inside the captive body. *Our ride is just beginning, you lizard-livered thief.*

As Mondo Xang screamed hysterically into the phone, Morio closed his stolen eyes and went back to feigning coma.

A Quick Note

If a book is going to have a chance at being successful, by far the most important factor is readers' opinions. So if you've got this far, please do consider leaving a quick review at your favourite on-line retailer – even just a line or two. It makes an incredible difference to all of us, and we would really appreciate it. Besides, writers always love to hear from someone who has read their work.

Thank you so much!

~ Everyone at Ghostwoods Books

Dramatis Personae

* *denotes important primary character*
** *denotes important secondary character*

Agnes Cornish is Darren Cornish's mother.
First (and only) appearance: 36. Kicking Off

Alexander is a young Greek man on a mission.
First (and only) appearance: 24. A Taste of Bitter Gold

** **Alice** is a possible former girlfriend of Jon Sutton's.
First mention: 2. What a Little Moonlight Can Do
First appearance: 23. Still Life

Alyssa (Vandenbussche) is Gloria's sister and Horace's daughter.
First mention: 14. A Brief Transaction
First appearance: 53. The Magus

* **Amber** Goodman is a young woman living in London, recently abandoned by her boyfriend.
First appearance: 2. What a Little Moonlight Can Do

** **Ambrose** is a former lover of Richard.
First mention: 12. Death's Dateless Night
First appearance: 28. Dear Time's Waste

* Lord **Amow** appears as a lion-headed man, and has some unfortunate hungers.
First mention: 15. Elsewhere
First appearance: 18. Here, Kitty!

** **Angus** is Iain's cousin, a Glaswegian chap with mystical ambitions.
First appearance: 1. Oh Aye, Crofton

Bernard is Jon Sutton's brother-in-law.
First mention: 33. Bullet Time
First appearance: 40. Nothing Happens, Endlessly

Brandon is an American student in London working on his master's degree.
First (and only) appearance: 29. Pushing Forward Back

** **Colette** Wilson is a woman whose journal Amber finds in the café.
First mentioned anonymously: 10. Past Tense
First mentioned by name: 38. Hell Hath No Fury
First appearance: 39. Heat and Rust

** **Corellwen** (aka **Cory**) is an emissary from an alternate reality.
First appearance: 7. All Things Considered

Darren Cornish lives in a barge on the Thames.
First appearance: 32. The Old Barge

* **Crofton Wingwalker** is a notorious occultist, author, and very bad man.
First appearance: 1. Oh Aye, Crofton

** **Mr. Dixon** is the head of a band of thugs and scientists.
First appearance: 3. For Whom the Phone Rings

Drinking in Cakewalk Kennington is a former world traveller who now resides in the park.
First (and only) appearance: 40. Nothing Happens, Endlessly

** **Elwyn** is one of Amow's lieutenants. She grew up with Corellwen but made some very different choices.
First named appearance: 21. Max

* **Gloria** Vandenbussche is the daughter of Horace Vandenbussche.
First mentioned: 2. What a Little Moonlight Can Do
First appearance: 13. The Go-Between

* **Henry** Bannister is a professor at McMurtry University. He is the boyfriend of Kelly David.
First appearance: 4. Tourist Trap

** **Horace Vandenbussche** is a wealthy philanthropist and antiquities collector.
First mention: 4. Tourist Trap
First appearance: 43. When the Phone Rings

Charles **Huntingdon-Smythe** is the disturbingly well-informed father of two of Maz Fishbein's childhood friends.
First mention: 17. The Storyteller
First (and only) appearance: 51. We Don't Like Cricket

Iain is Angus's cousin.
First appearance: 1. Oh Aye, Crofton

James is the porter in Amber's building.
First appearance: 2. What a Little Moonlight Can Do

* **Jarreth** Medlin is an American who recently moved to London.
First appearance: 3. For Whom the Phone Rings

* **Jon** Sutton is Amber Goodman's former boyfriend.
First mentioned: 2. What a Little Moonlight Can Do
First appearance: 32. The Old Barge

* **Kelly** David is a professor of antiquities at McMurty University. She's the girlfriend of Henry Bannister.
First mention: 4. Tourist Trap
First appearance: 13. The Go-Between

** **Lawrence** is a resistance fighter from the future.
First appears: 53. Who the Fuck is Kelly?

Papa **Legba** is the Haitian loa (god) who stands between humanity and the gods. He waits at the crossroads and mediates communication with the spirit world.
First anonymous appearance: 23. Still Life
First named appearance: 34. Convergence

** **Lorna** David is from the future.
First appears: 49. Cat Amongst Your Pigeons?

Margaret is a little homeless girl. She appears primarily with her mother.
First anonymous mention: 29. Pushing Forward Back
First appearance: 30. Phone Boxes Taste Bad

Mark is Mr. Ryder's caretaker.
First (and only) appearance: 8. Dementia

** **Mason** is a world-jumping vampire.
First appearance: 9. All Fall Down

* **Max** is a black cat who lives in Amber's neighbourhood. See **Corellwen**.
First appearance: 2. What a Little Moonlight Can Do
Max appears anonymously in some stories.

* **Maz** Fishbein is a spiv magician, and a finder of things and people for hire.
First appearance: 15. Elsewhere

Mondo Xang is a dead man, given a last chance to improve his score with the Goddess.
First (and only) appearance: Coda: Karma's a Bitch.

** **Mr. Ryder** (aka The Rider) is a dementia-ridden old man, apparently.
First appearance: 8. Dementia

** **Nadia** Zahradnikova runs Café McLaughlin.
First mention: 3. For Whom the Phone Rings
First (semi-anonymised) appearance: 10. Past Tense

(Not) Max, aka Nax. A black cat that seems to show up from time to time. See **Elwyn**.
First appearance: 21. Max
Nax appears anonymously in some stories.

** **Orbis** the Bookdealer (also known as just The Bookdealer)
First mention: 5. The Crimson Tower (This chapter is a journal article that Henry reads.)
First appearance: 54. Who the Fuck is Kelly?

Penny is Jon Sutton's sister.
First appearance: 33. Bullet Time

The **Phrygian** is an unpleasant collector.
First mention: 3. For Whom the Phone Rings

** **Richard** is Ambrose's former lover.
First appearance: 12. Death's Dateless Night

Robin is Cornish's former girlfriend.
First mention: 32. The Old Barge
First (and only) appearance: 42. Like the River Itself

** **Safran** Alef is a storyteller who works with kids. (Jesus was a carpenter.)
First appearance: 17. The Storyteller

** **Stuart** is Amber Goodman's current boyfriend.
First appearance: 2. What a Little Moonlight Can Do

* **Talbot** is a middle manager in a London call centre.
First appearance: 3. Echo

About the Contributors

Robert Bal (UK) is a Londoner currently living in British Columbia, Canada in the guise of an English teacher – a façade that quickly dissipates upon close inspection, revealing the careworn expression, chewed fingernails and ground-down teeth of an inveterate writer of fiction, short stories and poems.

Chris Bissette (UK) lives in a small house with too many books in Manchester, UK. He writes short pieces about the interstices between light and dark, and is currently at work on his first novel. You can find him online at **chrisbissette.com**, or on Twitter as **@pangalactic**.

Joff Brown (UK) is a magazine editor who sometimes writes stories for cash. He's written a series of six kids' detective stories, a few Doctor Who short stories for Big Finish, ghost stories, and a properly ridiculous number of fairy tales, amongst others. One day he would like to retire to a fictional seaside town called Elmore St Leonard.

Francesca Burgon (Canada) is a stagehand by career, a poet and a dreamer by her heart, and writes screenplays for fun. She lives with her son, a cat and far too many funky hats to make it practical to move easily.

David Church Rodríguez (France) started writing to avoid having to talk. He writes in both English and Spanish, and occasionally publishes short stories and translations here and there. A collection of his Spanish writing is due to be released in 2013. He currently lives near Paris and has a day job making people happy.

Gábor Csigás (Hungary) is a writer (with most of his short stories published in Hungarian) whose surname was, as far as he knows, not invented by H.P. Lovecraft, even though it might seem and sound so to some. He's also a designer (and a developer, where applicable) of book covers, websites and other weird things. You can find his portfolio at **gaborcsigas.daportfolio.com**.

Peter Dawes (US) is an author of urban fantasy, native to the United States. His stories often crawl from the inner recesses of a dark cellar and keep him up late at night until he finally succumbs to copying them down. One of these days, he might seek help for the voices in his head, but until then, they keep him amused. He is committed to a man named Victor, who has learned to tolerate the bouts of psychosis because the voices are rather fond of him. Peter also may or may not be a vampire. He leaves that for the reader to determine.

Tim Dedopulos (UK) is an unrepentant writer, editor, puzzle creator and game designer. A long-time lover of genre, he is particularly interested in the places where prose, film and game are coming together. He sometimes wakes up in the middle of the night crooning "Oculus Rift!" He blogs occasionally at **ghostwoods.com**, but can be found more reliably on Twitter as **@ghostwoods**.

James 'Grim' Desborough (UK) is an Origins' Award winning writer for tabletop role-playing games but also dips his toe into comics and fiction writing. Find him at Postmortem Studios, **postmortemstudios.wordpress.com**.

Hollis Dorian (US) is an artist, author, and supervillain. His paintings, illustrations, and velvet literary ramblings can be found at **hollisdorian.com**. Mr. Dorian currently resides on Earth.

Warren Ellis (UK) is a graphic novelist, author and columnist. His latest novel, *Gun Machine*, was released by Mulholland Books in January 2013, and is being developed for television by Chernin Entertainment and FOX. His first non-fiction book, from FSG, is due in 2014. *Red 2*, the sequel to the Bruce Willis/Helen Mirren film *Red* which was based on his graphic novel of the same name, will be released in August 2013.

erisreg (US) is an acerbic hermit in the woods of New Hampshire. He spends his time with chaos and magic, creating and trying to keep the damage to a minimum...

Kara Yoon Frame (US) was a traveler in the Himalayas for several years. She returned to study 3D Computer Graphics. Her cantastoria exploration continued with facilitating arts non-profits and production in intermedia performance only to rediscover her roots in illustration, sequential art, and educational transmedia. When she is not drawing, Kara makes synthetic tea while watching Sherpa-lined gondolas fly the landscape in digital Oakland. Find her at **karaframe.com**.

Lacie Grayson (US) is a former actress and circus performer with a film obsession. She loves her Holga and her family. When she's not taking pictures, she's writing. Lacie is committed to traveling and sharing her world. You can step inside her ever changing world at **snarkycompanion.com**.

Kate Harrad (UK) is the author of *All Lies and Jest*, a counterculture thriller from Ghostwoods Books, and also blogs in *The Huffington Post* and on her own site, Fausterella, at **loveandzombies.co.uk**.

Salome Jones (US/UK) is a professional writer and editor. You can seek out her editorial wisdom at **flourishediting.com** and find her on Twitter at **@call_me_salome**.

Tamsyn H. Kennedy (UK) is currently writing her second novel, fitting it between working, studying, gaming, dog walking and changing the nappies of her multiple children. She can also be found playing Rockband vocals on the Expert setting. Follow her on Twitter at **@xtamsynx**.

Sezin Koehler (US), a true third culture kid, had lived in five different countries on three continents by the time she was fifteen, and has lived in six more since then. A passionate defender of human rights, indigenous cultures and women's interests, Sezin has worked for UNICEF, the Sioux Nation, Davos, Interfaith International, and Mars, Inc – the last position as a researcher into the history of chocolate in America. Her post-modern feminist horror novel *American Monsters* is available on Amazon and other sites, published by Ghostwoods Books.

Uri Kurlianchik (Israel) is a game writer, translator, humanist, twitterist and storyteller from Israel, running RPGs in schools by day and being a freelance writer by night. Uri has written books, articles and short fiction for numerous publications, including Wizards of the Coast, Paizo and Mongoose. His current projects include *Israeli Storyteller*, a story cycle of Levantine Fantasy and *RATS!* an RPG about awakened rats' righteous struggle to reclaim the world humanity has stolen from them.

J.F. Lawrence (UK) is the name behind Hunter S. Blyton, Due South's legendary rock 'n' roll scribe, and the perpetrator of several aborted novels and screenplays. He is now posing as a cultural critic and poet, and still waiting for the call from Steely Dan to put down a hot guitar solo for their next album. Follow him on Twitter if you're *really* bored at **@Dzhimbo**.

Gethin A. Lynes (Australia) is a shameless cynic, habitual bridgeburner and, apparently, a reprobate. But when he occasionally crawls out of his self-indulgent, pitiful hole, he finds himself unable to keep down the emetic flow of stories disgorged by the sordid depths of his imagination... or maybe that's just the whisky. His countless novels, short stories and comics are forthcoming – really...

Remittance Girl (Vietnam) is the pen name of a Canadian writer who squandered the genetically inherited talent of two brilliant parents. Born in Toronto, she spent her childhood at bullfights and in the churches of Madrid. Her adolescence festered in a series of chilly boarding schools in the south of England. The persona of Remittance Girl was born on the web in 1998 when she moved to

Southeast Asia and began writing in earnest. As a perpetual expatriate, her stories often take the point of view of an outsider. They examine eroticism in the face of personal and moral dilemma, and cultural disorientation. Her short stories have been published in M. Christian & S. Vivant's 'Garden of the Perverse', Lisabet Sarai's 'Cream', Violet Blue's 'Girls on Top', D.L. King's 'The Sweetest Kiss' and M. Jakubowski's upcoming 'Mammoth Book of Best New Erotica, Vol. 9', among others. Most of her work is online at her website, `remittancegirl.com`.

Steven Sautter (US) hurls books at passersby from his cage in one of the west coast's major indie bookstores. He is one of the head writers for *The Terrible Zodin* and his comics journalism can be found flitting around the interwebs. His major claim to fame is interviewing both Captain Kirk and Luke Skywalker within 24 hours. He has experienced profound moments with cephalopods.

Matthew Scoppetta (US) cut his artistic teeth by putting finger-paint to wallpaper. Years later the wanton destruction of indoor living environments would, ironically, cultivate a passion for creation. An architectural designer/hyper-realistic renderer and artist currently occupying a southern portion of New Jersey, he hopes to bring a new perspective to fiction.

Joe Silber (Netherlands) earns his keep with his head in the cloud. In between manuals, he runs between paving stones conspiring to do him grave injury, writes the occasional poem, and employs the Oxford comma in the practice of composing bits of pulp, having determined the Great American Novel to be the greatest fiction of all. Follow him on Twitter at **@bishopjoey**.

Thadeus E. Suggs (US) is a deaf college student by day, and by night he's still deaf but that doesn't stop him from gambling with Hermes and out-drinking Dionysus. He blogs (sometimes) at `thadwld.wordpress.com` and is known on Twitter as **@thadwld**.

Chuck Walker (Canada) is a novelist, cartoonist, musician and artist. His creativity spans many disciplines and over the years has produced many books, music CDs, a number of works of art, and cartoons. In his words, "creativity is the heart of all things and without it, life would be meaningless." His latest work is called 'The Monk.' To examine some examples of his work and to order books or CDs go to **chuckwalker.net**. You can also follow Chuck on Twitter where he's known as **@chucklesink**.

Dan Wickline (US) is a published writer and photographer. Born in Norwalk, California, he currently resides in Los Angeles with his wife Debbie, dog Artemis and three cats: Tiger, Panther, and Crash. Dan has written for Image Comics, IDW Publishing, Humanoids Publishing, Zenescope Entertainment, Avatar Press, Cellar Door Publishing and Moonstone Books. Recently Dan has written the re-launch of ShadowHawk for Image Comics and the on-going Sinbad series for Zenescope. Visit his website at **danwickline.com**.

Cvetomir Yonchev (Bulgaria) divides his spare time between reading books concerning war atrocities, trying his luck as a writer and artist, and occasionally stepping out into the sun.

Acknowledgments

We owe a huge debt of gratitude to our backers on Kickstarter. Without all of you, this book would inhabit a strictly digital world, and might never even have reached complete book form. Here are the two hundred and sixty-odd **wonderful people** who believed in us enough to fund this project:

Abdullah Damluji, Ádám Ladányi, Adam Mayes, Adam Rajski, Agnes Kormendi, Aidan Howard, Aimee Carbonneau, AJ Hileman, Akshay Khanna, Alan R. Weaver, Albion Harrison-Naish, Alex Shiell, Alexis Ong, Ali Lemer, Alison Trace, Alison Van Hees, Amanda Hummer Young, Amber Keller, Andrea Maclam, Andrew O'Hara, Andy Haigh, Andy Molloy, Andy Oxenreider, Angus Abranson, Anne Austin, Anne Schroth, Anneka Hess, Anthony Iannazzi, Anthony Musa, Archaeogeek, Aris Alissandrakis, Bailey Shoemaker Richards, Barbara J. Gargano, Becky Guillett, Ben Ames, Ben Dedopulos, Ben Lovejoy, Ben Mitchell, Ben Pollard-Mathias, Benjamin Mialot, Bernd Pressler, Bethan Griffiths, Brendan Hanton, Brian Hicks, Brian McNamara, Brian Nisbet, Brittney Weaver, Cameron Horn, Chani Crow, chaosprime, Charles Neville, Chase Burton, Chris Bissette, Chris Newman, Chris Piazzo, Christine Henry, Christine Shaffer, Claire Butcher, Claire Tweed, Clare Jones, Colleen Desmond, Craig Oxbrow, Crimson Melodies, Csilla Kleinheincz, Dan Catron, Darío Villanueva, Dave Parker, David Church Rodríguez, David Matthewman, David Williams, Davva, Derek Ambrose, Devin McManus, Dimitrios Lakoumentas, Dominic Mooney, Donna Desborough, Duncan Fletcher, Edward D Cowling, Eisenhorn29, Elizabeth Anne Adler, Ellie Merchant, Erika Whillas, Erin Ewald, Eva Bradshaw, fantomas, François Lalande, Fritz Bogott, Fritz Freiheit, Gemma Wheeler-Carver, Gerard Gunnewijk, Gethin Lynes, Giles Lynes, Gordon Kennedy, Greg Draven, Gwa, Heather Royston, Heather Schultz, Helen Hui, Hernan Kowalsky, Holly Kish, Ian Kitley, Ian Ossher, James 'Grim' Desborough, James Turnbull, James

Wallis, Jan O'Malley, Jason Beamish, Jason Boyce, Jason Bruce, Jason Collins, Jason Gorringe, Jenn, Jennifer Day, Jenny Elliott, Jeremiah Gleim, Jesse Browne, Jo Howard, Jo Sansbury, Joan and Walt Walston, Joe Silber, John Conklin II, John Dodd, John Sullivan, John Wignall, Jon, Jon Bailey, Jonathan Korman, Jordan Hanie, Joshua Weiner, JR Wesley, Julian Solis, Justin, Karen MacLaughlin, Kat Player, Kate Epstein, Kate Minasian, Kate Oliver, Katie Jennings, Katie Noice, Keith Perkins, Ken Barnes, Kendall Talbot, Kerry Frey, Kevin Dixon, Kevin Going, Kevin J. Maroney, Kimberly Frixel, Komavary, Kristin, Krisztián Tóth, Larry Miller, _Lasar Liepins, Laura Pierce, Leath Sheales, Lewis Butler, Lindsay Conner, Littlepurplegoth, Liz Maguire, Lloyd Rasmussen, Luis Benitez, Lynda Naclerio, Maeve K. Cahiwat, Maggie Berney, Manuel Francisco Gomez Gomez, Marc Kevin Hall, Marcus De Giorgio, Maria Högberg, Marie Diamond, Mark Hirschman, Masha Gazizova, Mat Thomas, Matthew Porter, Matthew Rogers, Matthew Scoppetta, Matthew Walker, Maureen McColl, Max Fenton, Max Kaehn, Maxine Green, Melissa Donofrio, Melissa Pagonis, Merridew, Michael Austin, Michael Thome, Michael Ward, Michelle Masha Shannon, Mike Clampitt, Mladen Mrvelj, Monica Franz, moofkenubi, Muel, Murray Steele, Naomi Subtlety Saphra, Natasha Von Lemke, Nathan Atherfold, Neil Ford, Nell Lynes, Nicola Pedley, Nicole Mezzasalma, Noela Dillon, Noelle Estacio, Oddtwang, Papa Legba & friends, Patrick, Paul Braidford, Paul Clarkson, Peter Griffith, Philip Jucker, Philip Lautin Jackson, Rachel, Rahnia Collins, Randi Misterka, Rebecca Caldwell, Rémi Gérard-Marchant, Richard Deniz, Richard Fannon, Richard Hughes, Rob Crow, Robby Thrasher, Robert Edyvane, Robert Pait, Robin Zebrowski, Robyn Sitz, Rust Moon, Ruth Turner, rvdm, Ryan, Ryan Percival, Sally Hauser, Sarah Corn, Sarah Kirkpatrick, Sezin Koehler, Sharon Woolich, Simon Fell, Simon Tucker, Stephanie Wilson, Stephen Blackmoore, Steve Dempsey, Steve Wilson, Stuart Degnan, Sven Böyng, Tania, Tavey Be, Thom Dunn, Tim Meakins, Tim Moran, Tony Rett, Trypheyna, Ute Eberle, Viktor Juhasz, Volker Jacobsen, Whitt, Will, Will Lynes, William Alden, Zane Fleming, and Zizzy Yang.

Thank you all. Truly.

Thanks are also due:

To **you**, for reading this far. *hugs*.

To **all the writers**, who worked so hard not just on writing stories, but also helping to promote the Kickstarter. You have all contributed greatly to this work and to my general happiness.

To **Kara Yoon Frame**, who did a glorious job on the drawings in the book during a busy time in her life. Thank you, Kara. We love your work.

To **Gabor Csigas**, whom I can't really thank enough for his work on the cover, the dust jacket, and for contributing a story, while utterly swamped with life and work.

Very special thanks to **Warren Ellis**, who could so easily have said no when I asked him to write a story.

To **Sharon Woolich** for her help is setting up the Kickstarter. I don't know how I would have done it without you. Thank you so much, Sharon.

To **Gethin Lynes,** who not only wrote a lot of great stories, he edited one or two for me when I wasn't very well and had a deadline coming. Heart you, my friend.

To **Grim**, much love, and thank you so much for writing stories for me at the drop of a hat. You're the best. I won't tackle-hug you, but only because I don't want to make you blow your assault whistle.

And lastly, to **Tim Dedopulos**, the best weaver of stories I've ever met. May you become known for your many talents.

~ Salomé

6613720R00216

Printed in Great Britain
by Amazon.co.uk, Ltd.,
Marston Gate.